Carol Marinelli recently filled in a form asking for her job title. Thrilled to be able to put down her answer, she put 'writer'. Then it asked what Carol did for relaxation, and she put down the truth—'writing'. The third question asked for her hobbies. Well, not wanting to look obsessed, she crossed her fingers and answered 'swimming'—but, given that the chlorine in the pool does terrible things to her highlights, I'm sure you can guess the real answer!

Maisey Yates is a *New York Times* bestselling author of over seventy-five romance novels. She has a coffee habit she has no interest in kicking, and a slight Pinterest addiction. She lives with her husband and children in the Pacific Northwest. When Maisey isn't writing she can be found singing in the grocery store, shopping for shoes online and probably not doing dishes. Check out her website: maiseyyates.com.

D0813119

SECRET PRINCE'S CHRISTMAS SEDUCTION

CAROL MARINELLI

THE QUEEN'S BABY SCANDAL

MAISEY YATES

MILLS & BOON

First Published in Great Britain 2019
by Mills & Boon, an imprint of HarperCollins*Publishers*
1 London Bridge Street, London, SE1 9GF

Secret Prince's Christmas Seduction © 2019 by Carol Marinelli

The Queen's Baby Scandal © 2019 by Maisey Yates

ISBN: 978-0-263-27369-4

MIX
Paper from
responsible sources
FSC® C007454

This book is produced from independently certified FSC™ paper
to ensure responsible forest management.
For more information visit www.harpercollins.co.uk/green.

Printed and bound in Spain
by CPI, Barcelona

SECRET PRINCE'S CHRISTMAS SEDUCTION

CAROL MARINELLI

PROLOGUE

'THANKS, BUT I'M really hoping to be spending Christmas with my family.' Realising that she might have come across as ungrateful, Antonietta immediately apologised. 'It's very kind of you to invite me, but…'

'I get it.' Aurora shrugged as she carried on helping Antonietta to unpack. 'You didn't come to Silibri to spend Christmas Day with the Messinas.'

'Ah, but you're a Caruso now!' Antonietta smiled.

The cemetery in the village of Silibri, where Antonietta had loved to wander, held many names, but there were a few constants, and Caruso, Messina and Ricci were the prominent ones.

Especially Ricci.

The Ricci family extended across the south-west region of Sicily and beyond, but Silibri was its epicentre. Antonietta's father, who was the chief fire officer and a prominent landowner, was well connected and held in high regard.

'Do you know…?' Antonietta paused in hanging up the few clothes she owned. 'If I *had* married Sylvester then I wouldn't even have had to change my surname. I would still be Antonietta Ricci.'

'Yes, and you would be married to your second cousin

and living in a property on the grounds of your father's home, with Sylvester working for him.'

'True…' Antonietta started to say, but then faltered.

She had run away on her wedding day, five years ago, in rather spectacular style—climbing out of the bedroom window as her father waited outside to take her to the packed church. Sylvester was popular in the village, and a member of her extended family, so the fallout had been dire—her family had rejected her completely. Letters and emails had gone unanswered and her mother hung up on her whenever she called to try and make her case.

She had spent four years living and working in France, but though she had persisted with the language, and made friends there, it had never felt like home. So she had come back to Silibri, for Aurora and Nico's wedding, but there had been no welcome committee to greet her. Instead she had been shunned by both her immediate and extended family.

Rejecting Sylvester, and so publicly, had been taken as a rejection of them and their closed family values and traditions.

Since Nico and Aurora's wedding she had been working at Nico's grand hotel in Rome, as a chambermaid. But Rome was not home either, and she had often confided to her friend how she missed Silibri.

Antonietta had wanted one final chance to make amends, and Aurora had offered a solution—she could work as a chambermaid in Nico's new hotel in Silibri while training part-time as a massage therapist. The old monastery there had been painstakingly rebuilt, and refurbished to Nico's exacting standards, and it was more a luxurious retreat than a hotel. To train there would be a career boost indeed.

It was an opportunity that Antonietta didn't want to miss—but, given the level of animosity towards her, it was clear she would struggle to live in the village. Aurora had had a solution to that too—there was a small stone cottage, set on the cliff-edge, and Aurora had said she was more than welcome to use it.

'The internet connection is terrible there and it's too close to the helipad and hangar for the guests,' Aurora had explained, 'so it's just sitting empty.'

'Hopefully I shan't need it for too long,' Antonietta had replied. 'Once my family know that I'm back and working…'

She had seen the doubtful look flicker in her dear friend's eyes. The same doubtful look that flickered now, as Antonietta insisted she would be back with her family for the festivities.

'Antonietta…?'

She heard the question in her friend's voice and braced herself. Aurora was as outspoken as Antonietta was quiet, but till now her friend had refrained from stating the obvious.

'It's been five years since your family have spoken to you…'

'I know that,' Antonietta said. 'But it's not as if I've actually given them much opportunity to do so.'

'You came back for my wedding,' Aurora pointed out. 'And you were ignored by them.'

'I think they were just shocked to see me. But once they know I'm properly here, that I'm back for good…'

Aurora sat down on the bed but Antonietta remained standing, not wanting to have the conversation that was to come.

'It's been *years*,' Aurora said again. 'You were only twenty-one when it happened, and now you are close to turning twenty-six! Isn't it time to stop beating yourself up?'

'But I'm not,' Antonietta said. 'It's been an amazing five years. I've travelled and I've learnt a new language. It's not as if I'm walking around in sackcloth and ashes—most of the time life is wonderful. It's just at…'

Just at other times.

Times that should surely be spent with family.

'Christmas is especially hard,' Antonietta admitted. 'It is then that I miss them the most. And I find it hard to believe that they don't think of me and miss me also. Especially my mother. I want to give them one final chance…'

'Fair enough—but what about fun?' Aurora persisted. 'I get that it hasn't been all doom and gloom, but you haven't spoken of any friends. I never hear you saying you're going on a date…'

'*You* never dated anyone until Nico,' Antonietta said rather defensively.

'Only because I have loved Nico my entire life,' Aurora said. 'No one compared. But at least I tried once…'

They both laughed as they recalled Aurora's attempt to get over Nico by getting off with a fireman, but then Antonietta's laughter died away. There was a very good reason she hadn't dated. One that she hadn't even shared with her closest friend. It wasn't just the fact that Sylvester was her second cousin that had caused Antonietta to flee on her wedding day. It had been her dread of their wedding night.

Sylvester's kisses had repulsed Antonietta, and the rough, urgent roaming of his hands had terrified her. And her reluctance to partake had infuriated *him*.

It had all come to a head for Antonietta in the weeks before the planned wedding, when she had come to dread time spent alone with her fiancé. On more than a couple of occasions he had almost overpowered her, and Antonietta had been forced to plead with Sylvester and say that she was saving herself for her wedding night.

'*Frigida,*' he had called her angrily.

And very possibly she was, Antonietta had concluded, because to this day the thought of being intimate with a man left her cold.

At the time she had tried voicing her fears about it to her *mamma*, but her advice had been less than reassuring. Her *mamma* had told her that once she was married it was her wifely duty to perform '*once a week to keep him happy*'.

As the wedding night had loomed closer, so had Antonietta's sense of dread. And that feeling of dread, whenever she thought of kissing a man, let alone being intimate with a man, had stayed with her.

She wished she could speak about it with Aurora. But her friend was so confident with her sexuality, and so deliriously happy in her marriage that instead of confiding in her, Antonietta remained eternally private and kept the darkest part of her soul to herself.

'It's time to live a little,' Aurora pushed now.

'I agree.' Antonietta nodded, even if she didn't quite believe it herself. 'But first I have to give my parents this chance to forgive me.'

'For *what*, Antonietta?' Aurora was blunt. 'Sylvester was your second cousin; the fact is they just wanted to keep their money in the family and keep the Ricci name strong—'

'Even so…' It was Antonietta who interrupted now. 'I shamed my parents in front of their entire family. I left Sylvester standing at the altar! You saw the fallout, Aurora…'

'Yes…'

Apparently a huge fight had broken out in the church. Antonietta hadn't hung around to witness it, though; she had timed it so she had been on the train out of Silibri by then.

'I miss having a family.' It was the simple truth. 'They are not perfect—I know that—but I miss having them in my life. And even if we cannot reconcile I feel there is unfinished business between us. Even if it is a final goodbye then I want it to be said face to face.'

'Well, the offer's there if you change your mind,' Aurora said. 'Nico and I want Gabe to celebrate his first Christmas in Silibri...' Her voice trailed off as she pulled a swathe of scarlet fabric from Antonietta's case. 'This is beautiful—where did you get it?'

'Paris.' Antonietta smiled and ran her hands fondly over the fabric. 'I bought it just after I arrived there.' It had been a late summer's day and, having just written to her parents, she had been buoyed by the prospect of reconciliation. 'I was walking through Place Saint-Pierre and I wandered into a fabric store.'

She had decided to celebrate her happy mood and there amongst the brocades and velvets she had found a bolt of stunning crimson silk and bought a length.

'You have had it all this time and done nothing with it?' Aurora checked as Antonietta wrapped it back in its tissue paper and placed it in the bottom drawer of a heavy wooden chest. 'You *cannot* leave this hiding in a drawer.'

'I might make some cushions with it.'

'Cushions?' Aurora was aghast. 'That fabric deserves to be made into a dress and taken out!'

'Oh? And when will I ever wear it?'

'As a last resort you can wear it in your coffin,' Aurora said with typical Sicilian dark humour. 'You can lie there dead and people can say *Look how beautiful she almost was!* Give it to me and let me make something with it.'

Aurora was a brilliant seamstress, and would certainly make something beautiful, but it was almost reluctantly that Antonietta handed over the fabric.

'Let me get your measurements,' Aurora said.

'I don't have a tape measure.'

But of course Aurora did. And so, instead of unpacking, Antonietta stood, feeling awkward and shy in her underwear, holding her long, straight black hair up as Aurora took her measurements down to the last detail.

'You are *so* slim,' Aurora said as she wrote them all down. 'One of my legs is the size of your waist.'

'Rubbish!'

They were lifelong best friends and complete opposites. Aurora was all rippling curls and curves, and she exuded confidence, whereas Antonietta was as reserved and as slender as her shadow that now fell on the stone wall. The evening was cool, rather than cold, but the year was certainly moving into winter, and she shivered as Aurora took her time, writing down the measurements.

Antonietta tried to hurry her along. 'Nico will be here for you soon,' she warned.

He was checking on the hotel while Aurora helped her settle in, but soon his helicopter would come to return both him and Aurora to their residence in Rome.

'Aren't you going to drop in and visit your parents before you head back?'

'I am avoiding them.' Aurora rolled her eyes. 'Can you believe they want Nico to employ my lazy, good-for-nothing brother as chief groundskeeper for the Old Monastery?'

Antonietta laughed. Aurora's brother was lazy indeed.

'It's no joke,' Aurora said. 'You would need a scythe

to get to work if Nico relented. My brother is as bone idle as yours, but of course now me and Nico are married he seems to think that Nico owes him a job!'

'I hope Nico didn't feel obliged to employ *me*...'

'Don't be ridiculous.' Aurora cut her off. 'You are a hard worker and the Old Monastery is lucky to have you.'

Even so, it was a huge favour for them to give her this cottage as she worked on making amends for the past.

The sound of Nico's chopper starting up made Aurora look out of the window. 'There he is...' She kissed her friend on both cheeks and gave her a hug. 'Good luck starting work and I'll see you on Christmas Eve—if not before. And I mean it, Antonietta. If things don't work out with your family, the offer to join us is there.'

'Thank you,' Antonietta said. 'But Christmas is still a couple of months away; there is plenty of time for things to sort themselves out.'

'You'll be okay?' Aurora checked. 'You really are a bit cut off here.'

'I'll be fine,' Antonietta assured her. 'Thanks so much for this.'

Nico did not come into the cottage; instead he headed straight to the chopper and Antonietta watched as Aurora joined him. They were clearly both happy to be heading back to Rome and little Gabe, who would soon be turning one. She was glad that Nico hadn't dropped in. She was starting work soon, and didn't want her co-workers thinking that she had a direct line to the boss through her friend.

It felt odd, though, after Aurora had gone and she was truly alone.

The cottage was beautifully furnished, with a modern kitchen and a cosy living area, and she wandered through it, taking in not just the furnishings but the stunning view of the ocean from her bedroom. No beach was visible, just choppy waves and crashing foam. Despite the cool evening she opened the window, just to drown out the crippling silence that had descended since Aurora had left.

She was home, Antonietta told herself.

Not that it felt like it.

In truth, Silibri never had.

Antonietta had never quite felt she belonged.

CHAPTER ONE

Six weeks later

ANTONIETTA WAS UP long before the Sicilian winter sun. For a while she lay in the dark bedroom of her little stone cottage, listening to the sound of the waves rolling in and crashing on the rocks below. It might have worked in the meditation of monks of old, and it might be a tranquil backdrop for the guests, but it brought little peace to Antonietta.

It was two weeks until Christmas and since her return there had been little progress with her family. If anything the situation had worsened, with rude stares and muttered insults whenever she ventured into the village, and when she had gone to her parents' home the door had been closed in her face by her father.

Yet she had glimpsed a pained look in her mother's eyes from the hallway—as if her *mamma* had something she wanted to say.

It was for that reason Antonietta persisted.

Sylvester had married and moved away from the village, so there was little chance of bumping into him. And it was good to walk on the beach or in the hillsides she knew. Work was going incredibly well too; her colleagues were friendly and supportive and her training was first class.

Having showered, she went into her wardrobe to select her uniform. It varied—when she was working at the Oratory she wore white, but today she was working on cleaning the suites, so would need her regular uniform.

But as she went to take out her uniform her fingers lingered on the new addition to her wardrobe.

Yes, Aurora was a wonderful seamstress indeed, and the scarlet dress had arrived yesterday! However, just as Antonietta had been reluctant to hand over the fabric, she was even more reluctant to try it on. The dress was bold and sensual and everything she was not.

Still, there was not time for lingering. Her shift started soon, so she pulled out her uniform and got dressed.

The uniforms were actually stunning: the Persian orange linen went well with her olive skin and her slender figure suited the cut of the dress. Antonietta wore no make-up, either in or out of work, so getting ready didn't take long. She pulled her hair into a neat ponytail and then, having slipped on a jacket, made her way across the grounds towards the monastery.

Her little cottage was quite some distance from the main building. Still, it was a pleasant walk, with the sky turning to navy as the sleepy stars readied themselves to fade for the day, and there was a crisp, salt-laden breeze coming in from the Mediterranean.

And there was already activity at the Old Monastery!

A couple of dark-suited gentlemen were walking around the perimeter of the building and Pino, the chief concierge, was looking *very* dapper this morning as he greeted her warmly. '*Buongiorno*, Antonietta.'

'*Buongiorno*, Pino,' she responded.

'We have a new guest!'

The hotel housed many guests, but with the extra security visible Antonietta had already guessed there was a VIP in residence.

Pino loved to gossip and was determined to fill her in. 'We are to address him as Signor Louis Dupont. However…' Pino tapped the side of his nose '…the truth is he is really—'

'Pino…' Antonietta interrupted.

She adored Pino, and always arrived early to allow herself time to chat with him. Pino had recently lost his beloved wife of forty years, Rosa, and she knew that work was the only thing keeping him sane. Still, given that Antonietta was already a main source of gossip in the village, she refused to partake in it now.

'If that is how he wants to be addressed, then that is enough for me.'

'Fair enough,' Pino said, and then he took a proper look at her. 'How are you doing, Antonietta?'

'I'm getting there,' she said, touched that with all that was going on in his world he still took the time to ask about her. 'How about you?'

'I'm not looking forward to Christmas. Rosa always made it so special. It was her favourite time of the year.'

'What will you do? Are you going to visit your daughter?'

'No, it is her husband's family's turn this year, so I've told Francesca that I'll work. I decided that would be better than sitting at home alone. What about you—has there been any progress with your family?'

'None,' Antonietta admitted. 'I have been to the house several times but they still refuse to speak with me, and my trips to the village are less than pleasant. Perhaps it's time I accept that I'm not wanted here.'

'Not true,' Pino said. 'Not everyone is a Ricci—or related to one.'

'It feels like it.'

'Things will get better.'

'Perhaps—if I live to be a hundred!'

They shared a small wry smile. Both knew only too well that grudges lasted for a very long time in Silibri.

'You're doing well at work,' Pino pointed out.

'Yes!'

And the fact that she had committed to the therapy course was the main reason Antonietta had stayed even when it had become clear that her family did not want her around. With each shift, both as a chambermaid and while training as a therapist, she fell in love with her work a little more. Working at the Old Monastery was so different from the bars and café jobs that had supported her while she lived in France, and she preferred the tranquil nature of Silibri to the hustle and bustle of Rome.

'Work has been my saviour,' she admitted.

'And mine,' Pino agreed.

As she walked into the softly lit foyer the gorgeous scent of pine reached her, and Antonietta took a moment to breathe it in. Apart from the stunning Nebrodi fir tree, adorned with citrus fruits, there were no other Christmas decorations. As Nico had pointed out, many of their guests were retreating to *escape* Christmas, and did not need constant reminders—but Aurora, being Aurora, had insisted on at least a tree.

Still, thought Antonietta, as magnificent and splendid as the tree was, it was just a token, and somehow it just didn't *feel* like Christmas once had in Silibri.

Heading into the staff room, she dropped off her bag and jacket and made her way to the morning briefing from Maria, the head of housekeeping.

Francesca, the regional manager, was also in early, and was looking on as the chambermaids were informed that a new guest had just arrived into the August Suite, which was *the* premier suite of the hotel.

'I don't have his photo yet,' said Maria.

All the staff would be shown his photograph, so he could be recognised and greeted appropriately at all times, and so that all charges could be added to his suite without any formalities.

'Signor Dupont is to be given top priority,' Francesca cut in. 'If there are any issues you are to report them directly to me.'

Ah, so *that* was the reason she was here so early, Antonietta thought. She was always very aware of Francesca. Antonietta liked her, but because Francesca was a close friend of her mother there was a certain guardedness between them.

'Antonietta, that is where you shall be working today,' Maria continued with the handover. 'When you are not busy, you can assist Chi-Chi in the other superior suites, but Signor Dupont is to take priority at all times.'

Antonietta had been surprised at how quickly she had moved through the ranks. She was now regularly allocated the most important guests and Francesca had told her she was perfect for the role.

The August, Starlight and Temple Suites were sumptuous indeed, and the guests they housed could be anything from visiting royalty to rock stars recovering from their excesses, or even movie stars recuperating after a little nip and tuck.

The reason that Antonietta was so perfectly suited to working in the suites was her rather private nature. She had enough problems of her own and didn't care to delve into other people's. Nor did she have stars in her eyes, and she was not dumbstruck by celebrity, fame or title. Generally polite conversation was all that was required, and Antonietta could certainly do that. Silence was merited on occasion, and she was more than happy to oblige. She was polite to the guests, if a little distant, but she did her work quietly and well and let the guests be.

At the end of the handover, Francesca pulled Antonietta aside and gave her the pager for the August Suite. She offered a little more information.

'Signor Dupont has declined the services of a butler. He has stated that he wants privacy and is not to be unnecessarily disturbed. Perhaps you can sort out with him the best time to service his suite—he might want to get it over and done with—but I shall leave that to you.'

A guest in the August Suite could have the rooms serviced a hundred times a day if he so demanded.

'Also, Signor Dupont might need some assistance getting out of bed. If he—'

'I am not a nurse,' Antonietta interrupted. She had firm boundaries.

'I know that,' Francesca said, and gave her rather surly chambermaid a tight smile. 'Signor Dupont already has a nurse—although he seems rather testy and insists that he does not need one. Should he require her assistance, she can be paged. I should warn you that he is very bruised, so don't be shocked.'

'Okay.'

'Antonietta, I probably shouldn't tell you who he is, but—'

'Then please don't,' Antonietta cut in.

For her it really was as simple as that. She did not gossip and she did not listen to gossip either. Oh, the staff here were wonderful, and their gossip was never malicious. Certainly it would not reach the press, which was why there were so many exclusive guests at the hotel.

The same courtesy was extended in the village. The

locals were all thrilled at the vibrancy that had returned to the town with the new hotel, and so the Silibri people looked after its guests as their own. In fact, they looked after the guests *better* than their own—Antonietta had been treated shabbily by many of them.

'I don't want to know his real name, Francesca,' she said now, 'because then I might slip up and use it. Tell me only what I need to know.'

'Very well—he has his own security detail and you will need to show them your ID. He's booked in until Christmas Eve. Although, from what I gather, I believe it is doubtful he will last until then.'

'He's dying?' Antonietta frowned.

'No!' Francesca laughed. 'I meant he will grow bored. Now, he wants coffee to be delivered promptly at seven.'

'Then I had better get on.'

Francesca carried on chatting as they both made their way to the kitchen. 'I have just finalised the roster,' she told her. 'And I have you down for an early start on Christmas Day.'

Antonietta stopped in her tracks, and was about to open her mouth to protest, but then Francesca turned and she saw the resigned, almost sympathetic look on her manager's face. Francesca wasn't just telling her that she was to work on Christmas Day, Antonietta realised. Her mother must have made it clear to her friend that Antonietta would not be invited to partake in the family's festivities.

'Working is better than sitting alone in that cottage,' Francesca said as they resumed walking and headed into the kitchen. 'I shall be here too, and so will Pino and Chi-Chi...'

All the lonely hearts were working over Christmas then, Antonietta thought sadly.

'I'm on over Christmas too,' said Tony, the very portly head chef—which only confirmed Antonietta's thoughts.

Tony was married to his job, and put all his care and love into his food, and there was no exception this morning. There was a huge silver pot of coffee for their new guest, and cream and sugar, but there was also a basket of pastries and bread, a meat and cheese platter, and a fruit platter too. All the chefs, and especially Tony, could not refrain from adding Sicilian flair to every dish.

'Tony,' Antonietta pointed out as she checked the order, 'he only ordered coffee, but you have prepared a feast.'

'He is a *guest*.' Tony shrugged.

'And he's a big man!' Francesca said, holding out her hands high and wide. 'Huge! He needs to eat!'

It was the Silibri way—even in the poorest home there would be *biscotti* and *pizzelles* served alongside coffee. There was no point arguing, so Antonietta wheeled the trolley towards the elevator.

The monastery had been refurbished to perfection, and although it still looked ancient, it had all mod cons. Antonietta often saw the guests blink in surprise when they stepped behind a stone partition to reach the discreet elevator.

She took the elevator up to the top floor and, alone for a moment, slumped against the wall as she dwelt on the message behind Francesca's words. It really was time to accept that her family simply didn't want her. It was time to move on.

Where, though?

Back to France, perhaps? Or to Rome?

But she hadn't felt she had belonged in either place, and there was still her training to complete…

Catching sight of her reflection, she straightened up

and gave herself a mental shake. It wasn't the guest's fault that she was feeling blue, and she put on her game face as she stepped out and wheeled the trolley across the cloister, past the Starlight and Temple Suites, and across to the August Suite.

A suited man stood as she neared. She had known guests to bring their own security detail before, but never to this extent. What with the extra guards outside and within, this guest must be important indeed.

The guard was not exactly friendly, but without a word he looked at the photo on her lanyard and then checked Antonietta's face before stepping aside to let her past.

She knocked gently on the large wooden door. There was no response so, as she'd been trained to do, Antonietta let herself in with a swipe of her key card. Once inside, she turned on a side light and wheeled the trolley through the dimly lit lounge and over to the entrance to the main bedroom. She gave the door a gentle knock.

No response.

Another gentle knock and then, as she carefully opened the door, Antonietta called his name. 'Signor Dupont?'

Again there was no response, and though the room was in darkness it was clear to her that he was asleep. His breathing was deep and even, and judging from his outline Antonietta could see that he lay on his stomach in the large four-poster bed, with a sheet covering him.

'I have coffee for you,' Antonietta said quietly. 'Would you like me to open the drapes? The sun is just about to rise.'

'Si.' He stirred in the bed as he gave his groggy reply.

Antonietta headed to the drapes to open them, though it was not a simple matter of pulling them apart. The windows were vast and the dark velvet curtains heavy; pulling with both hands on the cord was truly like parting the curtains at a theatre, as if a play was about to unfold before her eyes.

The August Suite was her favourite. It occupied an entire wing of the Old Monastery, which allowed for panoramic views. The view from the lounge looked across the ocean, and the dining room looked over the valley, but here in the master bedroom there was a view of the ancient temple ruins.

Antonietta drank it in for a moment. There, as fingers of red light spread across the sky, the ocean danced to the rising sun and she felt she could happily gaze on it for ever. The view, though, was not hers to enjoy just now.

Antonietta turned around, and as she did so she started slightly when she first laid eyes on the guest.

He was *nothing* like she had imagined. From Francesca's description she had been expecting a possibly aging, somewhat bedridden and rather large man. But, while he was indeed large, he was certainly not overweight. Instead he was incredibly tall, judging by the amount of space he took up in the large bed. He was also broad and muscular, and thankfully covered by the sheet where it mattered.

And she guessed he might be around thirty.

Francesca had been right, though, to warn her about the bruises, for they really were shocking—purple and black, they covered his arms and chest and one eye, and his top lip was swollen. Signor Dupont, or whatever his real name was, had thick black hair that was rather messy, and also very matted—Antonietta guessed with blood. Of course she made no comment, but for the first time she found herself more than a little curious as to what had happened to a guest.

'Poor decision,' Signor Dupont said, and she guessed

he was referring to the sun, for he was shielding his eyes as he struggled to sit up in the bed.

'I can close them…' Antonietta offered.

'No, leave them.'

He would get used to the bright light soon, Rafe told himself, even as his pulse roared in his ears. But brighter than the sun were the shards of memory painfully surfacing in his brain—the absolute knowledge that this fall had been serious.

Rafe did not fear death for himself, but for a seemingly endless moment he had glimpsed the grief and chaos he would leave behind and had fought to right himself. He could not shake the memory of the looks of horror on his bodyguards' faces, the sense of panic all around, which seemed at odds with the soft voice speaking to him now.

'Would you like me to pour your coffee, Signor Dupont?'

For a moment he wondered who she was referring to. And then he remembered.

Ah, yes, security was extra-tight, for it would be disastrous if news of this near-miss leaked out.

So Rafe nodded and watched as the maid poured his drink, but as she removed one of the linen covers on the tray the sweet scent of bread and pastry reached him, and with it a wave of nausea.

'I only asked for coffee.'

'Ah, but you are in Silibri,' she responded. 'Here there is no such thing as "just coffee."'

'Please tell the chef that he is not to misinterpret my orders,' Rafe snapped.

'I shall pass that on.'

'Leave and take the trolley with you.' He dismissed her with a wave of his hand.

'Of course.'

Antonietta was only too happy to go. 'Testy' didn't come close to describing him. However, there was one thing that needed to be sorted out before she left. 'When would you like me to return and service the suite, Signor Du—?'

'Please!' His interruption was irritated rather than polite, and his dark eyes held hers in reprimand. 'Don't call me that again. Just use my first name.'

'Very well.' Antonietta felt a nervous flutter in her stomach, and it had nothing to do with his surly tone, and more to do with the deep navy of his eyes, which reminded her of the sky that morning. 'So, Louis, when would you—?'

'Rafe!' he snapped, and then softened his tone. It was not her fault there were so many restrictions on publicising his identity. 'You are to call me Rafe. And, no, I do not want my room serviced. If you could make up the bed while I have my coffee, that will suffice.'

He moved to climb out of bed, but then perhaps he got dizzy, because instead of heading to the bedside chair he remained sitting on the edge with his head in his hands, his skin turning from pale to grey.

He should be in hospital, Antonietta thought. 'Would you like me to—?'

'I can manage,' he snapped.

They'd both spoken at the same time, and Antonietta had not finished her sentence. Now she did. 'Would you like me to fetch the nurse to help you get out of bed?'

For some reason what she said caused him to lift his head from his hands and look at her. Antonietta was sure he *almost* smiled, but then his expression changed to austere.

'I *don't* need a nurse and I *don't* need the bed linen changed. Please, just leave.'

His tone was still brusque, but Antonietta took no offence. It was clear to her that Louis—or rather Rafe—loathed being seen in a weakened state. He was holding tightly on to the bedside table with one hand, while the other gripped the mattress, and she was certain he would prefer to be alone than have anyone witness him like this.

'Would you like me to come back later?'

'No.' He gave a shake of his head, which must have hurt, because he halted midway. 'I really don't want to be disturbed today—if you could let everybody know?'

'I shall.'

'And could you block out the sun before you leave?'

It was a slightly oddly worded request, and only then did she realise that Italian wasn't his first language. It took a second to place, but she soon realised that his Italian was tinged with an accent she loved—French.

She wanted to delve. For the first time ever Antonietta wanted to know more about a guest. He had asked that she use his real name—Rafe—and now she wanted to know it in full. She wanted to know where he was from and what had led him to this Silibri retreat to heal in secret.

Antonietta wanted to know *more* about this man.

But instead she wheeled out the trolley while the room was still light, and then returned. 'I'll close the drapes and then get out of your way. But, please, if you need anything then don't hesitate to page me.'

Rafe nodded and glanced at her, and was slightly bemused when he noticed her eyes. It wasn't so much that they were as black as treacle, and thickly lashed, it was more that he had never seen such sadness. Oh, it was not anything tangible—she was not downcast or grim—but there was an abject melancholy in them that tugged him out of deep introspection. And that was no mean feat, for Rafe had a lot on his mind.

An awful lot.

The black-eyed maid took out the trolley, and by the time she returned Rafe was back in bed. Before closing the drapes, she topped up the water by his bed.

'Thank you,' Rafe said, once the room was mercifully back to darkness. He actually meant it, for she had worked unobtrusively and had not, unlike so many others, pushed for conversation, nor dashed to help unasked. He almost smiled again when he remembered her offer to fetch the nurse rather than assist herself.

'What is your name?' he asked.

'Antonietta.'

And that was that.

Well, almost.

She wheeled the trolley back to the elevator and then went down to the kitchen and picked up the tablet to make a note of his requests. The internal computer system for the domestic staff was easy to navigate—she checked the box to say that he had declined having his suite serviced and added a note that he was not to be disturbed.

Yet she lingered a second.

His photo was up now, and she flushed as she looked at his elegant features. He wore black dress trousers and a white fitted shirt and there was a scowl on his lips and his eyes were narrowed, as if warning the photographer off.

She accidentally clicked on his profile, but there was only his pseudonym there.

Signor Louis Dupont.
VVIP

So, he was very, *very* important.

And in the box where normally a guest's requests were noted there was instead a direction.

All queries and requests to be directed to Francesca.
All hours.

'Is everything okay, Antonietta?'

She turned to the sound of Francesca's voice and saw she was chatting with Tony.

'Of course. I was just about to make a note regarding a guest but I'm not able to fill it in.'

'Because all Signor Dupont's requests are to be relayed first to *me*,' said Francesca.

'He didn't even *try* one of my pastries?' Tony was aghast when he saw that the trolley had been returned untouched.

Francesca, of course, thought she should have done better. 'You should have left a selection for him to nibble on.'

'He made himself very clear,' Antonietta said, blushing a bit as she did so, knowing that Rafe's lack of compliments to the chef would not go down well. 'I was just about to make a note—he has asked that the chef...' she hesitated and slightly rephrased Rafe's message '...should please not add anything to his order.'

Even that did not go down well.

Tony flounced off and she later found out from Vincenzo, the head of PR, that he had been discovered in tears.

'You know how temperamental Tony is,' he scolded her. 'And he's especially upset today because the Christmas rosters are out. Could you not at least have diluted such a prominent guest's criticism?'

'But I *did* dilute it,' Antonietta said. 'Anyway, I thought Tony was happy to be working on Christmas Day.'

Vincenzo just huffed off, leaving Antonietta wondering what on earth she'd said wrong this time. Still, there wasn't time to dwell, and for the rest of the day she worked with Chi-Chi. Or rather Antonietta worked while Chi-Chi did the *slowly-slowly*.

The *slowly-slowly* was a way to look busy while getting precisely nothing done, and Chi-Chi had perfected it. She had even tried to share her method with Antonietta.

'You can doze in the cleaning room, but keep some dusters on your lap, so that if Francesca pops her head in you can look as if you're in the middle of folding them,' Chi-Chi had explained when Antonietta had first started working there. 'But never cross your legs while you sleep or it will leave a red mark on your calf, and Francesca will be able to tell you've been in there for ages.'

'I don't want a bar of it,' Antonietta had told her.

She had known Chi-Chi her whole life, but she wasn't a friend, exactly, just someone she knew and, unfortunately, with whom she now worked. Chi-Chi's aim in life was to find a husband and do as little as she could get away with in the meantime. Once, Antonietta had actually seen her dozing on her arm as she supposedly cleaned a mirror, only to suddenly spring into action when Antonietta made her presence known!

'I saw your *papà* yesterday,' Chi-Chi said as she ate one of the turn-down chocolates while Antonietta dusted. 'He couldn't stop and speak for long, though, but he said he was busy getting things ready for the Christmas Eve bonfire. Will you be going?' she enquired, oh, so innocently.

'Of course,' Antonietta said. 'The fire in the village square is a tradition. Why wouldn't I go?'

Chi-Chi shrugged and helped herself to another chocolate. 'What is he like?' she asked.

'My *papà*?' Antonietta said, pretending she had no idea to whom Chi-Chi was referring.

'No, silly! The new man who is staying in the August Suite. I wonder what his real name is? He must be important. I have never seen so much security.'

'*All* our guests are important,' Antonietta said, refusing to be drawn.

Still, at the mention of the August Suite, and not for the first time, Antonietta glanced at her pager. But, no, Rafe had not paged her. Nor, when she checked, had he made any requests for in-suite dining. In fact later that afternoon she found out that his nurse had been given her marching orders for daring to make an unscheduled check on her patient.

Rafe had clearly meant what he'd said about not wanting to be disturbed.

At the end of her shift, as she walked back to her little cottage, Antonietta found she was glancing up in the direction of the August Suite. It was too far away for her to tell if he was on the balcony, but she wondered about him, wondered how he had spent his day and how he was.

For the first time ever Antonietta truly wondered about a man...

CHAPTER TWO

THE CHRISTMAS ROSTER was definitely the main topic of conversation over the next couple of days.

Antonietta was training in the Oratory, which was unusually quiet, but whenever she entered the staffroom it was all that was being discussed.

'It's not fair,' Chi-Chi huffed. 'Even Greta has got Christmas off and she only started three months ago.'

'She has children, though,' Antonietta pointed out.

'How come *you* are off, Vincenzo?'

'Because I live in Florence, and if I am to spend any time with my family then I need adequate time to get there.'

'But it is the Old Monastery's first Christmas,' Chi-Chi said. 'Surely the head of PR should be here and tweeting…or whatever it is you do.'

'I do rather more than play on my phone,' Vincenzo said, and then looked to Antonietta. 'How are things in the Oratory?'

'Quiet…' Antonietta sighed as she peeled the lid off a yoghurt. 'It's fully booked for next week, but the place was dead yesterday and it's almost empty today. I think people must be saving up their treatments for Christmas.'

She looked up as Francesca came to the door.

'Ah, there you are Antonietta. Could I ask you to service Signor Dupont's suite? I know you are meant to be doing your training in the Oratory today—'

'Of course,' Antonietta said, and went to get up.

'Finish your lunch first,' Francesca said. 'He has asked that it be serviced at one o'clock.'

'I'm glad she asked you and not me,' Chi-Chi said, the very second Francesca had gone. 'I've been working there the past couple of days, and he might be important, but he's also mean.'

'Mean?' Antonietta frowned.

'He told me to refrain from speaking while I do my work.'

'Well, I expect he has a headache,' Antonietta said, without adding that *she* certainly did when Chi-Chi was around.

Vincenzo looked at the time and then stood and brushed off his suit, smoothing his already immaculate red hair in the mirror before heading back.

'For someone so vain, you'd think he would have noticed that he's putting on weight,' Chi-Chi said the moment he was gone. 'His jacket doesn't even do up any more.'

'Leave him alone,' Antonietta snapped.

But Chi-Chi would not, and carried on with her grumbling. 'He's only got Christmas off because he's a manager.'

'No.' Antonietta shook her head. 'Francesca is working. I'd better go.'

'But you've barely sat down.'

She was happy to get up. Antonietta was more than a little bit fed up with Chi-Chi's rather grating nature.

'I need to get the linen ready to take up to the August Suite.'

Fetching the linen was one of Antonietta's favourite

tasks. Here at the Old Monastery the linen was tailor-made for each bed and was washed and line dried without a hint of bleach.

Antonietta breathed in the scent of fresh laundry as she walked in. Vera, who worked there, must be on her lunch, so Antonietta selected crisp linen and then walked across the stunning grounds.

A guest who had just arrived that morning had told her that it had been raining and grey in Rome when they'd left. Here, though, the sky was blue, and it was a little brisk and chilly, with cold nights.

The guard checked her ID and actually addressed her. 'He will be back by two, so please make sure you are done and out by then.'

'Certainly.'

Given that it took well over an hour to service the August Suite to standard, guests often went for a stroll, or down to the Oratory for a treatment, or to the restaurant while the maids worked. Usually she was relieved when the guests were out, but today she felt a stab of disappointment that she chose not to dwell on.

Of course she knocked before entering anyway, and when there was no answer she let herself in and stood for a moment, looking around. The place was a little chaotic, and she was wondering where to start when someone came in from the balcony.

Certainly she had not been expecting to see *him*.

'Buongiorno,' she said, and then immediately lost her tongue, for Rafe was dressed in black running shorts and nothing else.

'Buongiorno.' He returned the greeting, barely looking over. 'I'll be out of your way soon,' he added.

Indeed, Rafe had fully intended to go for a run—his first since the accident. But now he glanced over and recognised the maid from the fog of his first morning here. 'You've had some days off?'

'No,' Antonietta said. 'I haven't had any days off.'

'So why did they send me Chi-Chi?' he drawled, and rolled his eyes.

Antonietta almost smiled, but quickly recovered, because even if Chi-Chi drove her insane she would not discuss her colleague with a guest. Instead she answered as she headed into the bedroom. 'I've been working in the Oratory.'

She paused for a second to let him speak, as she should any guest, but truly she wanted to flee, for her cheeks were on fire and she hoped that he had not noticed. He did not reply.

'I hope you have a pleasant day,' she said.

'Thank you.'

Antonietta put down the list that she always worked from and immediately started stripping the vast walnut bed. She worked quickly, but the exertion was less out of necessity and more to match her heartbeat, which had tripped into a rapid rhythm at the sight of him semi-naked. And when he came into the bedroom to collect his trainers she had to force herself not to look—or rather not to stand there and simply gape.

'You work in the Oratory?' he checked. 'So you are a therapist?'

His voice caught her unawares; for she had not expected the terse gentleman she had met a few days ago to initiate a conversation.

'I'm training to be one,' Antonietta said, and glanced up from the bed.

And then it ceased being a glance, for she met his eyes and the world and its problems seemed for a moment to disappear.

'You look better,' she commented, when usually she would not, but the words had just tumbled out.

'I'm feeling a lot better,' he agreed. 'Although I still look as if I've been paint-bombed.'

She couldn't help but smile, for indeed he did. Those bruises were a riot of colour now, from blue to brown right through to a vivid pink, and they were spread across the left side of his torso and down to his shoulder and arm, and there were savage lines across his shoulder. Rafe's left eye looked as if he was wearing violet eyeshadow.

Yet he wore it well.

In fact, paint-bombed or not, Rafe looked stunning.

And as her eyes briefly travelled over his body, to take in his comment, she found that they wanted to linger on the long, yet muscular arms, and on his broad chest with just a smattering of black hair. More, she found that they lingered on his flat stomach. It was not bruised, so there was no real reason to look there. But Antonietta just found that she did, and a glimpse of that line of black hair had her already hot cheeks reddening as if scalded.

She wanted to ask, *What happened to you?*

Were those bruises from a fight? Or had he been in an accident? For once she wanted to know more, and yet it was not her place to ask.

'I shan't be long,' Rafe said, though usually he did not explain himself to maids, or even particularly notice that they were near.

Crossing the room, he took a seat by the bed she was making and bent over to lace his trainers.

Antonietta did her best to ignore him and not to look at his powerful back and the stretch of his trapezius muscles as he leant forward. Never had her fingers ached to touch so. To reach out with her newly trained therapist's fingers and relax the taut flesh beneath. Only she was self-aware enough to know that that kind of desire had precisely nothing to do with her line of work. He was so very male, and she was so very aware of that fact in a way she had never been until now.

Confused by this new feeling he aroused, Antonietta hurriedly looked away and resumed making the bed. But as she was fitting a sheet he must have caught the scent, and he made a comment.

'The sheets smell of summer.'

Antonietta nodded as she tucked it in. 'They smell of the Silibri sun. All the linen here is line-dried.'

'What about when it rains?'

'The stocks are plentiful—you have to make hay when the sun shines,' Antonietta said. 'Nico, the owner—'

'I know Nico.'

Rafe's interruption said a lot. Nico was prominent, and Rafe had not said I know *of* Nico, or I have *heard* of him. And then he elaborated more. 'It was he who suggested that I come to Silibri to recover.'

That admission made her a little more open to revealing something of herself. 'Aurora, his wife, is my best friend.'

'You are chalk and cheese.'

'Yes…' Antonietta smiled. 'I am drab in comparison.'

'Drab?'

'Sorry,' she said, assuming he didn't know that word. 'I meant…'

'I know what you meant—and, no, you are not.'

Rafe met a lot of people, and had an innate skill that enabled him to sum them up quickly and succinctly.

Yesterday's maid: slovenly.

The concierge, Pino, who had this morning suggested a running route: wise.

His assessments were rapid, and seldom wrong, and as he looked over to the maid he recalled asking her name that first morning. That morning he had not been able to sum *her* up in one word.

Admittedly, he had been concussed, and not at his best, but today he was much better. So he looked at those sad eyes, and, no, he still could not isolate that word.

Their conversation paused, and yet it did not end, for instead of heading out of the balcony and down the private steps to the grounds below he watched as, having made the bed, she headed to an occasional table, where she picked up her notepad and ticked off her list.

'So you are training as a therapist?'

'Yes,' she nodded. 'Although I'm not allowed to be let loose unsupervised on the guests yet. Well, I can give manicures, but that is all.'

'I *loathe* manicures.'

There were two types of men who had manicures, Antonietta had learnt. Those who chose to and those who had been born to. He had been born to, she was quite, quite sure.

She resisted the urge to walk over and examine his hands, but instead looked down at them… Yes, they were exquisite, long-fingered, with very neat, beautifully manicured nails.

'I find sitting there boring.'

'Then why bother?' Antonietta asked, and then pulled back the conversation. 'I'm sorry—that was personal.'

'Not at all,' Rafe said. 'I ask myself the same thing.'

'You could always listen to a podcast while your nails are being done,' Antonietta suggested.

'Ah, but then I wouldn't get to speak with you.'

It was a silly little joke but she smiled.

The girl with the saddest eyes smiled, and when she

did she looked glorious, Rafe thought. Her black eyes sparkled and her full red lips revealed very white teeth. She had a beautiful mouth, Rafe thought, and watched it as she responded to his light jest.

'I would not be allowed to treat a guest in the August Suite.'

He was about to say *What a pity*, but he rather sensed that that would have her scuttling behind the wall she had erected, which was just starting to inch down.

She rather fascinated him, and it was a relief to focus on their gentle conversation rather than deal with the problems he must face. He had intended to go for a run, just to clear his head. Yet instead he carried on chatting as she worked her way through the suite.

'You grew up here?' he asked.

'Yes, I left a few years ago.'

'For how long?'

'Five years,' Antonietta said. 'And though it was wonderful, I came to realise that you cannot drift for ever. Home is home—though it is very different now, and the hotel has changed things. There are more people, more work…'

'Is that why you came back?'

'No,' Antonietta said, and cut that line of conversation stone-cold dead.

It usually took an hour and fifteen minutes to service the suite to standard. Today it took a little longer, although they did not talk non-stop, just made gentle conversation as Antonietta got on with her work, diligently ticking off items in turn to ensure that nothing had been missed.

'Do you have family here?' Rafe asked, curious despite himself.

'Yes.'

Again she closed the topic, and headed into the lounge and dining area. There had been no fire lit last night, and no meal taken, but she dusted the gleaming table, then topped up the cognac decanter and replaced the glasses.

Tick.

He was leaning on the doorframe, watching her. Usually to have a guest watching her so overtly would be unsettling, yet it didn't feel that way with Rafe. She found him relaxing. Oh, her heart was in her throat, and beating way too fast, but that was for other reasons entirely.

She liked it that he did not demand elaboration. So much so that as she put the stopper in the decanter she revealed to him a little of her truth.

'We are not really speaking.'

'That must be hard.'

'Yes.'

The candles in the heavy candelabra were new, and didn't need replacing.

Tick.

She checked that the lighter worked.

Tick.

But she paused for a moment and wondered how used to luxury he must be not to light them each night. Not to need the stunning suite bathed in candle and firelight.

'The August Suite is my favourite,' Antonietta admitted. 'You should use these candles. I am sure it would look beautiful.'

'I'll keep that in mind.'

'I mean...' She was flustered, for she was not used to idle conversation. 'I've always wondered what it must look like.'

'I'll bear that in mind,' Rafe said again, and this time she flushed. 'Which is your favourite view?' he asked.

'The one from the dining room. From there you can see the valley.'

'Show me.'

As easily as that, he joined her at the window.

'When I left,' Antonietta said, 'that whole stretch of valley was black and scorched from wild fires.' She pointed to a large clearing atop a hillside. 'My family's property is up there.'

'Was it razed in the fires?'

'No, the fires stopped short of Silibri, but in the next village, where I also have family, there was a lot of damage. It's hard now to remember that it was so dead and black. I came back in spring, for Nico and Aurora's wedding, and the whole valley was a riot of colour. I have never seen it so alive. I find the view soothing. It reminds me that, as terrible as the fires were, they were good for the land.'

'So you stayed on after the wedding?'

'No,' Antonietta said. 'I went to Rome for a year, but I wanted to be back here for Christmas.' She gave him a tight smile. Certainly, she was not going to reveal that right now a happy family Christmas was looking less and less likely. 'I had better get on.'

'Of course.'

Nothing was left unchecked.

No cushion left unturned or unplumped.

And still Rafe did not go for his run. Instead he made a couple of phone calls, and it turned her insides to liquid to hear his deep voice flow in the language she loved.

'You are French?' she asked, after the second call had ended, although usually she would not pry.

'No,' Rafe said. 'But it is the language of my home.'

'Oh?'

'Tulano,' he added. 'It is between Italy and France…'

'I know where it is,' Antonietta said. 'I visited there once. Only briefly, though.'

His eyes narrowed a touch. In truth, Rafe did not believe she didn't know who he was. The maid yesterday had slipped up and called him by his full first name— Rafael—and the concierge had done the same when recommending a trail to run.

Soon, he was sure, his location would be leaked and the press would be here. The brief respite from the world would be over.

He asked her a question. 'Do you speak French?'

'Some—although not as much as I would like. I was there for four years,' she said, and then switched to French and told him that his Italian was better than her French. *'Votre Italien est meilleur que mon Français.'*

And he responded. *'Ta voix est délicieuse dans les deux langues.'*

She had been away from France for over a year, and it took her a moment to translate it, but as she did a heated blush crept up her neck.

Had he just said that her voice was delightful in both languages?

Were they flirting?

And if they were then why wasn't she halting it?

Why wasn't she running for cover, as she usually did whenever a man, let alone a guest, got a little too close?

Only Rafe wasn't too close for comfort. And Antonietta looked at the eyes that held hers as she responded. *'Ainsi est le tien.'*

So is yours.

It was the tiniest nod to his effect on her, and yet it felt rather huge to Antonietta.

There was another phone call for Rafe, and this time he answered in Italian, taking it out on the balcony.

Though she did not eavesdrop, his low voice reached her and it was clear that he was speaking with Nico. She felt a little flip of disappointment when she heard him state that he would not be staying for much longer.

The call ended and she looked over to where he sat, his long legs stretched out on another chair, his dark eyes scanning the grounds as a prisoner's might, as if looking for a way to escape. She could almost feel his restlessness, Antonietta thought as she headed out onto the balcony to finish her work.

'That was Nico,' he said, though he had absolutely no need to do so. 'Checking that I'm being looked after. He suggests that I take a wander into the village.'

'There are nice cafés there,' Antonietta said, and deliberately kept her voice casual. But there was a flip in her stomach at the thought he might be bored. 'Have you been down to the temple ruins?'

'No—that is where Pino suggested I ran.'

'And the ocean is glorious,' Antonietta said, and then stopped herself. It was not her job to sell the village to a reluctant guest.

'You live in the village?'

'No. Nico and Aurora have been very good to me. They knew coming back would be difficult...' She briefly closed her eyes, instantly regretting revealing so much, and then hurriedly spoke on. 'So they gave me a cottage in the grounds.' She pointed in the vague direction of the helipad, over to the far side of the Old Monastery.

'That must be very...' He hesitated, not wanting to say *isolated*.

Already, for Rafe, no matter how spacious and luxurious the August Suite, no matter how glorious the grounds, cabin fever was seriously hitting. This place really was in the middle of nowhere, and he'd been considering checking out later today.

Yet he was starting to change his mind.

Rafe wanted more of her smile, of her conversation— much, much more of her.

It was not as simple as that, though.

If their relationship were to evolve, then she needed to sign a non-disclosure agreement. She would have to be be vetted by his security staff and her phone would be confiscated before they so much as went out for dinner.

It could be no other way.

Yes, he had had a couple of relationships without such arrangements, but they had been with titled women and potential wives. This Antonietta could never be that. And he must test the waters to find out how she felt.

'That must be very quiet,' Rafe said.

'No,' Antonietta refuted as she watered the jasmine. 'I can hear the waves, and I am by the helipad so there are helicopters coming and going. Believe me, they are *loud* when they're overhead. But most of the time it is nice and peaceful.'

'Still…' Rafe said, and his voice was low as his eyes commanded hers to meet his. 'One can have too much tranquillity.'

Their eyes met and his words travelled through her like a current. Looking hastily away, she saw the slight shake of her hand as she watered the flowers and felt the devilish pull of his smooth voice.

Something told Antonietta that her response mattered, for his statement had felt like a question. More…it had felt like an invitation.

One she rapidly chose to decline.

'I am all for tranquillity,' Antonietta said rather crisply.

And instead of meeting his eyes, or thinking of something witty to add, she went back to her list and added a tick.

The flowers were watered, his suite was done and she gave him a smile—only this time, Rafe noted, it was a guarded one.

'I hope the rest of your day is pleasant,' Antonietta said, and let herself out, exhaling a long-held breath once the door between them was closed. She felt a little giddy.

When she entered the elevator to go down, she walked straight into Francesca.

'There you are! What on earth took you so long?' Francesca scolded the very second she clapped eyes on Antonietta, but then she must have regretted her tone, because she said, 'Oh, Antonietta, I apologise. I forgot that Chi-Chi has been working there for the past couple of days. The place must have been in disarray.'

It was Antonietta who was in disarray, though. Had Rafe been suggesting something?

There was little she could pin on his words, and yet there had been a wicked edge in their delivery—she was almost sure of it.

But she'd had no experience with men.

Not good ones, anyway.

For all Sylvester's attempts, his kisses and gropes had never, not once, made her feel the way that Rafe did with just his voice, just his eyes...

She was not only inexperienced in the kissing department, but in the flirting one too. And they *had* been flirting. Or was she romanticising things? Antonietta pondered as she went about her day. Certainly she was innocent, but she wasn't naïve, and she knew from her work in other hotels that Rafe might have been suggesting *'in-room service'*, so to speak.

She managed a soft laugh at that thought, for if that were the case Rafe was certainly wide of the mark.

And yet he had buoyed her up in a way she could not properly explain...

CHAPTER THREE

RAFE HAD BUOYED her up. The day felt brighter for the time she had spent with him.

And the night felt not so long, nor as dark, and Antonietta awoke the next morning with delicious anticipation.

Yes, even the *prospect* of seeing Rafe buoyed her up.

So much so that she decided to stroll into the village and do her shopping before her shift started.

In so many ways it was wonderful to be back. As Antonietta had explained to Rafe, when she had left Silibri it had been after a summer of fierce wild fires and the mountains and trees had been charred and black.

In fact the village had been slowly dying even before she was born, with shops and cafés closing and the youth moving on. Now, though, with the monastery refurbished, there was new growth all around. The trees were lush and there were winter wild flowers lining the roads. The village itself was thriving. Its produce and wares were now in demand, and the cafés were busy and vibrant.

She had already done some of her Christmas shopping— as well as presents for her parents and brother there was a lipstick for Aurora, which she bought faithfully each year. Just because her friend was newly rich, and could afford a lifetime's supply of the vibrant red cosmetic, some things never changed.

Some things *did* change, though. Aurora was married now, and so Antonietta bought some chocolate for Nico at one of the craft stalls in the village square. And not just any chocolate. Hand-made Modica chocolate, which was so exquisite that even a man who had everything could never have enough.

Bizarrely, she thought of Rafe.

Or perhaps not so bizarrely. Because she had been thinking of him on and off since the previous day. More accurately, he had been popping into her thoughts since the day they had met.

'Could I get the coffee flavour, too, please?' Antonietta said impulsively to the stallholder—and then jumped when she heard her name.

'Antonietta?'

It was Pino.

'Did I catch you buying me a gift?' he teased, when he saw her reddening cheeks.

'No, no…' Antonietta smiled back and then glanced at his shopping bag, which was empty. She knew that Pino was just killing time. 'Are you on a day off?'

'Yes, though I thought you were working?'

'Not till midday. But Francesca wants me to go in a little early. No doubt because of our esteemed guest.' She felt her cheeks go a little more pink.

'That's probably it.' Pino rolled his eyes. 'I heard he has asked not to have Chi-Chi service his suite again.'

'Really?' Antonietta's eyes widened. 'Why?'

'I thought you didn't like to gossip?' Pino teased.

'I don't,' Antonietta said, and hurriedly changed the subject. 'Now, I have to choose *two* presents for Gabe—it is his first birthday next week, and then Christmas too.'

Pino was delighted to help, and soon they had a little

wooden train for him, as well as a cute outfit, and Pino suggested they go for coffee.

'I don't have time,' Antonietta said, which wasn't quite true.

The sweet, spicy scent of *buccellato*—an Italian Christmas cake—wafted through a nearby café, and though she was tempted Antonietta was too nervous about bumping into her family to stop there for coffee and cake.

Instead, having said goodbye to Pino, she decided that she would bake her own, and headed into the village store. There she chose the figs and almonds that she needed to make the cake, and added a few other things to her basket before lining up to pay.

The shopkeeper was awkward with her, and did not make eye contact—and then Antonietta found out why.

'Stronza!'

The insult came from behind, and Antonietta did not need to turn her head to know that the word was aimed at her. She had been called worse on previous trips to the shops. Steadfastly, she did not turn around, and though she was tempted to walk out without her groceries, she held her ground.

Another insult was hurled. *'Puttana!'*

They all assumed there must have been another man for her to have run out on Sylvester, or that she had been sleeping with all and sundry in her years away.

Let them think what they choose, Antonietta told herself as she paid.

But as she picked up her bag she saw that it was Sylvester's aunt who was taunting her.

Antonietta said nothing. She just did her best to leave with her head held high—or not quite high, but nor was she head down and fleeing as she had previously. She was determined not to let the incident ruin her day.

But it was about to get worse.

Her parents were walking arm in arm towards her, and both were startled when they saw her.

'Mamma!' Antonietta called.

But together they looked away and crossed to the other side of the street. For Antonietta it was a new version of hell. That they should cross the road to avoid her was not only painful and humiliating, it made her angry too, and hurt words tumbled out.

'I tried to tell you, Mamma!'

Her voice was strangled then, but the words were true, for she *had* tried to reveal her fears about Sylvester to her mother. Antonietta watched as Tulia Ricci's shoulders stiffened. She stopped walking, and slowly turned around.

'You *know* I tried to tell you.'

'Antonietta.' Her father spoke then. 'What are you doing back here?'

And as she saw his cold expression she wondered the very same thing.

It was Antonietta who walked off, refusing to cry.

Even at the hotel she felt an anger building that was unfamiliar to her.

But her shift would start soon, and Antonietta decided she could not think about her family situation *and* do her work, so she fought to set it aside. Tonight she would examine it. Tonight she would sit down and decide whether to stay long enough to complete her training, to give them a chance for a Christmas reunion, but she would not think of it now.

She changed quickly into her uniform and then, with her heart fluttering in her chest and her breath coming too shallow and too fast, she crossed the monastery grounds.

Antonietta was usually a full fifteen minutes early

for work, but so shaken was she by the morning's events that she got there only just in time.

'*There* you are!' Francesca said by way of greeting. 'Signor Dupont has requested that his suite be serviced at midday, when he is out.'

Antonietta nodded and made her way up to the suite. After knocking and getting no answer, she let herself in. There was the scent of him in the air, but not his presence, and she was relieved to be alone and not have to make small talk. She set to work, ticking things off her list, trying to banish all thoughts of this morning.

Except Antonietta could not.

As she smoothed the sheets on the bed all she could see was the sight of her parents, crossing the street to avoid her. She plumped the pillow but found she was crushing it between her hands as the tears started to come thick and fast.

And they were *angry* tears!

She had come here to make amends.

To say sorry to her parents for not marrying a man who had treated her less than gently. A man who had tried to force her to do *that* more than once.

She had held on to her anger for so long, but it was more than seeping out now, and she buried her face in the pillow and let out a muffled scream.

'Agh!'

It felt good.

So good that she did it again.

'Agh!'

And again.

That was how Rafe found her.

He had finally gone for a run—in part to avoid *her*, for such was his cabin fever that he was getting a little too interested in a certain maid.

And that would *never* do.

However, he had not been for a run since his accident, and his endurance was not quite what it had been. He would soon get it back, he told himself, and the next run would be longer.

He made his way up the stone stairs to the private beach entrance of the balcony.

And then he saw her shouting into a pillow.

Rafe did not get involved with the dramas of maids. Ever.

But when she stopped shouting into the pillow and sobbed into it instead, something twisted inside him even though generally tears did not move him.

She was not crying for an audience; he was aware that he was witnessing something private that she would rather no one saw.

Indeed, Antonietta was mortified when she removed the pillow and saw Rafe.

He was breathing heavily from running, and he looked displeased.

'I apologise,' Antonietta said immediately, for an esteemed guest did not need anything other than quiet efficiency. She wiped her cheeks with her hands and started to peel off the pillowcase as her words tumbled out. 'I thought you were out.'

'It's fine.' Rafe shrugged.

'I ran into my parents...' She attempted to explain. 'They crossed the street to avoid me.'

'I see.' Rafe tried to remain unmoved. No, he did *not* get involved with the dramas of maids.

'I can send someone else up...' Antonietta hiccoughed, frantically trying to regain control. Except her tears would not stop.

'There's no need for that,' Rafe said. 'Carry on.'

'But, as you can see, I can't stop crying...'

'I said,' Rafe snapped, 'carry on.'

And though she did carry on with her work, she found that the tears carried on too, and the anger did not abate.

No pillow was left unthumped!

He ignored her.

Well, not quite. At one point, when anger gave way to sorrow, he gave a slight roll of his eyes and handed his weeping maid a handkerchief.

She carried on with her work.

She just dribbled tears, and she was so grateful for his lack of words, that there was no attempt at comfort, for there was nothing he could say.

She would never have her family back. Of that Antonietta was certain. And it was there in the August Suite that she finally mourned them. Oh, there was no howling. Antonietta just quietly let the tears roll.

Rafe did not involve himself.

He would have liked to have a shower, given he had just been for a run, except he did not want to have a shower while the weeping maid was here.

Of course he could dismiss her.

And yet he did not.

Instead Rafe stood on the balcony and looked out towards the temple ruins, wondering about his teary maid.

He recalled the slight triumph he had felt when she'd smiled, and he found he would like her to smile again.

In turn, she liked the silence he gave her. It did not feel as if she was crying alone, as she had done so many times. And neither did she feel patronised, for there had been no *there, there* or invasive questions.

He let her be, and finally she was done with both her work and her tears.

Every last thing on her list was ticked off and Antonietta felt surprisingly calm as she gathered her things and finally addressed Rafe. 'I am finished.'

'Perhaps before you go down you should go and splash your face with cold water...take a moment.'

She did as she was told, appalled to see her swollen eyes and red nose, but she appreciated the opportunity to calm down, and retied her hair before heading out.

'If you need anything else, please page me.'

'I shan't,' Rafe said, but then he reconsidered, for Antonietta really was proving to be the brightest part of his day... But, no, he would not make up reasons to call her. 'Are you working tomorrow?'

'Just a half-day,' Antonietta said. 'Then I have a day off.'

'Well, I might see you tomorrow, then?'

He hoped so.

So did she.

'Thank you,' Antonietta said as she turned to leave, instead of the other way around.

'No problem.'

Except there clearly was.

'Antonietta.'

He called her name as she headed for the door. And his summons hit her deep and low, and the word felt like a hand coming down on her shoulder. How could the sound of her own name make her tremble and feel almost scared to turn around?

Or rather *nervous* to turn around.

Slowly she did turn, and she knew in that second that she was not scared or even nervous to face him. She was fighting her own desire.

In the room behind him she could see the vast bed, and she wanted to lie with him on white sheets that smelt of summer. To know the bliss not just of *a* man, but of *him*.

Rafe.

Whoever he was.

'Yes?' Her voice sounded all wrong. It was too breathless and low and so she said it again—except it came out no better, was a mere croak. 'Yes?'

Rafe rarely—extremely rarely—did not know how to proceed. Not only did he not get involved with maids' dramas, neither did he take maids to bed.

Added to that, she had been crying for the best part of an hour. He never took advantage.

Yet the air was charged. She looked as if he'd just kissed her, and he could feel the energy between them and her increasing awareness of him.

His sad maid looked exactly as she might if he had her pressed against the wall.

'I could have one of my security detail come and speak with you?'

'Why would they need to speak with me?' She frowned, trying to untangle her thoughts from his words. Trying to remind herself that she was at work. 'Is there a problem with security in the suite?' She was desperately trying to hold a normal conversation as her body screamed for contact with his. 'If that's the case I can let Francesca know.'

She knew nothing about his ways, Rafe realised.

'It's fine,' Rafe said. 'My mistake.'

'Mistake?' Antonietta checked, and he could see that her eyes were perturbed, that she assumed she'd said something wrong.

But she'd said everything right.

For this was far more straightforward and yet way more complicated than a contracted affair.

This was pure, unadulterated lust.

From both of them.

And he actually believed now that she had no idea who he was.

Crown Prince Rafael of Tulano.

CHAPTER FOUR

'RAFAEL, BY ALL accounts you could have been killed.'

Rafe had spoken with his father since the accident, but the King hadn't called to enquire as to his health. 'Had you died as my sole heir,' the King continued in reprimand, 'the country would have been plunged into turmoil and well you know it. Did you think of that as you hurled yourself down the mountain?'

'Actually,' Rafe responded, 'I did.'

As he had fallen—as he had realised the seriousness of the unfolding incident—it had dawned on him that this might well be it and he had thought of his country. He had thought of the royal lineage shifting to his father's brother, of his idle, ignorant, spoiled cousins ruling the land that Rafe loved and their undoubted glee that finally the reckless Crown Prince had succumbed.

'Thank God it has been kept out of the press,' the King went on. 'Our people have thankfully been spared from knowing how close this country came *again* to losing its Crown Prince. But it is not enough, Rafe. You need to temper your ways.'

'Then give me more responsibility. Transition some of your power to me.'

It was the same argument they had had of old. Rafe was a natural-born leader who had been raised to be King and already wanted a more prominent role than merely making staged appearances. He did not want to be a pin-up prince; he wanted active power and to be a voice amongst world leaders, yet his father resisted.

'You know the answer to that,' the King responded tartly.

Yes.

Marriage.

And a suitable bride chosen for him by his father the King.

Rafe did not trust his father with that decision. After all, he had witnessed first-hand the hell of his parents' *suitable* marriage.

There was a reason that Rafe was the only heir to the Tulano throne—after he had been born his father had resumed his rakish ways.

His mother understood her duty to the country, and the impact of a divorce, and so it had never been considered. Emotions and feelings were rarely taken into account at the palace. The King and Queen's marriage was a working relationship only. The Queen met with the King daily, accompanied him on formal occasions and hosted functions with grace, but she had her own wing at the palace and had long ago removed herself from his bed.

And there was no 'family life' as such. Rafe had been raised by palace nannies and had later attended boarding school.

No, there was nothing Rafe had witnessed that endeared him to marriage or to the idea of starting a family of his own.

'I expect you back here on Christmas Eve,' the King said. 'Preferably in one piece and without scandal attached. Do you think you can possibly manage that?'

Rafe wasn't sure.

As luxurious as the Old Monastery was, he was already climbing the walls and ready to check out. In fact, he had been about to call Nico to thank him for his hospitality when the call from the palace had come.

'I shall put your mother on.'

To his mother, he was an afterthought. She would never think to call him herself. Instead, when he spoke to his father, she occasionally deigned to come to the phone.

As he awaited the Queen, Rafe decided that if he was going to hide from the public eye then it might as well be on a yacht. Somewhere warm, with requisite beauties. The Caribbean was calling, Rafe thought as he heard his mother's icy tone.

'Rafe.'

'Mother.'

'What a foolish waste of a great ruler it would have been had you been killed.'

'What a foolish waste it is now,' Rafe responded. 'I am told I'm expected to return for Christmas to inspect an army I can no longer fight alongside because you both deem it too dangerous. Perhaps the balcony I have to stand on and wave from is too high? Too much of a risk.'

'Don't be facetious.'

'I am not,' Rafe responded. 'I am bored with being an idle prince...'

'Then act accordingly and you will be given the responsibility you crave.'

Marriage.

All conversations, all rows, all roads led to that. And the pressure did not come solely from his family but from the people, who longed to see their reckless Prince settled.

'I don't require a wife in order to make decisions.'

'You need to temper your ways. At least in the eyes of the public.'

'So as long as I am discreet I can carry on as before?' Rafe checked, and there was no disguising the disgust in his tone.

But his mother was unmoved. 'You have your father's heart, Rafe,' Queen Marcelle responded matter-of-factly. 'No one expects you to be faithful—we all know that your love is reserved for your country. And that country wants to see its Prince married and with heirs.'

'I decide when.'

'Fine,' said his mother. 'Until then, enjoy waving from the balcony!'

They had had this discussion on many occasions, though the news that he could take mistresses, like his father did, was a new development. But not a welcome one. Rafe admired many things about the King, but abhorred plenty.

He had the last word, Rafe knew. But he could not force him to marry.

And yet he could feel the pressure to conform tightening.

Rafe had not been lying when he'd told the King that his country had been on his mind as he'd fallen. Perhaps it was time to take a break from his partying ways, for Rafe was surprised to find himself growing tired of them.

Back on the balcony, he was thinking of one particular beauty. It was too confined here. That must be the reason why his thoughts had again wandered to Antonietta, for usually he allowed himself to get close to no one.

Her tears had moved him.

He wanted to spoil her. He wanted that smile he had seen so briefly to return to her lips.

One more night in Silibri, Rafe told himself.

And he would not be spending it alone.

CHAPTER FIVE

WHO WAS HE?

For the first time Antonietta truly wanted to know more about a guest—or rather, she corrected herself, about a man.

Her no-gossip rule wasn't serving her well now.

But the Internet service in her tiny cottage really was *terrible*.

To her own slight bemusement, an hour after her shift had ended Antonietta found herself heading out of her cottage and standing on a cliff, typing *Rafe* and *Tulano* into her laptop.

No service.

Agh!

She stomped back to her cottage and told herself she was being ridiculous. Whoever Rafe really was, it was irrelevant, given he'd be gone in a matter of days.

Yet, she wanted to know.

She was too embarrassed to ask Pino, who would generally be her main source of information, having shut down his conversation that first morning. And Chi-Chi, who usually daydreamed aloud about any male she saw as a potential suitor, was unusually quiet. Vincenzo was too discreet.

Oh, how she regretted refusing to let Francesca reveal

his identify to her. She could hardly ask her for more information now—it would only raise suspicion. Nico, and in turn Francesca, were very strict about staff keeping a professional distance from their guests.

It was why she was doing so well.

A knock at the door startled her. No one ever came and visited her at the cottage. Well, except for Aurora, but usually she would text to say that she was on her way. Could it be her parents, feeling guilty about avoiding her earlier in the village? Was she finally going to get the Christmas she had craved?

There was a spark of hope as she pulled open the door. But that tiny ray of hope dimmed when she saw who it was.

Rafe!

Actually, it didn't dim. That little spark shrank and regrouped and then reignited, hot, white and blue, as if the collar of a Bunsen burner had been altered.

'Rafe!'

And it was a Rafe she had never seen before. He looked more like the man in the photo attached to his profile except in that he was scowling. In fact, he was smiling, making no attempt to hide his pleasure at her shock.

He wore a dinner suit, and he wore it so very well.

The first time she had seen him he had been rumpled and his hair matted with blood. Now it was black and glossy and brushed back from his elegant face.

There was still a deep bruise on his eyelid, but the swelling had gone, and he was so elegant and commanding, so unexpected and exquisite, that he was simply too much.

'You shouldn't be here,' Antonietta said immediately.

'I didn't see any signs warning me not to trespass.'

'How did you know where I live?'

'Thankfully there is only one cottage near the heli-pad.' Rafe shrugged. 'Or I might have ended up at Chi-Chi's—I'd never have got out alive...'

Despite herself, Antonietta found that she was laughing at the vision his words created. The most stunning man stood at her door, and instead of being nervous she was laughing!

But she stopped herself. 'I can't invite you in.'

'I'm not asking to be let in,' Rafe responded smoothly. 'I'm inviting to come out.'

'Out?'

'After the day you've had, I thought you might like a night of being spoiled.'

'I can't be seen in the restaurant with a guest.' Antonietta shook her head, but as one hand went to close the door her other hand resisted and held it part-way open—a kind of push-pull within her as she offered more reasons to say no. 'And I don't want to be seen in the village...'

'So we go further afield,' he said easily. 'My driver is waiting, if a night out appeals...?'

If a night out appeals?

Her mouth gaped at his choice of words. It more than appealed; pure temptation had come knocking at her door in the delectable shape of Rafe. And yet, as irresistible as his offer was, here came the voice of reason.

He's bored, the voice told her. *You are a mere diversion.*

And the voice became more insistent, rather unkindly pointing out that she was way too inexperienced to handle such prowess and likely it was not just her company he sought.

'I'm not allowed to date guests.'

'Who said anything about a date?'

Those eyes did, Antonietta wanted to respond. They

made her feel warm, and important, and deliciously sought after.

He played it down. 'It is dinner at a restaurant. I could use some company, that is all.' He looked at her. 'And so could you. It is my last night in Sicily. It seems a shame to leave without seeing some of it.'

Her heart sank at the news.

She had been told from the very start, even before they had met, when he had been simply Signor Dupont to her, that he undoubtedly would not last until Christmas Eve and would soon leave. Yet he was *Rafe* now, the man who brightened her day, and soon he would be gone.

Was that why she was considering his offer?

'Where?'

'I shall leave that to my driver. We have to try not to be seen, but it shouldn't be a problem…'

Antonietta frowned. Why would he worry about being seen out? She could think of only one thing.

'You don't have a wife?' she hurriedly checked. 'I know it's not a date, but…' Her voice trailed off.

'Antonietta, I don't have a wife, or a girlfriend. It's my parents who want me to lie low.'

His response gave her some relief, but also confused her. Rafe certainly didn't *look* like a man who worried about what his parents thought.

'Will you join me?' he asked.

A night of reheated pizza, ruminating over her parents' actions that morning and regretting her decision not to join this beautifully dizzying man for dinner? Such a night would be spent loathing her decision and her absolute inability to throw caution to the wind.

In fact, it might even become a lifetime of regret.

'Yes,' Antonietta said. 'I would love to join you.'

* * *

What were you supposed to wear when the sexiest man alive had arrived on your doorstep with a driver, and was waiting to whisk you to dinner?

Antonietta had but one possibility.

And, just as she had reluctantly handed the fabric over to Aurora, she now almost reluctantly slid the dress on.

Because it changed her.

Aurora was a brilliant seamstress. The silk had been cut on the bias, so the dress was as fluid as water and skimmed her body, enhancing the subtle curves The only issue she had was that it was so strappy it showed her bra, and Antonietta did not possess a strapless one.

Thankfully she was small-breasted, and Aurora had lined the top of the dress, but it still felt a little sinful to head out without one.

There was no time to fuss with her hair, so she simply brushed it and settled for wearing it down.

The dress needed no heels, but it certainly required lipstick.

Antonietta had no make-up of her own, and so, promising herself she would replenish it, she opened Aurora's Christmas present and painted her mouth crimson.

No, she would not save the dress for her coffin—and yet she felt like a liar as she stared in the mirror, for truly she was not the woman her reflection portrayed. She was not sexy, nor beautiful, Antonietta told herself, even if the dress said that she was.

Oh, but to Rafe she was.

Antonietta could not know the breath of fresh air that she was to him.

'I lied to you,' Rafe said as she approached.

'You *are* married…'

She knew it! He was simply too good to be true.

'No,' Rafe said, 'but this *is* a date, Antonietta.'

Her breath hitched and that flame spread warmth in her chest and down to her stomach.

'This can go nowhere…' he was very direct in telling her there could be no future for them '…but that doesn't change the fact that tonight I would love to get to know you some more.'

Before she responded, Antonietta knew she had to make something very clear. She did not know his motives, and she would not spend the whole night worrying about them, and so she would be upfront.

'I won't sleep with you, Rafe.'

'You would be a very boring dinner companion if you did.'

'I meant—'

'I know what you meant.' He smiled. 'Don't worry. *I* wouldn't sleep with me either—there's far too much paperwork involved.'

'Paperwork?'

'Come on,' he said, without clarifying what he meant, but she was glad she had told him the night would not end in bed, all the same.

He took her hand and led her to the waiting car, and it made her just a little dizzy that part of her didn't want to know that tomorrow she might wake up and think this had all been just a dream. Perhaps it was.

His driver took them through the village, and Antonietta was grateful for the blacked-out windows because of the number of people who turned and looked at the luxurious vehicle. But as they passed the tiny church—the one she failed to turn up to on her wedding day—Rafe must have felt her ripple of tension.

He turned and looked at her. 'Are you okay?' he checked.

'Of course.'

Except she wasn't. Because a short while later they passed her parents' property and she wondered what they would make of her going out on a date with a guest.

'Don't worry about your parents now.'

'How did you know I was thinking of them?'

'You pointed out where they live,' he reminded her. 'Forget about everything,' he told her. 'Tonight we escape.'

Only not quite.

They drove up the winding hillside and then down into the valley, and there was a certain exhilaration that swept through her at leaving the village she knew so well. But when she glanced behind them, the same car that had followed them out of the Old Monastery was still there.

'Are they following us?' Antonietta asked.

'It's just my security.' Rafe shrugged. 'Don't worry about them.'

But she did.

Not just because Rafe came with a full security detail, but because there was clearly more power to him than she could properly define. She felt as if she had run into the night with a giant—and not just in stature. There was an authoritative air to him that she had never encountered before, even in the most esteemed guests, a commanding edge that both enthralled and unnerved her.

Who *was* he?

Less than an hour ago she had been desperate to find out, but now she was scared to know.

'Do you like to dance?' Rafe asked.

'I don't dance,' Antonietta said. 'Well, I *can't* dance,' she admitted, and then frowned as he pressed the intercom and spoke with his driver.

'The lady likes to dance.'

The restaurant he took her to was stunning. His security team went into the trattoria before them, and she felt a little awkward when they were seated and she saw that the guards had stayed close.

'Do they *have* to be here?' Antonietta checked.

Rafe was so used to them that for a second he was about to ask to whom she referred, but then Antonietta spoke on.

'We're in the middle of nowhere.'

Only it wasn't just for *his* protection that they were close. It was to stop diners taking photos if he was recognised and also, Rafe knew bitterly, to report back to the King.

Rafe lived his life in the presence of staff—maids and aides, advisors and security—and barely noticed them. Yet he could see her discomfort.

'I'll have a word,' Rafe said.

He had several words, and none of them went down very well, for the Crown Prince's behaviour tonight was most irregular.

Still, soon enough they were dining alone.

Wine was poured and Antonietta realised just how hard it was to be in the village day after day after day. Being away from it, she could actually feel the tension leaving, and she let out a sigh as she put down her wine.

'That's better,' Rafe said. 'It's nice to see you looking...'

He didn't really know how to say it—it seemed there was a lightness to her that hadn't been there before. And he felt better being away from the hotel too. It was a relief from the constant weight of planning his next move forward.

'I don't know what to have,' Antonietta admitted, but then her eyes fell on the words 'pistachio pesto' and her mind was made up.

'I've never tried it,' Rafe said.

'Then you don't know what you're missing.' Antonietta smiled.

They ordered their main courses and then, finally alone, they clinked glasses.

'Saluti,' the French-speaking Rafe said.

'Santé!' Antonietta said, and looked him in the eye as they clinked glasses.

He was still looking at her as she took a sip of her drink and then rested back into her seat.

'It is good to be away,' Antonietta admitted. 'It's nice not to be stared at.'

'People were staring when we walked in,' Rafe said. 'Because you look beautiful.'

'Thank you,' Antonietta said. 'It's the dress.'

'Believe me, it's not just the dress,' Rafe said, and he realised he was more relaxed than he had been in a very long while.

It was a gorgeous restaurant, but the atmosphere was peaceful. And Antonietta was right: it was nice not to have his minders so close. Nice to tear bread and dip it in oil and to just…*be.*

Here, she was no longer his chambermaid. Which meant he could ask, 'What happened with your parents?' And she could choose whether or not she answered.

Antonietta looked at this delectable man and, though she would love his take on things, she did not want to bring the mood down. 'I don't want to bore you with it, Rafe.'

'So, give me the short version, then.'

He made her laugh. Oh, there was no *ha-ha-ha*, but his brusque humour teased a single note from her closed throat and stretched her lips to a smile.

He relaxed her. Even while she was nervous and out of her depth, still Rafe's presence somehow eased her soul.

'I was to be married,' Antonietta said. 'I have a very big family, across all the villages, and my father is very well connected...' She stopped herself. 'Sorry, you want the short version.'

'Take as long as you like.'

Her eyes widened, for he sounded as if he meant it. 'I've never really told anyone the whole thing. Then again, I've never had to—everyone already knows...'

'Ah, but do they know *your* version of events?'

'No.' She shook her head and thought for a moment. *'No,'* she said again, for even Aurora had not heard the news from her first-hand.

'It will go no further,' he assured her, 'and I would love to hear it.'

'The day I turned twenty-one I was told that I was to marry my second cousin, Sylvester.'

Antonietta had found that there were generally two reactions to this revelation—a slight grimace of discomfort or a nod of acceptance that said of *course* she should marry into the family, because that was where the money had to stay.

She looked at Rafe to gauge his reaction. There was no grimace and there was no nod. There was just patience.

She looked down. 'At the last minute I decided I couldn't go through with it. I jilted him.'

She dared not look up, but then his hand came across the table and closed around hers.

'Antonietta, can I have the slightly longer version, please?'

She gave a soft laugh, but it was laced with unshed tears—not just because of the subject matter, it was more the bliss of contact, the touch of his skin on hers that somehow cooled her endless scalding shame.

'I should have told him. I know that. Instead I left him standing at the altar. I ran away.'

'In your wedding dress?'

Still he held her hand.

'No. I pulled on some jeans and climbed out of the bedroom window. My father was waiting to take me to the church. By the time he worked out what I had done I was already on the train.'

To Rafe, the waiter coming over with their meals felt like an intrusion, and he wanted to wave him away.

For Antonietta, though, it felt like a reprieve, and her only reluctance at this break in conversation was that their hands had to part.

Then there were flurries of pepper and cheese, and their glasses were topped up, and Rafe could sense her relief not to be talking about herself any more.

He was not used to reticence.

The women he dated—for want of a better word— were only too happy to spend *hours* talking about themselves. Their upcoming photoshoot, their latest role, their clean and green diet, their blah-blah-blah.

And then they would casually ask if he knew so-and-so, which meant could he possibly have a word with them? Not that they wanted favours or anything, they would hastily add.

And then they would sip their thimble of champagne and pretend it had gone to their head, even as they kept all their wits about them, for this was their chance to get ahead, get seen, get a step up on the A-list ladder.

Oh, yes, Rafe knew their game well, because over and over he had allowed them to play it. And even as he told them that this could go nowhere, they countered with how much they liked him. No, no, they insisted, they *really* liked him. For *himself*. It had nothing to do with him being royal—they just liked him *incredibly* much…

He was bored with their fawning, and he knew that he was arrogant and not that nice—he knew there was nothing in him to like aside from his title.

He looked over to Antonietta, who gave an appreciative eye-roll that said her pasta was truly divine.

It was refreshing to sit in silence. To *want* to know more about someone else. And so it was Rafe who spoke. 'What made you change your mind?'

'I never got to make up my mind,' Antonietta said. 'He was the golden boy of the village.'

'Was?'

'He has married and moved away now, but at the time he was the star of Silibri—funny, charming, a hard worker. Everybody loves Sylvester. My father thought he was choosing well…'

'But?'

Antonietta did not know how to answer that. She did not know how to tell Rafe that Sylvester's kisses had left her cold, and that his hands had felt too rough. And that she'd had a sense of fear that had pitched in her stomach whenever she was alone with the man who had been chosen for her.

It wasn't loyalty to Sylvester that halted her, and nor was it Antonietta's propensity never to gossip. Instead it was a new layer of confusion that Rafe had inadvertently added to the mix—for she wanted *his* hand to close again around hers.

They were mid-meal, of course, but his earlier touch had bemused Antonietta, for not only had she liked it, it had felt like the most natural thing in the world. And touch had never come naturally to her.

'Have you seen him since?' Rafe asked when she refused to elaborate on what it was about Sylvester that had caused her to change her mind.

'No. When I got to Paris I wrote and apologised. He never responded and I don't blame him for that.'

'What about your parents?'

'They have had nothing to do with me since. I understand, though. I didn't just shame them. I embarrassed the whole family on both sides...'

'That's surely to be expected when the bride and groom are related?'

'Don't!' She gave a shocked laugh, but then it faded. 'I'm coming to realise that they're never going to forgive me.'

'The question is, can you forgive *them*?'

'Forgive *them*?'

'Antonietta, I'm sure you had your reasons for running away.'

She didn't answer with words. Instead it was Antonietta's skin that spoke, as a blush spread across her chest and cheeks.

'Quite sure,' Rafe said.

'They weren't to know,' she responded, in hot defence of her parents, but Rafe remained unmoved.

'I have known you for only a few days,' he said. 'And I *know* that you had your reasons. I don't know what they were, but I am certain they exist.'

Antonietta swallowed and then reached for her wine, took a gulp and swallowed again.

'You can tell me,' he offered.

'Why would I?' Antonietta retorted. 'You leave tomorrow.'

'That makes me the perfect sounding board,' said

Rafe, refusing to match her sudden anger. 'You never have to see me again.'

It was, she silently conceded, oddly appealing.

'However, if you don't want to speak about yourself any more you can ask about me,' he invited. 'Or perhaps you already know?'

'I don't know anything about you,' Antonietta admitted. 'Some of the staff have tried to tell me, but I close my ears to gossip and I never pry.'

'Pry away,' Rafe said, for although he had done his best to maintain their privacy, there was a chance she would wake up to the tabloids telling her she had dined with a playboy prince.

'You'll answer anything?' Antonietta checked.

'Not necessarily.' He would tell her his title, Rafe had decided. Generally, that more than sufficed.

Yet the question she had for Rafe was not about that. 'Where did you get those bruises?'

His eyebrows rose in surprise at her question. 'Skiing,' he said.

'An accident?'

'Not really. It was more recklessness on my part.'

'Oh. So you're here in Silibri to recover?'

'I'm here to lie low for a while,' Rafe said.

'And you're *not* married?'

'I've already told you, no.'

'Or involved with anyone?'

Rafe's jaw gritted a fraction. Couldn't she just ask the simple question and be done? Once she knew he was the Crown Prince of Tulano this attempt at a get-to-know-you would end.

For no one really knew the Crown Prince.

'I'm not serious about anyone.'

'Have you ever been?'

'Why all these questions?'

'You told me I was free to pry!'

So he had. 'No,' Rafe said. 'I have never been serious about anyone.' He thought back. 'I tried to be once,' he said. He glanced up and saw that she sat still and silent. Patiently waiting. 'Or rather, I tried to make things work. But I was barely in my twenties.' He looked into her sad treacle-black eyes and appreciated her lack of comment. 'I disappointed a lot of people when we broke up. Though I guess you would know all about that?'

'Were you engaged?'

'God, no!' Rafe said. 'If that had been the case there would have been no going back.'

The way he said it made her shiver. That dark note to his tone struck a warning that she had no idea of the power she was dealing with.

As delectable as her pasta was, Antonietta put her silverware down, and as the waiter removed her plate she braced herself to ask the final question.

But when push came to shove she found that she dared not. 'Rafe, on a couple of occasions I have tried to find out who you are. But the truth is I am a little nervous to know.'

'Why?'

'Because...' She flailed around for an explanation. 'Because I don't want to feel any more daunted than I already do.'

'You feel daunted?'

'A bit,' she admitted. 'A lot.'

'I don't want you to feel daunted,' Rafe said, and again he took her hand.

'Which is why I don't want to find out that you're a film star, or a world champion skier...'

She floundered in her poor attempts to label him, for

she was certain he was rather more than that. She knew it from the way he held himself, and the silent command of his presence. She knew that heads had turned as they entered the restaurant, and they had not, despite his kind words, turned for her.

She looked down at their entwined fingers. Oh, it was not just his hands that gave him away, but they had hinted at the truth from the start. Yes, there really were only two reasons that men had manicures: they chose to or they were born to.

She did not want to know.

'So you think I could be a film star or a world champion skier?' Rafe teased. 'Absolutely not, to the former, and I wish, to the latter.'

And then it was Rafe who had a question, and he both frowned and smiled when he asked it.

'Why wouldn't you want me to be a champion skier?'

She blushed instead of answering.

'Why?' Rafe asked again.

'I would like to see the dessert menu,' Antonietta said, and sidestepped the question.

Rafe left it.

For now.

'I can't decide!' Antonietta groaned as she read through the menu, because everything sounded sublime.

'When there is Modica chocolate mousse on the menu,' Rafe said, with barely a glance at the other offerings, 'the choice is already made.'

He gave her a quizzical look as she started.

'What?'

'Nothing,' Antonietta said, thinking of the purchase she had made that morning with Rafe in mind. It would be foolish to tell him, surely? But then she looked into the eyes of the man who had been so very kind to her today and it made it a little easier to reveal. 'I bought some for you.'

'For *me*?'

Antonietta nodded. 'For Christmas. Well, that was when I thought you were staying until Christmas Eve.'

In Silibri, gifts were often exchanged then. Though it wasn't often that a chambermaid bought a gift for a guest, and they both knew it.

She opened her mouth to say that she had bought it because he had been kind when she cried. But of course that would be a lie, for she had bought it before that had happened.

'It's just a small thing,' she settled for instead. 'A tiny little thing.'

Yet it touched Rafe.

'Coffee-flavoured,' Antonietta said.

'With a breakfast banquet at the side?' he checked, taking them both back to the morning they had met.

'No!' Antonietta smiled.

'You were the only good thing that happened that day.'

'I didn't do anything,' she pointed out.

'Antonietta, I find your silence golden.'

Their desserts arrived, and with them a silver platter which, the waiter told them, held real snow from the Nebrodi range. Nestled in it were two tiny glasses of icy Limoncello.

'Is this really snow?' Antonietta asked, pressing into it with her fingers.

'Apparently so,' Rafe said, pushing his own fingers in and finding hers. '*Not* what I need after a skiing accident. It's lucky it's not triggering a flashback.'

He made her laugh.

And to see her laugh felt like a reward.

The mousse was perfect and the Limoncello, though

icy, was warming and a delectable end to their meal. Though the night did not have to end, suggested Rafe. Because they could dance.

'I told you, I don't dance,' she attempted to say. But when he ignored her and stood up, held out his hand, she decided that Aurora was right and this dress did deserve at least one dance.

Or two. For how could he be so tall and so broad and yet so graceful? Antonietta wondered as she melted in his arms.

He carried her through it—not physically, but through her missteps and clumsy efforts. And he only winced once.

'Did I step on your feet?' She gave a worried frown.

'No,' Rafe told her, and he said no more—just held her until she knew how to dance…but only with him.

He felt the tension slide out of her during the second dance, and he knew certain triumph as she relaxed in his arms. Somehow he knew this was rare for her. And he could not remember enjoying a night so much.

A night that could be considered tame by his usual standards, but by royal standards was both reckless and wild. Because she hadn't been palace-approved, as a true date would be, and neither had she signed disclaimers, as his usual companions would.

It was uncharted waters for both of them.

The music slowed further, as if the band had heard his silent request, and now he moved her closer.

Antonietta made no protest, for she wanted more contact and she liked the shield of his arms. The heat from his palm was in the middle of her back and his other hand was on her bare arm. He did not put a finger wrong.

Not one.

Yet her bare arm wished that he would.

She could feel the slight pressure of his fingers and she ached to know their caress. She wished the hand on her back would go lower, so much so that she suddenly found she was holding her breath.

'Antonietta?'

His head had lowered and his mouth was near her ear. His voice, so close, made her shiver.

'Yes?' she said, though she did not lift her face to him. Instead she opened her eyes to the fabric of his suit.

'Why don't you want me to be a world champion skier?'

She didn't answer straight away, and instead swayed to the beat as every exposed piece of flesh—and those hidden away beneath the red silk—burned in his arms.

'Because...' she started.

'I can't hear you.'

Now she lifted her head, and she had to stretch her neck so that her red-painted lips were close to his ear.

'Aren't sportsmen supposed to be insatiable?'

'I don't know,' Rafe said. 'I have never been with one.'

She laughed, but then she was serious. 'I won't sleep with you,' she said again.

It was stated as fact, yet she knew it was a lie, because she was on fire in his arms and she was weak with want.

'Can I ask why?' Rafe said, for he could feel her desire.

She could have told him that she was scared to, or that she did not know how, and both of those answers would have been true, but there was another reason that was holding her back, and Antonietta voiced it now.

'Because I have a feeling that you would pay me.'

'I would pay for your discretion,' Rafe responded calmly. 'Not for the act.'

She pulled back and looked up into his eyes. 'I don't understand...'

'You would have to sign an NDA.' He registered her frown. 'A non-disclosure agreement.'

'That's the most unromantic thing I have ever heard.' She actually laughed.

'Tell me about it,' Rafe said. 'It is very inconvenient at times.'

How was she *laughing* at such a subject?

Why was she imagining them tumbling into bed and Rafe whipping out a contract for her to sign?

'It is just as well,' Rafe continued, 'that I am the least romantic man.'

Except he didn't seem unromantic to her. She had never felt more looked after, or been held with such care and skill, and she had never looked so deeply into a man's eyes while sharing a smile.

'But you can carry on dancing with me,' Rafe said, 'without signing a thing.'

He pulled her in so close that she could feel all she would be missing pressing into the softness of her stomach. His other hand was on her shoulder, toying with the spaghetti strap of her dress and making her breasts ache and crave for the same attention.

'Can you kiss me?' Antonietta asked, and her voice was husky and unfamiliar. 'Without me having to sign a thing?'

'Of course,' he said, in a voice that was completely steady. 'But later.'

Kiss me now, she wanted to plead as his hand moved down to the small of her back and pressed her in a little more.

He smoothed the hair from her hot face and then slid his hand under the dark curtain and stroked her neck and the top of her spine. They hadn't even kissed, yet she was weak and breathless in his arms, and just when she thought she might die from wanting him he released her a touch.

'Why don't I take you home?' Rafe suggested.

He made her wait for her kiss.

Through handshakes with the owner and then out to the delicately lit street.

Now, she kept thinking. *Let it be now.*

But, no.

He took her hand and held it tightly as they walked to the car.

Now, please now, she thought, with the moon high in the sky as they drove through the hillsides.

But of course it would not be now, for she did not want the audience of his driver for their first kiss, even if there was a partition.

Rafe sensed that. He had done far more than kiss in the back of a luxury car, but he wanted this to be right.

He still held her hand, carefully moving it to his thigh, but that was all. And then he loosened his grip and left it there.

She felt the solid muscle beneath her hand and of course she was too shy to move her hand higher. But there was actually no need, for to rest her hand on his thigh was bliss enough.

And then the girl with the saddest eyes spoke and made her first joke to him. 'Champion skiers have very powerful thighs.'

He smiled. 'Perhaps I missed my vocation.'

He made her wait even longer as they arrived at her little stone cottage at the end of a perfect date, and he made one thing very clear.

'Don't ask me to come in, for I might find it impossible to leave.'

'I won't.' Antonietta nodded. She would not lower

herself to deal with 'paperwork', but she did have one request. 'Can you ask your minders to leave, though?'

She was not just quiet, Rafe realised, she was shy, for the cars were all parked well away. He was about to point that out, and even possibly to add that they could not be less interested in a mere kiss, for they had seen far more. In truth, should he be asked in, they were the men who would speak with her first and get her signature on a page.

Except it was not a *mere* kiss.

And he would not be asked in.

'One moment.'

Dismissing Royal Protection Officers was not that easy, for though they were minding *him*, they answered to the King. And this was irregular indeed.

But in the end Rafe was Crown Prince, and when the Crown Prince told you, in no uncertain terms, to back the hell off because you were dismissed for the night, then—albeit reluctantly—you left.

She heard the crunch of gravel as the cars drove away and watched as Rafe walked back towards her—alone. She was nervous, but no longer daunted. He took her little purse from her hands and he took off her shawl. But it wasn't the night air that made her shiver as he placed them on the stone wall, it was the thought of the kiss to come.

He looked right at her as his fingers went to the spaghetti strap of her dress. They made a new language, one without words, for as his fingers toyed with the strap his eyes told her that he had wanted to do this on the dance floor. She swallowed as he pulled the strap down her arm, and she was shaking like a trapped bird as he lowered his head and kissed the bare skin.

Oh, his mouth was warm and soft, and then not so

soft, more thorough and deep, and her lips parted, and her knees did not know how to keep her standing up.

No matter, for his hand slid around her waist and his mouth worked up her neck and then came to her mouth.

'All night,' Rafe said, 'I have wanted to kiss you.'

Antonietta had dreaded Sylvester's kiss, let alone the thought of anything more. She had never envisaged that she might ache for a man's kiss. But now, with her neck damp from his mouth and his hands on her cheeks, she was wound tight with anticipation, and desperate to know the weight of his lips on hers.

It was a soft weight, and at first it satisfied. The graze of his lips had her own mouth pouting to reciprocate and her eyes simultaneously closing. He kissed her slowly until she returned it, and when her lips parted she shivered at her first taste of his tongue.

She had never imagined that a mouth could be so sublime, that his tongue could dance her to pleasure. His hands slipped from her face and moved down her bare arms, and Antonietta remained in his kiss, felt the pleasure building. He kissed her harder, and she felt as if she were nailed to the wooden door by his mouth, by the hands that were on her ribcage and the stroke of his thumb on her breast.

It had her weak and yet faintly desperate. Yes, desperate. For his kiss no longer satisfied. Instead it shot need into her veins. And the way his hand cupped her breast and lightly stroked her felt as if he was stroking her on the inside.

Rafe wanted her.

Badly.

But she had stated her case. So he removed his mouth and looked down at her, flushed and wanting and desirous.

'Go inside,' he told her.

Yet she remained.

For it felt as if the sky had parted and she had glimpsed behind it—as if everything she had been told and all that she had assumed was wrong.

Her body *worked*.

She wanted Rafe's kisses.

She craved Rafe's touch.

Sylvester's taunts had pierced her, embedded themselves so deeply, and yet she felt them lifting now.

Rafe did not daunt her.

If anything, she felt as if he had freed her.

This elusive man, who housed so many secrets, had set her body on fire.

Antonietta glimpsed all that she had avoided and all she had never truly known she was missing.

But would that change if he knew about her lack of experience?

Rafe was used to sophisticated women—something she doubted she could be. Would her innocence douse his desire? For he had made it clear he wanted no strings. And in that moment neither did she.

For the first time in her life Antonietta wanted to be intimate with a man. To taste his kiss again and to know the bliss denied to her until now.

This was so different—so new and so transforming.

And her choice entirely.

Her usual caution lay somewhere between the furthest star and the moon. She knew now how good a kiss should be, and only wanted more of the same.

And so she said what was in her heart.

'Take me to bed.'

CHAPTER SIX

RAFE DID *NOT* recall his minders.

Antonietta removed her high heels and they walked hand in hand across the moon-drenched grounds of the monastery on a clear Silibri night.

Where there had been years of turmoil and angst, now there was clarity and certainty. For there was no thought as to the outcome, or to tomorrow, just the bliss of now and this night.

'We can't go through the foyer,' Antonietta said.

'Of course not,' Rafe agreed. 'I have my own entrance. Though you would…'

His voice trailed off and she felt his grip tighten on her hand. She looked up to see what had stopped him from speaking, though his stride did not falter.

Antonietta looked to where his gaze fell and there at the foot of the steps was a suited man—one of his security detail. She attempted a small joke. 'He can't stop you from entering, surely…?'

And then it was her voice that trailed off as she realised that of course it was not *Rafe* who was the problem.

It was her.

But the security man said nothing. He merely stepped aside. And as Antonietta glanced up at Rafe she saw why—the man would surely not dare to question him, for the look Rafe gave him could freeze molten lava and halt a lion's approach.

'Is there a problem?' Antonietta asked, recalling their conversation about 'paperwork'.

'Of course not,' Rafe said, for he knew he would deal with the issues raised tomorrow. And there would be issues—of that he was certain. For Antonietta had been neither vetted nor approved. And the security guard had unnerved her.

Rafe could not know of her trepidation as he pushed open the French windows and they stepped into the lounge of his suite.

The turn-down service had been in and a fire was lit.

'Would you like a drink?' he offered.

She was about to decline, but then she glanced at the open doors to the bedroom and saw the vast bed. She decided she needed to pause things for a moment, if only to slow her heartbeat down.

'Please.'

She took in a deep breath as he poured, and could not decipher whether it was terror or desire that coursed through her.

Both, she decided as they clinked glasses.

But a drink didn't hold him back for long.

'Come here,' he told her, and put down his glass.

Antonietta did the same, and as she walked towards him it felt less seamless, and his kiss was different too.

It was thorough, it was hungry, and she felt her bravado fading.

She was tumbling with confusion, on an impossible see-saw as she kissed him back. Because he sent her skywards with his hands, with his mouth, with the way he held her against him.

He took her hand and guided it to where he was hard,

and she felt as if the giddy high of the sky and then her nerves had her meeting the ground with a thud.

And she did not know how to reach the sky again.

And she could not fake her way through it.

'Rafe...' She had to tear her mouth from his, had to force her breathless throat to form words. 'I've never...'

Rafe did not care if she had never been into one-night stands.

He did not care if this was not something she often did.

But then he saw her pupils were dilated—and not just with desire. He recognised fear, and though he held her still, he froze absolutely.

'I've never slept with anyone before,' she said.

He dropped her.

Oh, she did not actually tumble to the ground, but she felt the see-saw crash down and she sank further without his touch.

'And you didn't think to tell me?'

'I was hoping you wouldn't notice.'

'Not notice! What the—?'

How the hell could she possibly think he might miss such a detail? But then his eyes narrowed in suspicion.

'Or were you hoping that I'd be too far gone to care?' he accused.

'I don't know what you mean.'

She really didn't.

He watched as she pulled up the straps on her dress, her pert nipples visible beneath the sheer fabric because their arousal remained. It was a fire that would not die, and had her words not halted him they would have been locked together now, with no thought to the consequences.

Rafe knew it.

Absolutely he knew it.

And it was an unfamiliar thing—for he always maintained a semblance of control and never forgot he was royal.

'I don't know what you mean,' Antonietta said again, her voice rising this time, and Rafe felt the anger recede, for she *really* didn't know. She wasn't trying to trap him, he realised. She was clueless, not ruthless.

'You should have told me.'

'Yes,' Antonietta agreed. 'But if I had I would be tucked up in bed alone now.'

'Do you know why?'

'Because you want someone experienced. You want—'

'Antonietta,' he interrupted, 'I leave tomorrow.'

She didn't blink, he noted. At least not until a log on the fire dropped, and it spat sparks and hissed for a moment before it settled.

'I know that,' she said finally.

'If you have waited this long—'

'Oh, please don't!' Antonietta interrupted him now, a little embarrassed and a lot angry. 'Please don't tell me that I must be saving myself for marriage, for Mr Right...'

'Why have you waited, then?'

'Because.'

Now she was embarrassed, and she reached for her shawl rather than answer him. She picked up her bag, ready to head out into the night, but he caught her arm.

'Because?' he demanded.

'I've never wanted anyone until now!' She shouted it, and continued to shout. 'My fiancé kept trying and I loathed it. I loathed every touch and every kiss and every attempt—' Her chest shuddered as she took in ragged gulps of air.

'Every *attempt*?' Rafe checked. 'What do you mean?'

'He tried—several times—but I fought him off.'

There—she had said it and the sky had not fallen. She had told someone. In fact she had admitted to this man whom she had known only a few days, something she had never revealed to her family or even her dearest friend.

Perhaps it was because she knew Rafe was leaving, she pondered briefly.

'I told *him* that I was saving myself for marriage; it was the only way I could keep him back. So please don't assume you know my reasons for waiting.'

'Did he hurt you?' Rafe was aware of the anger in his own voice and fought to check it, for his anger was not aimed at her. Then he answered his own question. 'Of course he did.'

'No,' she countered. 'Not really.' For even all these years later there was no neat category for what had taken place on those long-ago nights, and she didn't want to discuss it. 'You are not a counsellor—and I came here to move on, not to look back.'

She looked down to his hand, still closed around her wrist, but looser now.

'I'll say goodnight,' she said.

Yet Rafe could not leave things there. He let go of her wrist, and as he watched Antonietta gather her things there were two people that Rafe loathed right now.

The man who had attempted to force her.

And the man who had tonight denied her.

'Antonietta…' He could see her confusion, could still feel the hum of angry words that hung in the air, and he did not want her leaving like this. 'I would never have brought you back here had I known you were a virgin.'

'We've already established that,' she clipped.

'Listen to me!' he snapped back.

And she liked it that he snapped. She liked his impatience, and the fact that he did not suddenly treat her like fragile glass, that her past did not change them.

'I am trying to explain…'

'You don't want me,' Antonietta said. 'I think you have made that exceptionally clear.'

'Of *course* I want you!'

He sounded cross, and yet his tone did not trouble her. It felt like a row. Yet it did not unnerve her.

For when she looked, when she met his navy eyes, there was desire rather than ire blazing in his eyes.

And it almost floored her.

'Antonietta.'

He took a breath and it seemed to her as if he was preparing her for bad news.

'I *will* be leaving tomorrow.'

Was that it? The bad news? She knew that already.

'Rafe…'

She did not know how best to put it that she was not terrified of his leaving. She was terrified of being sent away!

Tomorrow? She had dreaded so many tomorrows. And she had loathed so many yesterdays.

'I don't care what happens in the morning.'

It sounded reckless, yet right now she felt no caution.

Rafe knew more about her than any other person on this earth. He knew her secrets. And with his kiss he had disproved her own theory, for it turned out that Antonietta *could* want, could be folded over with desire and crave a man's touch.

'I don't care that you're leaving tomorrow,' she told him. 'I care only that you're asking me to leave *now*.'

He weighed her words as he stood there. And they were heavy ones, for she was trusting herself to him.

'I'm not asking you to leave,' Rafe said. 'I'm just asking if you are sure.'

She was.

Absolutely.

As certain as she had been at the door to her cottage.

More certain than she had been as they'd walked on the moon-drenched grass.

Completely certain now.

And nervous.

Yet excited as Rafe took her hand and led her to the master bedroom.

It was warm in there. The turn-down service had been in and the fire was roaring. She wondered if he would open the French windows to let in some cool air, but instead he threw two more logs on the roaring fire and then came over to her.

'What am I to do with you?' Rafe asked, and she did not know how to answer. He smoothed back the hair from her face and his gaze was assessing. 'Are you scared?'

'No,' Antonietta said. 'Well, a bit—but not like I once was.'

The room was too hot, and they stood just a little too close to the fire. But she liked it. For the fire felt like an iceberg and the air seemed cool compared to the heat pooling low in her belly and spreading down her thighs.

Yet Rafe touched her not.

Deliberately so.

This would be no *attempt*.

He loathed it that she had been touched while unwilling, and he would not move even so much as a finger until she approached him, though he'd offer direction.

'Take off your dress,' he told her, and she blinked, because she had thought that Rafe would take care of that. But Rafe did not cajole her, he did not sweet talk or wheedle, he simply made her want.

And it felt delicious.

For the first time ever she rued Aurora's dressmaking skills, for it took her a moment to find the tiny concealed zip at the side. She pulled it down with shaky hands and then stood trembling and a little shy as it fell to the ground.

She stood only in her knickers. As a reflex, she covered her breasts with her arm. But then she pondered her own disappointment if Rafe were to undress and do the same, and she took a breath and peeled her arm away, let it fall to the side.

Rafe cast his gaze the length of her slender frame, to her pert breasts and the dark areolae, the stiffened nipples that he ached to touch—but resistance was a turn-on, he was finding.

She pushed her knickers down without his instruction, and had to put a hand up, resting it on his chest to steady herself. He hissed out a long intake of breath.

He reached out and traced one manicured finger from her collarbone to her breast, until her own breath choked her. The feel of his hand on her breast was sublime and she looked down, somewhat fascinated. For the room felt like a sauna, and yet her dark nipples peaked to his touch as if they were smeared in Nebrodi snow.

He was sure that she was sure.

So sure that he lifted her by the hips and their mouths met as if deprived. She coiled her legs around his torso and his hand roamed her naked body as they kissed.

She did not know how sexy she was, Rafe thought, for he had thought her shy and reticent and yet she came alive in his hands.

He wanted to tear off his clothes, just to feel her naked

against him, but there was a supreme pleasure in her naked warm body wrapped around him.

He placed her down on the bed that she had made that very morning. The sheets that smelt of summer were cool and yet soft on her naked skin, and she made no attempt to cover herself, just lay and watched as he undressed.

She had seen him nearly naked, but on those occasions she had averted her eyes and tried not to look. Now there was no need to be chaste, or embarrassed by her inquisitiveness, and she watched unashamedly as he peeled off his shirt and revealed his chest.

Rafe was impatient to be naked and to join her. Rarely did he have to tell himself to slow down, and yet her hungry eyes beckoned. The rosy blush spread as if she held a fan across her chest and cheeks, and the way she bit down on her lip as he unbuckled his belt made undressing a less than seamless task, for he could not tear his eyes from her.

Nor could she tear hers from him. For she might have seen him *nearly* naked and considered him perfection, but completely exposed Rafe was magnificent.

Far more magnificent than she knew what to do with.

And when she saw him, so strong and erect, there was a stroke of desire so low in her stomach that she pulled up her knees.

'Don't be scared,' he told her.

'I'm not,' Antonietta said, in a voice that sounded too thick and too low.

And then she looked at him again, and wondered how they might possibly fit.

But she was *not* scared. She knew that because before fear had made her fight like a cat and slam her legs closed.

Fear had never made her approach. And it was not

fear that had her rising to her knees and prowling across the bed towards him.

For the first time they were face to face, and yet only for a moment did they look into each other's eyes. There was so much to explore, to touch and to feel, and Antonietta had been resisting doing so almost since they had met, since their first conversation.

But now she could touch those wide shoulders, feel their strength and his warm skin beneath her fingers. Now she could run her hand down his chest and explore the mahogany nipples, pressing the pads of her fingers in. She ached to kiss them, and yet there was even more she ached to feel. She perused the taut planes of his stomach and then turned her hand so the backs of her fingers brushed the snaky line of dark hair.

Daring herself, she touched his thick member, surprised when it twitched as she held him alive and firm in her nervous palm. He slid through her hands and Rafe let her explore him, though his teeth were gritted together, for he longed to wrap his hand tight over hers. But to show her his rhythm would finish him, so he sank into her untutored perusal and explored her instead.

His hands were light on her breasts, yet her nipples hardened further and almost stung, so that she yearned for the wetness of his mouth. He did not give it. Instead his hands slid slowly down, past the curve of her waist, and held her hips, pulling her closer to him and rocking her, so that he nudged against her and left a silver trail on her stomach.

Her breathing hitched and she did not know how to get it back to its rhythm. When his hand slid between her thighs she gave in, and just rested her head on his chest.

Her soft moans spoke of her pleasure as he parted

damp curls. Feeling her warm and ready, Rafe slid his fingers into her warm folds and explored her.

'There…' she breathed.

It was a needless instruction, because he already was there, but she pressed her face into his chest and inhaled his scent. One large hand cupped her buttock as the other burrowed into her tight, warm space.

And she didn't just let him—Antonietta *wanted* him.

She wanted the tiny volts of pleasure he shot through her, and she wanted the salty taste of his skin on her lips and tongue, and the tears that squeezed from her eyes were absolutely ones of pleasure.

And when he was sure she was ready—when he could feel she was on the delicious edge, and when he knew that her pleasure might finish him—Rafe withdrew his hand and opened the bedside drawer.

The tearing of foil felt like a zip tightening low in her stomach, and Antonietta watched, held in a spell of his making, as he sheathed himself.

She bit down on her lip rather than admit that she preferred the velvet skin naked.

But then her lip broke free, and unwittingly she voiced her thoughts. 'I want to feel you in me…'

Rafe pulled a breath in. Those words from anyone else would have served as a warning. Yet tonight those words were a mirror of his own thoughts.

'And you shall,' he told her as he laid her down.

The room was almost stifling, yet it only heightened the pleasure. Her body was flushed and pliant, and when he came over her Antonietta's mouth met his.

He nudged at her entrance and she closed her eyes as he finally took her—took her there and back on a spectrum of pleasure and pain as he filled her.

Her hands gripped his shoulders and he gritted his teeth. 'Your shoulder...' she gasped.

She knew then what his grimace on the dance floor had been about, but as she went to remove her hands his pain was forgotten, and she dug her fingers further in as he filled her so absolutely that it felt there wasn't even enough space to gather in a necessary deep breath.

Instead, she held on to her breath and to a scream.

She had been right. They did not fit.

Yet for Rafe the tight grip of her was so intense that he let out a moan as he fought to stay still while she grew accustomed to the feel of him inside.

She would never accustom herself, Antonietta was sure. Except now his ragged breathing in her ear was coming into focus, and her grip was loosening on his shoulder, and she was so warm she felt she might faint.

'I want a drink of water,' she said, and heard his low laughter in her ear.

He gave her his mouth and he kissed her softly, so that she forgot the agony she was in. More velvet-soft kisses and then he moved deep inside her until she could no longer focus on his kiss.

She slumped back on the bed and he slid an arm under her, and when he moved she did the same.

'Rafe...' She said his name and he tempered himself, fought to slow down, but that was not what she was asking. 'More...'

She had never known anything so delicious—until he put his elbows to the sides of her head and looked right down into her eyes, sweeping damp hair from her face. Then Rafe started to thrust, and she held not his chest, nor his shoulders. She stroked her fingers down his back and felt his taut buttocks, pressed him harder into her.

How did he know? she wondered, because she'd

closed her eyes and told him nothing, but he was thrusting harder now.

'Rafe...' she said again, but there was no instruction she could give when he was playing her like a master.

He felt the shivers of her orgasm even before Antonietta knew what was happening.

He was moving faster, and she could see the concentration on his features. The tension seemed to rip through her, and she clenched tight, but he thrust harder.

Rafe came in blessed relief, and her deep pulses dragging him in were his reward. And then his breathless moan reverberated through her as she convulsed beneath him. He felt her soft collapse as her body relaxed.

'I never knew...' Antonietta was breathless as he lay atop her, dragging in air. 'All I was missing...'

'Because you never knew *me*.'

CHAPTER SEVEN

Just as she always was, Antonietta was up long before the Sicilian winter sun. And for a moment she languished in bliss. Her head lay on Rafe's chest and she listened to the *thud, thud, thud* of his heart, and in the silence of predawn she focussed only on the sheer pleasure of waking next to him.

The hurt that had become so familiar was held at bay when she was in his arms, and it was incredibly tempting to sink back into the sleep that beckoned. She fought it, though. The consequences of being caught in a guest's bed had started to impinge and Antonietta forced her eyes open.

'Rafe...' She tried to untangle herself from the heavy arm that lay over her. 'I had better head back to the cottage.'

'Not yet,' he said sleepily.

'Yes,' she insisted. 'Your coffee will be delivered soon, and I had better not be here! I ought to leave while it's still dark.'

'I'll walk you back.'

It was an offer without precedent, for while Rafe always ensured that his dates were seen home, it was generally under the care of his driver. Not that Antonietta could know that.

Even so, she immediately shook her head. 'No, the staff will soon be starting to arrive,' she said as she hauled herself from the warm bed and pulled the drapes open enough to allow her to see and scramble for her clothes. 'I cannot be seen leaving your room.'

It really was unthinkable.

Most certainly she would lose her job. And, worse, her reputation in the village—already shaky at best—would flatline completely.

Last night it had felt so simple and straightforward, but the encroaching light of dawn cast shadows of doubt.

Rafe had promised one night, which meant their time was over, but how could this be goodbye? How did she simply walk out of his life as if their parting did not matter to her?

Because it did.

It very much did.

Rafe turned on the bedside light and Antonietta hurried to finish dressing. She turned her back to him, though not because she was suddenly shy—she was trying to hide her eyes. She did not want Rafe to glimpse, even for a second, that last night's bravado had gone.

'Tomorrow' was here.

Which meant he was leaving today.

Antonietta couldn't say that she hadn't been warned. The potential for hurt had been clearly labelled, just as a pharmacist added stickers to a medicine bottle.

May cause heartbreak.
In case of sudden tears do not attempt conversation.

And so Antonietta did up the tiny zip on her dress, pulled on her shoes, and then turned to Rafe and attempted a smile. 'Thank you for a wonderful night.'

He lay with his hands behind his head, watching her dress and wanting to haul her back into bed. Sex had made him hungry, and he would love nothing more than to confuse the chefs and cancel his strict order for coffee only, then tear into pastries and make love to her all over again.

'Stay a little longer. I'll order breakfast.'

'I'm not hiding in the bathroom, Rafe. Anyway, I really do have to go to work.'

She did not want prolonged goodbyes and to be told by him that it had been good while it lasted.

Make that *great*.

Or rather, make that the single best time of her entire life.

And it wasn't just the sex, though her body felt deliciously bruised and awoken. More, it had been the talking and the dancing, and walking across the Old Monastery grounds hand in hand.

And, even more than the sum of all that, it had been the honesty she had found with him. Even if it was impossible to be honest now, and admit that leaving with a smile was the hardest thing she had ever done.

Absolutely the hardest.

She went over and gave him a kiss.

A light one was her intention—except Rafe moved his hand behind her head and pressed her close. Antonietta closed her eyes to the taste and the bliss. She was tempted, so tempted to give in. Was he subtly guiding her to lie atop him, or was she actually drifting that way to the command of his kiss?

Their tongues were more urgent, the kiss deeper as his other hand moved to her breast, toying with it through the fabric of her dress, and Antonietta knew he would have far less trouble with the zip than she.

Rafe's moves were seamless, and Antonietta knew that any moment she would be naked and knotted with him, locked into bliss with no thought as to the ramifications there would surely be.

And she would fall deeper.

Self-preservation had Antonietta removing her mouth, and she looked down for a moment into his deep navy eyes and knew she could very easily drown in them.

Do not take more than the stated dose...

Or she might never recover.

'Be good,' she said.

He gave a slight mirthless laugh. 'I don't want to be good.' But then he was serious. 'You're okay?'

'Of course.'

'You're sure?' Rafe checked, and watched as her eyes narrowed a touch.

Would he prefer that she cried? Antonietta wondered. Well, she refused to allow him back into her thoughts. She had been a willing participant last night and did not regret it for a moment. It was just that she had missed the part in life's guidebook about how to walk from someone who mattered. The lesson that taught you how to be incredibly close one moment and say farewell the next.

'Goodbye, Rafe.'

Yes, walking through the French doors and climbing down the stone steps really was the hardest thing she had ever done.

Leaving a packed church full of people waiting for the bride to arrive had been a very public hurt. Being disowned by her parents had caused anguish and pain. But it was the price she had paid for rejecting Sylvester, and despite the consequences she knew she would do it again.

This was a private hurt that no one knew of.

The guard gave her a bored look as she passed, which told her that a woman leaving Rafe's bed was hardly noteworthy.

The birds were starting to sing and the sky was starting to lighten as she crossed the grounds, and the world carried on as if nothing had changed.

Yet for Antonietta, everything had.

She looked back to the Old Monastery, and more specifically to the August Suite, from which she had just come. The master bedroom was in darkness, and she could almost picture Rafe reaching out and flicking the switch on the lamp before drifting off to sleep.

But Rafe had not gone back to sleep. Instead, he lay in the dark, in a bed perfumed by their union.

He had come to Silibri not just to lie low but to prepare himself for the enormity of what lay ahead, and all that awaited him when he returned to Tulano.

He had come to Silibri to clear his head.

Not to lose it to a maid with sad eyes.

Just this once Antonietta would have liked to do one of Chi-Chi's *slowly-slowly* acts. She was sore, and tender, and she wanted to dwell on last night and wallow a while. But then nothing would get done.

'I think it is mean of Nico to make us work on Christmas Day…' Chi-Chi huffed as she refilled the selection of toiletries in one of the regular suites.

It was stunning, of course, and looked out towards the valley, but it was nowhere near as luxurious as the August Suite.

In truth, Antonietta was happy to have been allocated to the suites well away from there. Her ears were on ten-

terhooks, waiting for the sound of a helicopter's approach
that might signal his leaving.

'Of course some staff have to work,' said Antonietta,
dragging her mind to their conversation as she dragged
the vacuum cleaner from the doorway. 'Are the guests
supposed to make their own beds and get their own food?
What would be the point of people taking a Christmas
Break?'

'Well, there could be a skeleton staff,' said Chi-Chi,
as she needlessly rearranged the herbal teabags. 'That
way some of the staff who have been here since the place
opened could have the day off.'

'Tell Nico.' Antonietta shrugged.

'I intend to,' Chi-Chi said. 'In fact—'

Whatever Chi-Chi's grand plans were, Antonietta
chose not to hear them and switched on the vacuum
cleaner. She turned it to full suction and wished that
drowning out her thoughts of Rafe was as easy as drowning out Chi-Chi's whining voice.

'Antonietta!'

She heard her name and then heard it again.

'Antonietta!'

'What?' she snapped, wondering what gripe Chi-Chi
had this time that couldn't possibly wait—except it was
Francesca who was calling her.

'*Scusi,*' Antonietta said and turned off the vacuum. 'I
didn't see you there.'

'That's fine. I can see that *you* are busy…' Francesca
shot a look at Chi-Chi, who was suddenly polishing a
mirror. 'Signor Dupont has asked for his room to be serviced and he has requested you.'

'But I thought he was checking out?'

'Checking out?' Francesca frowned. 'Where did you
hear that?'

'I'm not sure...' Antonietta attempted to cover her mistake. 'I thought you said he wouldn't last until Christmas Eve?'

'Well, that might be the case, but for now he is here—and, given that he has been in the August Suite for a week now, it requires a deep service, so I shall come with you.'

Oh, God! Please, no, Antonietta thought as they left Chi-Chi to it and collected linen before taking the elevator and heading along the cloisters.

What on earth was Rafe thinking, requesting *her*? She had visions of him lying naked on the bed as she and Francesca walked in, and was actually sweating as Francesca knocked and then opened the door.

It would seem Rafe had better manners than that, though.

'He's out,' Francesca said, after she'd made herself known but got no response.

Thank you, Antonietta breathed to herself.

'Let's get started,' Francesca said.

It felt odd, being back in the August Suite after last night. There on the table were the glasses that they had drunk from, but Francesca soon whipped them away.

'It looks as if he had company last night. Antonietta, why don't you get started in the master bedroom?'

From riches to rags.

Well, not quite. But she was no longer his lover and she was back to being his maid.

First she swept out the fire before which he had slowly undressed her. It felt as if it had been a dream. And then she rebuilt it, adding kindling under the logs and kneeling back for a moment. But there was no time to daydream, so she went to make up the bed.

As she pulled back the heavy cover she had lain beneath she saw the evidence of her lost virginity.

It had not all been a dream.

Quickly, and with her cheeks burning red, she bunched up the sheet. She was about to toss it to the floor when, glancing up, she saw Francesca standing in the doorway, watching her.

'You're a good worker, Antonietta.'

'Thank you.'

'It doesn't go unnoticed.'

Was it still the bloodied sheet that she held in her hand that made her blush, or was she hearing a warning behind Francesca's words? Had Rafe asking for her to service his suite set off an alarm? Or had they been seen driving off last night?

Surely Francesca didn't know?

'Let me help you,' Francesca said, and together they made the bed with fresh linen, chatting while they worked. 'After this we need to set up the Temple Suite.'

'Is there a guest arriving?' Antonietta frowned, because there had been no mention at handover.

'Nico is flying in to take lunch with Signor Dupont in the restaurant.'

'Oh.'

'Birds of feather.' Francesca gave a tight smile as she wrestled a pillow into its case.

'I'm sorry?'

'Oh, I know Nico is happily married now, but let us not whitewash his past and make him a saint. He was as much a playboy as Signor—'

'Francesca,' Antonietta interrupted, even though Francesca was her boss. 'You know I don't like to gossip. Aurora is my dearest friend and Nico is her husband. Gabe is my godson.'

'Of course.'

The silence between them was a bit strained after that.

With the bed made, Antonietta swept out the fire in the main lounge and then ticked that off the list. Because it was a deep service there was high dusting and ledges to be wiped, but finally it was all finished. And then, because Francesca seemed to be watching everything she did, Antonietta checked each and every candle, despite knowing they hadn't been lit.

It was possibly Antonietta's only regret from last night—not to have seen the August Suite bathed in candlelight.

'I think we are done,' Francesca said. 'Why don't you head off? I shall head down to greet Nico.'

'But we have the Temple Suite to prepare.'

'You're on a half-day,' Francesca pointed out, and then stopped speaking as the door opened and Rafe walked in.

He wore black jeans and a black jumper and his hair was dishevelled. From the sand he'd brought in, Antonietta guessed he had been walking on the beach.

'*Buongiorno*, Signor Dupont,' Francesca said. 'We have just finished.'

'*Buongiorno, signor,*' Antonietta added dutifully, although her voice was barely a croak.

Rafe didn't return their greetings and gave only the vaguest of nods as he walked past them with barely a glance.

She could have kissed him there and then for his arrogant ways, for surely this must put paid to any suspicions Francesca might have.

'Have a nice half-day and a good day off tomorrow,' Francesca said. 'Do you still have Christmas shopping to do?'

'No...' Antonietta said, but then remembered the lipstick. 'Yes—I still have Aurora's present to get, and I would like to get something for Pino.'

And she wanted to get something for Francesca too, Antonietta thought as she left the Old Monastery. Oh, and Vera in the laundry. And then there was Tony and Vincenzo...

She had come back to Silibri to be reunited with her family, and if that didn't work then her plan had been to leave and never look back. Yet, despite making no progress with her family, she was starting to make friends here. Real friends.

But still, it was going to be a very lonely Christmas. And for different reasons than those she had imagined when she had first arrived in Silibri. Christmas meant that Rafe would be gone, and she did not know how she would deal with that.

Nico's chopper was hovering as she crossed the grounds, and she watched as the pilot skilfully landed the beast. To her delight it was not just Nico who stepped out but Aurora too, and she was holding little Gabe!

Aurora looked stunning. She wore a kingfisher-blue dress with killer heels and her hair was a tumble of raven curls as she waved and ran towards her friend. Gabe was all black curls too, and huge black eyes, and Antonietta simply melted when he smiled as she held out her arms to him.

'See,' Aurora said as her son went so readily to Antonietta, 'he knows you.'

'He really does.' Antonietta beamed. 'I didn't think you were coming back until Christmas Eve?' she said.

'I wasn't intending to,' Aurora explained as Antonietta let them into the cottage, 'but Nico has a friend in residence over at the hotel. They are having lunch so I thought Gabe and I could come and see you. I'll join them for coffee afterwards and then we'll head over to my parents'.' She gave a dramatic eye-roll.

'How are they?'

'Still demanding that Nico gives my idle brother work. I have said no, but Nico has backed down. He's going to tell him this afternoon he's got him a role. God help us,' she muttered. 'He didn't even move the logs from Geo's house when there were those wildfires.' Geo was Nico's late father. 'Instead he left it to *me*.'

'That was a long time ago,' Antonietta pointed out.

'And he has grown fatter and lazier since. Honestly, families are—' She stopped herself. 'Sorry. That was insensitive of me.'

'It's fine.'

'Has there been any progress?'

Antonietta gave a non-committal shrug. No, there had been no progress with her family—if anything, they seemed to be going backwards. But there had been progress in her life. She was making friends—real ones—and she was putting down roots too.

And as for Rafe...

That felt like progress too, because even if they could go nowhere he had taught her so much about herself.

'I've brought your Christmas present,' Aurora declared. 'I'll put it under your tree. No peeking...' she said, and then looked at the little lounge, which was pretty much exactly as she had left it some weeks ago. 'No tree!'

'There's only me here.'

'But you love Christmas! Here,' Aurora said, and handed her a parcel—only Antonietta had nothing to give her surprise guest in return.

'I did have yours...' Antonietta blushed. 'Then I borrowed it. I have to get another.'

'Well, hurry up.' Aurora smiled. 'It is only a few days till Christmas.' She looked over at her great friend and gave a quizzical frown. 'Since when do *you* wear red lipstick?'

'Who said I got you red lipstick?' Antonietta attempted, but Aurora knew her too well.

'You always do,' Aurora answered. 'Even when you were in France, and we were barely in touch, you sent the same present each year. So how come you borrowed it?'

'I just decided to give it a try.' Antonietta shrugged. 'You've been nagging me to wear make-up for years.'

'With no luck, though!' Aurora's shrewd eyes narrowed. 'What's going on?'

'Nothing,' Antonietta said, and set about filling the coffee pot, even though Aurora said she didn't want one.

'Just water for me. Antonietta…is everything okay? You seem on edge.'

'Of course.'

Antonietta knew she was holding back, but though she wanted to confide, in this case she felt she could not. Aurora might be her best friend, but her husband was Nico—the owner of the Old Monastery. He wouldn't appreciate a maid fraternising with a guest.

Still, she was saved from explaining her sudden need for lipstick by the sight of little Gabe, tottering around the table on unsteady legs.

'You didn't tell me he was almost walking!'

'Watch this,' Aurora said, and held out her arms to Gabe. 'Show Antonietta what you can do!'

Antonietta held her breath as Gabe turned from the table and took two tottering steps unaided, and then fell into his *mamma*'s arms.

'Oh, look at you!' Antonietta beamed and clapped her hands. 'He's adorable.'

'He is,' Aurora agreed. 'And he knows it. Though he's in for a big shock when his little sister comes along…'

It took a second for the news to sink in. 'You're expecting?'

'Yes! Although only you are allowed to know for now! We're thrilled,' she added. 'I know it means we'll have two under two, but we want them to be close...'

It was wonderful news. This time last year Aurora had been pregnant and practically homeless. Now she was deliriously happy and with *another* new baby on the way!

'I feel sick this time, though,' Aurora admitted.

'Then what are you doing in a helicopter?'

'Flying is fine—it is food that upsets me. That is why I decided not to join Nico for lunch. I don't think me vomiting in front of the Crown Prince of Tulano would go down too well.'

It was the second big piece of news in as many minutes—not that Aurora could know the effect her throwaway comment had had.

'Crown Prince...?'

The smile Antonietta had been wearing slipped from her face, and as her legs turned to water she reached for the couch and sat down. On some level she had always known, but on hearing Aurora confirm it Antonietta crumpled and buried her face in her hands.

'Whatever's wrong?' Aurora said. 'Antonietta, what did I say...?' She came and put her arm around her friend's shoulder. 'Tell me.'

'I can't.'

'Is it Rafe?' Aurora asked—because she had seen her friend pale when she had mentioned his title. When Antonietta neither confirmed nor denied it, Aurora pushed for more. 'Has he been causing problems for you?'

'Problems?' Antonietta frowned. 'No...no.'

'You don't have to put up with it just because you are staff...'

'No, Aurora.' Her friend was on the wrong track. 'The only problem is how much I like him.'

She felt the hand on her shoulder tense and wondered if she had been wise to say anything. But apart from being the boss's wife Aurora was also her best friend, and in truth she desperately needed her trusted advice.

'I *really* like him,' Antonietta admitted.

'You've never said that about anyone before.'

'I've never felt like this before. Rafe took me out for dinner last night and it was absolute bliss. I wore the red silk dress that you made for me and I knew *happiness*, Aurora. He was wonderful to me.'

She saw the doubt in her friend's eyes. The same doubt Antonietta had seen there when she'd insisted her family would forgive her.

'He really was…' she said.

'You're in over your head, Antonietta.'

'I know that,' Antonietta said. 'I already knew that even before I found out he was royal.'

'He has the most terrible reputation with women.' Aurora was both abrupt and upfront. 'Rafe makes Nico look tame, and I don't even know half of what Nico got up to before we were married.' She was genuinely concerned. 'Antonietta, don't let him use you.'

'*Used* was how I felt with Sylvester,' Antonietta admitted. 'I've never felt that way for a moment with Rafe.'

'Listen to me,' Aurora urged. 'Crown Prince Rafael is his father's son—everybody says so. You must have heard all the scandals attached to the King of Tulano?'

Antonietta had. Oh, they weren't sitting there at the forefront of her mind, but there were little memories of her mother tutting over a magazine. And there had been some scandalous articles she'd read laboriously when she'd been trying to improve her vocabulary in France.

'Rafe is exactly the same.'

'Rafe isn't married.'

'That doesn't give him free rein! He is irredeemable, Antonietta, and a complete rake. You must have looked him up?'

'No! I make up my own mind about people,' Antonietta said rather piously, and then stepped down from her high horse and admitted the truth. 'I've tried to look him up, but I can't get on the Internet here and I daren't risk it at work.'

'Well, don't bother—just heed my advice and stay well away from him,' Aurora warned, and then she looked at Antonietta's pale cheeks. 'Or am I right in guessing it's too late for that and he didn't just take you for dinner?'

Antonietta said nothing.

'Oh, Antonietta…'

It wasn't the best catch-up with her friend. Antonietta had wanted advice—only not the advice she had got.

And although Aurora wanted to be delighted for her friend, who had tucked herself away for far too long, she could not bring herself to it.

'I have to go over there now,' she said, picking up Gabe's little jacket. 'I'll try not to kill Rafe when I see him.'

'Please don't say anything,' Antonietta begged.

'Of course I won't.'

'Why don't you leave Gabe with me?' Antonietta offered. 'I can give him his birthday present…'

'You're sure?' Aurora checked. 'He's due for his afternoon sleep and it would be so much easier.'

'Of course I'm sure.'

'I'll leave my phone too,' Aurora said. 'It's got a good signal.'

Antonietta frowned, wondering for a moment why

Aurora would leave her phone here when she was heading out, but then realised she was being given an opportunity to look Rafe up.

'That won't be necessary,' she said, but Aurora was blowing kisses to Gabe as she headed off for coffee with her husband and Rafe…

Rafe had found, during a long and luxurious lunch, that he'd had to keep pulling his focus back to the conversation with Nico. His mind had kept drifting to last night. Or rather it had kept honing in on *tonight*, and seeing Antonietta again.

All thoughts of checking out had gone and, knowing that she was on a half-day, he had decided that he would not wait until evening. If he walked Nico to his helicopter he could make a diversion to the cottage unnoticed…

'Ah, here is Aurora now,' Nico said, and both men stood as she approached the table.

As Rafe greeted her with the familiar kiss to the cheek, it was confirmed that she and Antonietta really were chalk and cheese. A person had to dig deep to get so much as a glimpse of Antonietta's thoughts, whereas Aurora wore her heart on her sleeve.

'Rafe,' she said as they greeted each other.

And, though it wasn't quite the Sicilian kiss of death, he could feel Aurora's wrath and suspicion even as they brushed cheeks, and was certain that she knew what had transpired last night.

'It is lovely to see you again,' Rafe said.

'Likewise.' Aurora gave a tight smile.

'Is Gabe with Antonietta?' Nico checked.

'Naturally,' Aurora said. 'Why wouldn't I leave him with my dearest friend? She *is* his godmother, after all.' She looked over to Rafe. 'I consider Antonietta family.'

'Of course…' Nico frowned, with no idea of what Aurora was alluding to.

Rafe knew, and he could feel Aurora's contempt when she addressed him.

'I was sorry to hear of your accident, though clearly you are feeling much better.'

'Much,' Rafe agreed. 'And I was just telling Nico how much I've enjoyed my stay here.'

'Any time,' Nico said. 'You are always welcome here, and I shall always do my best to ensure that your time in Silibri goes unreported. Consider the August Suite your bolthole.'

'I am sure,' Aurora said, 'that Rafe will soon grow bored with all Silibri has to offer.'

He could feel her animosity, and in truth it was merited. Rafe knew that he had earned his poor reputation with women. And he knew, too, that his time had run out and very soon he would have to settle down.

Nico's suggestion that he use Silibri as a bolthole had rattled Rafe—because it appealed. He sat making polite small talk with his hosts as visions of regular returns to Silibri scrolled in his mind.

And then he shocked himself by imagining how much nicer this gathering would be if Antonietta had joined them.

Rafe had always enjoyed Nico's company, although it had taken a new direction since his friend had settled down, and now took the form of tame lunches rather than parties aboard Rafe's yacht.

But to say there could be no future for himself and Antonietta was the understatement of the century.

Well, no tangible future, anyway.

She could be vetted, of course, and liaisons arranged beyond the reach of a camera lens. But Rafe knew even at this early stage that Antonietta deserved far more than that.

'We should get going,' Nico said now, but as farewells were exchanged, Aurora took another shot.

'So you will be going home for Christmas?' she checked. 'Or, given how well you have recovered, perhaps sooner?'

Rafe heard the veiled threat and was about to make a smart reply—for he did not appreciate being told what to do by anyone, let alone a newly married friend's wife. Except her concern was merited. And in truth he was grateful that Antonietta had Aurora on her side.

'There is a lot to take into consideration before I leave.' Rafe met her gaze, and with solemn eyes told her he had heard her concerns. 'Believe me, I am giving it much thought.'

So much thought that instead of strolling across the grounds to wave them off, and 'dropping in' on Antonietta, Rafe resisted the pull and headed back to his suite.

The thought of being with Antonietta appealed way more than it should. But he was a prince who needed no distractions, and it was time to pull back.

For Antonietta, the conclusion was the same.

She had spent an adorable hour playing with Gabe and the little wooden train. He was an absolutely beautiful baby, with dark curls and big brown eyes, and just the distraction she needed for a confused and troubled heart.

Aurora's phone, resting on the table, had called to her, but Antonietta had resisted.

'Look,' she'd said, waving the train again. But after an hour it had become clear, even though Gabe took it, that all he wanted to do was sleep. Eventually Gabe had thrown the toy down, and Antonietta had only been able to smile, because he'd reminded her then of Aurora.

'You win,' Antonietta had said, pulling cushions from the sofa.

She'd made Gabe a little bed on the floor and in a matter of moments he'd been asleep.

By then Aurora's phone had developed its own magnetic pull, and she hadn't been able to help walking over to it.

You don't want to know, Antonietta had told herself.

Oh, but she did.

It hadn't taken her long to find out that Aurora's dark assessment of Rafe had been correct. Crown Prince Rafael of Tulano did indeed live a life of excess. There were endless photos, taken from a distance, but zoomed in enough, capturing the depravity taking place aboard his yacht. On land he was no better, be it *après ski* or falling out of casinos, and always, *always* with a beauty hanging off his arm.

Yet his lovers remained nameless and they *never* told all.

She'd been able to find no interviews, no bitter tears spilled in the glossies. He paid for their silence, Antonietta guessed, and finally she understood his reference to 'paperwork'.

His life of excess was not just with women. Antonietta had winced at the photos of a sports car wrapped around a tree, from which he had been cut out. And there had been falls from horses and an accident involving jet skis.

Yet through it all his people still adored him, despite seeming to wish for their Prince to slow down.

He showed few signs of doing so.

There were a couple of relationships she'd found, although they went way back. A Lady from England and a minor European royal it seemed he had dated for a while. Although on closer inspection she'd seen that it had been close to a decade ago. The press had gone wild with speculation both times, anticipating marriage, but those relationships had quietly faded and Crown Prince Rafael had reverted to his wild ways.

When Aurora had come to collect Gabe, it had been a shaken but resolute Antonietta who'd opened the door.

'We've got five minutes,' Aurora had said. 'Nico is just meeting with Francesca. How was Gabe?'

'Perfect,' Antonietta had said. 'He's sound asleep. How was your catch-up?'

'You mean how was Rafe?'

'No.' Antonietta had shaken her head firmly. 'I've decided you're right. I won't be seeing him again, even if he asks. And I won't—'

'Antonietta.' Aurora had interrupted her and plonked herself down on the floor beside her sleeping baby, playing with his little black curls. 'What if I'm wrong?'

'You're not wrong, though! I just looked him up and you gave me good advice.'

'Perhaps...' Aurora had sighed.

'Anyway, he's leaving.'

'He gave no indication that he was.' She'd looked up at Antonietta. 'Do you remember that night when the whole village was threatened by fire and you knew Nico was back and staying at my parents'...?'

'Of course.'

'Everyone had told me to get over Nico, yet you told me to go and fix what I could.'

'There was something there to fix, though. You and Nico had been promised to each other for ever...'

'Antonietta, the fact that you like Rafe speaks volumes to me. I don't *want* to like Rafe. I want to tell you to stay the hell away from him and I want to tell him the same, but…'

Then Aurora had taken a breath and told her friend something she never had before.

'When I was in Rome for staff training last year and I ran into Nico he wanted a one-night stand. Another one,' Aurora had added, and given a mirthless laugh. 'I denied him, of course. I refused to be used again. And I walked away. I was so proud of myself for resisting him, but by the next morning it had turned into the biggest regret of my life. I regretted it so much that I threw a coin in the Trevi Fountain and pleaded to have that time over again. And I got it!'

'There's no future for Rafe and me,' Antonietta had pointed out, and then she'd given a wry smile. 'And there's no Trevi Fountain here.'

'What I'm trying to say is that even if Nico and I had never come to anything I would not have regretted the time we spent together in Rome.' She'd looked over to Antonietta. 'You just have to—'

'I know what you're going to say,' Antonietta had interrupted. 'If I see him again I just have to hold on to my heart.'

'No.' Aurora had shaken her head. 'Do you trust him?'

Antonietta had thought for a moment.

Oh, there was a whole lot of evidence not to, but while her head told her to be cautious, her heart said otherwise. She thought of her time with Rafe. The man who had taught her to dance and so much more.

'Yes, I believe that I do.'

'Then you have to do the bravest thing and let go of your heart.'

CHAPTER EIGHT

BUT THERE WAS no opportunity to let go of her heart. No chance to proceed, even with caution, for there was no gentle knock at her door that night.

She slept fitfully and awoke with a jolt, unsure if she had missed the sound of Rafe's chopper leaving. It was her last day off before Christmas, and though Antonietta knew she should head into the village to finish her shopping, she couldn't face it.

This afternoon, perhaps, but right now she had never felt less Christmassy in her life.

She pulled on a denim skirt, a thin jumper and flat shoes and decided a walk might clear her head.

The temple ruins had been her and Aurora's playground. As little girls they would go there to play and lose an entire day, sitting on the steps and watching each other sing, or running through the columns. Aurora had loved the remains of the altar in the cellar area and would dress it with flowers and dream out loud about her wedding to Nico.

Aurora had always known what she wanted—family and home, Nico and babies, and all that she held dear on this very spot on earth...

But Antonietta had always looked beyond. Even as a little girl she had sat hugging her knees and looking out, dreaming of places, some near, some far. Picking up the orange dirt, she would run it through her hands and imagine grains of Saharan sand. There was a whole world she hadn't seen, and as Aurora sang, Antonietta would lie back on the stone and imagine that she lay in a glass igloo, looking up at the Northern Lights, or that she was stretched out on a manicured lawn at the Palace of Versailles…

She had tried that, Antonietta told herself now, and she had been told off for being on the grass.

Her ponderings were interrupted by the sight of Rafe, running in the distance. He was still here, then, and that brought a sense of relief in itself. His form was magnificent, his body a masterpiece, and she admired it for a stolen few moments before he noticed and ran in her direction.

'Hey,' she said as he approached. 'No minders?'

'I'm on the hotel grounds.'

'Not technically.'

She smiled, because the ruins were outside the boundaries of the Old Monastery. Then her smile slipped and she felt suddenly a bit awkward and shy. It had nothing to do with their lovemaking. Now she knew about his royal status, she couldn't pretend. It had been far easier not to know.

'I thought you were leaving yesterday?'

'That was the plan.'

'Why did you tell Francesca that you wanted me to service your suite?'

'I didn't,' Rafe said. 'I told her I did *not* want Chi-Chi.'

'Really?'

'Absolutely,' Rafe said.

He held out his hand and helped her to stand and they

started walking. She offered him her water bottle and he took a long, refreshing drink.

'The ruins are spectacular,' Rafe said.

'I love them,' Antonietta agreed. 'Aurora and I used to play here when we were little. Or rather, Aurora used to play and I used to daydream.'

'About what?'

'The world,' Antonietta said. 'This is where she and Nico were married.' She glanced sideways at him. 'You weren't at their wedding?' She would certainly have remembered if he had been.

'No, I had prior engagements,' Rafe said.

And usually he would have left it at that. Certainly, he rarely explained himself, and yet he found himself telling Antonietta more than he usually would.

'Nico and I are friends, yes, but perhaps not in the way you and Aurora are. It's more that we shared the same social scene for a while.'

'But not now?'

'No, not now. If that were the case I doubt Aurora would be pleased.'

'So, a bit wild?'

'Quite a bit.' He gave a wry laugh. 'You don't want to know.'

'But I do.' And then she was honest. 'I know who you are,' she admitted. 'Aurora told me.'

'And how does that make you feel?'

'Better and worse.'

Rafe frowned.

'Better because I understand now why this can go nowhere,' Antonietta said. 'And worse because I understand now why this can go nowhere.'

Rafe laughed ruefully and they carried on walking.

The air was cold on his cooling body and yet the company was invigorating. As they walked he told her something of his life. The endless calls to duty interspersed with a jet-set lifestyle, and the endless stream of heavily vetted company aboard luxurious yachts and invitation-only parties. And he told her how boring it got, for there was no fear of missing out when you were the draw card. And there was no thrill to the chase when all the women in the room had already signed a document to be discreetly yours.

But there were penalties to be paid for living in the fast lane, and he knew his reckless ways upset his people. 'I'm supposed to lie low until the bruises heal,' he said.

'They're still pretty spectacular,' she said, looking at his blackened shoulder and the purple lines there to match the yellow and grey ones she knew were on his ribs. 'And your eye is still black...'

Her voice trailed off because it could easily be covered with make-up, if he chose, since the swelling had all but gone now. Or she could paint him!

Antonietta gave a soft laugh as she recalled a time from her childhood.

'What's funny?' Rafe asked.

'I painted a rash on myself once. I was trying to get out of school.'

'Did it work?'

'I thought it did,' Antonietta said as they walked on in the crisp morning air. 'My *mamma* was worried and told me to stay in bed. I said I thought I might be strong enough to lie in the lounge and watch television.'

Rafe smiled.

'Then she said it was a very serious rash, and she would make me Sopa de Pat...' She glanced over and translated. 'Pig's feet soup. It is the thing I hate most in the world. But my *mamma* said it was the only cure for the rash I had.'

'And was it?' Rafe smiled.

'I did not wait to find out. I washed off the rash and told my *mamma* I felt better…'

And now she would be honest, which would take almost more courage than the other night.

'I would like to paint a rash on you, so you can stay a while.'

'I would like to stay a while too,' Rafe agreed. 'But it won't change the fact that I have to be home in time for Christmas. I am expected to join my family on the palace balcony on Christmas morning.' There was more to it than that, though. 'I've been rather reckless in my ways and those days are over.'

'Have you been told?' she asked.

'I have been told the same for more than a decade,' Rafe admitted, 'but I know that the time is now. I want to work hard for my country, and to do that I have to marry.'

'*Have* to?'

'I have been told that if I want more responsibility then I must tame my ways.'

This was not a conversation he had ever expected to have with a lover, for he always kept his distance, even in bed. Not with Antonietta, though, and Rafe tried, as gently as he could, to explain the future that had been dictated for him before he had even been born.

'I am to marry a bride my father and his advisors deem suitable. One who will further our country's connections and who understands the role of Crown Prince's consort.'

She asked him the same question he had asked her. 'And how does that make you feel?'

His answer was not so direct, though. 'I am the sole

heir to the Tulano throne. The people have been patient long enough.'

'But how do you *feel*?'

'I prefer not to feel,' Rafe said. 'Feelings tend to complicate things.'

'So you choose not to have them?'

'Yes.'

Only that wasn't strictly true, for walking and talking with Antonietta gave him a feeling he would like to capture and store. This morning, walking free, with the winter sun high and Antonietta by his side, his life felt exhilarating rather than complicated.

'And the women you…' she swallowed '…you date? Are you saying that you don't have feelings for them?'

'I am not a machine,' Rafe said. 'Nor am I an utter bastard.' He looked sideways and saw that her head was down. She was frowning slightly as she tried to understand him. 'It is said by many that I have my father's heart…'

Antonietta flushed, because Aurora had said much the same thing. 'And do you?'

'No,' Rafe said. 'I have my mother's heart. I don't get close to people, Antonietta. I am cold like that.'

'Is she cold to you?'

'Especially to me. My parents were young when they married and I think she blames my arrival for my father's philandering ways. She is the epitome of the Ice Queen.'

'Perhaps so—but *I* don't find you cold, Rafe.'

'Because you haven't seen me when I choose to move on. Then I am as detached and indifferent as she. That is why I prefer to pay for company; that is why I choose to have a contract.'

'Yet I haven't signed anything.'

'No.' He gave a tight smile at this.

'So what if I go to the press?' Antonietta asked. 'What if in a couple of years' time I'm on some chat show, revealing all?'

'All?' Rafe checked. 'You mean you would tell the world about the night I took your virginity...?'

He loved it that she blushed, and he loved it that he knew she would never reveal it, and yet he teased her all the same.

'Would you tell them about the morning I took you in the temple ruins...?'

'You didn't, though,' she said, even as he pulled her towards him. 'And you won't—we can be seen from the monastery.'

'If people have binoculars,' Rafe pointed out, but as he moved in to kiss her he could taste her tension and feel her distraction, so he halted their kiss and held her a moment.

Rafe thought of how happy she had been when they'd been away from here. How the tension had lifted from her shoulders, how she had laughed and danced and relaxed in his arms. He thought of his yacht, and the privacy that would be afforded them there.

And he decided.

'Come with me to Capri.'

CHAPTER NINE

He made it happen.

Antonietta waited at the cottage while Rafe headed off to change. She would have loved to do the same, but apart from her red silk dress there weren't many options.

She pulled on some tights, and her most comfortable boots for all the sightseeing ahead, and decided she would just have to do.

By the time Rafe returned, dressed in black jeans and a jumper topped with a fine grey woollen coat, his helicopter was out of the hangar.

Antonietta had only ever heard the choppers, or seen them arriving and leaving, but now she sat in Rafe's private one, her stomach lurching as it lifted into the sky.

Capri was well known for the capricious nature of its weather, but it turned on the sun today, and the ocean was azure beneath them. She stared at the white cliffs as they approached the island.

'There it is…' Rafe spoke to her through headphones and pointed down to his yacht in Marina Grande—possibly the most exclusive marina in the world.

But Antonietta was not looking at it. 'I've always wanted to see the Christmas decorations in Capri,' she said, with her hands pressed to the window. 'And to eat *struffoli*. I can't believe you've brought me here!'

They were not in Capri to see the Christmas lights and eat *struffoli*, Rafe thought to himself. He had brought them here for the opulent privacy of his yacht and an awful lot of sex.

Yet his self-proclaimed cold indifference seemed to elude him around Antonietta, and he did not want to disappoint her.

As if his yacht had ever disappointed!

But Antonietta clearly thought they were here on some sort of day trip, so a word was had with his pilot in rapid French, and Rafe had to quickly rethink their day...

'You'll freeze in what you're wearing,' he told her as they sat in a sumptuous café and shared a plate of the famous *struffoli*. 'You need to get something warmer to wear.'

'I'll be fine.'

'We're going out to the Blue Grotto,' Rafe said. He'd go anywhere if it meant getting her out of those appalling tights—and for once he wasn't thinking about sex. 'You'll need to rug up.'

'It's closed in December,' she told him, for she had heard the tourists on the next table grumbling about it.

'It's not closed for me.'

And so they headed to Via Camerelle, with its designer boutiques, and he sipped coffee and insisted that the pale grey woollen dress that hugged her slender frame required a coat, and boots in the softest suede.

'And you'll need a dress and shoes for tonight,' Rafe told her.

'I have to be back at work tomorrow,' she told him.

'And you shall be,' Rafe told her. 'Get a dress.'

He told her he had an appointment to keep, and suggested that while she waited for him she might as well get her hair done.

'Rafe,' Antonietta protested. 'Please don't try to change me.'

'I don't want to change you,' Rafe said. 'But I have never known a woman to turn down a couple of hours in a salon in Via Vittorio Emanuele just to wait in a car.'

The suited men were back. Hovering discreetly, but annoyingly present. And Antonietta could tell they were less than pleased with her.

So, yes, she chose to get her hair done—rather than sit in a car with a driver who looked at her through slightly narrowed eyes.

That was the very reason Rafe needed some time away from her. He headed to the private royal residence for a less than straightforward meeting with his aides and minders, who were all appalled that he had brought a woman onto shore. Not just that, the same woman who had been in the August Suite the other night.

'She has not been vetted,' his advisor warned. 'And you still haven't had her sign the NDA.'

Neither would he. For this was too precious. And he told them none too gently to back off, and that he would deal with the fallout that would inevitably come from a run-in with the King.

It was worth it for this.

Antonietta's long, straight dark hair was still long, straight and dark, but just a vital inch shorter, and so glossy and thick that he put up a hand just to feel it.

And then he looked into dark eyes that were painted smoky and seductive. He took the coat from the doorman, just so he could help her into it himself, and handed her expensive shades.

'Wear these,' he suggested, 'if you don't want people at work to know.'

For Crown Prince Rafael was in Capri, and there was a

stir in all the best restaurants, where they put a 'reserved' sign on their very best table in the hope that he might dine there tonight. And in the cobbled streets the locals soon heard that the Playboy Prince had a woman on his arm.

'Who is she?' they asked—because usually Rafe did not bring his dates in from his yacht, where he tended to party. Perhaps he was finally serious about someone.

His luxurious yacht would not fit into the Blue Grotto cove, of course, so a speedboat took them in. There they transferred to a small wooden row-boat with a single skipper.

'We'll have to lie down,' Rafe told her.

'Really?' she checked, unsure if he was teasing.

'Really.'

He wasn't joking, but she wouldn't have minded if he had been, for it was bliss to lie side by side with him.

And then they entered the grotto. And it was like sliding into heaven as they were bathed in sapphire light.

'It's wonderful…' Antonietta breathed, for the water and its reflection was magical, the cavern illuminated spectacularly. And today, just for them, music was playing, inviting them further in. 'I've never seen anything more beautiful.'

'Nor have I,' Rafe told her.

And she decided that even though he might have used that line many times she would let that thought go. For when he looked at her like that, when he kissed her so slowly, she felt like the only girl in his world. She felt as if she belonged.

Rafe felt Antonietta still in his arms and, concerned, he halted. 'Is everything okay?'

'Yes,' she answered.

And all those years of searching, and yearning, and

never quite fitting in, ended then, and she found her place in the world in his arms.

Oh, it made no logical sense, for it was not about the *place* she was in, it was the connection she had found.

Only then did she understand what Aurora had meant when she had advised her to let go of her heart. For letting go meant no thoughts of tomorrow and a cold, indifferent end. And to let go meant she didn't examine the impossibility of them. She just had to let her heart go and it would fly straight to Rafe.

'Keep kissing me.'

'I can do that,' Rafe said.

He kissed her so deep and so long and with such smouldering passion that she felt as if she were floating, and that if he let go of her she might rise to the ceiling of the cove.

But even Blue Grotto kisses must end.

It was cold and getting dark when he held out his hand and helped her into the speedboat. Instead of going to his yacht, they headed to shore.

The Christmas lights of Capri were truly an amazing sight—not that he'd really paid attention before. They strolled through the square, with its carpets of fairy lights on the buildings and in canopies above them. It was like walking through a nativity scene, with towering musical trees draped in a million lights.

'This is the best day of my life,' Antonietta told him. 'The best Christmas.'

For *this* was her Christmas she decided. Tonight, here with Rafe.

It was cold, though, and their time on the water and the salty ocean breeze meant that not even his arm around her and her new thick coat could keep her from shivering.

'Let's go and eat,' Rafe said.

'I want *ravioli caprese* while I'm here,' Antonietta said, 'and chocolate torte...'

Any restaurant in Capri would serve that. And all the best restaurants, he knew, would have a table reserved for them.

Yet he was sick to the back teeth of restaurants.

There was somewhere else he wanted to take Antonietta.

'Come on, then.'

He called for his driver, and as he saw Antonietta into the vehicle he told the driver where they were headed.

The driver asked him to repeat the location.

'You heard,' Rafe said, although he knew it was *un*-heard of for him to take a date to one of his family's private residences.

They drove slowly up a hill and then turned in at a concealed entrance. She peered out of the darkened windows for a sign that might tell her the name of the restaurant he had chosen, but there wasn't one. Antonietta looked over to Rafe for an explanation as some gates slid open and they drove slowly up a steep path canopied in trees.

'Where are we going?'

'My family has a private residence here.'

'You *family*?' she croaked. 'They won't be here?'

'Of course not,' Rafe said. 'I thought it might be pleasanter than a restaurant.'

Antonietta wasn't so sure... A polite greeting awaited them, but she could sense the caution in the staff when they arrived.

The entrance to the villa was vast, with high vaulted ceilings that seemed to shrink her as they stepped inside. Rafe took off his coat and handed it to the butler, who waited for Antonietta to do the same.

Rafe could feel her discomfort as she handed over her coat and was already ruing his decision to bring her here as he led her through to the lounge.

A huge fire was waiting, and Antonietta stood and warmed her hands as the butler poured drinks.

'They must have been expecting you,' she said, referring to the fire and the fleet of staff. 'But from their surprise I thought you had arrived unannounced.'

The surprise was Antonietta.

Not that he told her.

'They are used to me arriving at all hours,' Rafe said. 'I'm sorry if it feels awkward to be here. I never thought...'

'No,' Antonietta said. 'I'm glad to be here. I'm just...'

She was just overwhelmed—not by her surroundings, but by the fact that he had brought her here. The fact that this man, who had told her he was cold, had lit a flame in her heart. How this man, who was a prince, somehow made her feel not just equal but as if she had found her missing part.

'I'm hungry!' she said, because that felt safe.

'Then let's get dressed for dinner.'

They climbed the stairs, and it felt so different from the monastery—for, no matter how luxurious, that was still a hotel. This was a home, with pictures lining the stairwell, and though it might be one of many homes there were personal touches that no hotel could replicate.

When she stepped into his bedroom it was Rafe's books upon the shelves and his chosen artwork on the walls.

And there was *his* bed.

A high, ornate, dark wooden bed, dressed in jade velvet. She couldn't resist sitting on the edge and bouncing up and down. It felt as delicious as it looked.

He took her leg and removed one of her gorgeous suede boots.

'I would love to sleep here,' she said.

She wanted to know what it was like to sleep in Rafe's own bed, and to know a little more of his life.

'Then do.'

'I have to be back for work,' she reminded him as he removed the other boot. 'I have a shift in the Oratory.'

But she forgot about work after that, liking how deftly he undressed her, lifting her bottom as he removed her stockings, and her panties too, and then pushed her shoulders down so she toppled back onto the mattress.

She lifted up onto her elbows and watched as he parted her legs and exposed her. And then examined her with desirous eyes. She should be shy, Antonietta thought. Yet she was not.

There was no kiss, no preamble. And her legs were pliant, rather than resisting, as Rafe placed them over his wide shoulders.

'I *have* to taste you,' Rafe said.

'Then do.'

He had been right to bring her here. Rafe knew it then. She deserved better than exposed temple grounds, and she did not need the ghosts of his past on the yacht, nor another nameless hotel, Rafe thought as he parted legs that were still cold from their day out.

She was warm *there* though.

He looked at her glistening folds and all he could do was taste...

Antonietta did not know, had not even imagined, that a mouth could deliver such bliss. His unshaven jaw was rough, and though his tongue was soft it made her feel exquisitely tender. There was no desire to pull away. He tasted her slowly and leisurely as her heart seemed to beat in her throat. He explored her more thoroughly, just a little roughly, and her thighs trembled as he tasted her deeply, dizzied her with light suction, then with decadent flicks with his tongue.

And never—not once—did she ask him to stop.

He was probing, and thorough and she found that she was panting, desperate—but for what she didn't quite know. Her hands went up and grasped at the bedcover, but it kept slipping away, like her own control.

'Rafe!' she pleaded—except she didn't know for what she was pleading.

She was back in the Blue Grotto on the crystalline waters. She was floating again, yet held by his mouth. She could hear her own voice calling his name as her fingers knotted in his thick hair.

He moaned into her, and his mouth was more insistent now. He was kneeling up and pulling her deeper into him. There was nowhere to go and nowhere to hide from the bliss he delivered. Every nerve in her body seemed arrowed to her centre, every beat of her heart felt aimed at her sex—until she sobbed and shattered and pulsed to his skilled mouth.

And he tasted her all through it. Even as her orgasm was fading he tenderly caressed those last flickers from her and then knelt back.

His swallow was the most intimate sound she had ever heard.

Antonietta dressed for dinner in the silver-grey dress she had bought earlier that day, then sat at the large dressing table and got ready. Her hair fell into perfect shape as she ran a silver comb through it and Aurora's red lipstick was worn again.

Rafe had never known a woman to take so little time

to get dressed for dinner and to look so breathtaking when she did. But it was not the dress, nor the hair that had transformed her. It was the sparkle in her eyes, Rafe realised, and he felt proud that he had brought joy to her.

'You look amazing,' he told her.

'Thank you.' She smiled and then added, 'You *always* do.'

And never more so than now. Rafe had shaved, his raven hair was brushed back, and he had changed into a deep navy suit.

She understood better the merits of dressing for dinner, for she felt a certain thrill that he had dressed so smartly, so immaculately, even though they were not to be seen, for they were not going out. Rafe had shaved and dressed with care only for *her*.

He took her up to a moonlit terrace, looking out to the Faraglioni rock formations. They sat at a beautifully dressed table, under burners that kept them as warm as a real fire.

'I can't believe I'm here,' Antonietta said.

'I can,' Rafe said.

It felt right.

Dinner was served, and somehow it was an intimate affair, and she gasped when *ravioli caprese* arrived.

'How did the chef know?'

'I told him,' Rafe said. 'Though we might have to wait a little while for the chocolate torte.'

'I don't mind waiting,' Antonietta said. Then asked, 'Do you come here a lot?'

'Not often,' Rafe said. 'My father uses it as a retreat, but I tend to give it a miss and stay out on my yacht.' He saw her slight frown. 'Growing up, I would come here sometimes in summer.'

'With your family?'

'No. My mother felt holidays were pointless. I came here with the nanny, and later I would bring friends.' He gave a wry smile. 'Vetted, of course.'

'But I am not vetted.'

'You have been by me,' Rafe said. 'And I like everything I see.'

'You have my discretion.'

'I know that.' And for the first time in his life he really did.

'This has been the perfect day.'

'An unplanned day,' Rafe admitted. 'I was going to take you to my yacht, but then you said you wanted to see the Christmas lights and eat *struffoli*...'

'You were taking me to your *yacht*?' Antonietta checked. 'For what? Sex?'

'And fine dining.' Rafe smiled. 'Thankfully, I realised just in time that you wanted a day trip.'

And now he had been so honest, she could be honest too. 'I just wanted a day with you, Rafe.'

Well, she'd got it. Rafe had given her a perfect day. And yet the moon moved too fast behind the clouds, and their time together was slipping away.

Dessert was served, and it was delicious—especially when fed to her from his silver spoon.

The second Rafe dismissed the staff she slipped from her side of the table to his knee and they tasted each other again.

She wanted his bed. His velvet bed. She wanted to lie there tonight and to wake with him tomorrow and for their time together to never end.

'We should head back,' Rafe told her. 'If you *have* to be at work.'

She heard the unsubtle emphasis.

'I do,' Antonietta said. 'I can't let them down...'

Rafe would be gone soon, and right now work was the only constant she had.

'I have to get back.'

'I know that.'

'But not yet…'

Not before he took her to his velvet bed.

CHAPTER TEN

ANTONIETTA WASN'T LATE, EXACTLY.

The helicopter pilot made excellent time and they arrived just before the winter sun rose above the horizon—which gave Antonietta just enough time for a quick shower and to change, though she was cutting it fine.

There was no morning chat with Pino.

Antonietta had got away with it.

Rafe hadn't.

Before he had even shrugged out of his coat his father was on the phone. The call was neither unexpected nor pleasant.

'What the hell were you thinking, parading this woman in Capri?' his father demanded.

'Hardly "parading",' Rafe said. 'It hasn't even made the papers.' He knew, because while Antonietta had been dozing beside him on the flight home he'd checked.

'Only because your PR team have been working all night to silence it.' The King was incensed. 'You are supposed to be recovering—'

'I am fully recovered,' Rafe interrupted.

'Then come home.'

'I'm not due back until Christmas Eve.'

'That wasn't a suggestion, Rafe. You have been given an extremely generous length of rope, yet you choose to ignore all the conditions that come with it. Well, no more. You are to return home. And in the New Year there shall be an announcement as to your upcoming marriage. The party is over, Rafe.'

'I am in no position to get engaged,' Rafe answered curtly. 'As you are clearly aware, I am currently seeing someone.'

It was more than he had wanted to reveal—more than he had even acknowledged to himself. But the fact was he was more involved with Antonietta than he had ever been or intended to be with anyone.

'Then *un*see her,' the King said.

Rafe walked out onto the balcony and there, crossing the grounds, was Antonietta. She was dressed in a white uniform and tying her hair back as she walked briskly to begin her shift.

'It's not that straightforward—'

'Are you forgetting who you are conversing with?' his father cut in.

For a moment Rafe had. But he was not under the thumb of his parents—it was the full weight of his title that came crashing down as the King spoke on.

'Your accident caused great concern, Rafe. You have a responsibility to marry and to produce heirs.'

'It is too soon,' Rafe said.

He was not even thinking of himself—more of Antonietta finding out he was engaged a few days after they'd ended.

'As I said, I am seeing someone, and she—'

'*She* has no bearing on this discussion,' the King said. '*She* is a lowly maid, who has been disowned by her own family because of a chequered past…'

'Don't even *go* there!' Rafe shouted.

'I should say the same to you,' his father shot back.

'Rafe, if you are particularly enamoured of this woman, then after your marriage, after an appropriate length of time, you can discreetly—'

'Don't!' Rafe interrupted, and his voice was low and threatening, even if his father was the King. 'Don't even try to give me relationship advice or instruct me on how to conduct my marriage.'

'Again, I remind you of to whom you are speaking,' the King said. 'I shall grant you this day to conclude matters and then I expect your return to the palace this night.'

The King had spoken and he was calling him home.

It was a busy day in the Oratory. As Antonietta had predicted, a lot of the guests had saved their treatments to be taken close to Christmas. And even if Christmas was a somewhat muted affair out in the main building, here in the Oratory it was festive indeed.

She painted many nails red and even performed her first massage on a paying client.

'Busy day?' Pino asked, long after six, when the last client had finally left.

'Very.' She sighed. 'How about you?'

'Lots of activity…' He halted. 'Never mind.' It would seem that Pino had found his discretion button. 'Ready for Christmas?'

'Pretty much.'

'Is that for Aurora?' Pino asked, when she showed him the large bottle of fragrant oil she had purchased with her staff discount.

It was easier to nod—though of course it was for Rafe. Antonietta had decided that chocolate wasn't enough, and had been racking her brains as to what she could get him. What was a person supposed to buy for a prince who had everything?

Including her heart.

She had let go of her heart and lost it to Blue Grotto kisses, and now she had spent half a week's wages on a bottle of neroli oil and had it wrapped in a bow.

Antonietta had never been happier in her life and it had not gone unnoticed—even Pino commented now that she looked brighter.

'I'm just...' But Antonietta could not explain the joy that radiated from her, nor her sudden exuberance, for fraternising with guests was strictly forbidden. So she blamed the season of goodwill for her wide smile. 'Looking forward to Christmas, I guess.'

Which was a lie, because she was actually dreading it, for by Christmas Rafe would be gone.

'Only four more days,' Pino said, and then his phone started to ring. 'Do you mind if I get that? It's my daughter—she's with the in-laws and worried about me.'

'Sure.' Antonietta smiled. 'Say hi from me.'

He gave her a wave and as she stepped into the night she saw that Pino was huddled over his phone, with his back to her, engrossed in his conversation.

There were no guests coming in or out to concern him. No cars arriving or helicopters approaching, nor guests checking in or out.

She could walk the fifteen minutes it would take her to get home, quickly get changed, and then walk the fifteen minutes back to Rafe's suite's private entrance.

Or she could go there now and have an extra thirty-five minutes with him.

And when you only had three days until Christmas Eve, when the man you were falling for was leaving, those minutes counted. And so, instead of walking home, Antonietta walked back inside the monastery.

If Pino saw her she would say she had left her phone, or something.

But there was no need for the excuses she had practised, for so deep in conversation was Pino that she entered unseen, slipped behind the stone partition and took the elevator without being spotted.

Past the Starlight and Temple Suites and through the cloister she walked briskly, wondering which excuse she would give if she was caught.

There was no guard on the door, and Antonietta frowned, because she had never known Rafe's suite to be unattended. And it was not just his suite that was unguarded. As she swiped her card and pushed the door open Antonietta realised that her heart was unguarded too.

For almost the first time since his arrival she *hadn't* spent the day with her ears strained for the sound of his helicopter, signalling that he was leaving. Or for Francesca's voice informing her that Signor Dupont had departed and she should turn over his suite.

And now she stood there, silent and completely unprepared, for she held his gift in her hands and her face still bore the smile she had been wearing when she entered, as if the wind had changed and set it there.

An ill wind.

When she had expected it least, Rafe had gone.

'Antonietta!'

She jumped at the sound of her name, and as Rafe flicked on the light he frowned, for her face was alabaster-white.

'You're early.'

'I didn't go home.' Her voice was strained and she cleared her throat. 'I came straight here. Why are you in darkness?'

'I was taking a shower.'

And that made sense, for he wore nothing more than a towel, but the fire wasn't even lit.

'There's no guard on the door.'

'No,' Rafe said, and he could see the questions in her eyes.

To avoid them, he turned and lit the fire. The guards had not just been there for his protection, they had reported back to the King. And they were not mere 'guards', they were Royal Protection Officers, which meant they were completely within their brief to carry out background checks on her. And when he had told them to leave they had retreated only to the perimeter of the hotel.

But his senior RPO, who had worked with Rafe for years, had stayed back, warning him that he should be back in Tulano by now, by request of the King.

It had been one step down from an order.

'I'm aware of that,' Rafe had told him. 'This is my doing.'

His doing.

'Antonietta...' he started, and loathed the austerity of his tone—but it was surely kinder in the long run, and there was no point prettying up his words.

'I got you a present...' she said.

He glanced down at the bottle she held, dressed in a red velvet bow.

'That was not necessary,' Rafe said.

'Presents shouldn't be *necessary*.' Antonietta smiled, but it wavered. 'It was just something I saw...'

Rafe was more than used to gifts. So *very* used to them. But none had ever shot to his heart in the way this did.

Not only could she not afford it, but it had been chosen with care, and he was loath to cause offence.

'Thank you,' he said.

'Smell it.'

He would rather not, and yet she was already unscrewing the lid.

Rather than offering him the bottle, she poured some into her palm and held out her hand for him to sniff.

'I was worried about your shoulder,' Antonietta said, and attempted to place her oiled hand there, feeling him actually wince at her uninvited fingers, while berating herself for thinking she could possibly spoil a man who could have anything he wanted.

Even her.

'It's too cold in here, though,' Antonietta said, and removed her hand.

She wasn't referring to the temperature of the room. Even though she had tried to ignore it, she could pick up his resistant vibe.

And she refused to beg.

'Enjoy,' she said, and placed the bottle on the table.

Unsure of him for the first time, she turned to go.

'Antonietta.' He caught her oiled hand but it slipped from his grasp, so he caught her more firmly and turned her around to face him. 'Don't leave.'

'I don't feel very welcome all of a sudden.'

'You are *always* welcome.'

He took her hand and placed it back on his shoulder. The contact was her undoing, for she had craved this moment for so much longer than today.

His bruises had all but gone, though there were still two dark lines where the rotator cuff had sheared, and now, when he winced at her touch, it was not in recoil more in targeted relief.

'Did I hurt you that night on the dance floor?' Antonietta asked, and she watched his arrogant mouth edge into a smile.

'A bit,' he said. 'And then you dug your nails into me when we were in bed…'

'I don't have long nails,' Antonietta said, and she pressed her fingers in, exactly where it would hurt.

He sucked in his breath and then exhaled as the muscle was released. 'They felt like long nails,' Rafe said.

He was already hardening, and turned on, and his resolution to avoid break-up sex was fading.

'What pain we both felt that night,' Antonietta said. 'When you took me I thought I might die.'

And as she took him back to that moment Rafe knew that he, the practised seducer, was being seduced by the shy maid with the sad eyes. It was he who had brought this side out in her, Rafe lamented, and he felt a snap of possessiveness at the thought of her out in the world without him. It was a coil in his gut that was unfamiliar as her fingers dug and pressed and kneaded.

She traced a finger around his flat mahogany nipples and then nipped him there with her teeth.

'Antonietta…'

She lifted her head and looked right at him. There was no trace of sadness, and nor was she shy, but he could not bring himself to do what he must and end it.

And so he ripped open the poppers of her white therapist's uniform and scooped her breasts from their flimsy bra. He took some of the oil and warmed it in his palm before playing with them, at first gently, then increasingly roughly.

His towel was gone, and he pushed her dress down over her arms and down past her hips. She stepped out of her knickers along with the rest of her clothes.

Once they were naked, Rafe pulled them both down to

the floor and lifted her hips. It was her hand that guided him as he slipped into her tight space. And they were panting and hot on this cool December night, as he held her hips so he could fill her with his thick length.

Antonietta was up on her knees, holding onto his oiled and slippery shoulders, watching the delicious sight of him sliding in and out of her. Her hair was on his face, and as he brushed it back their mouths met in frenzied, swollen kisses.

They both knew they must stop.

But he could feel her abandon and he craved just a little more.

'We should…' He attempted to speak. He knew he ought to lift her off him, for the protection was in the master bedroom. Except there was no going back now. The condoms might as well be locked in a vault in Switzerland for all the hope he had of getting to them.

He grew careless, as he never had before. It was unthinkable that he should have unprotected sex—not least because Antonietta wasn't on the Pill. But it was *such* a building need… And he *had* to feel her come around him.

'Rafe…'

She delivered her warning that she was close and he hit the snooze button on his thoughts, sinking into the flickering bliss of her grip.

She felt the final swell of him and yelped as he crashed over the edge and lost himself in the hot pulse of her tender flesh.

So careless. Because now he ignored the world outside, and the conversation that needed to be had, and carried her to his bed.

Everything else could wait.

CHAPTER ELEVEN

FOR ONCE, ANTONIETTA was up long *after* the Silibri sun.

Dizzy from lack of sleep, they had crashed at dawn.

Last night Rafe had hit the proverbial snooze button on his mental alarm.

This morning Antonietta had hit the real one.

Outside the warm bed the room was cold, so it had been easy—too easy—to give in to the arm that pulled her into his warmth and drift back to sleep.

'Shall I open the drapes for you, Signor Dupont?'

The sound of Francesca's voice jolted Antonietta awake, although her eyes did not open. Rafe's hand tightened on her bare arm and she lay as if set in stone, with her heart fluttering like a trapped bird in her chest.

'No,' Rafe said. 'That will be all.' And then he added, 'Thank you.'

Antonietta heard the bedroom door close and it felt like for ever until the main door opened and shut. Only then did she sit up and let out a low moan. 'Francesca knew I was here.'

'Of course she didn't. You could have been anyone,' Rafe said. 'The lights are not on...'

'No,' Antonietta said. 'Francesca is the manager. She doesn't bring guests their coffee—not even royal ones. She *knew* I was here...'

'How?'

'She's been checking on me.'

Antonietta climbed out of bed, pulled a throw from the top of it and wrapped it around her. 'That day when she suddenly came to check your suite with me...'

'You're reading too much into things,' Rafe said with stoic calm even as she dashed into the lounge.

'No, Rafe, I'm not.'

Francesca knew—of that Antonietta was certain.

'Did you fold my uniform after you removed it from me?' Antonietta asked as he joined her in the lounge. 'Did you carefully place it over the chair?'

His hand came down on her shoulder and he turned her to face him. Of course he had not.

He wrapped her in a strong embrace. Her head was on his chest and she listened to the steady *thud, thud, thud* of his heart and wished hers could match it.

'I will speak with Nico,' Rafe said.

'No,' Antonietta said. 'I don't need you to do me any favours. I will handle it myself.' She pulled her head from his chest.

'You don't have to.'

'Of course I do.' She removed herself from the haven of his arms. 'How can your intervening possibly help? You weren't the one caught—that was me...'

'Antonietta...' Rafe attempted reason. 'It was both of us.'

'No.' She shook her head. 'You can sleep with whomever you choose, Rafe.' She gave him a tight smile. 'And from everything I've heard you frequently do.'

'Don't do this, Antonietta,' Rafe warned. 'Don't turn this into something cheap.'

But in her head Antonietta already had.

She had struggled to justify sleeping with Rafe even to herself, while all the time knowing that it could go no-where. In the cold light of day she saw it was impossible to defend it now—especially to others.

She showered quickly and then dressed in her uni-form, and came out to find Rafe lying on the bed with his hands behind his head, looking grim.

'I don't blame *you*,' Antonietta said, 'I should have set the alarm…'

'Why does blame have to be apportioned?' Rafe asked.

'Because we are in Silibri,' Antonietta said. 'Finding someone to blame is our national sport.'

'Antonietta,' Rafe said. 'I won't let you lose your job because of me…'

Damn, he hadn't even told her he was leaving today.

'I've lost more than my job to you, Rafe.'

'You speak as if you were an unwilling participant.' His voice came out defensive and derisive, as it tended to when he was feeling caught out.

'I'm talking about my virginity,' Antonietta replied, loathing her own tone, but she felt caught out too.

He didn't know what to do as she flounced off. His immediate thought was to call Nico and put in a word, but he knew she would hate that. Or he could head down and apologise to Francesca…

Rafe felt as if he was back at school.

And then the weight of his own problems arrived at his door.

Antonietta would have barely made it through the cloister when there came a heavy knock.

It was his RPO, looking grim. 'You are to call the palace.'

'I have already spoken with the King,' Rafe responded

tartly. He did not need to be told again that it was time for him to leave.

But he had not understood the message.

'It is the Queen who wishes to speak with you.'

Rafe could not remember a time when his mother had requested to speak with him, and for a moment he felt ice run down his spine. It must be bad news. His mother never called. Not during his schooling, nor when he was injured.

So rare was this request that by the time he had been put through to the palace Rafe had almost convinced himself that his father must be on his deathbed and he was about to become King.

Not now, Rafe thought. *Not like this.*

'Rafael.'

His mother's tone gave him no clue—it was brusque and efficient as always.

'I spoke with your father at length last night.'

'He is well?' Rafe checked.

'Of course he is.' Marcelle sounded irritated. 'Rafe, I understand you are involved with someone?'

'Yes.'

'I have heard your father's poor advice to you.'

For a second he thought he had an ally. That possibly his mother was on his side. But this was not a gentle lead-in. There was no preamble with the Ice Queen.

'End things with her and do it immediately.'

'That's your advice?'

'Of course,' Marcelle said. 'Or would you prefer your father's suggestion to keep her on call? It *is* doable, of course,' Marcelle said. 'I should know.'

Rafe drew in a breath and found that he was holding it. His mother had never discussed his father's ways. At least not with Rafe.

'You took her to Capri?' Marcelle checked.

'I did.'

'You can take her there again...'

Rafe frowned.

'But I will tell you this much, Rafe,' his mother said. 'Your wife must never set foot on that island.'

Rafe had always found his mother cold. In that moment he knew she burnt with humiliation and pain.

'I would never do that to my wife.'

'Good,' Marcelle said. 'Because right now your future wife is being chosen and your engagement is to be announced on New Year's Day. Do as I suggest, and end it with this woman cleanly and quietly. Leave her in no doubt that the two of you are completely through.'

For Antonietta it was quite a walk of shame to Francesca's office.

Yes, she had lost more than her virginity to Rafe. She had lost her pride. For there was little pride to be salvaged when you were found in an eminent guest's bed. But more than that she had lost her heart to Rafe, and that was the part that hurt the most.

It came to her then that this would never have happened had she not been falling in love.

She pressed her eyes closed on that thought as she knocked at Francesca's door.

'Come in.'

Francesca's voice was hostile and so were her eyes as Antonietta stepped in and closed the door.

'Are you here to deliver your resignation?' Francesca asked.

'No,' Antonietta said. 'I am here to apologise. I know it looks terrible, but—'

'Don't make excuses,' Francesca broke in. 'It is forbidden for staff to fraternise or offer favours to guests for reward. Signor Caruso is very clear on that fact.'

'Yes, but I was not offering favours. Aurora knows and—'

'Oh, that's right—you are friends with the boss's wife.' Francesca again cut her off. 'Very well. You can tell your friend that Nico shall have my resignation by lunchtime.'

'No,' Antonietta protested. 'Why would you leave because of me?'

The very thought that Francesca would resign over this appalled Antonietta, who knew the manager loved her work. Francesca worked both day and night, greeting their most esteemed guests, ensuring that every detail of their stay was perfect. She couldn't understand why her actions might force Francesca out.

'If I'd wanted to be a madam then I would have applied for a job at Rubina's.'

Rubina's was the bordello in the next village.

'I am not a whore,' Antonietta said. 'I am not being paid or anything like that…'

'Oh, *please*,' Francesca sneered. 'I don't believe you for a moment.'

'But it's true,' Antonietta insisted, and then admitted a truth she had been trying to resist until now. 'It has nothing to do with money. I love him.'

There was silence from both of them at the enormity of her words, for Francesca knew that Antonietta was not one for passionate declarations.

'Oh, Antonietta…' Francesca sighed. 'You foolish, foolish girl.'

But she said it kindly, and Antonietta knew that Francesca really cared. In truth, she ached for a more mature woman's advice. 'Why foolish?'

'I thought that you at least knew what you were doing and that it was a business arrangement.'

'You'd rather that he was paying me?'

'Yes,' Francesca admitted. 'I'd rather that than you give your heart to a man who is using you.'

'But he *isn't* using me.'

'No—you offered yourself to him on a plate.'

She had.

Antonietta's eyes screwed closed as realisation started to hit and she recalled that first night, outside her cottage, and her reaction to her very first kiss. *Take me to bed.* It had felt at the time as necessary and straightforward as that.

'Sit down, Antonietta,' Francesca said gently.

She offered tissues, and poured water, and then pulled her chair around so she sat next to Antonietta.

The older woman took her hand. 'I won't tell anyone, and neither will I lose my job over this, or you yours, but there is a condition.'

'What?'

'You are to go and tell Signor Dupont—or rather, Crown Prince Rafael—that you have kept your job only on the condition that, after your conversation, you will never speak to him again.'

Antonietta swallowed.

'You are not to be in his suite and he is not to come to your home. There will be no more contact between the two of you.'

'But—'

Francesca spoke over her. 'And after you tell him that I can guarantee that within hours he will leave. Crown Prince Rafael was not expected to stay here for even a few days. I was told that as soon as he was even partway healed he would grow bored and fly out.'

'He didn't leave, though.'

'Of course not. He was getting sex and nightly entertainment. Tell me, Antonietta, why *would* he leave?'

'It wasn't like that—'

'It was *exactly* like that, and I should know,' Francesca said. 'I was taken advantage of by a man a year after my husband left me. I'm guessing that you were lonely?'

Antonietta opened her mouth to argue, but the truth was she *had* been lonely—desperately so. 'Yes,' she admitted. 'But Rafe did not take advantage of that fact. I was complicit.'

'You were out of your depth,' Francesca countered. 'He is a notorious playboy. Have you not seen him in the scandal rags?' Francesca answered her own question. 'Of course not—you wouldn't read them. But, Antonietta, not all gossip is bad. It can serve as a warning.'

'I doubt I would have heeded any warning.'

Antonietta thought back and knew that there might have been a group of protesters on the lawn that first night, as she had walked to his suite, and they could have been holding placards attesting to his reputation, and still she would not have let go of his hand.

'He told me from the start it could go nowhere...'

'Of course not.'

'Even before I knew who he was.'

'And now that you do, be the one to end it.'

Francesca gave her shy and somewhat naive chambermaid a little cuddle, and felt angry on her behalf—and not just with Prince Rafael.

'Antonietta, for what it is worth, I will not tell your mother.'

'I don't care any more.'

She would have dreaded that a short while ago, but

no longer. She had spent these last years frozen at age twenty-one, desperate to reclaim their approval.

'I cannot keep apologising for being me.'

'No,' Francesca said. 'And neither should you. I think your parents' treatment of you has been terrible and I have told your mother the same. We are no longer speaking.'

'I'm sorry.'

'No more saying sorry,' Francesca said.

'One more apology,' Antonietta replied.

In the last hour she had learnt many lessons, and she now felt all of her twenty-six years. She knew that Francesca was being stern out of kindness and to protect her.

'I will always be Aurora's best friend, but I will never use that friendship again. At work, I answer only to you.'

'Thank you,' Francesca said.

It felt right. And for a moment the world felt a lot better than it had in recent years. But now came the hard part. The hardest part.

To let Rafe go with grace and not let him see the agony in her heart.

Antonietta knocked on the door, and instead of being called to come in, or using her swipe card, this time Rafe opened it.

He wore black jeans and a black shirt and was unshaven, yet somehow he seemed so immaculate and regal that Antonietta wondered how she had not known he was royal on sight.

'Come in,' Rafe said. 'How did you get on?'

'Okay, I think,' Antonietta said.

And because she felt as if her knees might give way she chose to take a seat opposite the chair on which Francesca had folded her uniform dress, on the sofa on which they had made love the previous evening.

'I have assured her that it will never happen again.'

'You are hardly going to make a habit of sleeping with the guests.'

'I think she understands that it won't happen again. And I won't be coming to your suite again.'

Rafe actually opened his mouth to dispute that. To wave his royal wand, or rather have things smoothed over, but to what end?

He was leaving, and it was far better to end it now. Cleanly. He did not want to follow his father's example.

Rafe glimpsed it then—a future for them of the kind his father had described. He could return to Silibri at every whim. Take out a permanent lease on the August Suite…

No. Better he followed his mother's example and killed this now.

Or let her think that she had.

'Perhaps that would be for the best.' His voice was steady and he watched her rapid blinking.

'So I'm dismissed?' Antonietta could not keep the hurt at his cold reply from her voice.

'You are the one saying that you won't be returning to my suite,' Rafe pointed out. 'You are the one saying that you cannot see me any more.'

'Yes, but…' She had hoped for some protest, some indication—*any* indication—that this was hurting him even a fraction of how much it was killing her. Yet he seemed unmoved.

'I told you this could go nowhere.'

'You did, but…'

That *but* again. He could hear her attempting to defend them. Worse, he was still glimpsing that future.

And so he killed it, with brutal but necessary words, for he could not drag it out any longer. 'I am to marry,' Rafe said. 'My engagement will be announced in the New Year.'

'Why are you telling me this?'

'At least I have the difficult conversation, Antonietta. At least I don't run from it.'

'That's unfair.'

'Why? Would you prefer it if I just take off and leave and then write you a letter in a few months, explaining my actions? Would you prefer that I return in five years and expect to resume where we left off?'

'Of course not.'

'So what *do* you want, Antonietta?' he asked. 'You tell me that you are no longer coming to my suite and yet you secretly want me to dissuade you?'

'No!' she protested, but that wasn't quite true. 'Perhaps…' she conceded.

Her honesty floored him and made it hard to remain cold, for he could see the confusion in her eyes.

Cleanly, Rafe.

He didn't want it to be over, though. And neither did she.

'One moment.'

He went into the bedroom and from the dresser there removed a slim black velvet box. Then he returned to the lounge and handed it to her.

Antonietta opened it with some difficulty, for she could feel him watching her. She refused to gasp, but held her breath when she saw the gorgeous pendant, with a stone so bold and blue that for a moment she could imagine she was back in the Blue Grotto.

'Thank you,' she said, 'but I cannot accept it.'

'Of course you can.'

'No.' She held out the box to him but he refused to take it, so she placed it on the desk. 'Rafe, I don't know its value, but I am certain that sapphire would buy me a house—not that I would ever sell it.'

He did not tell her that it was a rare blue diamond. Instead he let her speak.

'But how on earth could I keep it?' She looked at him. 'When my life moves on, am I to wear it for special occasions? Perhaps on my wedding day?'

His jaw ground down.

'No,' she answered her own question. 'For that would be crass. So just on dates, or birthdays, or whatever? Or do I buy a safe? And when my lover asks how I came upon it do I tell him that for a few nights I slept with a prince?'

She looked at him, this girl with the saddest eyes, but still there were no tears.

'I don't think that would go down too well.'

She held it out but still he did not take it from her.

'Please, Rafe, don't mark the end of us with this.'

'Take it, Antonietta. Sell it if you have to.'

'I already told you—I refuse to be your whore.'

She stood and placed the box on an occasional table.

'I'm going.' No more kisses, no promises, just one plea. 'Don't get in touch with me. Don't enquire about me from Aurora or Nico. Don't keep me on a thread.'

And so he did what Antonietta wanted and what his mother had suggested—he pushed them to the point of no return.

'That's very conceited of you, Antonietta. I won't even remember your name by the middle of next week. Certainly I won't be looking you up for a replay. You weren't *that* good.'

Ah, yes, Antonietta thought, *he warned me how cold he would be at the end.*

But she had so little to compare this with—so little to go on apart from her heart, which was braver than she. So she walked over to him and looked up to meet his eyes.

And as it turned out she *could* have the difficult conversation.

'Liar.'

She was met with silence.

'I'm going to get on with my life now.'

She walked out of his suite and there, waiting in the cloister, was Francesca.

'I'm proud of you,' Francesca said.

'So am I,' Antonietta admitted.

And so too was Rafe.

'I hope you have had a wonderful stay,' said the concierge.

'Indeed,' Rafe replied, and handed Pino a handwritten note of thanks, as a royal prince was expected to do to someone who had taken such care to ensure his every demand had been met. 'Thank you for your help. The running route you suggested was most excellent.'

'It was a favourite of mine.'

'Was?' Rafe checked.

'I used to walk there with Rosa.'

Ah, yes, Rafe recalled that Pino had lost his wife earlier this year. What *was* it with this place? Usually he did not get involved in staff's lives or dramas.

'It's still beautiful,' Rafe said.

'Not without Rosa,' Pino responded, and held out his hand to the Prince. 'It's been a pleasure having you at the Old Monastery, and I know we are all looking forward to your return.'

But he would not be returning.

Like Pino, the thought of being here without his love meant Silibri had lost its charm.

Love?

Instantly he refuted that. His life would still be beautiful without Antonietta, Rafe told himself. He would return to his country and marry a suitable woman, if it pleased the people, and then he would have the power he required for the changes he craved.

He would no longer be the reckless Playboy Prince.

And Antonietta would move on with her life.

She had been expecting that sound.

Chi-Chi was eating a guest's grapes in one of the standard suites as Antonietta switched off the vacuum. She could hear the whirr of the rotors in the distance and headed to the window.

First she saw Pino and one of the bell boys, carrying luggage, and then she saw Rafe, running across the ground and bounding up into the helicopter.

'He's leaving, then,' Chi-Chi said with a distinct lack of interest.

Antonietta didn't have the energy to respond, and she watched as it lifted into the sky until it was just a tiny black dot on the horizon.

Without his 'amusement' Rafe had not even seen out the day…

CHAPTER TWELVE

RAFE'S HELICOPTER TOOK him to Palermo, and from there it was a private jet to Tulano.

Rafael did not reside at the main palace. He had his own court. As the gates opened it was already dark. But there was no question of sleep. He sat with a pen and tried to work on the most important speech of his life.

It took all night, and, when he finally stood before his father, to his disquiet his mother was there, and her cool gaze was less than encouraging.

At least she was listening. His father didn't even let him past the second line.

'She's a commoner?' the King interjected. *'Non.'*

'Will you at least hear what I have to say?' Rafe bit down on his frustration, for he knew it was imperative that he stay polite.

'There's no point,' the King said. 'So I don't need to hear it. I have been giving your marriage a lot of thought, and we need someone who is well-versed in royal tradition—someone who understands that the crown comes before everything...'

'So a loveless marriage?' Rafe checked.

'Rafe, you have had your freedom, and you have abused that freedom to the nth degree. You are thirty years old and the only heir to the throne—'

'Whose fault is that?' his mother interrupted.

Rafe closed his eyes in frustration. *Here we go*, he thought.

Except his mother truly was the Ice Queen, and Rafe watched as she spoke of the most painful part of her life without a shred of emotion.

'You married me because your father instructed you to. You have stayed married to me purely to avoid a royal scandal, and yet you have created many a royal scandal of your own.'

'And whose fault is *that*?' the King retorted, and he shot a reproving look at the wife who for so long had refused to share his bed.

'Don't speak to her like that,' Rafe warned his father.

'May I remind you to whom you—?'

'I don't need to be reminded,' Rafe retorted. 'I have lived it, and so has your Queen.'

His mother was on his side, Rafe realised. And suddenly he understood her cold nature better and looked back on his childhood with adult eyes. No wonder she had never set foot on Capri, for Rafe could not even fathom taking his future wife there after what he and Antonietta had shared.

He did have his mother's heart after all. She was not cold. She was just bruised by an unfaithful husband, and yet she spoke out for her son now.

'I shall never recommend that you force our son to do the same,' she said.

'I tell you this much,' Rafe said, for though he was grateful to his mother for speaking out he knew his own mind. 'I will never conform to the same.' He faced his father. 'As I have stated, I refuse to take marital advice from you, but I venture to give you some in return: sort out your own marriage before you meddle in mine.'

'How dare you?' the King roared. 'Have you forgotten I am your King?'

'Never,' Rafe responded. 'And for that reason, and that reason only, I stand before you and petition for your permission to propose to the woman I love.'

'She is a commoner,' the King dismissed.

'I have made my choice,' Rafe said.

'A poor one! I will *never* approve this marriage.'

Rafe knew his father well enough to know that he would not back down.

'Will you abide by my decision?' the King demanded.

Would he?

Rafe knew that although his father was King in truth it was Rafe who held the power, for he could simply say no, he would *not* abide by his father's decision. And he would get his own way for his father would loathe the thought of the succession continuing with Rafe's cousins rather than following his own line.

But marrying without the King's permission, even if he remained Crown Prince, would prove a living hell for Antonietta. She would be frozen out by the courtiers and treated with derision by the aides. There would be division in the palace and ramifications that he would not wish on the girl with the saddest eyes, who had only ever wanted to belong.

'Rafe?' the King pushed. 'Will you abide by my decision?'

'Yes,' Rafe said finally. 'I will abide by your decision but I will never forgive you for it.'

'Don't threaten me, Rafe.'

'It is not a threat—it is a fact. And one you should consider. Unlike you, I will do everything in my power to make my marriage work. My wife will never know that I did not wish to marry her. When she asks why I am cold with my father the King I will never tell her the true reason. And when she asks why I don't stand by your side on the balcony I will tell her that it is to do with ancient history and not something she should trouble herself with. And when the heirs you seek are born, and they ask why they only see their grandparents on formal occasions, I will tell them to ask their grandfather to explain why relationships are strained.'

'How dare you threaten me?'

The King stood, but Rafe did not flinch.

'It is a mere glimpse into the future,' Rafe said. 'So think long and hard, Your Majesty, as to how you wish to proceed.'

CHAPTER THIRTEEN

'You are tense,' Antonietta commented as she massaged Vincenzo's shoulders.

As part of her training she was still practising on the staff, but they were actually asking for her now, and a couple of them had told her that they would be her clients if she ever set up on her own.

'Isn't everyone tense at Christmas?' asked Vincenzo, who was lying face-down.

'No!' Antonietta smiled. 'It's supposed to be a happy time.'

'Well, you should be happy!' Vincenzo said. 'It would seem you made the right choice!'

'Sorry?'

'With Sylvester. You know…because his wife left him?'

Her hands stilled on Vincenzo's shoulders.

'You haven't heard?'

'No,' Antonietta said.

As Vincenzo spoke on she discovered that it had been a terrible break-up—and, no, it did not make her happy to hear it.

She poured more oil on her hands and got to work on Vincenzo's knotted neck. Some clients preferred silence, which Antonietta was very good at, and usually Vincenzo was one of them, but today he seemed keen to talk.

'I am so over Christmas, and it isn't even here yet,' Vincenzo said.

'You're off to Florence tonight?' Antonietta checked.

'Yes, but my family are driving me crazy.' He sighed. 'They expect me to come home, yet they don't want me to bring a guest…'

Antonietta's hands paused and, unseen by Vincenzo, she frowned, though she kept her voice light. 'My family don't want me home with or without a guest, so I win.'

He laughed and relaxed a little. 'I don't know how to keep everyone happy,' he admitted.

'I think it's time to make your own traditions, Vincenzo. I know I've been relying on other people to make this Christmas a happy one.'

An idea was forming, though she did not share it with Vincenzo as he was now half asleep. But when he was done, and it was time for her break, Antonietta knocked on Francesca's door.

'Come in, Antonietta,' Francesca said.

'I lied to you.'

Antonietta saw Francesca's curious frown as she took a seat in her office.

'About what?' Francesca asked. 'Are you intending to open a bordello here?'

They shared a small smile before Antonietta answered. 'Of course not. But I do want to take advantage of my friendship with Aurora and Nico. I wanted to speak with you about it beforehand. I don't want to go over your head.'

'I'm curious,' Francesca admitted.

'I came to Silibri hoping for a wonderful Christmas,'

Antonietta said, 'and I've realised I have done little to bring it about.'

Francesca frowned.

'I have left my fate in other people's hands for too long,' Antonietta said. 'I have been waiting for my parents to decide how I spend my days, and what will make me happy, but no more.'

'What do you have in mind?'

'Cake,' Antonietta said. 'And lots of it. And decorations. And a feast shared with the people I care about and who care about me.'

'Who?' Francesca asked.

'You!' Antonietta smiled. 'And anyone else who isn't getting the Christmas they hoped for. Of course it would only take place after all the guests have been taken care of...'

'I have loathed Christmas ever since my divorce,' Francesca admitted—and then perked up. 'We could use the grand dining room,' Francesca said. 'Tony would cook, I'm sure of it, and Pino...' She gave a pained sigh. 'I have been so worried about him spending Christmas alone.'

'And me,' Antonietta admitted.

'I was going to invite him over for dinner,' Francesca admitted, 'but you know how the villagers talk...'

'Believe me, I know,' Antonietta said. 'But of course you are just being...' She was about to say that of course Francesca was just being friendly, but her voice trailed off as her manager went a little bit pink.

Francesca and Pino?

But Pino was grieving Rosa so deeply he would never look at Francesca in that way, Antonietta was sure.

Oh, love was so difficult and cruel—but, given that she couldn't fix her own love-life, she certainly couldn't help anyone else with theirs, so she got back to organising the party.

'We would need Nico's permission.'

'He will never give it.' Francesca shook her head. 'He is like the Grinch. He didn't even want a Christmas tree in the foyer.'

'It's his first Christmas with Aurora and his first as a father...'

'Do you think Aurora could persuade him?'

'Oh, yes.' Antonietta smiled.

'Then on this occasion,' Francesca said, 'I have no problem with you going over my head.'

Antonietta called Aurora. And since Aurora thought it a brilliant idea she said she would be delighted to 'work on Nico'.

'Ha-ha!' Aurora added.

Antonietta would have frowned at that just a few short weeks ago. She had been utterly clueless back then.

'Enjoy!' Antonietta said instead, and then communicated her response back to Francesca.

'We have the go-ahead? Nico approves?' Francesca checked.

'Aurora is working on him.'

'Lucky Aurora!'

Soon they had gathered all the staff who would be working on Christmas Day.

'Do we get paid for staying on?' Chi-Chi asked.

'It's a party,' Francesca said. 'Of course not.'

'Then you can count me out,' Chi-Chi said, and left.

'Well, I think it's a great idea,' Pino said. 'I've been dreading Christmas. I know I said I didn't mind that my daughter is with her husband's family, but really...'

As it turned out, he wasn't the only one who felt lonely at this time of year.

Vera, who worked in the laundry, and could have had the day off but had chosen to work, was another who admitted she struggled. 'I can make a lasagne,' she said.

'No, *I* am making the lasagne,' Tony insisted. 'But, Vera, your cannelloni is the best I have ever tasted...' His voice trailed off as Vincenzo came in.

'What's going on?' Vincenzo asked.

'We're having a meal—a staff party for those who have to...' Antonietta paused '...for those who have *chosen* to work on Christmas Day.'

'Oh!' Vincenzo just stood there.

'Well, it doesn't apply to *you*,' Tony said rather spitefully. '*You're* spending Christmas with family.'

Though it was not quite the perfect remedy for getting over a broken heart, it was fun to organise everything, and in her time off Antonietta baked.

And cried.

But mainly she baked.

Or mainly she cried.

But there was cake involved, which always helped.

What didn't help was finding on Christmas Eve the coffee-flavoured Modica chocolate that she had bought for Rafe.

Well, not really. But she had certainly bought it with Rafe in mind, never knowing that that very night they would make love.

It had been so good.

At least it had been for her.

But then she reminded herself of his cruel departure, and those horrible harsh words, and told herself to get over him.

And she would.

Oh, she would...

But first she had to weep for him.

Yet she knew that once she'd started she wouldn't be able to stop.

She would have to mourn him later, Antonietta decided. For now, the show must go on.

And so, dressing for the Christmas Eve bonfire that night, she put on the gorgeous dress, tights and boots he had bought her.

And though there was no sign of Rafe's black helicopter, still a chariot awaited…

Well, the hotel put on a car to take the people who were working till late into the village for the last hour of the bonfire before everyone headed to church.

Poor Pino, Antonietta thought as she climbed in. He looked pensive as they drove up the winding hill.

But then he gave her a little pep talk. 'If there are any problems tonight, just come and find me.'

'I'll be fine, Pino. My family might not be talking to me, but they're not going to make a scene at the Christmas Eve bonfire.'

'You probably haven't heard the news,' said Francesca.

'I know about Sylvester,' Antonietta said.

'It's nothing to do with you, of course,' Francesca soothed, 'but from what I've heard emotions are a little raw.'

'Emotions are always a little raw with the Riccis.' Antonietta shrugged. 'You're right—Sylvester and his marriage are nothing to do with me.'

She shut down the conversation—and not just because she refused to gossip. She shut down the conversation because it hurt. Though she had no feelings at all for Sylvester, another person's misery still didn't feel like a triumph. There was enough sadness in the world, and right now she was busy dealing with her own.

Antonietta was at the start of her life without Rafe. Oh, they had been together for only a short time, but it had been long enough for her heart to know it was love.

The bonfire would be a nice place to weep unnoticed.

It was huge. The children were all laughing and playing, and there were cheers and celebrations as the orange flames licked up towards the sky—she would blame the smoke for her watery eyes, should anyone see. But she refused to break down completely.

'Antonietta…'

She turned at the sound of her name, and there stood her *mamma*.

'Have you heard about Sylvester?'

'What does that have to do with me?'

'It would seem you were right to have doubts,' her mother said. 'Come to us tomorrow,' she offered. 'Have Christmas Day with your family.'

It was everything she had once wished for. Everything she had come to Silibri for.

And yet Rafe had been right when he'd asked her if she would ever be able to forgive her parents. It had seemed a ridiculous question at the time, but it made perfect sense now.

Antonietta looked at her mother, and though she could stand there now, vindicated and redeemed in her mother's eyes, there was too much hurt.

'I have plans for tomorrow,' Antonietta said.

'Antonietta, don't do this. I have missed you so much…'

'Then why didn't you pick up the phone?' Antonietta retorted, and walked off.

'Hey,' Pino said. 'Is everything all right?'

'I got what I wanted,' Antonietta said. 'Or what I thought I wanted. But it's too little, too late.'

'So carry on the fight, then,' Pino said. 'And we can all be miserable this Christmas.'

He made her smile.

'I know that I don't want to be miserable any longer,' Pino said. 'I was talking to Signor Dupont before he left. He told me to go and look at the ruins. Said that life can still be beautiful even without Rosa.'

'He told you that?' Antonietta said. It angered her rather than soothed her, for she loathed the thought of Rafe just going on with his beautiful life.

'He did. And if he hadn't been a guest—and a royal one at that—I might have hit him,' Pino said.

'But you didn't?'

'No, because I think he might be right. I want to make peace with the past, and I want to embrace the rest of my life. Call me old-fashioned, but I believe life is better with family.'

'Even when they hurt you?'

'Of course,' Pino said. 'Love isn't always easy. My daughter has hurt me...'

'Have you told her?'

'No,' Pino said. 'For there might come a time when I hurt her too. I just have to hope she'll be happy for me...'

Was he talking about Francesca? Antonietta pondered. Surely it was too soon? But then, who was she to judge?

She looked at Pino's tired, kind face and gave him a little squeeze on the arm. 'I'd be happy for you, Pino.'

He'd given her good advice. And so she walked over to her mother, who stood by the fire, when it would have been so much easier, even justified, to walk away.

'I have plans tomorrow, Mamma, but I could come over in the evening, perhaps, for a drink.'

And biscotti and cake and *pizzelles*, no doubt. For there was no such thing as *just a drink* in Silibri.

It would be awkward, and difficult, but it would be a start—and, wrongly or rightly, she could not turn her back on her family.

'I'd love that,' said her *mamma*.

'I'll see you tomorrow.'

'You're not coming to church?'

'No.' Antonietta gave a wry smile. 'That would be too many Riccis under the same roof for me.'

Her *mamma* actually smiled.

And Antonietta smiled too, until she got home. And then she gave in to tears and cried more than she ever had.

She was home.

All was sorted.

Except she had let her heart go to a playboy.

And she didn't know how to even start to get it back.

CHAPTER FOURTEEN

'*Buon Natale!*' Pino said as she came to the door.

'*Buon Natale!*' Antonietta smiled.

And then she laughed as she stepped into the foyer. Nico had let them pull out all the stops, and there was now a small nativity scene on the reception desk.

'We have bon-bons.' Francesca beamed as she came over. 'And Signor Caruso is throwing in champagne. Aurora must have been working overtime on him.'

And, despite her blue heart, Antonietta laughed. '*Buon Natale*, Francesca.'

She was so grateful for her wonderful friends and colleagues who had supported her. And she was grateful too for Francesca. Yes, her words had hurt at the time, but Antonietta knew she had got off very lightly.

Well, not that lightly, because she still had to work with Chi-Chi, and they had been given a full list of suites to service in an impossibly short amount of time while the guests were at breakfast or the Oratory or church.

'My back is killing me,' Chi-Chi grumbled.

'One more suite,' Antonietta said, and knocked on the door.

'Good,' Chi-Chi said. 'They're out.'

The suite looked like a tornado had hit it. There were champagne bottles and glasses in the lounge, half-drunk mimosas on the bedside tables, and wrapping paper all over the bed.

'Don't just throw it away,' Antonietta barked, as Chi-Chi scooped up the paper. 'There might still be gifts in there...'

Foolish words.

'My back is killing me,' Chi-Chi grumbled. She sat on the sofa and commenced her *slowly-slowly*, folding the wrapping paper piece by piece as Antonietta made the bed. 'I just need five minutes.'

Antonietta rolled her eyes as Chi-Chi turned the television on. Really! She wanted a few moments alone and so, having made the bed, she went and serviced the bathroom. For a tiny second she allowed herself the dream of her and Rafe sitting in bed on Christmas morning, sipping mimosas as they unwrapped their presents.

Did she regret her time with Rafe?

No, not for a single second.

Oh, she regretted that they had been doomed from the start...and perhaps she regretted how hard she had tumbled into loving him.

But no, she refuted, she did not regret that.

As she came out of the bathroom she glanced at the television and saw the Vatican, and the Pope giving his Christmas address.

Antonietta stood watching for a moment, and saw an image of the Christmas celebrations in France, and then Germany, and then the British royal family heading to church...

And then her difficult Christmas became an impossible one—for there were the King and Queen of Tulano on the palace balcony, and beside them stood Crown Prince Rafael.

It was a mere glimpse, but it burned in her brain: the

sight of Rafe in all his military splendour, looking so impossibly handsome and so utterly beyond her, and worst of all so happy, for he had been smiling. Smiling a natural, relaxed smile that told Antonietta he was truly happy.

Of course she wanted him to be happy—but not quite yet. Not when her own heart was so raw and bleeding.

But even as Antonietta cried out in recognition the footage moved on to Austria, and how Christmas was being celebrated there.

'He's mean,' Chi-Chi huffed. 'Do you know, he left letters for all the staff who had dealings with him, and a tip, yet he left nothing for me?'

'Nor me,' Antonietta said.

Well, he had tried to give her a necklace. But that was one thing that didn't make sense.

It could not be a coincidence that the sapphire he'd tried to give her had been the exact shade of the water in the Blue Grotto. Surely?

Get over yourself, Antonietta, she warned herself.

He probably had a collection of sapphires. And all the women he took to the Blue Grotto and made love to were probably gifted one.

There was probably a Blue Grotto Sapphire club, Antonietta decided bitterly.

'Time for me to go,' Chi-Chi declared at five minutes to three. '*Buon Natale*, Antonietta.'

'*Buon Natale*, Chi-Chi.'

But *was* it a happy Christmas?

Antonietta brushed her hair and applied Aurora's red lipstick, which clashed a little with her Persian orange dress.

She had managed to get a replacement lipstick for her friend, and had baked gifts for everyone else. Well, everyone except Pino.

Antonietta collected her gifts from her locker and arrived only a little late to the party she had herself organised. And suddenly it really was a *Buon Natale*.

There was a canopy of lights that stretched across the ballroom, and in the corner stood a huge tree dressed in ropes of lights. It reminded her so much of her magical time in Capri that for a moment tears filled her eyes.

'Who did this?' she asked.

Francesca didn't even have to answer her, for a moment later there were footsteps, and Antonietta turned to the sight of Nico carrying little Gabe, with Aurora by his side.

'You're here!' Antonietta beamed. 'And you've been so busy!' she exclaimed. 'The ballroom looks beautiful.'

'Doesn't it?' Aurora said as she hugged her. 'And of course I'm here. To tell the truth, my family were driving me crazy. It is wonderful to escape!'

'There is no escape…' Nico sighed. 'And we have to head back by five for an announcement.'

'Announcement?' Antonietta frowned.

'Don't pretend you don't know,' Aurora said, and then blinked. 'My brother is getting engaged.'

'Oh!'

'To Chi-Chi!' Aurora groaned.

'No!'

'Yes,' Nico groaned. 'How the hell do I fire her now! Antonietta, you cannot leave Silibri. I swear the two of them will move into the cottage and we'll never get them out.'

For the first time since Rafe had left, Antonietta found that she was properly laughing. 'Every pot has its lid!' she said.

'And that lid is going to be my sister-in-law!' Aurora sighed, but then brightened when she saw Vincenzo arriving, weighed down with presents. 'I thought you were off!'

'I am,' Vincenzo said. 'But since when did I ever miss a party?'

Antonietta frowned, a little surprised that Vincenzo wasn't in Florence. But then Tony walked in, carrying silver trays laden with seafood and all kinds of delicacies, smiling proudly. He almost overbalanced when he saw that Vincenzo had arrived.

She turned and looked as a flush crept up Vincenzo's cheeks when Tony smiled at him. *Oh, my!* No wonder Vincenzo was putting on weight. Imagine if Tony was trying to constantly feed you!

'Is Tony the reason you aren't home for Christmas?' Antonietta asked with a smile.

'I *am* home for Christmas,' Vincenzo said. 'Here is home. It just took me a little while to work that out. My family have refused to accept Tony and me. So it is time to start our own traditions...'

'Good for you,' Antonietta said.

The table was groaning with the most delicious food. Christmas Eve was the Feast of the Seven Fishes, and there was lobster, *scungilli*... And as they sat and laughed it was impossible not be happy.

As the feasting ended the speeches started, and she looked around the table and saw that these people were the ones she loved.

Nico started by thanking his staff, and Antonietta for her marvellous idea. And there was clearly too much champagne flowing, because they all toasted Aurora for persuading him.

Then Francesca spoke. 'My staff have never let me down...'

Antonietta flushed a little at that.

'Never,' Francesca said. 'There is nowhere I would rather be than here this Christmas.'

And then Antonietta stood, and though her speech was short and sweet it came from her heart. 'I am so lucky to have you all.'

She truly was, Aurora knew. She finally had her magical Christmas.

'I might go for a walk in the temple ruins,' said Pino. 'And burn this dinner off.'

'A good idea!' Francesca smiled.

For a second Antonietta thought Francesca was going to suggest joining Pino, but there was something in his stance that suggested he wanted to be alone.

'Enjoy your walk,' Francesca said.

'Thank you.' Pino smiled.

But one day Francesca would join him. Antonietta just knew it.

It really was a two-by-two world, Antonietta thought as she bounced little Gabe on her knee and looked over to Vincenzo and Tony, who were happily holding hands.

'Antonietta,' Francesca whispered in her ear. 'Sorry to pull you away, but I need someone to take a trolley up to the August Suite.'

And it seemed that 'someone' would be her.

'Here,' Antonietta said, and handed little Gabe back to Aurora. 'I have to take a trolley up. I shouldn't be long.'

'We ought to get going,' Aurora said.

'Yes.' Antonietta forced a smile. 'You have an announcement to get to.'

Antonietta could hear the laughter wafting up from the ballroom as she pushed the trolley along the cloister. She hadn't been back to the August Suite since her cruel parting from Rafe, and it didn't help that it was Christmas Day.

And that everyone was happy except her.

She pressed her fingers into her eyes and rued the champagne she had drunk, because guests did not need a chambermaid with tears in her eyes.

'Service,' she called after knocking.

When she got no reply, she swiped her card and let herself in.

'Service,' she said again.

And then stepped into a room that was not in complete darkness, for though the drapes were drawn, every candle in the suite had been lit. The August Suite was softly illuminated with twinkling lights that stretched and danced to a gentle breeze she hadn't even been aware existed.

It felt like a church, or a ballroom, as if the stars had been brought down from the sky.

'*Buon Natale*, Antonietta.'

She jolted at the sound of his voice.

'Rafe!'

She must be dreaming. Hallucinating, even. For he was dressed in military finery, and now that her eyes were adjusting she saw that the August Suite had a Christmas tree, with presents beneath it. And a dining table set for two.

Yes, she was dreaming, Antonietta decided. She would wake up in a moment and her pillow would be wet with tears and she would be late for duty...

'I forgot my present,' Rafe said when she could not speak.

'I gave you your present, Rafe. The neroli oil, remember?'

'Of course. It is on my dresser at home. I meant the chocolate.'

'I gave it to Pino,' Antonietta said, utterly unsure as

to what was going on, and expecting him at any moment to disappear.

Except he did not disappear. In fact, when she walked over he wrapped her in his arms, but that only served to confuse her further.

'I saw you on the balcony...on the television,' she said.

'That was a couple of hours ago. It would be a break with tradition if I did not appear...'

'Rafe.' She pulled back. 'I cannot do this. Does Francesca—?'

'Stop,' he said. 'There is no conflict—this is no clandestine meeting. She knows that I am here, and so do Nico and Aurora.'

'They know?'

'Of course. And they agree that Christmas Day should be spent with the people you love. *Oui?*'

Yes. Did that mean birthdays too? And all the other special days? Would he return to Silibri on a whim?

'I have *ravioli caprese* for us,' said Rafe, 'and chocolate torte too...'

'I've eaten, Rafe.'

Perhaps it was not the kindest reply, when he had gone to so much trouble, but Antonietta didn't know what his being here meant.

When she didn't lift the cloche, Rafe did.

But it was not a romantic dinner for two that lay beneath.

It was her Blue Grotto stone. She would recognise it anywhere, even set in a ring.

'It's beautiful, but...'

Rather than pick it up, she cast anxious eyes up to him.

'Please don't play with my heart, Rafe. Please don't tell me that this sapphire means you will one day return...

that we will kiss and be together again in the light of the Blue Grotto…'

'I would never do that,' Rafe said. 'And it is not a sapphire, Antonietta. It is a diamond. Forgive me for ever thinking it should be a pendant. We *shall* kiss and be together again in the light of the Blue Grotto—but as husband and wife…'

'How…?'

'How not?' Rafe said. 'How could I ever marry anyone else? It would not just be unfair to us both, but it would be cruel to my wife also. I have my mother to thank for that insight.'

He told her the truth.

'My father used to take his lovers to Capri, and I confess, for a while I considered doing the same with you. And Nico said that Silibri could be my bolthole…'

'Never!' Antonietta shook her head.

'Silibri can be *our* bolthole,' Rafe said. 'I know it will be a huge change for you, and I know you might need time to think, and it's a lot to take in…'

'No,' Antonietta said. 'I don't need to think—you are my lid.'

'Scusi?'

'Every pot has its lid. And you, Rafe, are mine.' She picked up her Blue Grotto ring and placed it on her own finger. 'I would love more than anything in the world to be your wife.'

And then, when her bravery ran out, when she was daunted by all that lay ahead, Rafe carried her to the candlelit bedroom where he made her his lover for life.

EPILOGUE

'I HAVE TO go to my parents' house later…'

They lay in bed as she stared at her ring, which sparkled in the fading candlelight.

'I said I would go there for a drink.'

'You are speaking to each other now?' Rafe checked.

'It would seem so.'

'That is good,' Rafe said. 'Tell them that I have married you.'

'Not yet!' Antonietta laughed. 'You must ask my father's permission!'

'Oh, no,' Rafe said. 'We will be married by then.'

'Don't be ridiculous.'

'There will be a huge formal wedding in a few weeks,' Rafe told her. 'And there will be duty and cameras and parades…' He looked over at his bride-to-be. 'But I want you to know how committed I am before I take you home. Life is going to change for you, Antonietta…'

'I know.'

'But my love for you never will.'

'I know that too,' Antonietta said. 'But, Rafe, I have nothing—and I mean *nothing*—to wear.'

Enter Aurora. The best friend, the best seamstress and the best keeper and sharer of secrets that a girl could ever have.

Antonietta's dress was a sheath of Italian white lace, so slender that for a second Antonietta was sure that Aurora had got her measurements wrong.

'Hold still,' Aurora warned. She wore gloves just to do the zipper up. 'Oh, Antonietta, look!'

Aurora was crying—she actually was—as she admired not only her handiwork, and the pretty shoes she had selected, but her best friend's happiness.

And then Francesca arrived and dotted her hair with flowers, handed her a little posy.

'I am so happy for you,' Francesca said. 'And I take back every word I said about him.'

It was the most intimate and unofficial wedding in Tulano history. But what it lacked in paperwork, it made up for with love.

Rafe slid a heavy ring on her finger and said, 'I loved you the morning I met you, though I told myself I had a head injury.' Everyone smiled. 'And I hope every day to see your eyes smiling.'

And Antonietta smiled up at her impossibly handsome groom and said, 'I love you, and that is never going to change.'

'I know,' Rafe told her, and he kissed his shy bride who melted solely for him.

He held her hand as Pino read her favourite verse from Corinthians and choked up a little, for it was the one that had been read at his and Rosa's wedding. One that was still relevant now...

'"And now these three remain: faith, hope and love. But the greatest of these is love."'

And Nico did a speech, during which both Aurora and Antonietta sat, just a little tense, hoping he would not share too much of the groom's chequered past.

He did not.

'Aurora considers Antonietta family. So I guess,' Nico said, looking over to Rafe, 'that my old friend is now almost my brother-in-law. Welcome to our family.'

Christmas had delivered its magic.

With Rafe by her side she belonged in this world.

And with friends like these surrounding her as she danced with the love of her life, Antonietta had got her for ever family...

* * * * *

THE QUEEN'S
BABY SCANDAL

MAISEY YATES

To Jackie, Megan, Nicole and Rusty.

Finding true friends who understand you, relate to you, make you laugh and even try to politely respond to the 100 raccoon pictures you send them a day is a rare thing. I think it might even be magic.

Thank you for being my friends.

CHAPTER ONE

QUEEN ASTRID VON BJORNLAND had never been to a club before. But she was reasonably familiar with the layout of the Ice Palace, nestled in the Italian Alps, hidden away from commoners and social riffraff—as defined by Mauro Bianchi, the billionaire owner of the establishment—in spite of the fact that it was a place she'd never before visited.

She and Latika had done an intense amount of research on the subject prior to hatching their plan, and image searches of the facility itself had been involved. Though, the findings had been sparse.

Mauro was intensely protective of the image of the club as exclusive. And the only photographs that existed were photographs that had been officially sanctioned by Mauro himself, and included only the main areas, and none of the VIP locations that the many articles Astrid had read stated were stationed throughout the club.

Her palms were sweaty, but she knew that the invitation that she held in her hand was good enough.

Latika had assured her of that. And Latika was never wrong.

When Astrid had been looking to hire an assistant the year before her father had passed, she'd made discreet inquiries among the circle of dignitaries and royalty she knew, and Latika had appeared the next day. Polished, sleek and just a bit too good to be true.

It hadn't taken long for Astrid to realize Latika was hiding something.

"I had to get away from my father. He's a very rich man, and looking to consolidate that wealth by marrying me off to a man who is... He's not a good man. I will need to stay out of the spotlight completely. So all of my work will be done quietly, efficiently and with me out of the picture."

That was all Astrid had needed to hear. She knew all about the looming specter of potential arranged marriages and overly controlling fathers.

And so, she had hired Latika on the spot.

She was a whiz of an assistant—and had become an even better friend, and ally—and able to conjure up near magic with the snap of her fingers. In this case, magic had included: an excuse for Astrid to go to Italy, a car rented on the sly, an extravagant and extravagantly skimpy designer dress, jewels and shoes, and a near impossible invitation to the party.

And now Astrid was standing and waiting behind the thick velvet rope, in line, for entry.

Astrid had never waited in a line before. Not once in her life.

Astrid had never waited full stop.

She had been born five minutes before her twin brother, Prince Gunnar, much to the dismay of her father and the entire house of nobility. And that had essentially set the tone for her entire life.

A tone that had led to this particular plan, as dangerous, unlikely and foolhardy as it was.

All of those adjectives had belonged to Latika. Who had scolded Astrid the entire time she had aided her in putting the plan together.

Latika had *many* opinions, but none of them really mattered. Both in terms of what she would help Astrid accomplish, and in terms of what Astrid would choose to do. She would make happen whatever Astrid asked her to make happen. And that was the simple truth of it.

Astrid tugged at the hem of her impossibly short white dress. It was daring, and nothing like she would wear in her real life, but that had been part of the plan.

She could not look like Queen Astrid. If her brother found out, he would come down to the club and physically drag her out. Not to mention if any of the various government officials found out, they would do the same.

But she was doing what had to be done to wrest control of her kingdom into her own hands. Control of her future.

She would find other ways if need be, but this plan had come together with so much expert timing that Astrid was willing to chance it for several reasons.

And, she had been willing to wear a gown that was essentially a suit jacket with nothing beneath it. The neckline gaped, showing curves and angles of her body she normally kept well hidden.

Her red hair was loose, cascading over her shoulders, and she was wearing a single, long emerald on a chain, which swayed perilously between her cleavage and made her feel like she was drawing attention.

Of course, if she wasn't drawing attention to her cleavage, then she was calling attention to her legs, with that abbreviated hemline in the sky-high heels. And perhaps her rear, where she knew the white dress clung with a kind of saucy cheekiness. At least, that was what Latika had told her.

But the final thing that Latika had said to her as she had dropped her in front of the queue for the club was that she absolutely had to be back out at the curb by two in the morning.

The timing was essential, and if she missed the timing at all, not only could the plan be in jeopardy, but Latika's job *certainly* would be. And by extension possibly Latika herself, given that her position at the palace had been insulation for her for the past three years.

Astrid was the figurehead for her country. And she had power, it was true. But her father's antiquated board, along with the elected government, had authority and if something was ever put to a vote, whether it be a member of staff or law, then Astrid would be outweighed. It would be thus, she had been assured, even if Gunnar had been made king. Even if he were not born five minutes *after* his sister.

Though, Astrid was not convinced of this.

And she had found a loophole. And that loophole was why she was here.

It certainly had nothing to do with Mauro Bianchi. Not in the personal sense. She didn't even know the man, after all. But she knew about him. Everyone did. A self-made billionaire who had risen up from abject poverty thanks to his grit and determination.

In Astrid's opinion, had this been the Middle Ages, he would have been a marauding conqueror. And as she was dealing with arcane laws more firmly in the Middle Ages than in the modern era, that had only made him all the more attractive to her as she set about hatching her plan.

She took a step forward in line as all of the people

shuffled upward, and she found herself facing a large, grim-looking bouncer with a pronounced scar running across the length of his face.

She squared her shoulders, and then, changed tactics. She arched her breasts outward instead, and rather than affecting her typical severe glance, she went with a pout, just as she and Latika had been practicing in her hotel room tonight before they had gone out.

"Here is my invitation," she said, somehow feeling like she hadn't quite gotten down the simper that the other women in the line had thrown out when they had presented their invitations to the bouncer.

But it didn't matter. The invitation—while for a person who didn't exist—was for the person she was playing, and it was legitimate.

"Of course," he said, looking her over, something he did in his gaze that Astrid had never had directed at her before. "Enjoy the party, Ms. Steele."

He kept the card firmly in his hand, and ushered her inside.

It was a strange and wondrous place, some rooms carved entirely of ice, and requiring coats for entry, others fashioned of steel and glittering lights, everything fading into each other like a twisting, glittering paradise.

Astrid had grown up surrounded by luxury. But it was not a modern luxury. Not in the least. It was velvet and drapes, gold and ornate wrought iron. Cold marble and granite.

This was color, twisted metal and light. Fire and ice all melded together in an escape for the senses that verged on decadent.

There was a dance floor that was suspended up above a carved icy chamber. It glittered and twisted, casting refracted light all around. Railings around the outside of the platform prevented the revelers from falling below. She had never seen anything quite like it.

It was like something from a dream. Or a fairy tale.

If fairy tales contained house music.

And for the first time, a slight thrill went through her.

She had come about this entire plan with the grimness of a general going to war.

At least, that was what she had told herself. She had told herself that it had nothing to do with the fact that she wanted one night of freedom.

Had told herself that Mauro Bianchi had not been her target because he was attractive. Because he had a reputation for showing women the kinds of pleasure that was normally found only in books. No.

She had told herself that he was a *strategic* target.

A man with no royal connection or blood, which would make the claiming of her position even more unquestionable. Had told herself that a known playboy was sensible because as an unpracticed seductress, she would need a target that would have very low resistance.

Because she knew where to find him.

She had told herself all of those things, and the more she had read articles about him, the more she had seen images of him, his face, his body, the dark tattoos that covered his skin…

She had told herself that none of that mattered. That his beauty was secondary, and indeed only a perk in that it was a genetic point of desirability.

But now that she was here… Now that she was here in this club with dance music wrapping itself around her skin, and the thrill of her deceit rocketing through her like adrenaline, a smile spread across her lips.

Freedom.

This was a moment of freedom. A moment to last a lifetime.

Yes, she was doing this to claim the maximum amount of freedom a woman in her position ever could. But even so, she would go back to her life of service when all this was said and done. But this… This was a moment out of time.

Not a moment to think about the future. Of what it would be like to finally have the power over her country she deserved. To finally get out of her father's stranglehold. Not a moment to ponder how the ache of loneliness she felt inside might finally be assuaged by holding a child of her own. A child she would love no matter what.

She was Alice, through a looking glass. Not Astrid.

And she was going to seduce a man for the first time in her life. Possibly the last.

All she had to do was find him. And then she saw him, there could be no mistaking him. He was up on a platform above the dance floor, surveying the party below. It could be only him. That dark, enigmatic gaze rolling over the crowd with an air of unquestionable authority.

Astrid was royalty in Bjornland. She was the queen.

But there was no mistaking that here in this club, Mauro Bianchi was king.

The king of sin, of vice, of pleasure.

The kind of king who would never be welcome in a state and steady nation such as hers. But the perfect king for tonight.

She took a breath and made her way over to the stairs, thanking a lifetime of deportment for her ability to climb them with ease even in those spiked, crystal heels she had on her feet. She let her fingers drift along the rail in a seductive manner, the kind that she had been warned against as a girl. She had been taught to convey herself as cool. Sexless, really.

She was the first female monarch in Bjornland since the 1500s. The weight of the crown for her could never have been anything but heavy.

Her father had ever been resentful of the fact that it was the daughter who had been born first. Resentful. Distrustful. Doubtful.

But her mother… It was her mother who had made absolutely certain that there would be no creative shifting of birth orders.

Astrid had been born first. And her mother had had the announcement issued with speed and finality.

Her mother had also made sure that Astrid's education had been complete. That she had been trained in the art of war. Not just the kind found on the battlefield, but the kind she would face in any and all political arenas.

There was a ruthlessness, her mother had told her, to all rulers. And a queen would need to hone her ruthlessness to a razor-sharp point, and wield it with more exacting brutality than any king.

And so she had been instructed on how to hold herself, how to be beautiful, without being sexual.

She was throwing all of it away right in that moment. Allowing her hips to sway, allowing her fingertips to caress the railing like she might a lover.

She had never had a lover.

But it was the aim of tonight.

And so, she could forget everything she had learned, or rather, could turn it upside down in this place that was like a mirror of her normal life.

That was how she felt. As if she'd stepped through the

looking glass. As if she was on the other side of wealth and beauty. Not the weighted, austere version, but this frivolous palace made of ice. Transient and decadent. For no purpose other than pleasure.

She tossed her hair over her shoulder, and the moment she stepped onto the dance floor, she looked up.

Her eyes collided with his.

He saw her. He more than saw her.

It was as if there was an electric current in the air.

And so she did something she would have never done on any other day when her eyes connected with a strange man's from across the room.

She licked her lips. Slowly. Deliberately.

And then she smiled.

She tossed her hair over her shoulder and continued onto the dance floor.

There were many women, and men, dancing by themselves and so she threw herself into the middle of them, and she allowed the rhythm to guide her movements.

She knew the steps to any number of formal dances. Music composed to complement a dance, not music created to lead it.

But she let the beat determine the shift of her hips, the arch in her spine. And for one, wonderful moment she felt like she was simply part of the crowd. Exhilarating. Freeing.

And then she felt the crowd move. But it was more than that. There was a change in the air. In everything around her.

And she knew already what it meant.

The king was on the dance floor.

She turned, and she nearly ran into a broad chest, her face coming just to his collarbone.

He was wearing a black jacket, black shirt with the top two buttons undone, exposing a wedge of skin and dark hair, tantalizing and forbidden—in her estimation—as no dignitary she had ever encountered would approach her without his tie done up tight.

She looked up, and her heart nearly stopped. And then when a smile tipped his lips upward, it accelerated again.

Photographs had not prepared her.

She'd first seen him in a gossip magazine a year ago when Astrid had brought in a copy of a particularly vile rag that had featured a scandal about Astrid's brother—who had not spent life on his best behavior in the slightest.

But it wasn't Gunnar and his naked exploits with a French model that had held Astrid's attention. First of all, it was a terribly *common* thing. Even for Gunnar. It wasn't even interesting.

But second of all…

Oh, there had been Mauro. A dissolute, salacious, scandalous playboy in a tux, with one woman clinging to each arm as he walked through one of his clubs.

Her heart had stopped. The world had stopped.

That was just a photograph.

In person…

He was beautiful, but not in the way the word was typically used. He was far too masculine a thing for simple beauty. Hard and angular like a rock, his jaw square and sculpted, his lips perfectly shaped and firm looking. His dark eyes were like chips of obsidian, the lights on the dance floor swallowed up in those fathomless depths.

He said nothing, and she wouldn't have been able to hear him anyway. But he extended his hand, and she took his, the spark of fire that ignited at that point of contact spreading over her body like a ripple in the water. Sharp and shocking at its core, rolling over her wider and broader as it expanded.

He caught her and held her against his body.

She had danced with men before, but they had not held her like this. So close that her breasts were crushed to hard, muscular midsections, a large commanding hand low on her back.

And then his lips touched her ear, his whisper husky. "I've never seen you before."

She moved back, tipping her chin upward so that she could see him, so that she could look him full in the face. Except, she could hardly sustain it. She looked down.

And he captured her chin, forcing her to meet his gaze again. If she hadn't been wearing those heels she would have been so incredibly dwarfed by him there would have been no responding. But he lowered his head, and she leaned in.

"Because I've never been here before."

"It's always nice to see an unfamiliar face," he said, this time brushing her hair back from her face as he whispered.

"Dance with me," she said, not bothering to whisper this time.

The way that the rather predatory grin slid over his mouth told her that he understood.

That she wanted to do more than dance.

His eyes burned into hers as he gripped her hips, dragging her toward him as they moved in time with the music. She felt his touch everywhere, not just where he had his hands, but all the points in between, down deep, in the most intimate parts of her. She had danced with men before, but it had never been like this. Of course, the perfectly polished aristocrats who had always attended the balls she'd been at had never been anything like this.

There was an element of danger to this man. And she found herself drawn to it.

In fact, she found she wanted to fling herself against it. Against him. She had always been asked to be strong, but she had also been sheltered in many ways. Her take on the world was theoretical. And now, she was being tasked with ruling an entire country, while still suffering from that same fate.

Power, but with chains around it.

She wanted to test herself. To test those bonds.

It was what she was here to do.

"Maybe you could show me your club."

His grip tightened on her, and he looked at her for a long moment, before taking her hand and leading her from the dance floor. He held on to her as he took her down the stairs, away from the pulsing music. But they didn't go back to the entry, where people had crowded in. Instead, he moved her down a slim corridor with black flooring that had gold light shooting through the spaces in the tile. He pushed open a door that simply looked like another obsidian panel. "You will want a coat," he said, not taking one for himself, but offering her a snow-white one from a rack by the door.

"Thank you," she said, taking the coat from him and putting it on.

She quite wondered if covering her body might put her out of this advantage, but he was the one leading her, so she supposed she had better follow instruction.

Another thing she had never been very good at. But unlike waiting, it was something she had been asked to do quite a bit.

Something she now wished to avoid.

The room he led her into was made entirely of ice, the walls carved in intricate designs, crystalline, nearly see-through. By a deep navy blue couch was a wall that allowed a mirror view, however rippling and obscured, of revelers next door.

"You are quite bold," he said. "Asking me to show you my club."

"And yet, you seem to be showing me."

"I don't know that you realize just how rare it is for me to take a woman up on such an offer."

"And here I thought you took women up on such offers on a nightly basis. I've read about you."

His lips twisted upward in a cynical impersonation of a smile. "Of course you have."

"I'm sorry," she said. "Should I pretend I don't know who you are? Should I pretend that this is simply a chance encounter, and I came to your club with no prior knowledge of who you were?"

He affected a casual shrug. "Many women would."

"Perhaps those women have the luxury of time. I don't."

"You don't have a bomb strapped to your chest, do you?"

She swallowed hard, letting the edges of her coat fall open, revealing the only thing she had against her chest, that emerald, which immediately felt cold in the icy room. "You're welcome to look for yourself."

His gaze flickered over her body, and it didn't stay cool. "I see. Someone waiting for you at home, then?"

That was close enough to the truth. "Yes," she said.

"Can I have your name?"

"Alice," she said.

"Alice," he repeated. "From?"

She knew her English was quite good, but that it would also be colored by an accent. His was too, though different from hers. She liked the way it sounded. She wanted to hear his voice speak his native tongue. And hers. What sort of accent would it give to her own language? And what sorts of words might he say…?

"England," she said. "Not originally. But for most of my life."

"What brings you to Italy?"

"Your party," she said.

"I see. Are you an enthusiast when it comes to clubs, or are you a sex tourist?"

The words were bold, and she knew that she was playing a bold game and she needed to be able to return in kind.

"In this instance, I suppose it's sex tourism."

"Am I to understand that you saw my picture in the news and decided to make a trip all the way to my club for sex?"

Nothing he'd said was a lie. There might be more in her reasoning, but she had seen his photo. And she had wanted him on sight.

"Chemistry is a fairly powerful thing."

"Can you feel chemistry with a photograph?"

"I didn't even have to go looking for you," she said. "You came to me. So that makes me wonder if it's possible."

And that was the honest truth.

She had never expected Mauro Bianchi to approach her. No, she had expected that she would have to chase him down. That she would be the one pursuing him. And yet, he had simply appeared. And now, he had taken her to a VIP room. So it all rather did beg the question if chemistry could be that obvious.

The expression on his hard face did something then, and she couldn't quite put into words what that was. He looked quite irritated, but at the same time perhaps a bit impressed with her boldness and her reasoning. And he couldn't argue. Because here they were, sitting in this private suite, strangers who had never met until only a moment ago.

"I think the only thing to do then is perhaps test your theory," he said, his voice lowering to a silky purr.

"That is what I'm here for," she said, fighting to keep her voice smooth.

"Perhaps you would like to see my private suite."

"I would like that very much," she said.

This was moving much quicker than she had anticipated. But it was also going exactly according to plan.

She had expected...obstacles. Resistance.

Perhaps because the last year of her life had been marked by such things. Endless resistance from her father's officials. Endless proclamations being made. Demands that she be married. The concern over her producing an heir, as for her, there would be a time limit, unlike with men.

But they had not counted on one thing. Because they had not educated themselves, not to the extent that she had.

Men. With their arrogance. Their certainty that they were right. That they could not be bested, least of all by her.

She had read the laws. She had studied. She had made sure, above all else, that she was prepared for her position, and that she would not be taken by surprise.

Because for the protection of the queen, for the protection of the throne, if she claimed that her issue had no father, that it was the queen's alone.

And there were no questions of legitimacy. A law set into motion to protect the queen from marauders, Vikings and barbarians, anyone who might seek to use her to claim power.

And at this point in history, in time, used to protect the queen from forced marriages, and politicians who overexerted their power, and sought to keep a nation in the dark ages.

All she needed was her marauder.

And she had found him.

"Yes," she said. "Let's go to your room."

CHAPTER TWO

BY THE TIME they had gone through a maze of high-gloss marble corridors and arrived at Mauro's suite, Astrid was trembling. She did her best to try to disguise it, and hope that he would perhaps assume it was because they were surrounded by ice. But the fact of the matter was, the pieces of the structure that were not made of ice were quite comfortable, and she imagined he assumed no such thing.

She was so good at pretending to be confident, serene and as if she were in possession of every secret in all the world, that sometimes she even convinced herself such things were true.

Sometimes she forgot what she really was.

She was a queen, that much was true. A queen with quite a lot of power, education and confidence that was rightly earned.

She was also a woman who had been kept separate from peers for most of her life while she focused on her education. A woman who had danced with a man, but never, ever kissed one.

She was a virgin queen, above reproach as her mother had always instructed her to be.

But matters had become desperate, and so had she.

And she was waging war in a sense, and that meant she could not afford nerves. Even as they rolled over her in a wave, the reality of the utter disparity between the two of them a strange and intense sort of drug.

An aphrodisiac and a bit of a terror.

She was used to having a mantle of power over her, but he didn't know who she was. And here, in this private room he had just ushered her into, he was the experienced one. He was physically so much more powerful than she could ever hope to be, and her guards were well and truly dismissed. She had no one to snap her fingers for and call for rescue. She didn't even have her phone, as she and Latika had agreed that her being traceable to the club in any manner wasn't acceptable.

It was why the timing of everything was so crucial.

His suite was warm, wonderfully appointed with furs in a dark ebony, and bright white cotton spread over a massive mattress.

She looked over at him, and his lips curved as he closed the door behind them.

"Second thoughts?"

"No," she said, squaring her shoulders. "Not at all."

"I did not take a woman who would freely admit to being a sex tourist as one who would be overcome by the nerves of an innocent."

She laughed, so very grateful for all the years she had spent at various political events dodging barbs of every sort, allowing her an easy smile and confident stare even while verbal daggers were being thrown her way. "Naturally not. It's only that… We haven't even kissed yet. And I do want a bit of certainty regarding chemistry."

"A woman of high standards."

"Exceptionally," she said. "I should have mentioned

to you that I am—as far as sex tourists go—not a back-packer. I only go first-class. And if things are not to my liking, I don't stay."

A dark flame burned yet higher in his eyes, a clear response to what he obviously took as a challenge.

"I was going to offer you a drink," he said.

"Why? Because you think you should fare better if my senses are dulled?"

He chuckled and moved to her, wrapping his arm around her waist and pulling her against his body. He took hold of her chin, keeping her face steady as he stared down into her eyes.

"Let us test the chemistry, then," he said, his voice rough.

He bent down, closing the distance between them, and it was like a flame had ignited across her skin.

His kiss was rough, commanding and intense in ways she had not imagined a kiss could ever be. And this was why she had chosen him. It was why he was the only one she could fathom being with.

She had known, somehow, that he would be the one who could make her forget, for just a moment, what she was. That he could be the one who made her exult in feeling delicate. Fragile.

His masculinity was so rough. So exciting. His kiss that of a conqueror. And how she reveled in it. Gloried in his touch. His hands, large and impossibly rough, held her face steady as he angled his head and took the kiss deeper, deeper still, his tongue invading her, making her tremble, making her knees weak.

When they parted, he stared down at her, those eyes shot through with intensity. "Is that quite enough chemistry for you?" he asked.

"Yes," she whispered. "I think that is exactly the chemistry I was looking for."

He stood back and shrugged his jacket off, tossing it carelessly toward the couch on the opposite side of the room, and then he began to unbutton his shirt.

Astrid's mouth went dry as she watched him expose his body. His chest was hard looking and muscular, his abs clearly defined, with just the right amount of dark hair dusted over those sculpted ridges. And he had tattoos. Dark, swirling ink that covered his shoulder, part of his chest geometric patterns that she couldn't quite divine the meaning of.

But the beauty of tonight was that it didn't matter.

It didn't matter what any of this meant to him. All that mattered was what it meant to her.

Freedom. Wildness.

A night with her very own barbarian.

The kind of man she would scarcely have been allowed to speak to if her handlers were present. Much less be alone in a room with.

Much less be on the verge of…

"Pictures don't do you justice," she said.

"I have a feeling that dress doesn't do *you* justice," he returned. "But I would like to see for a fact if this is true."

With shaking fingers, she reached around behind her back and slowly lowered the zip to her dress, letting the soft white fabric release itself from her body and fall to the ground, a pale, silken pool at her feet.

She was still wearing those impossibly high heels and a pair of white panties. Nothing more. He seemed to approve.

Her breasts grew heavy, her nipples tight, her body overcome with restless anticipation.

Then he sprung into action, his muscles all languid grace and lethal precision as he took her in his arms and swept her up off the floor, carrying her over to that large bed and setting her down on the soft, black fur that was spread over the top.

He said something in Italian, something completely unfamiliar to her, something she assumed was something like a curse, or just something so filthy no one would have ever seen fit to teach her. Anticipation shimmered deep and low inside her.

He drew away from the bed, his eyes never leaving hers as he slowly undid his belt, drawing the zipper on his pants down as he divested himself of the rest of his clothing, leaving him completely naked in front of her.

Astrid was one for research. For being prepared when going to war. And as such, she had done a fair share of figuring out just what happened between men and women in bed, not simply in the perfunctory sense. She had done a bit of pictorial research.

But it had not prepared her for this. For him. All of him.

He was quite a bit more of a man than she had ever seen, and she had certainly never been in the same room as a naked man before. So deliciously, impossibly male.

"You are stunning," he said, advancing on her, moving toward the bed. Her stomach twisted, fear and excitement twining together and becoming something so exciting, so unbearably potent she could scarcely breathe, let alone think. She licked her lips, grabbing hold of the waistband of her panties and pushing them down her legs as she arched her bottom up off the mattress, managing to pull them only down to her knees, then uncertain how to continue. He clearly took her uncertainty as an intentional coquettishness, and she was happy to have him think so. He growled, moving down to the bed and grabbing hold of the scrap of lace and wrenching it from her body. Leaving her bare and exposed to him.

His eyes roamed over her hungrily, and there was something so incredibly close and raw about the moment that Astrid had to close her eyes.

Because there was no title here to protect her. No designer clothing, no guards. Nothing between her and this man. This man who seemed to want her, though he'd had many other women.

Astrid was used to being special. Singular. But she had none of the hallmarks here that made her any of that. She was simply a woman. She was not a queen.

And yet.

And yet he still wanted her.

She began to push the shoes off she was wearing, and he moved over her, gripping her wrists and drawing them up over her head. "Leave them," he said, pressing a kiss to her mouth before skimming his hand over her curves, his thumb moving over her nipple, an arrow of pleasure hitting her down low, making her feel aching and hollow. And then he kissed her neck, her collarbone, down to the plump curve of her breast, his tongue tracing a line around the tightened bud there.

She squirmed, arching against him, but he held her wrists fast with one hand while he continued his exploration with his mouth, and his other hand, which had moved to her hip, and was now drifting between her thighs.

Her hips bowed up off the bed when he touched her there. His fingers delving expertly into her silken folds, finding her embarrassingly wet for him.

But then, there was no point to embarrassment. Not now. Not with him.

This was her one night of freedom.

Her one night to claim a lifetime of greater freedom.

And she would not do it with a whimper. But with a roar.

She moved her hips sinuously, in time with his strokes, with the soft suction of his mouth on her breast.

He moved his thumb over the most sensitive place between her legs, stroking back and forth, and she cried out, caught off guard by the intensity of the sensations he created there. When her release broke over her, it was a shock, shattering her like a fragile glass pane, the sharp, jagged edges of her pleasure making her feel weak and vulnerable.

She clung to his shoulders, kissing his mouth, moving her hands over his finely muscled back as she did. She shifted beneath him, feeling the hard, heavy weight of his erection against her thigh. He began to move away.

"It's okay," she said in a rush, while she still had her wits about her.

And she knew what he would interpret it to mean.

She also knew, from much of her reading, that he was a very careful man when it came to these matters.

But she was counting on him being lost in the moment. She was counting on him being mortal.

This was her killing blow, so to speak, and she had to deliver it and not falter.

"Please," she whispered against his mouth and she rolled her hips upward, so that his erection was settled against her wet heat, and she arched back and forth, the pleasure making her see stars.

She could see, mirrored in his own eyes, no small

amount of that same pleasure. Of that desire. That need. He was no stronger than she, and she had been counting on that.

He growled, wrapping his hand around his arousal and positioning himself firmly against her before he slammed inside.

His savage kiss swallowed her cry of pain, and she knew that he misinterpreted it as pleasure as he lost control and pulled out slowly before thrusting back home again.

Astrid closed her eyes tight, willing herself to make it through this without crying, without embarrassing herself.

She simply hadn't anticipated it would hurt quite so badly.

He was lost to it, and she needed him to be. She only wished that she could join him.

She held his shoulders, burying her face in his neck.

And then he seemed to grasp some kind of hold on himself, his movement slowing, his pelvis rocking forward, hitting her just so, and creating a spark inside her she had been convinced would be lost in this encounter.

But it wasn't. Oh, it wasn't.

Suddenly she felt it. Deep and pleasurable and building inside her. Overcoming the pain. Overcoming everything else. It was wonderful. Beautiful and real.

He kissed her as he held her hips and drove home, hard and relentless, and welcome now. It was like she couldn't get enough. As if he couldn't go deep enough, hard enough.

There was something mystical in this joining that she couldn't figure out, but it had something to do with that instant spark that had happened when they laid eyes on each other.

Maybe even with the spark she felt when she had first seen his picture.

And when her release broke over her, it was different from before. Her body gripped his, drawing him deeper, pulsing around him as light exploded behind her eyes. And she didn't feel shattered. She felt renewed. Reinforced as he broke apart, as he trembled in her arms, this large, muscular, experienced man, reduced to shaking as he spent himself inside her.

They lay there, not for long. Only a few moments. While Astrid tried to catch her breath.

And then she heard the sound of a clock strike two chimes.

"What time is it?"

"Two?" he asked, his words muffled, sleepy.

"I have to go," she said. She scrambled out of bed in a panic, hunting around for clothing, getting dressed as quickly as possible while Mauro looked on.

"You're not going to just leave."

"I have to," she said, desperation clawing at her.

"Give me your name."

"Alice," she said.

"Your full name. I wish to find you again."

"Alice Steele," she said, the lie tripping off her tongue.

"That's wrong," he said.

"No," she said, panic like a wild thing inside her. "It's on the invitation."

"That isn't your name," he said, his dark eyes seeing straight into her.

She straightened and looked at him for one last, lingering moment, before she fled. She made her way down the halls, thankful that he was naked, and therefore wouldn't be able to move as quickly as she.

By the time she made it out to the main part of the club, Mauro was right behind her. She kept on running, one of her shoes flying off as she did, as she made an uneven escape down the stairs and tumbled straight into the limo that Latika was driving.

"Go," she said.

"Were you successful?"

She looked back at the doorway and saw him standing there, holding her shoe in his hand.

"Just go," she said, panic and emotion rising up in her throat.

And Queen Astrid escaped into the night, without her virginity, but very hopefully, carrying her heir.

CHAPTER THREE

"FORGIVE ME FOR saying so, sir, but you do not seem yourself."

Mauro Bianchi, dissolute playboy and renowned billionaire, looked over at his assistant Carlo, and treated him to a fearsome scowl. "You are *not* forgiven."

Not because his assistant was not wrong in his observation. No. Mauro was not himself, and had not been for the past three months. He could not pretend he didn't know why. He did.

He was held utterly captive by memories of a bewitching redhead, and a stolen hour in his private suite of rooms.

By the way she had run from him, leaving him holding her shoe.

And by the discovery he'd made when he had gone back to his bedroom.

The blood left on the sheets.

It was entirely possible the woman had started her period, he supposed.

Also... Also a possibility that she had been a virgin. Though he could not fathom a virgin speaking as boldly as she had.

A virgin going back to a man's room for sex, and only sex.

And she had said there was someone waiting for her at home.

He was captivated by the mystery of her, by the erotic memory of her, and nothing he did allowed him to shake it.

Apparently his staff was beginning to notice.

Certainly, the paparazzi had.

Wondering why he'd yet to turn up anywhere with a new woman on his arm, and there was endless speculation about that.

Some even suggesting that he might be in a real relationship, rather than just engaging in one of his usual transient sexual dalliances.

Of course, the press could not be more wrong.

His bed was cold and empty. And Mauro Bianchi could not remember a time in his life when that had been true before.

As soon as he reached sexual maturity, he'd not been alone unless by his own choosing. As a homeless boy, he'd found quite handily that if he were to seduce a woman who did have a bed, he could get not only sex but a nice place to stay.

He had never been shy about using his body. It was one of his many tools. Something that could bring him profit and pleasure, and why not?

He behaved thus even still.

But since his encounter with Alice. Alice Steele, who he knew was not real. He had searched high and low for women bearing that name who resembled her even slightly. Women who resided in England, and then indeed anywhere, and none fit her description.

As he suspected, her name was not real.

She was like a ghost. And the only thing he had to assure himself that she had been real at all was the shoe.

The shoe that sat on his nightstand. Not the act of a man who was in his right mind. Not at all. But knowing that did not entice him to change it.

He didn't feel in the mood to be in his right mind. That was the problem.

He was in the mood for *her*. Hungry for *her*.

He'd told himself he'd never be hungry again. Never want without having.

She'd forced him into that position and it made him feel...

Powerless.

Which was a foolish thing. He was a man at the top of the world. At the top of his field. She was... She was nothing. Just a woman in a club. He was a man who'd risen from the slums of Italy in defiance of his father, a man who had been rich and titled and had wanted nothing to do with his son.

On the far wall, between the windows that overlooked a view of Rome below, news was playing on the TV. He always had news on. It was imperative that he keep up with world events, and he was well able to absorb information without giving it his full attention. His ability to multitask another part of his storied rise to success. His aptitude for numbers, and investments, and indeed for picking places that would become the hottest locations in terms of real estate and trends, had made him incredibly wealthy.

That required him to work constantly, and to pay attention to a great many details at once.

Of course, he could pay people to do much of the day-to-day things now, but still, if he didn't have a lot of input he was bored easily.

Without a female in his bed for the past three months he was growing intensely bored and incredibly bad tempered.

But no one appealed to him. None at all. None save…

Suddenly, a flash of red hair caught his attention and he gave his full focus to the TV, where a woman was sitting in a private-looking room, pale legs crossed at the ankles, hands folded in her lap. She was dressed incredibly demurely. Her red hair was pinned into an elegant bun, her butter-yellow skirt falling below her knees, her high heels sensible and sedate.

She looked so very like the woman—*his* woman—from three months ago, and yet like a different creature entirely.

She was regal in her posture, her every movement elegant, each slight turn of her head intentional.

"Sir," Carlo said.

"Shut up," Mauro said, grabbing the remote and turning the TV up.

She was speaking, but it was in a different language, something like Norwegian, but slightly different, and he didn't speak it either way. They were not putting up subtitles on the screen, but the news commentators were going over the top in his native Italian.

"Queen Astrid von Bjornland issued a statement today to her people, that she is about to embark on an unusual path for a woman in her position. The queen is pregnant, it seems, and is determined to raise the child alone. Invoking an old rule native to the country, the queen is able to claim herself as the sole parent of the heir to the throne."

The camera panned away from the woman, shrinking the video down to a small square, where two news anchors were sitting at a desk now, a man and a woman.

"And only women can do this?" the man asked, looking somewhat incredulous.

"Yes." The female news anchor nodded gravely. "An old, protective law that ensured a queen would not be bound to one of the country's invaders, should she be forced against her will."

Against her will? She had…

That lying bitch.

She was pregnant with his child.

More than that, she was denying him his right as a father.

It took him back in an instant. To what it had been like to be a boy. Knowing his father was there in the city, an omnipresent being in his mind who had been potentially around any corner. Who had, to him, been possibly any well-dressed man walking by.

He'd known his father was a rich man. A powerful man.

A man who didn't want him.

And he had done his best to be careful—with every woman except this one—but he'd always known that with sex there was a chance birth control would fail. And he'd always known that should that ever happen he would not be like the man who'd fathered him.

He would never let a child of his wonder like that. Would never leave him abandoned, unanchored to what he was.

Would never deny him anything he had.

Yes, Astrid von Bjornland had money, had a title. But

their child was more than her. That child deserved *all*, not half.

And yet there she was. Claiming his child as hers and solely hers, when both of them knew he was well involved.

He remembered the way she had looked up at him, the way she had trembled just before he'd entered her body.

"It's fine," she had whispered.

It had bloody well not been fine. He hadn't realized he'd stood up until he looked over and saw Carlo's shocked expression.

"Sir?"

"Ready my plane," Mauro said, his tone hard. "I'm leaving."

"Where are you going?"

"Bjornland. I hear it's lovely in summer, and a bit harsh in winter. However, I hear their queen is a lying snake all year round. And that is something that needs addressing."

"Mr. Bianchi…"

"Don't worry," he said. "I'm not going to make an international incident. Provided she falls in line."

CHAPTER FOUR

"WHAT THE HELL were you thinking?"

The voice boomed.

"Excellent," Latika said, her tone dripping with disdain. "His Majesty King Gunnar has arrived. Oh, wait. But he is not king, is he?"

"I still outrank *you*," Astrid's brother said, sweeping into the room, each one of his thirty-three years evident on his face thanks to years of hard living. "And lest you become confused, darling Latika, I don't covet my sister's position. In fact, I would rather die. However, I do have some opinions on how she might conduct her business."

"That's *very* fascinating," Astrid said. "Except it is not."

"Why didn't you tell me?" he asked, his tone turning fierce, and she felt momentarily bad for her anger. Momentarily.

"Because. Telling you defeats the purpose. This is no one's business but mine. And that's the entire point of it. My heir. No one else's."

"Except, there is someone, isn't there?" Gunnar asked. "I know how these things work."

"Science is a wonderful thing," Astrid said drily. "Perhaps that was the method I employed to find myself with child."

"I don't suppose you're going to tell me," Gunnar said.

"No," she responded. "But you didn't have to return to Bjornland on my account."

"I fear *very much* that I did. You have created an incident."

"You create incidents nightly, brother dear."

"I am not the heir, Astrid. And I am a man. You know that unfair as it is… It is different."

"There is no incident," Astrid insisted. "I am well within my rights to do this. I have done all of the research required to discern that."

"Father's council will oppose you. That is their function. To keep control and power, to keep traditions. To curb your power, because father believed that men were best left in charge and not women at all."

"They can try," Astrid said. "But they won't succeed. They will not, and they cannot. Don't you think, Gunnar, that I made absolutely sure I could not legally fail in this before committing?"

Gunnar shook his head. "You underestimate the power of old men who feel their traditions are being threatened."

"This is a very old law," Astrid said, looking square at her brother. They could not be more opposite in temperament. Gunnar was a risk taker. The rebel prince who spent his life skydiving out of planes, serving in the military and piloting helicopters. Who would have been perfectly at home at a club party like the one Astrid had attended only three months ago. When she had turned her world upside down, and made a choice to wrest control of her life away from the hands of those men he was talking about now.

He was like a Viking. His eyes the color of ice, his hair

blond. His beard a darker gold that gave him a roguish appearance the press waxed poetic about.

The Viking Prince.

He was also her very best friend in the entire world, in spite of the fact that he was a massive pain. Latika saw him *only* as a pain, that much was clear. The feeling, it often seemed, was mutual.

"I have not underestimated anything. And I'm prepared for a fight. But there is a reason that I could let no one know before I made my announcement public. I also made sure that every media outlet was aware of the law in Bjornland. The one that protects the queen should she need to claim an heir as solely hers. Well, Latika ensured that made its way out to everyone."

"Did you?" Gunnar asked. "Just how involved with all of this were you?"

"Latika does what I ask her to," Astrid said.

Latika held up a hand and arched her dark brow. "It's all right. I don't need you to protect me from him. I have done my duty by my queen. And by this country. I may not be a citizen by birth, but I swear my allegiance, and you well know it."

"For now. Until you go back to America. And then, all of these problems will be ours and ours alone."

"Problems that I willingly took on," she said, her tone firm. "I am a queen, I am not a child."

"Your Majesty." One of her guards rushed into the room, his expression harried. "It seems that we have an uninvited guest at the palace, and while we had thought to shoot him on sight, he is quite famous."

Astrid blinked. "I'm not sure I understand."

"A man has walked into the palace without permission," the guard clarified.

"Then why didn't you shoot him?" Gunnar asked.

"The fame," the other man said. "We would be liable to create an international incident."

"Who is it?" Astrid asked.

"Mauro Bianchi."

Astrid's stomach clenched, the blood in her veins turning to ice. There was no way. No possible way that he could know. She just didn't give him that much credit. That he would recognize her. That he would care.

"What does he want?"

"He wishes to see you."

"Now I really don't like this," Gunnar said. "Please tell me that this man was not involved in the creation of your child."

"Define *involved*," Astrid said.

"You know exactly what I mean. Don't play coy, particularly if you don't want to be treated like a child."

"The child is mine," Astrid repeated. "And mine alone."

"Please speak to him?"

"Yes," Astrid said. "I will speak to him."

"And I shall accompany you," Gunnar said.

"No," Astrid said. "I will speak to him alone."

"You're not *my* queen," Gunnar pointed out.

"I was unaware that you had become an expat of our beloved country, my dear brother."

"You are my sister," he said. "And that takes precedence over any title."

"Then as my brother I ask you to respect my wishes. The fact that men would not respect my wishes is the reason this is happening."

"I understand," he said. "I understand full well why

you feel you had to do this, Astrid. But you're not alone. You have my support, and you will have my protection."

"I don't need it," Astrid said. "I possess the power to command that he be shot on sight. Frankly, I could ask the same of you."

"Were you... Issuing an order?" her guard asked.

"Not yet." Astrid flicked a glance between her brother and Latika. "Will you please keep an eye on him?"

"I don't get paid to babysit," Latika pointed out.

"And I receive no compensation for spending time in the company of a snarling American," Gunnar bit out. "But here we are."

Astrid left, muttering about how she wouldn't have to have him shot on sight, as he and Latika were just as likely to kill each other during her absence.

She made her way out into the antechamber of the Royal Palace, her heels clicking on the marble floor. When she saw him, her stomach dropped. His impact had not been diminished by their time apart. Not in the least. In fact, if anything, her response to him was even deeper. More visceral. Possibly because she knew exactly what he could make her feel now.

"May I help you?" she asked.

He stopped and reached into his jacket, and all of the guards in the room put their hands on their weapons.

"Stand down," Astrid said. "He isn't going to shoot me."

"Not at all," he responded. Instead, when he pulled his hand out, he was holding a shoe. *Her* shoe.

"I had thought that you might possess its partner."

"I'm not sure I know what you're talking about."

"Is that so? *Alice*."

She stiffened, straightening her shoulders. "I am

Queen Astrid von Bjornland. And I do not know anyone by that name. You are mistaken, sir."

"And I am not blind. Your hair down, a bit more
makeup and a bit more skin is hardly a convincing disguise, my Queen. If you wished to truly fool me you will
have to try much harder than that."

Irritation crept up her spine, irritation that he was not
minding what he said in front of her guards. Irritation
that he was here at all.

"Leave us," she said, gesturing toward the guards.

The room cleared, every man leaving at her behest.
At least she commanded authority over her own guards.
There was that.

"Does every man in your life defer to you in such a
manner?"

She met him full on, making her expression as imperious as possible. "Not just the men."

"I am no one's puppet," he said.

"I did not need you to be a puppet."

There was no point in lying to him. He wasn't stu-
pid. It was entirely too clear that they had met before.
And there was something… Something between them,
an electricity that arced across the space. There was no
pretending anymore. She simply had to find out what he
wanted and provide him with that, and try to end this encounter as quickly as possible.

"I need my freedom," she said. "I am queen, and there
are a great many people who don't respect my position.
I did what had to be done."

"You tricked me into getting you pregnant."

"I *seduced* you. I didn't trick you. You went along with
everything happily."

"You said everything was all right. You said it was fine to have sex without a condom."

"I said it was fine. And for my purposes it was. I sincerely hope that you don't treat every hookup in such a casual manner when it comes to protection."

"I don't," he said, the words gritted out through his teeth.

"Just with me, then. But still. I did not trick you. The fact that you assumed *fine* meant what you wanted it to mean and went along with it speaks to how foolish men are where sex is concerned."

As if she would have been capable of making a more rational decision in the moment.

"I want my child," he said.

"It's *my* child." Hers. Her child to love and to raise as she saw fit. To support and protect. And give all the things her parents never had. "By law. I can declare my child fatherless, and I have done so."

"That might be a law, Queen Astrid, but it is not reality. I am the father of your child whether you speak it or not. And I am not one of your citizens."

"No. But you are in my country. Which is where my child will be born. And my child is one of my citizens."

"You underestimate me. You are so arrogant because of your position. You have no idea who you are dealing with. You feel that you face opposition? Do you truly understand what opposition is? It is not a disgruntled cough during a meeting that makes you feel as if someone might be challenging you. No. I will give you so much more than that. If you would like to learn about opposition, I will give you a study in it."

"You should know that I don't respond well to threats,"

she said, her tone like ice. "Indeed, I don't respond to them at all."

"You don't respond to *empty* threats. Because that is all the red-faced, posturing men that you've dealt with in the past have ever issued. But I will tell you, my Queen, my threats are never idle. They are very real. I might be a bastard of ignoble birth, but the power that I possess is very real indeed. What will the public think if I were to claim my child?"

"Why?" she asked. "It is my understanding that a man in your position will want nothing to do with the child. And that is one reason I selected you, lest you think that I meant you any harm or wanted anything from you."

"You assumed you knew what manner of man I was based on the press and what they had written about me, and that was your first mistake. Tell me, Astrid, what does the press say about you? How true is it?"

"The press has never had occasion to write about a scandal of mine. And I knew full well going into this that I was inviting that. You cannot scare me."

"You have imagined the wrong sorts of headlines, I think. I doubt what you want is a long-term custody battle looming over your head. The problem here is that you imagined me as a prop. A means to an end, but what you failed to see as you read all of those headlines, as you examine all those photos of me in the articles and imagine me touching you. Imagine me claiming that body of yours, and we both know you imagined it. That you got wet thinking of it late at night in your bed. You forgot what I am."

Astrid drew back, her heart thundering. Because he was so close to the truth, it cut her close to the heart. He wasn't wrong. She had imagined him as a chess piece.

Capable of strategy, certainly, but she had also imagined that she could see ahead to every move he might make. That she understood what sort of man he was, and what he might want. But his standing here had proved already that he was not anything like she had anticipated.

She had thought of him as a barbarian, as a conqueror so many times. But in a vague, fantastical sense. In a sexual one. She had not thought in concrete terms about what it would mean to go up against this man.

Because she had not imagined he would oppose her. On that score, he was correct. She had imagined nothing like this.

She had underestimated him. And it galled her to admit it.

"What else could you want?" she said. "Anything else. I know you don't need money, and I will not insult you with such an offer. There are business opportunities to be had in Bjornland, and I am more than willing to facilitate easing the way for you. Whatever it is you want, I will give it. Only don't ask me to sacrifice this. This is what I need to claim the throne, and I will not…"

"I will not be managed. I want nothing less than what I have demanded. I want my child."

"Why?"

"Because as a boy I sat back and watched my father live in excess while my mother earned her meager pay in ways that cost. A man with money who does not care for his own is not a man at all. He is weak. Vile. The lowest form of being to ever walk the earth. If indeed you can call what he does walking. He would be better suited to crawling on his belly. I am not that man. And I will be damned if I will allow you to manipulate me. To think that I can be bought."

"What do you suggest?"

"I suggest shared custody, my Queen. But I imagine that's going to damage the optics of your little kingdom."

She blinked, not entirely certain how that would work. "There is no way that I can do that. You have to either be out of the picture entirely, the secret to the world, or you must…" Her stomach rolled. "You would have to marry me."

"Why not?" He shrugged a shoulder. "You had no intention of marrying, clearly."

"I had no intention of being maneuvered into a political marriage that wasn't of my choosing. That isn't quite the same thing."

"And yet I find in this moment the end result could likely be the same. There would be no downside to a marriage between the two of us. You can consolidate the power as you see fit, you will not be forced to marry a man chosen by this council that you're so opposed to, and I certainly have no interest in meddling in the affairs of your country."

"And you are a prime candidate for marriage?"

"Not at all. But aren't games of infidelity stock standard for royals?"

"It would require a bit more discretion than you seem capable of exhibiting."

"I can be very discreet when I choose. Tell me, my Queen. Have you seen a single headline about my sexual exploits with a virginal redhead in my private suites? No, I don't think you have. Had I wanted a headline there would have been one." He stepped forward, and tossed her shoe on the ground in front of her, the crystalline material glimmering in the light. "It seems I was able to find you without resorting to such tactics. Or trying this on any of the feet of all the eligible maidens in the country."

She thought suddenly so clearly. The queen was in check. The king had her cornered.

She could not see a way out.

"What is a queen without a king, after all?"

"According to the history of the world, more powerful."

"Not if the queen has been shamed and disgraced in the media."

Panic tightened around her throat, and as he advanced on her, shamefully, something other than panic took hold of her. A sense of shameful, heated desire that she despised.

"I have no designs on your kingdom. What I want is to give my son or daughter validity. To ensure that they have all that is rightfully theirs. And if I benefit from having my name attached to Bjornland, and to royalty, then so be it."

"Is that what this is to you? A game?"

"That's what it was to you. The fact that you don't like the outcome of that game is not my concern. You played with me."

"Whether you think so or not, I wasn't playing with you. I was helping myself."

His expression shifted, a deadly light in those dark eyes. "Do you know what a child who was born in the gutter dreams of? What it must look like from the very top. When you are born looking up, it concerns you greatly. How it must feel to look down. I know the answer to that now. And yet, any real sense of belonging in high society escapes me. I am looked upon as a trinket often, to women who wish to slum it. A bit of rough on the side. And surely, you must know that, as you did not see me any differently. In fact, I would suggest that you thought I wasn't smart enough to find out what you had done."

He began to circle her, a wolf, a predator now, looking at her as if she was a sheep. "Did you think that somehow my impoverished, low-born eyes would not be able to recognize you when you went from common club slut to queen? What you, and all of your kind, would do well to remember is that the odds are greatly stacked against someone born in my position, and if I make it to where I am, the chances are I am much smarter than you've ever had to be. Much more determined. My patience undoubtedly greatly exceeds yours. And that means that on this score I will win. My ruthlessness exceeds yours too. Yours is all theoretical. You have no idea the things I've done to get where I am. And I don't regret a single one."

Her heart was thundering. A sick feeling invading her body. Because what could she do? He was correct. He could flay her in the media.

Expose what they had done as something seedy. Call it a one-night stand, expose the parentage of her child, and the origins of it. Or, she could take hold of it now. Say the two of them had fallen in love. Yes. A love match. She could control the narrative. She could find a way to spin it.

"You must pretend to be in love with me," she commanded.

"You've already suggested to the entire world that your child had no father. How do you profess to shift that now?"

"I will say that we had a whirlwind romance. But that I was not brave. And I was afraid that you might be rejected by the council, by my people. But in the end, you came after me, and my heart won. I will say that I trust that my people will honor what I want in my heart. We will live separate lives. We will be married only in the eyes of the law. You may conduct your affairs as you see fit as long as you do it quietly. And as long as you wait."

"Wait?"

"You will remain celibate for the first two years of our marriage. If anyone were to get wind of the fact that you are having affairs so soon after our child was born, and so soon after I professed that the two of us had fallen in love, it would cast everything into doubt. Already having you as my husband will be an incredibly difficult thing for the nation to accept."

"More difficult than you staking your claim as an unwed mother?"

"Possibly not. But I was prepared for that fight. Because this position is one that I was born to be in. And I must fight for it daily because of my sex. And you tell me what you would have done in my situation."

"Likely exactly what you did. Though, I would have chosen someone with transparency, and paid for their silence."

She could have done that. She had thought about it. But the fact of the matter was she had seen him and become captivated. It was something that she had a difficult time admitting, because it made it clear that there was a personal element to what had occurred. That was something she didn't really wish for him to know.

That when he'd said she had thought of him at night, thought of him and become aroused, he wasn't wrong.

No. He wasn't wrong at all.

What she had done had been clouded by desire. And

it was easy for her to try to pretend it had been a clinical maneuver on her part. But the inclusion of Mauro Bianchi had always been suspect. She had tried to tell herself there were many reasons apart from the fact that she wanted to touch his body. To kiss him. To have him.

Well, now she'd had him. But not in the way that she had once wished.

She was queen, and he had come into her palace. Her country. She should feel a sense of power, regardless of his threats. This was her house. Not his. And yet, all she felt was the sense that she had let a tiger inside. One that didn't care about hierarchy or blood.

One that cared only for what he might possess and how. He might exploit the weaknesses of those around him.

"You have a deal," he said. "An engagement, more accurately."

"Good," Astrid said. "That means we have a lot to do. A lot of training to prepare you for your role as consort."

"I thought you would have known by now," he said, a dangerous smile curling that wicked mouth of his. "I am not one to be trained. I am not the one who will be receiving instruction. What you will have to learn is how to be a woman who would stand at my side. A woman who would compromise her kingdom for me. At the moment, you're not believable in such a role."

She narrowed her eyes. "I don't understand the need for a farce."

"You're the one who demanded it. It isn't my fault if you didn't think about what that might mean."

He took his phone out of his pocket and pressed a number, holding it to his ear. "Carlo," he barked. "For the time being I will be relocating to Bjornland. You will have my things sent here until further notice."

Astrid bristled, trying to regain control of the situation. "Of course you will move into the palace."

"No," he said. "I will not. When we are married, we can perhaps share the same residence for part of the year. Until then, I am more than comfortable procuring my own lodgings."

"There's no point," she said. "There's no point, everyone already knows that I'm pregnant."

"Yes, but what must be made clear, to you and everyone else, is that I am not a pet. I will have nothing to do with the day-to-day running of your country. I am not a man who needs to rent a space in a woman's bed to have a roof over his head. I am not a man you can control. You would do well to remember that."

He then turned and walked from the throne room, leaving Astrid standing there wondering how all of this had spun out of her control. It had started out as the perfect plan, and now it wasn't even her plan anymore.

Mauro Bianchi had given her many firsts.

Her first time waiting in line.

Her first time having sex.

Her first time feeling utterly and completely at the mercy of another person.

She was trapped. And she could see absolutely no way out.

CHAPTER FIVE

It took Mauro less than twenty-four hours to acquire a penthouse in the small business district of Bjornland's capital city, only three miles from the palace.

It was a simple thing to figure out a temporary work setup, where he could call in to any meeting he might be needed at over the next few weeks.

He wasn't leaving Astrid unattended. Not now. Not until everything was settled between them. Legally.

He also wasn't a dog that could be brought to heel, which was why he was refusing to move into the palace.

It took less time than that for him to acquire an engagement ring for his royal bride.

He had no doubt that she would be expecting to use a piece of jewelry belonging to the royal family, but he would not have it be so. He was not a house cat, and he would be damned if he were treated like one. That meant consolidating as much of his own power in the moment as he could. And what he had found was that there really wasn't much that couldn't be solved with money. Money was the universal way of gaining power and control. He might not have a title, and he might be theoretically beneath Astrid in this country, but he had no doubt he could buy the government of this country many times over.

And he found that as long as he made it clear that was the case, people rushed to accommodate him.

He also managed to procure a reservation at what he had been assured was the queen's favorite restaurant. It was the most highly coveted in the entire country.

The next step had been ensuring that he could get the queen to the restaurant. He'd thought about kidnap, but, with as many guards as she had, it would be needlessly complicated.

He had discovered through his research that the queen had an assistant. And he intended to use her if necessary.

He picked up the phone and waited while it rang. "Yes?"

"Is this Latika Bakshmi?"

"How did you get this number?" He could hear her lips go tight, could sense that her gaze had gone narrow and cold.

"I have connections," he said easily. "This is Mauro Bianchi. I hear that you are the minder of my new fiancée."

"She is not your fiancée. At least, not yet. As it is not printed in any papers anywhere."

"Is that the standard by which engagements are measured?"

"In this world."

"We have a verbal agreement. More than that, she is carrying my child."

"I would kill you myself to protect her," Latika said. "I hope you understand that."

He was impressed. It took real leadership to inspire that kind of loyalty. Real friendship. He had not been able to get a read on his betrothed, not in a meaningful sense, since meeting her outside of that initial encounter, when she had been pretending to be someone else entirely. She seemed frosty. Distant, and completely unlike the beautiful, witty woman he had met that night. But the fact that Latika seemed quite so dedicated to her indicated that there was something more than she had shown him. Not that it mattered either way.

None of this had anything to do with her.

Not in a personal sense. It was all about his child.

He would no sooner touch her again then he would allow a snake in his bed.

"I admire that," he said. "But I would also like to remain unmurdered. I do not want to hurt your princess. I simply want to ask her to dinner."

"You *are* hurting her," Latika said. "By pushing this marriage the way that you are."

"What do you suggest? That I allow my child to grow up without my name? Without me?"

He would not let his child grow up alone.

There was a long pause. "She didn't think you would care."

"I do," he returned. "I don't know the relationship you had with your own father, but surely you must understand that it is a loss to me to think I might not know my child."

The pause on the other end of the line was longer this time. "What exactly did you need to know?"

"I would like to take her out to dinner tonight. I was hoping you could facilitate that."

"I think that I can."

By the time Mauro pulled up to the palace that night in his newly acquired car, he had every puzzle piece in place. What he had said to her about the way that he maneuvered the press was true. If he wanted to be seen by the press, then he was. Likewise, he knew how to avoid them. He was more than happy to cultivate a certain image in the media as it suited him. And more than happy to be left alone when it suited him, as well.

Tonight he needed an audience. And he had made sure that there would be one.

The restaurant itself was built into the side of a mountain. The views it offered of the valley below, a broad swath of mist and green, made him understand why Bjornland was listed as one of the world's most pristine undiscovered gems.

Staff in the kitchen had ensured that the photographs he wished to have taken tonight would be taken. A bit of money in the right palms, and the paparazzi would be let in the back doors at the appropriate time. He was bound and determined that he would secure this union and bind Astrid to him as quickly as possible.

He did not get to where he was in life by waiting. Or by leaving anything to chance. The palace doors opened, and she appeared.

Dressed in an immaculate emerald green dress with a wide, square neck that showcased her delicious breasts. The dress skimmed her curves, falling down below her knee, hugging each line and swell of her body like a lover.

It was a shame she was so beautiful. Considering he knew exactly what she was. Even knowing, his body responded to her. That connection that he had felt from the moment he had first seen her defied any kind of logic, and it continued to do so.

A valet came to the car and opened the passenger side, and she paused before getting in.

"It is you."

"Did your faithful sidekick not tell you?"

"She did not. She was rather intentionally vague." Astrid sank down into the car with a great deal of overly dignified posture. She looked like an arched hen, stiff and tall, but visibly ruffled. "She may in fact find herself looking for a job."

"I would only hire her in my company," he said, treating her to a grin he knew was wicked. And it had the desired result. Her color mounted, her indignation increasing.

"Why would you do that?"

"She helped me. And I am loyal to those that help me. Make no mistake."

"That's interesting," she said as he put his car in Drive and roared away from the palace. "It's interesting because you have rather a reputation for treating people as if they're disposable."

"You mean women," he said, pointedly.

"Yes," she said.

"I have many women that work at my company, and they will tell you differently."

"I mean *lovers*," she clarified.

"And yet, here you are."

"That's different," she said.

"If you say so. The media makes much about my reputation, and a good portion of it is deserved. I am a man with a healthy sexual appetite, and I have never seen the point in pretending otherwise. However, I am a man from a particular background. And I learned long ago that only people with a disposable income could afford to treat others as if they were disposable. I was dependent upon the kindness of others for a great many years, and I have not forgotten it."

"But to hear the press tell it…"

"I'm ruthless," he said. "Relentless in my pursuit of the almighty dollar. And that might be true. I have thought nothing of buying property out from under the rich and titled. But I have not—and will not—send anyone to the poorhouse. I have scruples. Isn't that an inconvenient thing for you to learn?"

She said nothing.

"Does it bother you?" he pressed. "The idea that I might not be a caricature that you can easily pin down? You wanted me to be a villain, did you not? Someone that you could easily say deserved to have his child hidden from him. After all, if I am everything you seem to think, I should not have a child in my presence, should I?"

She was frozen now, that stiff posture adding to her silence.

"I am not a nice man," he continued. "On that score you are correct. I like excess. There you are correct, as well. But there are certain things that I cannot endure. That I will not abide by. I do not treat human beings like trash. Not the poor. And certainly not children. Least of all my own."

"How kind of you," she said, archly, making it clear she still found his standards of humanity beneath her.

"Do you actually want this child?" he asked as they continued up the winding mountain road that he knew would lead them to the palatial restaurant.

"Yes," she said, her tone fierce. "I want this child very much. My life has been incredibly lonely. Filled mostly with tutors and sycophants. My brother has been my primary companion for most of that time, but he had a very different life than I did. He had a lot more freedom."

"You are the queen," he pointed out. "You have more power than he does."

"More power in this case is not more freedom. I'm five minutes older than my brother," she said. "*Five min-*

utes. My brother is everything the old men of my father's council could possibly want in a leader. A tall, strapping man. An alpha male with the kind of immediate presence that gives a sense of confidence and intimidation. And me?" She shrugged. "I'm a woman. But, if not for a little bit of acrobatics in the womb, they would have the leader they wanted, and not the one they're stuck with. Do you have any idea how much that galls them? How much they resent it? I can feel it every time I'm in their presence. And make no mistake, a great many citizens of this country feel the same way. When my father passed away, I think they all hoped that there would be some secret switch. That I would abdicate. That I would do the right thing. That is what some people think. That it would be right for me to abdicate because of my gender. I have been above reproach all this time. And I have been opposed every step of the way for no other reason than that I was born a woman. It was my mother's deepest wish that I would not allow them to take what was rightfully mine. And I have not. I will not."

"And the child… The child helps you accomplish this."

"The issue of me needing a husband was being pushed. And there was a possibility that they would have the right to select a husband for me. There is also a great deal of responsibility placed on the production of an heir. Once I have produced one, some of the council's oversight is removed. This is a protective method that has been in place in the country for generations. To ensure that a royal is doing their duty by the country, and if not, then decisions may have to be made."

"And there is some arcane law that says the queen can be considered solely responsible for her own issue."

"Yes." She sighed heavily. "It seemed the smartest thing to do."

"It might've been," he said. "Had you chosen any other man."

"Do you know what I liked about you?" she asked. He heard a slight smile in her voice.

"No," he returned. It was true, he didn't. Based on his interactions with her he would have assumed she liked nothing about him at all.

"You reminded me of a warrior. I liked that about you. I thought… That is the kind of genetic material I need for my child. And you might judge that, I understand. But it made sense to me at the time. I was feeling a bit desperate."

He let silence lapse around them for a moment. The only sound that of the tires on the road, the engine a low hum running beneath. "The problem with warriors," he said finally, "is that you cannot control all that they might do."

She laughed. A small, humorless sound. "Understood. Understood all too well at this point."

It was then that they reached the summit of the mountain, the restaurant glittering against the stone.

"Oh," she breathed. "This is my favorite."

"Good," he said, and he fought against the strange curl of pleasure in his stomach that he had pleased her in some way.

There were glittering Christmas lights around the perimeter of the restaurant, green boughs hanging heavily over the doors and windows.

"It's a bit early for all of this," he commented.

"Perhaps," she agreed. "But it's nice all the same."

She softened a bit, talking about Christmas. It confounded him. He didn't much understand the joy of Christmas.

He'd never had a Christmas, not really.

They left the car with the valet, and he looped his arm through hers as he led her into the restaurant. She was like ice beside him, but he didn't pay attention to that. Instead, he leaned in, his lips brushing against her ear. "You will have to look as if you enjoy touching me."

"I didn't realize this was an exhibition."

"You are Queen Astrid von Bjornland, and I am Mauro Bianchi, the most famous self-made billionaire in all the world. Everything we do is an exhibition."

"Most famous?" she asked drily. "You think very highly of yourself."

"I didn't realize that ego and honesty were considered the same thing in your world."

"I consider ego very important. Never think that I'm insulting you for pointing out that you have a healthy one. After all, I'm the queen that millions think should not have a crown. How do you think I walk with my head held so high?"

"Well, now," he said. "That I can respect."

"Whatever you think about me," she continued. "I guarantee that you don't have the first idea of what it means to operate in my world. You might be rich. But you don't understand the expectations that have been placed on me. No one does. My brother… He tries. It cannot be said he doesn't. He is my twin, and the closest person to me in the entire world. But he can't fully understand. I don't know that a man ever could."

"Is that so?"

"Yes. Now, I imagine that being of low birth, as you are—"

"Low birth," he said. "What a delicate way to phrase it."

She shrugged. "I wasn't trying to be delicate in particular. But being from the kind of station you are, I imagine that you reached some opposition when you were trying to ascend. I also imagine that once you proved yourself capable, then it was assumed you were capable."

"I confess, my prowess has never been called into question. In any arena."

"I was born to this," she said. "My blood runs blue. My education, my upbringing… It was all geared toward me finding success in this career that I was born for. And yet whether or not I am capable of handling it… My marital status, whether or not I'm carrying an heir, all of those things, seem to matter more. I am a pass-through ruler. And believe me when I tell you they will all pray this child is a boy."

"England seems to have done all right for itself," he pointed out.

"It isn't the same. Our country is smaller, the government is run differently. We don't have parliament."

"Let us go inside," he said.

They were standing out in the chilly air, Astrid looking up at him, and he had a feeling that she was putting off the moment that they would have to go in and face the public. But then, she had no idea the level of public that would be in attendance.

"All right," she said slowly.

She allowed him to lead her into the restaurant, and he knew that he was being allowed. After all, this woman did not seem to cow under any threat or circumstance. Whether or not the council respected all that she was, he did. He could see what she was. It oozed from her every pore. From the very way in which she carried herself.

He moved his hand to her lower back as they walked into the warm restaurant. It was very Scandinavian, with a sparse design aesthetic, the windows looking out over the impressive mountain view, the trees inky and black against the backdrop of the rich velvet sky, the stars glittering like diamonds.

"This is a beautiful place," he commented, keenly aware of the fact that all of the eyes in the room had turned to them.

"Yes," she said, somewhat absently. "It truly is."

He leaned in, conscious of the fact that they would be being photographed now. "And what is your favorite thing on the menu?"

"I always get the special," she said. "Whatever is seasonal. Oh, and if there's an appetizer with one of the Bjornish aged cheddars, I always get that."

"You have a fondness for cheese?"

"I would distrust anyone who doesn't."

"I see. So that is how you arrive at conclusions regarding who you can trust and who you can't? Which foods they have an affinity for?"

"I've yet to surmise a more adequate way of parsing a person's character.

"Well," he said, "I like cheese. What does that say about your metric?"

She looked at him, those lovely, green eyes appraising. "I chose you, didn't I?"

The words were cool and unsettling. They made him feel much more like she might be in the driver's seat than he was comfortable with.

The maître d' appeared and quickly ushered them to a semiprivate table, which Mauro liked because it gave the appearance that they were attempting to stay out of the way, while still allowing for the paparazzi to be able to get discreet photos.

In his experience, the quality of the publicity was all in how you courted it. Or how you appeared not to.

And just like that, he was reminded of who was in control.

At least tonight.

She was a fascinating woman in some ways. He was not accustomed to dealing with women—with anyone— who had even a comparable amount of power to his own. Astrid was a queen, and the idea that she could snap her fingers and have him executed infused him with a particular kind of fascination he had not dealt with before.

He hadn't anticipated a powerful woman being quite such an aphrodisiac, and yet it made sense. What good was strength and power if it went untested? What good was strength and power when pitted against someone weaker?

Far more interesting to spar with an equal.

When a waiter appeared, Mauro spoke quickly to him, procuring the specials, and requesting a special appetizer with local cheese for the queen.

"You did not have to order for me," she said.

"Perhaps not," he said. "But I thought it might make an interesting challenge." He looked at her. "You did not have to let me order for you. I imagine you could have stopped me at any point."

"It's true," she bit out.

"I imagine that you could call the waiter back now and reverse my order if you find it unsatisfactory."

She sniffed. "Well, you got what I would have ordered anyway."

He smiled. "That isn't true."

"Oh, yes?"

"Yes. It isn't true because you would never have asked for a special entrée to be made for you."

She sniffed again. "I told you, I was raised to be a queen. Why do you think that is beyond my scope?"

"Because you were raised to be very careful. That is something else I know."

"It's true. My mother always stressed that I would be scrutinized much more closely than a potential king would be. It's impossible for me to know if it would have been different for Gunnar if he were the heir. But he gets much more leeway in the press, and his behavior is considered something of a national pastime. Of course, he is not in immediate line to the throne. So perhaps that's the reason why. But it really is impossible to know."

"I imagine you could never risk looking overly commanding."

"No," she said. "Neither could I… Neither could I ever risk dancing too close to a man."

"And so you disguised yourself in something unsuitable and went to my club?"

"The truly amazing thing," she said, "is that people don't look closely at other people. We never search for the unexpected. I've never put a foot out of line, and so no one would ever think that they might spot me at your club. Least of all wearing the dress I had chosen. It was the perfect moment to engage in a small rebellion."

"It was coup in many ways, it could be argued."

"I suppose. To claim the power that should've been mine all along."

The two of them began to eat in silence and Mauro became aware of the sound of a camera. It was subtle, but it was evident, and he made sure to reach out and brush his fingertips across Astrid's knuckles. She startled, drawing her hand back.

"Your Majesty," he said. "Never make the mistake of thinking that we might not be in the presence of an audience."

"An audience?"

"I made sure the press knew that we were here."

She went still, as if she'd transformed into a pillar of salt, the stony expression on her face one of biblical proportions. "What are you up to?"

"Did you honestly think that I called you here without a plan?"

"I suspected that we would discuss these things together." She said the words through tight lips, her expression serene, even as the waves emanating from her were not.

"Smile," he said.

As if on cue, she did so, and to anyone observing them it would seem that they were having a friendly exchange.

"This is not your show," he continued. "That is one thing you need to learn about me. I am subject to no one and nothing. Least of all you. You made a choice. You stepped into my world. And now, you have ensured that you'll never fully be free of me. This was your decision, not mine. And now, here I am. I am the thing you must contend with. You assume that your consequence would be carrying my child. No, my Queen. *I* am your consequence."

"Damn," she said, keeping that smile stretched wide. "A consequence I had not foreseen. How unusual."

"Indeed."

And he knew that his next move was one she had not seen coming either. It would be cliché to wait for dessert.

The move of a man who was calculating the entire event. But he was determined to make it look as if theirs was a spontaneous proposal. If this was what she wanted, the look of love, the look of a real couple, then he would give it to her. But he would give it to on his terms. If she thought that she could be in charge of creating their narrative, she was about to be sadly disappointed.

He reached into his jacket pocket, and he produced a small ring box.

The shock on her face was not manufactured. Not in the least. It was clear to him that she had not been expecting this. Not at all. And it gave him an illicit rush, a thrill, to have her at his mercy. Because that night when he had first met her, he had felt a connection between the two of them that he had never felt with another woman before. And she had been using him.

That that bothered him at all was laughable. It shouldn't. And yet, it did. His every emotion tangled up in this thing that he had neither anticipated, nor ever thought to protect himself from.

And then it had turned out the connection was a creation. All a part of a tactical war she was waging, unbeknownst to him. He did not handle such things well.

And now, it was her turn. Her turn to be caught off guard.

He dropped to one knee in front of her, a position that she probably saw men in often, but this was not a pose of submission. Not a gesture of deference on his part.

He opened up the ring box, the piece that he was presenting her a true marvel of design. Clean and simple, like this restaurant that she favored so much. Something that reminded him of what she had worn the night they had met. A creation designed to complement who she was, rather than adding unnecessary adornment.

A large, square cut diamond, clear and bright, in a platinum setting.

Something that worked with the lines of her elegant hand, rather than overwhelming them.

"Queen Astrid," he said. "Would you do me the honor of becoming my wife."

It was not a question. And she seemed to know it.

He could sense the electricity around them, the entire restaurant now rapt at the scene in front of them. Shutters were going off, cameras raised, while people snapped completely obvious cell phone photographs of the moment. And now he had her. Now he truly had her.

"Yes," she said, her answer wooden, stiff. "Of course I'll marry you."

Her smile was effortless, the result of years of practice and breeding, he could only assume. And to anyone else she would look positively joyful.

But he could feel her rage.

Her desire to make him pay.

And it only fueled that damnable fire in his veins.

"You've made me the happiest man in the world," he said.

Then he grabbed her hand and tugged them both to their feet, drawing her up against his chest and gripping her chin between his thumb and forefinger.

The look in her eyes, that glinted there, threatened to cut him. But her actions remained agreeable.

For a woman for whom reputation was everything, this was a hostage situation. And as a man who didn't care at all what anyone thought, it was a victory.

Then, he lowered his head, and claimed her mouth with his own.

And that was the moment he had not planned for.

He hated this woman. Despised the way that she had deceived him, used him. The way that she had been intent upon hiding his child from him.

But this remained. This spark.

The electricity of the room wasn't simply coming from the excitement of the spectators around them. No. The electricity was in them. Arcing between them with uncontrollable sparks.

He wanted to devour her. Part her lips and slide his tongue against hers. Luxuriate in this until it consumed them both.

And it was that feeling. The sense of being out of control. Of wanting…

That was what pulled him back. Because he would be damned if he would crave a thing that was out of his reach ever again.

He pulled himself away from her, staring down in triumph at her swollen mouth, her stunned expression.

"I believe this makes you my fiancée."

And just like that, he had the queen in check.

CHAPTER SIX

"How dare you make a move like this without consulting the council."

"Which move?" Astrid asked as she faced down the long board table of very angry men. Men her father had appointed to their positions over the course of his rule. It was traditional for the monarch of Bjornland to have consult of a council. With more freedom being handed over to the ruler after marriage, or after an heir was produced.

But the way this particular council had been established, without her approval, even as her reign was approaching, and with life terms given to those who sat in their positions, was unheard of. And allowed only, she imagined, because she was a woman.

Her father had installed babysitters for her.

He'd never cared that she'd done nothing but demonstrate her ability. He couldn't see past what he considered her fundamental flaw. She was female, and would therefore be a weaker ruler. Inclined to lead with her emotions. To be swayed by her hormones in a way a man was never led about by the member of his body.

The very idea sent Astrid into a small internal rage.

Men were always so concerned with what women might do during a certain time of the month, and yet they were slaves to the whims of the lower halves of their bodies at all times of every month.

That her father had considered her weak and fallible because of her sex was, in her mind, a sign of the weakness in him.

But with her upcoming marriage, and the baby coming, they were on the way to becoming less powerful, and they were certainly sitting there looking as though they knew it.

"The one where I decided that I would be taking control of the child that I carry, or the one where I got engaged?"

"Either," Lars, the lead councilman, replied.

"Both are done," she said causally. "There's nothing to discuss."

She had whiled away her time letting these men occupy their seats. Not making waves. So that when she had the moment to consolidate her power they would be blindsided. And that was clearly what had occurred.

She would remain calm even now. Better to have them unable to anticipate her next moves.

To the outside world it might appear as if she was taking orders. As if she was allowing herself to be walked on.

But she had the trump card. And she refused to waste energy flailing when she was in the process of succeeding in a tactical strike.

The ring on her left hand felt heavy. And her lips still felt tingly from the kiss she had shared with Mauro at the restaurant. Perhaps *share* was too strong of a word. That kiss had been a conquering. Truly, the barbarian had reached the gates, and no amount of planning on her part had been sufficient to keep it from being so.

She had handed him the keys to her kingdom. She might as well tilt her head back and let him slit her throat.

And if it were ancient times, perhaps that's what would have been done. At least, after she had produced his issue.

But he claimed that he wanted nothing to do with the kingdom specifically, and right now, looking at all of the faces staring back at her, feeling the rage emanating from them, she could only take comfort in the fact that the only people more upset about this development than she, were them.

As much as she could feel her plan spinning out of control, she imagined that they could feel their control on the kingdom slipping out of their grasp.

And as long as that was the case, she would be happy enough.

"He is the father of your child?" Lars pressed.

"That is the question on the lips of everyone in the world at the moment, it seems," she said, keeping her expression serene and her shoulders straight.

"You claimed there was no father," another of the men said from the other end of the table.

"Well, I think we all know that's a lie. Even men such as yourselves don't spring from holes in the ground. They are made the typical way." She received raised eyebrows in return for that statement. "Do not all of you go looking so shocked that I am a woman. After all, if I were not, you would not be here, with the layers of additional power my father bestowed upon you. To protect myself I was willing to invoke that particular law written in our books. But it turns out, I didn't have to. The issues that Mauro and I were having—personal issues—have been resolved. And now we will be able to present a united front for the kingdom. I fail to see how this is not a winning proposition for the entire nation."

"A playboy," a dissenting voice said. "And one from the gutter at that. He is well beneath you, and beneath this kingdom."

"Is he?" she asked, with no small amount of ice in her voice. "Have I not lowered the kingdom sufficiently to reach his level? I should think that by mere virtue of the fact that I am a woman, I would have slipped us down several ranks in your estimation. Not to mention my very nonsecretive pregnancy, which the whole world knows occurred out of wedlock."

"My Queen," Lars said. "You know that you have nothing but support from the council. That is why your father solidified our position before his death. To make sure that we could support you."

"Support. Undermine. In the grand scheme of things is there any difference? I knew that in order to claim my independence I had to either marry or produce an heir. Handily, I will be able to do both very soon."

"How soon shall the marriage take place?"

"Two weeks," she said, the words, the commitment, sending a stab of terror through her body. She had not discussed this with Mauro. But she imagined that the sooner the better as far as he was concerned. After all, he had taken control of the timeline by making their engagement so visible, and thrusting it upon her without giving her any time to be coordinated. He could hardly get angry at her for keeping up with that push forward.

Well, maybe he could. But maybe it would do him some good to be angry.

She had the terrible feeling that she was going from

one battle of wills straight into another. She also had the terrible feeling that the council wasn't going to go quietly.

She suddenly had the distinct vision of being pulled between Mauro and the table full of councilmen.

She also had the clear vision of Mauro being able to pull her away from all of them.

She disliked that.

She had intended to rescue herself. The idea of needing his help was galling indeed.

"That is impossible," her largest dissenter said, rubbing his hand over his face. "You know we cannot coordinate a wedding in that time."

"Then don't coordinate it. I assume you don't want a heavily pregnant queen wandering down the aisle, which means expedience should be welcome. And if that's too difficult for you, I will arrange it myself. It will coincide with the tree lighting, and other Christmas festivities Bjornland will be celebrating, and I can think of nothing better."

"You will add unnecessary duties to the staff at this time of year?" Lars sneered.

"Not at all. I will boost the economy and provide with it extra money for the season. And I am well able to ensure it all goes to plan without involvement of anyone in this room."

"How?"

"I have an assistant for a reason. And believe me, she is more efficient than this group of people all on her own. If the idea of helping to coordinate this wedding intimidates you, then I'm certain that Latika will happily take up the banner."

"This is *unprecedented*."

"That's fine. I don't mind being unprecedented in this

manner, as I am unprecedented in every other way. You were the only ones that seem to have an issue with that. You are beginning to drag down the entire country."

"Mark my words," one of the men in the back said. "If the country is to fall, it will be on your head."

She firmed her jaw, calling on all the strength she'd spent her life culminating. "Then so be it. But it will not be my head alone, but my new husband's, as well. You will find he is nothing but a staunch supporter of me. You might be able to oppose me, but when I am joined with him I will only be stronger. Two are better than one. And the two of us will be vastly better than twelve," she said, looking at them all meaningfully. "I will send you an invitation to the wedding if you wish. Otherwise, you may take a backseat. You will have to get used to that."

On that she turned on her heel and walked out of the room, listening with satisfaction as each step echoed loudly around her.

She had been angry at Mauro last night about what he had done. She had been uncertain with how to proceed. But she knew now. Everything had a purpose now.

Suddenly, this marriage actually seemed like the best idea.

It might never be a real marriage. She didn't need it to be a real marriage.

He would be a figurehead, and she… She would finally be able to be the queen that she was always meant to be.

Dinner that night was at the palace, and it was filled with pronouncements. Mostly made *at* him. Mauro wasn't used to such things, and he found he had limited patience for it.

Though there was something exceptionally alluring about Astrid, even when she was being a pain in his ass.

Sometimes, especially when she was being a pain in his ass, and he didn't fully understand that.

"We are to be married in time for the tree lighting in the palace. It will be integrated into the ceremony in point of fact."

"Is that so?"

"How pregnant did you expect I should look on the day of our wedding, for all the papers to see?"

For some strange, inexplicable reason the idea of her looking pregnant—her stomach round with his child—did something to him that he could not explain. Something he didn't want to explain, even to himself.

"How pregnant you are or aren't when you walk down the aisle doesn't matter to me," he said. "The only reputation I have to maintain is one of total debauchery and general disdain for social niceties. For me, this is on brand."

"How nice for you," she said, drily. "We will marry in a month."

"When do you suppose you will learn I don't respond well to commands?"

"I don't know. I suspect we have a lifetime to discover that."

"Surely not a whole lifetime," he said. "Only while the child is…a child, I'd assume. Do we really need to be so pedantic that we stay together for eighteen years?"

"I hadn't considered it," she said, her expression bland. "Marriage, to me, is forever, but it certainly doesn't have to mean together."

"Elaborate," he said. "I am not from a household that contained a marriage. My view of it is limited to sitcoms and crime dramas. Both give a very different idea of what it means to be married. I imagine the truth lies somewhere between happy hijinks and murder."

Astrid chuckled softly, pushing food around on her plate. "Yes, something like that. I think that middle ground is called 'quiet disdain.'"

"Speaking of your parents' marriage?" he asked.

"Yes. You know, my father never wanted me to be queen. My mother was stubborn about it from the beginning. From making sure the announcement that the press received was unambiguous about which child was born first."

"But he was the king. Couldn't he override her decision?"

"Yes," she said. "He could have. There were many reasons he didn't. That he would suffer in the eyes of his people, and the world, being a large part of that. Also... He knew I wasn't incompetent. If I had been I think he wouldn't have hesitated to have Gunnar named the official successor to the throne. My father wasn't an easy man, but he had a strong sense of duty. I don't know that he... I don't know that he loved anyone. But he loved the country. As for my mother..."

"Did she love him?"

"I don't think she did. Mostly they spent their marriage sleeping with other people, once Gunnar and I were born. Heir and spare in one go. Exceedingly handy."

"Before your idea to circumvent the council, what was your thought on who you might marry?" He didn't know why he was curious. He shouldn't be. Not about this minx who had upended his whole life, forcing him into a situation he didn't want to be in.

No, he didn't want to want this child. But he did.

His mother was dead now, gone. Years of hard living

having taken their toll on her. Installing her in a luxury penthouse for the last six months of her life had probably extended her time on earth, but not by as much as he'd hoped.

His father still lived, but he'd vowed he'd never speak to the man again.

The child, his child, would be a real flesh-and-blood connection he could have here on this earth. This child was something real to care about. To want to care for.

He didn't…want to need those things, and yet he found he did. It was more than just a feeling of responsibility. It was something that called to a deeper place inside him.

One he'd done a great job pretending wasn't there for the past thirty-five years of his life.

Just another reason to find Astrid enraging.

But he found he was still curious.

"I didn't think about it," she said. "I imagined my parents would be involved in helping curate a selection of acceptable suitors. But they never did. My father died when I was twenty-nine. I still don't know why he didn't try to marry me off before then. A year ago, I thought of this plan. Oh, I hadn't chosen you specifically but I had decided I would have a baby alone."

"You never wanted love?"

She lowered her head, shaking it slightly. Then she laughed. "All I ever wanted was for the people around me to see that I was competent. Not in spite of being a woman. Not barely acceptable when they could have had a man. But qualified. A passionate leader, a good leader. One who loves her country and all of its people. Fantasies of romantic love have never factored into my life. I can't even get respect, why would I hinge any great thing on love?"

He could relate to that feeling, though his was not a sense he did not deserve love, but the deep, abiding belief it did not truly exist.

Love, in his mind, was an illusion. When life became bleak, love was always the first thing to crumble. In the end, people would always choose themselves. They would not choose another person. Not really.

It didn't make him sad anymore to know that. As a boy, it had. He'd been convinced if only his father could love his mother, they would be a family and be happy. He'd been convinced that if only his father would meet him, he would love him and he would want to give him and his mother the money they needed to live.

But his father loved himself. He loved the life he had in the palazzo on the hill with his wife and their real children. The children he'd made intentionally, with the aristocrat woman he'd chosen. Not the gutter trash he'd knocked up during a dalliance.

His mother had made it very clear where she'd stood in his father's eyes. Never to make him feel sorry for her. Never to cry about injustice.

Only to make it known why any reconciliation was impossible.

Still, he'd always thought it could be so as a boy.

He'd found out as a young man he'd been wrong.

"What about you?" she asked. "Am I interrupting any marital plans?"

"No," he said. "I intended to whore my way around the world. I intend to continue doing so when our need for total discretion is resolved."

"Excellent," she said, though her tone sounded quite crisp.

"Does it bother you?"

She shook her head. "Not at all. You recall I intended to walk away from you and never see you again. I hardly intended to own your sexuality for the rest of your life. I intended to forget your name."

He smiled. "And now, here we are."

"What *the hell* is happening?"

He turned to look, at the same time Astrid nearly gave herself whiplash twisting around when a large man, who had slightly different coloring, with blond hair and a beard, but was identical to her in the stubborn set of his jaw, came striding into the formal dining room.

"It's five in the evening, Gunnar," Astrid said, as she recovered herself. "I hope you didn't get out of bed so long before your typical wake-up time just to question my life decisions."

"I'm questioning *his*," Gunnar said, the anger in his expression making abundant sense now that he knew for sure this was Astrid's brother.

"Your sister is having my baby," Mauro said. "What precisely should I have done to treat her in a more respectful manner? I have proposed marriage to her."

"And you'll get your hands on the kingdom?" Astrid's brother was like a very large, angry Viking barreling down on him, and if he weren't an accomplished street fighter, he might have been concerned for his safety.

"Whatever your plan is… It is not going to succeed," the other man continued. "Astrid is much stronger than that."

"I'm aware of that. It's one reason I'm so fond of her."

"Your stories are conflicting," Gunnar said. "My sister made it very clear there was no father of her child. Then suddenly, you appeared."

"We had a disagreement. That disagreement has been resolved."

"It's a political marriage," Astrid said, sounding tired. "There's no point lying to him. Neither of us can get away with lying to each other ever. It's one of the worst things about having a twin."

"You don't have to do this," Gunnar said.

"I do," she insisted. "I overplayed my hand and I lost. But now we have a scenario that helps me in the end."

"In what sense?" Gunnar asked.

"The council is madder at me than you are," she said, her mouth lifting up into a small smirk.

"That is something," Mauro said.

"I assume," Gunnar said, turning his focus to Mauro, "there are official documents that can be drawn up and kept secreted away in your personal vaults well away from Bjornland?"

"Of course," Mauro said. "Discretion is key in my line of work."

"I didn't know *discretion* was part of your vocabulary," Gunnar said.

"Because you've never gotten wind of a single thing that I appeared to be obscuring. I find hiding in plain sight is often the best plan."

Astrid's brother regarded him with what appeared to be grudging respect.

"Now that you're through treating me like a child…" Astrid said.

"Yes, I'm sure that if I appeared with a random fiancée you'd take it in your stride."

"Of course not," Astrid said. "I'd renounce her as a gold digger."

"Then don't expect me to sit back and allow you to make choices I find...deeply suspicious."

Mauro leaned back in his chair. "You should find it deeply suspicious. Though, as I said, I have no designs on your country."

"What do you have designs on?"

Mauro leveled a gaze at the other man. "Is it so difficult to believe it's your sister?"

Gunnar shook his head once. "Not at all. But there are easier women in the world to be with. My sister has an obligation first to her country. My sister will never be able to take her husband's name, or be his housewife."

"What a happy thing, then, that my name means less than nothing to me. I am a bastard son of a whore. My name is dirt in civilized circles. But I do have money. And money allows me to go where I like, to get what I like. Better still, I have no house. A series of penthouses, yes. Private apartments nestled in exclusive clubs. But nowhere one would expect a wife to put on a twinset and pearls and...bake. My lodgings are reserved for more exotic uses."

"You may have to childproof them soon enough."

Astrid's response to that was to treat her brother to an evil glare. But she said nothing. She was a strong woman and certainly more than capable of speaking up in a situation like this and yet now she chose to remain silent.

He could only assume there was a reason. One that had nothing to do with being intimidated.

"My clubs are no place for children. But then, that is another issue. I want my child. Is that so hard to believe?"

"Most men of your sort do not."

"Then they are not men," he said. Simple. Hard.

And that seemed to earn him the most respect of all.

Eyes that were like chips of ice appraised with a coldness that would have sent a lesser man running from the room. Then finally, Gunnar turned his focus back to his sister. "Proceed with planning your wedding, Astrid, by all means. I won't stop you."

"You *couldn't*," Astrid pointed out. "I command an army."

The corner of her brother's mouth tipped up in defiance, and at that moment he could truly see that they were twins. "I said I *won't* stop you. Not that I can't. My choice of words was no accident."

"Then we're all on the same page," Mauro said. "Including those of us who had no choice in the matter."

After that Mauro had the feeling that whatever other obstacles might rise up in the future, his brother-in-law wouldn't be one of them.

"It's actually a good thing you're getting married so quickly," Latika said, staring appraisingly at Astrid in her close-fitting lace gown.

"And why is that?" Astrid asked.

"Because this dress would no longer fit you if you waited even another week. It's getting snug as it is."

"I'm pregnant," Astrid sniffed.

The word sent a sudden jolt through her.

Words like *heir* made it all detached. But the fact remained she was going to be a mother and no matter how much she wanted to be, the reality of it felt weighty, and infused with the weight of the unknown.

But then, everything in her world felt inverted right now and there was no finding normal. Mauro was… He was a presence even when he wasn't in the palace. He had committed to working mostly in Bjornland until the wedding, leaving only a couple of times, and even then never staying overnight. He had a residence in town but she swore she could feel him.

And the feeling was…

It was electric and it was unsettling.

She wanted him. And there was no room in this situation for want. Especially when he was a brick wall she couldn't read.

He didn't seem to want her at all.

The night of the engagement he'd kissed her, and then he'd pulled away like nothing had happened while her entire body had continued to burn like a wildfire had been set off in her belly, spreading out over everything.

They could talk, and it felt cordial, but even that seemed…calculated.

She'd come closest to knowing the man the night she'd met him in his club, of that she was certain.

With no names, and no truth, she'd seen pieces of the real Mauro somehow.

He wasn't giving her any of that now.

He asked her questions. He shared his own information with an easy defiance. As if he enjoyed his disreputable history, and lived to shock people with it.

But none of it was real.

None of it was what existed on the other side of a wall she shouldn't even want to scale.

He had been a means to an end. He continued to be.

The world was agog over their union, but they'd quickly recovered from her declaration that her child had no father becoming a shock engagement. Mostly because, more than anything, the world wanted a love story.

Even if it was improbable and unbelievable.

Maybe most especially then.

"I wasn't insulting you," Latika said.

Astrid looked at the wall, refusing to look at her assistant. "It sounded like it."

"Well, I wasn't." She tilted her head to the side, her glossy black hair sliding over her shoulder. "You truly will make a magnificent bride."

"I don't care about that. I want to be a magnificent *queen*."

Latika sighed. "You're already that. You don't need a husband to make it true. Even if you need one to help insulate you."

"Somehow this is starting to feel a little bit like the forced marriage I was avoiding."

"Except…" Latika trailed off, as if she thought better of what she'd been about to say.

"What?"

"You've already slept with him," she pointed out. "You *are* attracted to him."

"It isn't a factor now," Astrid said, her cheeks getting warm.

"Isn't it?"

"No," she scoffed. "He's no longer interested in me anyway."

"Why do you think that?"

"He's… Well, he's completely cold toward me, and anyway…" She sighed. "I don't know. I don't know what I want from this. What I want to do. What would you do?"

Latika blinked. "Do you mean in this exact situation? Because I don't think I can answer that."

"Okay," Astrid said slowly. "I grant you that my current situation is a little bit unorthodox."

Latika snorted. "A little bit?"

Astrid turned around, facing her assistant instead of

the mirror. "What do you do with men? I don't have any experience with them. Except for that one night. And I hardly think that counts."

Latika sighed heavily. "I can't say as I have any brilliant suggestions on how to handle a man like Mauro."

"But surely you must have some idea how to handle men?"

Astrid could see Latika decide to dodge the question. While she valued that skill in Latika when it came to her acting as a shield between Astrid and the rest of the world, it was deeply annoying at the moment.

"Latika, we don't speak overly much of your past because I can see that it hurts you, but if you could offer me some insight…"

"I can't. I always knew I would be married off to a man I didn't love, and I was sheltered from men to…preserve me. When the man my father chose turned out to be an ancient European with a reputation for treating women ill… Well, now I am here. I know how to plan and organize any event, how to make casual conversation with people from all walks of life. I might have been roped off from having my own social life, but I was forced to participate in the social lives of my parents. I've planned your wedding, but I can't help you here, I'm afraid."

"If nothing else, it's very helpful to have you. To have a friend."

Latika treated her to a small smile. "What is it you want from him? Because it seems to me that while you might have failed in the first iteration of your plan, this one is going to work just fine."

"That's the problem," Astrid said. "I'm really not sure what I want. I should want to keep things compartmentalized. We have a good agreement. We really do."

"But…"

"There's no *but*," she said quickly. "Not really."

Latika sighed. "You have a crush on him. You have ever since you saw his picture in that magazine."

Astrid sputtered. "One cannot have something so… benign as a crush on a man like Mauro Bianchi. Anyway. I'm a queen. Queens don't have crushes."

"You're human. A human woman. You would have to be blind not to notice his appeal."

"So you've noticed it, then."

Latika laughed. "International playboys aren't really my thing."

"No. If they were you might not want to pinch my brother's head off every time you were in the same room with him."

Latika shifted. "Maybe."

"I need to stay strong with him," Astrid said. "I need to make sure that I don't blur lines between us."

"If you think so," Latika returned.

"You think I should do differently?"

"I wouldn't dare question you. But mostly… I had a high-handed…unorthodox upbringing, you could say. I was very cloistered, and protected. Something I know you understand. Even now sometimes I feel like I'm hiding. If I had the ability to claim freedom the way that you did, I would take it. And I know that I was a little bit disapproving of your entire plan, but it was only because I worried for you."

"So you think that I should continue on with a physical relationship with him?"

Latika shrugged. "If not him then with someone. But it seems to me that you have feelings for him. Also, you're pregnant with his baby and marrying him, so it seems that he's the most convenient target around."

"He hates me," she said. She was suddenly very aware of exactly what that strange emotion she could feel vibrating beneath the surface of the man was. "He really does. And he wants the child, and I don't understand why. I mean, he says it's because it's a man's responsibility to be a father…"

"And you don't believe him?"

"I just think there's more." She shook her head. "It's the strangest thing. It isn't that I think he's lying. Just that I can sense there's something else. And he's never going to tell me."

"Have you asked him?"

"Why would I ask him? I just said I'm fairly certain he hates me."

"You should ask him about that too. About whether or not he actually hates you. It seems to me that he could have taken a much more extreme tactic with you than he has."

"Oh, than forcing me into marriage?"

"You have to admit, as things go… His version of forcing you into marriage is fairly kind."

"*Kind* is not the word I would use for it."

"Okay. Maybe that was an overstatement. But he isn't after your country. He isn't after any of your power. And you have to admit that when compared to basically every other man in your life—except for Gunnar—that's fairly significant."

"That might be the first nice thing I've ever heard you say about my brother."

Latika rolled her eyes. "Well, it's not going to happen again. Don't get used to it."

"I'm getting married." A sick feeling settled in the pit of her stomach. She couldn't even blame morning sickness. "I wonder what my mother would think of all this."

"She would be proud of you," Latika said. "I didn't know her, but from everything you've told me I think she would approve greatly. Think of all she did, the way she put her marriage in jeopardy to ensure your position on the throne. She would understand why you were doing all of this."

Astrid had nothing else to anchor her. Nothing that made her feel particularly assured, or like she even knew which way was up. But if she could just imagine her mother being proud. It was the one thing she'd worked for all these years, really. And even if she'd never get the words of approval she'd always longed for, she knew that she was doing what her mother had always wanted her to do.

That she was becoming what her mother had wanted her to be.

For now, that would be enough.

And the mystery of Mauro, and the problem of what she was going to do about him, would have to wait to be solved.

However, the countdown to the wedding night was ticking down... And she imagined she would have to make a decision before then.

CHAPTER SEVEN

MAURO HAD NEVER given much thought to the Christmas season. As a child it had meant next to nothing. Something for other children to celebrate, for other people to enjoy. As for his life, it had always been a reminder of the ways in which he had very little in comparison with those. Not in a monetary sense. He hadn't cared about that so much, at least apart from being fed.

But in the sense of family.

While he'd had a long succession of uncles throughout the course of his childhood, it certainly wasn't the same as the sorts of families—whatever shape they took—who gathered around Christmas trees and dinner tables during that most festive season.

As an adult, it had meant little more to him than an excuse to throw themed parties at his clubs across the world. Everyone enjoyed the excuse to engage in revelry. All the better it was an excuse to cover up past pain and breakaway issues with family, and lovers new and old.

He was under no illusion that many of the people who patronized his clubs were doing just that. But, it wasn't his job to worry about the emotional well-being of the people who danced their way to oblivion in his establishments on a nightly basis. He envied them their oblivion, in point of fact.

Typically, he felt nothing.

That sense of blurry freedom that came with alcohol and other substances didn't resonate with him. Not anymore. It violated his sense of control, and that was an unpleasant place for a man like himself to be in. He could not have what he wanted.

But then, that was true of a great many things lately. Astrid dominated his dreams, and now here it was, attending a Christmas tree lighting, on his wedding day. As the holiday held such little significance for him in general, this would be the marker for it for the rest of his life, whether he wanted it to be or not.

A marriage that wasn't a marriage. For a child who was no larger than an avocado at the moment.

But the child wouldn't stay the size of an avocado. Indeed, that child would grow. A son or daughter. One that he... He would have to hold it. Care for it. Granted, both he and Astrid could hire enough people to make sure that neither of them ever had to interact with their progeny if they chose. But he failed to see the point of that. It would make him barely a shade better than his father. And that just wasn't... It was a strange thing to him to discover he had standards, but it turned out he did.

A fact that was in ample evidence as he stood there in his bespoke tux, custom made for this day.

His wedding.

And tonight would be his wedding night. A wedding night that would herald the beginning of two years without sex. That was something he had not yet fought his bride on. There would be no way he would fall in line in such a way for that long. It simply wasn't reasonable, not for a man like him.

If nothing else, it was the principle of the thing. And he would not be dictated to.

"Two minutes."

The order from Astrid's petite, efficient little assistant came almost in defiance to that thought.

She was a pretty woman. With jet-black hair and golden-brown skin. Her glittering eyes and sharp features gave the impression of an astute field mouse, always in motion, and never missing even the faintest twitch of movement around her.

"Don't worry," he said, "I'm not going to leave your princess at the altar."

"I didn't think you were. Considering you were the one who pushed for this in the first place."

"I get the feeling you don't trust me."

She squared her shoulders. "I don't trust anyone. Not in the least."

"Interesting."

"Why?"

"You don't seem like the type of person who would be that hard."

"Very few of us are exactly what we seem. Astrid might be. Utterly and completely who she seems to be. And if you hurt her, I will have you executed."

"I have no plans to hurt your queen."

"Good. Then we have no problem."

She turned and left, and Mauro lingered for a moment, waiting until it was time for him to walk out of the holding room, as he thought of it, and toward the chapel. He was ushered to a back door that took him to the front of the sanctuary. All eyes were on them, and he knew that only approved photos were allowed. There were no cell phones present in the sanctuary. Only official photographers.

Thus was the royal protocol demanded by the very angry council that had been hands-off in every way in regards to the wedding, except for things like that. Things that made it all feel like a circus performance, more than anything else.

Not that he was opposed to a circus.

He was quite an accomplished ringmaster. But he preferred to have greater control of the show. And not the kind being exerted here.

He took his position, and music began to play, a hush falling over the room. Neither of them had attendants. It was not a tradition in Bjornland, and anyway, it made no sense for him or for her. So it quickly became a bridal march, and the guests rose, turning toward the doors, which opened slowly, as if building anticipation for what they would reveal.

And what they did reveal was as a punch to his stomach.

She was exquisite. The first time he'd seen her she'd been in white, but she had been draped in fabric designed obviously to seduce. And he was a man who enjoyed the obvious. This was something more.

The lace gown clung to her curves, lovingly shaping to her beautiful body. The neckline was scalloped, the rounded curves drawing attention to breasts that he knew were soft and plump, and just the right size to fit in his hand.

She was like a goddess, her red hair cascading around her shoulders like a copper-gold halo, the light from behind seeming to ignite it. She did not have a veil, but rather a simple, jeweled circle that draped across her forehead.

She did not carry flowers. Her elegant hands were empty, her engagement ring glittering on her finger as she moved toward him, slowly, with purpose.

And suddenly, inspiration for just how he would handle his wife hit him, like a falling anvil.

She had used her body to bring them to this moment. She had used him.

And he had absolutely no qualms now about using her. Until his desire for her was spent. Until his lust for her had been quenched. How long had she tormented him?

Months.

Months before he had found her again, and in the months since returning to Bjornland. Since their engagement. He had wanted her, and not allowed himself to have her. He had desired her, and not allowed himself to stake a claim.

Celibacy for two years? Why? When the most beautiful, intoxicating woman he'd ever had in his bed would be with him. Bound to him. When he would be living part-time in the palace of a necessity. He had easy access to her, and there was no reason he shouldn't make free use. At least, not in his estimation. There was terror in her eyes when she approached him, her hands trembling as she clasped his.

He wanted her to tremble before him. But for a different reason.

He wanted her out of her mind with need, as he had been. So incredibly naive. And he had not been naive.

He had never considered himself naive. But that was what she had done to him. And why shouldn't he reclaim himself?

He felt a slow smile cross his lips. And as the priest led them in their vows, he allowed himself to skim over the words. They didn't matter. Neither of them were forsaking all others for as long as they lived. There was no point to such a thing. Death would not be what parted them. But rather a calculated move on both their ends.

Love was not what had brought them together, so it did not matter what tore it asunder.

What mattered was tonight. Tonight, he would make his queen beg. Tonight, he would stake his claim in the marital bed.

She might not be his for life, but she was his for now. And he would make sure that the time they did have was spent naked.

That was what was wrong. Of course it was. Those moments when he felt compelled to understand her… They had never been about that. They had been replacement for what he truly desired. Her body, pressed against his. Her body, pliant and willing. His inside hers.

That thought got him through the ceremony, and then on to the reception.

And there was a moment, where the dance floor was cleared, and he and his bride were meant to dance together.

"Quite an elaborate party for a farce," he said the moment they were joined together, his voice nothing more than a husky whisper.

"What's the point of engaging in a farce if you don't go all the way?" Her spring-green eyes met his, and his gut tightened.

Indeed. There was no point engaging in a farce if it didn't go as far as it could. And that was what he intended to claim for himself tonight. All of it. Everything.

"The food is good," he said. "At least."

"What an odd detail to focus on."

"I also like your dress," he said, lowering his voice. "Or rather, I suspect that I like the body beneath it."

Her cheeks immediately turned pink. "Really? I mean… I don't know…why you would say that either. I would rather talk about the food."

"I like food a great deal," he said, very intentionally moving his hand so that it rested lower on her spine, hovering just above the curve of her ass. "You see, I spent a good deal of my childhood starving. And when you have experienced something like that… You become very protective of your next meal. And you appreciate it when you get it."

"That's terrible," she said, clearly uncomfortable. With the change in subject being so sudden, with everything.

"There's nothing to be sorry about. But you see, this is why I enjoy the many vices I do. Because there were very few in my life as a child. Very little I could depend on. As I got older I learned to depend on myself. To make my own way. I have not been hungry since. It is a powerful thing, realizing you can change your own world."

Astrid nodded slowly. "I know. I know because that was what I had to learn. That I could change my world. That I could change my world and not violate my duty. Not the part of it that counted."

Something turned over inside him, and he felt a sense of grudging respect for her. And more than that… Understanding.

"We should be making our departure soon," he said.

"Should we?"

"A married couple very much in love is eager to escape on their wedding night. At least, that is my sense for it."

She looked away from him for a moment, and then back. "Right. I hadn't thought of that."

"Of course not," he said. "I did. In fact, I've thought of little else beyond the fact that it's our wedding night since you stepped out in that dress."

Her eyes met his, wide and full of uncertainty. A strange thing with Astrid, who made it her business to at least appear certain at all times. "We have an agreement."

"Cannot agreements be amended?"

"You didn't give any indication that you wanted ours to be amended."

He was tired of talking. He was tired of being civil. This was the problem with business negotiations. It was the problem with needing to be civilized. At least when he had lived on the street there had been an honesty about it. About the transactions he'd engaged in with women who wanted his body, and would allow him to share their beds. In honesty and all motivation. It was clear. In the upper echelons of society, things like tact were required, and in Mauro's world those things were overrated.

He was done with words. He was done with verbal sparring.

He tightened his hold on her and she gasped, her head falling back, her eyes wide as she looked up at him. And he smiled. Because this reminded him of that night in the club. This reminded him why even if he could go back and undo what had happened between them knowing what he did now, he probably wouldn't.

He lowered his head, claiming her mouth with his. He parted her lips ruthlessly, sweeping his tongue in deep so that he could taste her. Taste this one thing between them that was utterly, completely honest.

They had an audience still. A captive one. They were

out on the dance floor, and he was kissing her as if she were air and he was a man deprived of it. She clung to him, shaking, and that was when he knew he was going to get exactly what he wanted. Her, trembling beneath him. Begging for him.

He pulled away from her. "We should make our way to our room, don't you think?"

"Is that what this was about?" she said in a hushed whisper.

"No. You will find out exactly what this is about. When we go to your room." He thought for a moment that she might protest. But instead, she lowered her eyes, and then when she met his gaze again, they were blazing. "Then let's go to bed."

Her heart was racing, threatening to thunder out of her chest.

Yet, she had gone with him.

She had allowed him to lead her from the room. She was… She didn't know what was happening. He flew in the face of everything they had agreed, everything she had decided was appropriate. But he had kissed her, and then she didn't care. And then the idea of being married to him and not sharing his bed had seemed like an impossibility.

Because from the moment she had seen his picture for the first time in the papers, the idea of *not* being in his bed had been torture. She had been contending with that part of herself for the past few months.

Badly.

Because what did it say about her? That she was merely another groupie of his? One who had dressed up her motivations for being with him into something a bit more noble, when her reasoning was as base as anyone else's.

Right now, she felt base. Utterly and completely. Was reduced to a grasping creature made entirely of need and desire. That was all she was, it was all she could remember being. This woman who needed his touch more than she needed anything else.

That kiss the night they'd gotten engaged had been kerosene. And the kiss tonight had been a lit match against it. She was not strong. Not with him. Not with this.

She had stood tall and steady, with a will of iron since she had started to rule the country two years earlier. Before that she had been a model citizen. Studying, completing vast amounts of charity work. She had been strong. She had been for so very long.

She wanted something else now. She wanted to be held in someone else's strong arms. To let him hold on to her, and in so doing, take some of the weight of the crown, of her duty, off her. Even if it was just for a night.

How twisted was it that even her one and only time being with a man was rooted in a lie she told herself about it being all for her country?

When what it was had been… She had done it for her country. For herself. The baby part. But there had been other ways. But she had been willing to use him first. Before she resorted to science. Because at the end of the day she had wanted him. And it was all fine and good to try to make excuses, to try to tell herself she'd been selecting the finest specimen genetically.

She had told herself a lot of pretty lies.

What she had been was a girl with a crush. Latika had been right about that.

A girl who had a crush and no understanding of how to handle it.

She had spent a life dealing with people who catered to her too much, counterbalanced by constantly feeling opposed and undermined. Great authority, but with a very short leash. It made it difficult for her to figure out how to actually know people. How to relate to them.

The fact of the matter was she didn't know. And she never had. Her brother was her friend, but he was also a royal.

Latika was someone she also considered a friend, but Latika worked for her, and that created a strange sort of dynamic. She was isolated. And a bit spoiled. And she had behaved that way with him. Like a child entitled to something, one who had seen a shiny toy that she wanted, and had come up with all sorts of reasons why she deserved it.

But he wanted her now. And she wanted him. Even as remorse for her behavior flooded her, she still wanted him. Their rooms were next to each other. As was custom. He had not spent the night in the palace yet, and she wondered if he ever really would. But for appearances, they had readied the standard royal bedchambers. She wondered which room this would happen in. And what would happen after.

What would happen during.

The very thought made her shiver.

He dragged her down the empty corridor, and then suddenly pushed her up against the wall. His dark eyes blazed into hers, fearsome and filled with the dark emotion she couldn't name. It was like rage but hotter, desire but with a knife's edge.

He had not looked at her like this the night of the club.

This was something more. Something deeper. Something that carried the layers that their relationship contained. A relationship she had forced him into.

Because he was here out of a sense of duty, she understood that all of a sudden. Not because he wanted to be her husband. Not because he was drawn to the idea of being married to a queen.

Not because he hungered for power or lusted for money.

Because of his own integrity.

She had convinced herself that she was acting with some kind of integrity when she had fooled him. But it had been self-serving.

Guilt lashed her like a whip. And for the first time she wondered if she was much more her father than she had ever previously imagined.

She had always thought of herself like her mother. And Latika had said, just tonight, that her mother would have approved of what she done.

But her mother had never harmed anyone. Would have never lied.

Her mother had told the truth when Gunnar and Astrid had been born. At great cost to herself in terms of her marriage.

Her mother believed in honesty, if not in showing love. It was her father who would have stooped to subterfuge to do what he had imagined he might have to do to save the kingdom.

Her actions were the same.

Right because she had found a loophole, because she imagined her own sense of justice to be the one true version of it.

And this was her penance. This man. This large, muscular angry man who was paying it right along with her.

She didn't know what he might do next. But he didn't make her wait long to find out.

He cupped her cheek, his touch gentle, and almost all the more terrifying for it. All that leashed strength. She could feel it. The force of his rage, and the way that he held it in check so that he could softly move his thumb over her cheekbone.

He lowered his hand then, gripping her hips tightly and surging forward, letting her feel the evidence of his desire. And then he lowered his head, kissing her, harder, deeper than he had back in the ballroom.

She was drowning in it. Drowning in him.

There was no more time for thought or self-flagellation. If this was her punishment she would submit to it. Because it was also her salvation.

Her moment.

Because he was strong. And he could hold her.

Because he was angry, and he could feel it in a thousand ways she had never really allowed herself to feel it.

Because he wanted her. It opened the door to allow her to feel her own want.

"Your room or mine?" he asked, his teeth scraping along the side of her neck. "Where shall I take you, out here in the hallway?"

The idea made her shiver with need, but she couldn't allow something like that. No.

"The bedroom," she said softly.

"As you wish."

He hauled her to him, lifting her off the ground and carrying her a few steps toward the bedroom, opening the door and propelling them both inside before he slammed it behind them. The room was familiar to her. She had inhabited it for the past couple of years. And yet, somehow with this man inside it, it felt completely different. He should look civilized in that custom-made tuxedo of his, the dark, elegant lines conforming gracefully to his body. But he didn't.

Instead, it seemed to provide a greater contrast to that strength, to his feral nature.

He tugged at his bow tie, letting it drape over his shoulders, and then he advanced on her, his movements quick and decisive as he grabbed hold of the zipper on the back of her dress and dragged it down, letting it fall to the floor, that custom creation that was worth thousands of dollars. He stepped over it as if it didn't matter and picked her up, carrying her to the large, ornate bed and placing her at the center of it, where she was surrounded by lush, velvet pillows, the cool, soft texture such a contrast to that hot, hard man above her.

"I would say that the night you approached me in Italy was your show. Tonight it is mine, *cara mia*. And I will enjoy every moment of it."

He grabbed hold of his bow tie, tugging it from his shoulders, and then he took hold of her wrists, encircling them easily with one hand and drawing them up over her head. He smiled, then in one fluid motion took the strip of black fabric and tied it securely around her wrists, leaving her bound.

Desire and fear raced through her in equal measure, electricity shooting down between her thighs, the sensation of being hollow almost unbearable.

"Just making sure you stay where I want you."

"Mauro…"

"How badly do you want this?" he asked, tracing the edge of her lace bra cup with his fingertip. "How badly?"

"I need you," she whimpered.

"Well, let's see how long you can withstand this." He let his fingertips drip beneath the edge of the fabric, one calloused pad skimming her nipple, and she cried out.

"So sensitive," he said, chuckling darkly as he pressed a kiss to that vulnerable place between her rib cage, down to her belly button, down farther. He pressed his mouth over her lace-covered mound, his breath hot against her skin as he scraped his teeth over the delicate fabric. She shivered, arching into him.

"That's the thing about going into a lion's den, *cara*," he said. "Sooner or later he's going to eat you."

He hooked his finger through the fabric on her panties and tugged it to the side, revealing her to his gaze. And then he moved in, laughing at her with bold, intense strokes. He curved his arms around her thighs, locking his fingers together and dragging her toward his face, holding her firmly against him as he continued to lavish attention on her with his lips, his tongue, his teeth.

He drove her to insane heights, and then brought her back from the edge. Over and over again until she was sobbing, crying with her need for release.

He traced circles around that sensitized bundle of nerves with his tongue, before lapping her in one slow lick, her climax pouring over her, leaving her spent and shaking and breathless.

But he wasn't finished. He began to toy with her, using his fingers, stroking her and teasing her until she found her release again. And again, this time with his mouth at her breast and his fingers buried deep inside her.

He brought her up to her knees, turned her away from him, where he lowered his head and laughed at her from a different angle, until she was trembling, begging for him to stop.

"Please," she said. "Finish."

"We are finished," he said, his voice rough. "I think you've had enough."

"You didn't… We didn't…"

"I said that was enough. It was a very long day."

He moved away from her, and she rolled onto her back, her hands still bound. He took hold of one end of the knot, freeing her in one easy tug that seemed to make a mockery of the way she had felt at his mercy.

Had she wanted to escape, she could have. The whole time.

The captivity had been only an illusion, and she had been so willing to sink into it because of what she wanted from him.

Because she had wanted him to hold her captive, to force her to feel those things, so that none of it was her responsibility.

He had proved that he could. But now… Now he was leaving.

"I'll see you tomorrow."

She was about to ask if he wanted her, if he had ever wanted her, but she could see the thick, hard outline of his erection pressed against the front of his black pants.

She could see that he wanted her, and he was still walking away.

"Good night," she said, the words thin and shaking.

"Good night."

And he didn't even have to get dressed to leave, because he was still fully clothed, and she was… Destroyed. Her bra was wrenched up over her breasts, but still clasped, her underwear shifted and torn in places.

She was humiliated. She had a feeling that he had intended to leave her humiliated.

She couldn't even feel angry, because she kept remembering the things that had occurred to her out in the hall. What she had done to him.

The humiliation he must've felt when she was on TV saying their child had no father.

Tonight he had demanded submission from her. He had exerted his control.

And now he was finished.

But she was not.

It took only a moment for Astrid to come to a decision.

She couldn't exist in this. In this world where he took his anger out on her body in such a way. She would give him an apology.

And she would make it one he would never forget.

Apologizing was another thing that Astrid had never done. But she was sure that she would do it well.

CHAPTER EIGHT

MAURO STRIPPED HIMSELF NAKED. He needed a cold shower. Something. Anything to deal with the desire that was still riding through his body. He had intended to make her feel out of control. To give her a taste of what she had done to him that night at the club.

When she had pushed him past the point of thinking clearly. Past the point of being sensible at all. And he had. He had, but in the end, she had somehow still done something to him. Overridden anything sensible. Destroyed every barrier that he had placed between the two of them.

The fact that he had been able to walk away had been a damned miracle. And now…

He was shaking. He was. He had wanted to make her tremble, had wanted to make her boneless, mindless, and he had done it. But at what cost?

What cost to himself?

He did not know the man he was when he touched her.

He went up in flames.

The connecting door between their bedrooms suddenly opened, and he turned.

It was his wife.

And he was completely naked, so there was no hiding the fact that he was aroused, that his cock was hard, and ready for her. That he was in no way in control of his needs or desires.

"What are you doing here?"

She was still naked, her entire body bare and exposed to him, her pale curves temptation he was not sure he could fight. Was not certain he could overcome.

"I came because I owe you an apology."

She began to walk toward him, her hips swaying gently, her lush curves and wild, glorious hair, tumbled around her shoulders, making him think of an ancient goddess.

"You owe me an apology?" he asked, the words sounding stilted.

"Yes. I owe you a great many things. And one evening will not be sufficient in making amends. But I would like to try."

"What are you doing?"

She moved nearer to him, pressing her palm against his chest, her touch soft, bewitching. "If you have to ask, then I'm not doing a very good job."

She walked a circle around him, slowly, appraising his body, her fingertips grazing lightly over his skin as she did. She stopped in front of him, those green eyes intent on his, blazing.

"I am a queen," she said. "I have been, my entire life, even before I bore the title. That's how it works. When you are the heir, you must behave as if you are from the beginning. There is no other option. There will be no quarter given. And I have… I have lived my life that way. Above reproach in many ways, as we discussed. But also without nuance. Without subtlety. There is no humility in me. I didn't learn it. I like to think there's compassion. Caring. And that mostly in my life I have acted in a way that would not do harm to others. But I have always been set apart, and I have always lived that way. My connections with those around me... I'm incapable of separating them from my status. I am not like you."

"Indeed," he said, grabbing hold of her wrist and holding her fast. "Because I'm not blue-blooded like you?"

"Yes," she whispered. "Yes."

Rage fired through him, but it wasn't because of that. It was because of all of the feelings inside him. The deep, roaring desire that he had to take her now, in spite of the fact that he had told himself he would not.

"You've lived more than one life," she continued. "And because of that I think you understand more. I think you see more. I have my struggles. Things that I have had to overcome. But they are in this world. My battlefield has been an ivory tower. I see my country from an elevated stance. My people. It is a necessity in many ways so that I can have an overview. So that I can know as much, and have time to look at it all. I fear sometimes that leads me to see people in general as statistics. Or chess pieces. I saw you as a chess piece. And I used you and for that I owe you an apology." She looked up at him again, and desire made his gut tighten.

"I am a queen," she repeated. "And I bow to no man. I never have. But for you... For you I will get on my knees."

And without warning she did just that, her red hair sliding over her shoulders as she went down. And then, she looked back up at him as she raised her hand, wrapping it around his hardened length.

And he knew he was lost. Knew that there was no way he could fight this. Not now.

He was finished. His control was at an end. And when

that slick, pink tongue darted out over his arousal, when she closed her lips over him and took him in deep, there was no more thought.

She clung to him as she lavished attention on his body with that imperious mouth.

He had heard it issued demands, had heard it whisper lies. And now that same, traitorous tongue slid effortlessly over him and stoked the flame of desire in his stomach.

Women had done this for him many times. It was not an unusual act, but there was something in the way she did it that made it something entirely new. Because she was queen. Because she was Astrid.

Because she made him feel the way no woman ever had before.

Because. Because many things he didn't want to think about. Didn't want to acknowledge.

He was at the verge of being able to hold back no more. And he didn't want that. Didn't want it to end that way. Not now.

"Enough," he growled, pulling her away from him.

"I haven't finished," she said, a small smile tilting her lips upward.

"If you wish to truly bow before me, my Queen, if you truly wish to make amends, and allow me use of your royal body, then I have a decidedly better way for you to kneel."

He swept her up off the floor and into his arms, carrying her over to the bed and positioning her there, on her hands and knees, her deliciously shaped ass on full display for his enjoyment.

He stroked himself, looking at her, at the image that she created there.

He was a fool. An absolute fool. He should have turned away from this long ago, but now it was too late. Now, he had to have her. Now, there was no going back.

If she wanted to apologize for her treachery, then he would take it out on her body. It would be no hardship. She was giving herself to him freely, and it was because of the ruthless seduction he had subjected her to only moments before.

This was control.

He still had control.

He pressed his fingers between her legs, pushing inside her tight, wet body as he tested her readiness.

She was ready. So very ready, and so desirous of him that it nearly made him lose his control then and there.

He joined her on the bed, positioning himself at her entrance and pushing inside slowly. She was so tight, so impossibly perfect.

She moaned, slow and long as he withdrew and thrust back home. And as he pounded inside her, he watched. The way that her elegant spine arched as she felt her pleasure build, the way she curled her fingers around the bedspread.

He couldn't see her face, but there was no denying it was her. His queen.

On her knees for him.

He held on to her hips, showing no mercy as he pushed them both toward a release he knew would consume them both.

And as his pleasure roared through his blood, screamed through his system like a freight train, there was one last thought before his release burned each and every one away like stubble and hay beneath the flame.

She was on her knees for him.

But he was on his knees too.

And then there was nothing. Oblivion. Sweet, desperate need being satisfied as he poured himself inside her.

His queen. His wife.

When it was through, she collapsed onto her stomach on the bed, then rolled to her side, curling up into a ball, her expression sleepy and satisfied.

And he remembered the way she had run out on him the first night.

How he had tried to run out on her not long ago.

It would be better to keep her with him. To keep her here.

He had tried it the other way, and he didn't like it.

If this was to be about him staking his claim and finding his place, then he was free to make that decision.

And so he wrapped his arm around her waist and drew her up against him, holding her tight.

He was on the verge of deciding on an entirely new plan.

One where Astrid being his wife meant her spending her nights in his bed. And only his.

For there was no way he would ever allow another man to touch her, he realized that now.

She was his woman. And she was carrying his child.

And the decision to hold her all night seemed to make everything clear.

His.

Only his.

CHAPTER NINE

OF ALL THE things Astrid expected to wake to the morning after her wedding, a scandal wasn't one of them.

After all, there had been ample opportunity for a scandal to break over the past couple of weeks, and yet none had.

But then, Bjornland being isolated as it was, it was often cloistered from the rest of the world, with news filtering out slowly. But, given that Mauro was arguably more famous than she the world over, she would have expected something like this to break sooner.

The breakfast table was covered in newspapers. And she didn't have to be terribly insightful to figure out that someone from her father's council was responsible for the delivery of the day's tidings.

"What is this?" Mauro asked, taking his seat at the table with utter confidence.

He did everything with supreme confidence. As he had shown her last night. Repeatedly. Until he had made her shake. Made her scream. Until she could no longer tell where her body ended and his began.

Something had changed between them last night. What had started in anger had ended with something else. It wasn't absent anger. It was imbued with an intensity that spoke of nearly every emotion.

All she knew was that by the time it was all over, the most natural thing in the world had been to curl up against him.

In many ways, she felt like a lamb choosing to sleep nestled up against the side of a lion. Mostly, she just had to trust that he wasn't going to eat her.

She had the feeling that Mauro was undecided as yet.

"Our reckoning," Astrid said, lifting one of the papers up. "At least, that's what it appears to be."

"I see my past has caught up with me."

Astrid began to read past the inflammatory headline.

The brand-new consort to the queen of Bjornland used to work as a rent boy.

There was no real escaping from the truth inherent in the headline. There were some seedy details included. Though, it didn't sound as if Mauro had been working the street so much as being passed around among bored older women.

"Why didn't you tell me?" she asked. "More interestingly, why has this not been in the press before?"

"Because, one of the women would have had to be willing to admit the fact that they paid me for sex. And apparently Lady Catherine is just close enough to death's door to do such a thing now." Astrid continued to stare at him, trying to figure out what he was feeling. He didn't look upset, nor did he look ashamed.

Being connected to such a scandal was the stuff of nightmares for her, and it made her skin feel like it was too tight for her body. Mauro was simply... He didn't seem to feel a thing at all.

"Also," he continued. "I make my living from scandal, Astrid. My clubs are all about debauchery. At what point do you suppose this would have been an interesting headline for a man famous for immoral acts? No, it's only interesting now."

She pressed her fingers to the center of her forehead. "This is a fantastic look to show the world," she said.

"You chose me as the father of your child."

"And now these are things our child will see. It's printed in black-and-white…"

"Do you have regrets, my Queen?"

The words were so cold and hard, and they hit her square in the chest. "No. Not in the way that you mean. But there are consequences for this. For our son or daughter. That's what I care about."

"Not about your own pristine reputation?"

She took in a labored breath. "I would be lying to you if I said I didn't care at all for the reputation of my country, and myself. But I can't deny my own involvement in bringing myself here. Is there anything else that you need to tell me?"

"I came from the gutter, Astrid. You do not ascend to success in the amount of time I did without crossing a few barriers between one side of the law and the other. Without making bargains with morality. You simply don't. I regret nothing of what I did, because it brought me to where I am. Once I figured out that I could control my fate, I took every opportunity to do so. At a certain age I discovered that women quite enjoyed me. And if it was something I was going to go out and do anyway for recreation, why not get a place to stay for the night, a hot meal. And some cash in my pocket. I have no moral qualms about what I did."

For the first time, she saw a spark in his face. In his

eyes. "The rest of the world does," he continued, stabbing a headline with his forefinger. "The rest of the world that leaves people behind, blames them for accidents of birth that see them thrust into a guaranteed lifetime of poverty. And believe me, we will be able to overcome this. Were I a woman in the same position... I fear my reputation would be beyond salvation. Fortunately, I'm a man, and one that now has money."

"Is that what you think?"

"It's what I know. My mother was nothing but a whore in the eyes of the world until the day she died. No one ever admitted her to their parties. Not even with me as her son. Of course, by the time of her death I wasn't quite as well-known as I am now. I imagine at a certain point any amount of money can erase a life of harlotry. My mother did what she had to. For us. Because my father, though he possessed the ability to support us, decided to pretend we didn't exist. No, don't ask me to apologize for selling what I had. Anymore than she should apologize for it. People with money are willing to buy it, and they're willing to pay quite a bit. They would rather buy sex than buy dinner for anyone in the slums, so you tell me what's to be done."

"I didn't say I was judging you," she said, but at the same time, she felt like something had shifted. Because what had happened between them last night was not a simple transaction. Then she wondered if it was for him.

It was deep and elemental and intimate. Had been from the first time. She couldn't imagine simply handing her body over for a few dollars and a place to sleep.

Because you've never been asked to do it. You've never had to. You were protected and you were insulated, and

*the most despicable thing you ever had to put up with
was your father not believing in you.*

She gritted her teeth. "How long did you do that?"

"Truthfully? Not even quite a year. Just something
I did to save up money and move myself on to the next
thing. I did that. I also worked as a bouncer at a club.
That's where I got familiar with that sort of environment."

"Did you… Did it bother you? To be with women you
didn't want?"

"I could make myself want them all. And if I didn't
want them specifically, I could make myself do it for the
money. A soft bed is quite arousing when the alternative
is the streets."

She blinked, ignoring the scratchy feeling behind her
eyes. "What did your mother think?"

"We never discussed it," he said, chuckling darkly.
"Clearly. But then, she always behaved as if I might not
know what she did with men coming through the house
at all hours."

"So, you had a house?"

"Yes. For a time. I left when I was sixteen, because
I couldn't bear it anymore. To watch her submit herself
to that. Neither could I tolerate the ones who came to
my room after, seeing if I would give for free what my
mother had charged for. Don't worry. No one ever did
anything to me. I was lucky. And that's the other thing,
in the grand scheme of things, given my background, I
was quite lucky. What I did, I did with a certain amount
of choice involved. It's more than I can say for many like
me. Don't waste any sympathy on me."

"I have sympathy for the headlines."

"They don't bother me. Though, I wonder if I should be concerned about you."

"There need be no concern," she said, pushing herself into a standing position.

She despised the weakness that had settled into her limbs. Hated that the press had been able to make her feel this way. That her father's councilmen were succeeding in trying to sabotage them so soon after the wedding.

This idea that bad press should be avoided at all cost, that being scandal free was an essential, was old thinking. Old thinking that was part of the Astrid she'd been before. Before she'd decided to take control of her own life by having her own child.

That Astrid could not care so much for scandal.

That Astrid would do things differently.

She took a breath. "I will be damned if anyone is allowed to write the story but us. We have done our best to control it from the beginning, and I don't see why we can't continue on as we began. We should go. We should go to Italy, visit your clubs. Show that I am in absolute support of you and all that you are."

He arched a brow. "Are you sure you don't just want to have a press release where you stand behind me looking regretful while I confess my many sins?"

She waved a hand. "No. I have no interest in that. None at all."

"Reputation is of no concern to me," he said.

"Well, it is of a concern to me," she said. "And I will not allow the press to decide what that reputation is. I'm clearing my schedule."

"Shall we take your private plane or mine?" he asked.

"We both have private planes?"

"Yes indeed," he said.

"Well, that just borders on absurd."

"It might, but I think it would be difficult for us to consolidate, given our busy schedules."

"I suppose."

"Mine, then," he said. "It has the whiskey I like on board."

"That isn't fair. I can't drink any."

"I never said any of this was going to be fair."

Astrid frowned. "I don't suppose you did."

The doors to the dining room burst open, and in charged one of the men from the council, his face red. "Do you see the censure you have opened us up to?" he railed against Astrid. "If your father were alive to see the disgrace that you have brought on his country…"

Mauro stood, slowly and decisively, his manner intimidating, his body radiating with a dark energy. "If your father were alive, he would see a woman standing strong in the face of embarrassingly tiny adversaries. And that is what you will continue to see in the coming days. I never met the old king, so I cannot speak confidently of what would give him pride. But he would at least not be able to deny the strength and sense of honor that Queen Astrid exudes."

Astrid said nothing, she simply watched as the councilman turned and walked out of the room, clearly not at all mollified by Mauro's interference, but likely gone off to lick his wounds, as he clearly didn't possess the wherewithal to stand against a man of Mauro's presence.

She could have defended herself. She had done it for years now. This was hardly going to be the straw that broke the camel's back. But she was tired, and she was reeling from the revelations in the paper in front of her.

And for all that Mauro was tangled up in the challenges she was dealing with now, she was grateful to have had him there to stand with her. It wasn't always about needing to be rescued or defended. But sometimes it was good to know that someone was there to stand with you. To be the first to speak in defense.

To know that someone else was on your side.

She didn't know when that switch had occurred. Mauro had felt like yet another in a line of adversaries, and suddenly now she felt as if they had melded into a team. If nothing else, Mauro would want a stable environment for their child.

She took a breath. "I think we have a plane to catch."

By the time the plane touched down in Italy, yet another scandal had broken.

Mauro was ready to track down journalists and cockroaches from his past and present alike and create some real scandal.

He minded the rumors about his life as a prostitute less than the stories that greeted them the moment they touched down in his homeland.

His father had come forward.

Dominic Farenzi, titled old duke and part of one of Italy's oldest aristocratic families, had finally claimed his son.

Oh, not for a happy reunion, no, the duke would never do such a thing. He wanted his name in the press. To attach himself to the scandal by dragging Mauro's name down further.

And, of course, it made perfect sense. Mauro had taken a different last name as he had ascended the ranks, partly because he didn't want every old relative of his mother's coming out of the woodwork to demand endless paydays. He had wanted to avoid situations that involved blackmail.

His former clients—the women he slept with—would have most certainly recognized him, but Dominic would have no reason to recognize him on sight. They had met only once, and Mauro had been young.

He had looked up at the old man with all of the hope only a boy could still possess after such a miserable upbringing—and the old man had gazed back with a sneer. And told Mauro exactly what he was. Not a part of that lineage, but a mistake. A mistake that should have been nothing more than a stain on his sheets.

But now... Now that his profile had been raised, and now that he was royalty by marriage, his father had made the connection, and more than that, had seen his opportunity to use the connection. Money... The old man had that. This was something more, and obviously he wished to use it.

"So, you're not a commoner," Astrid said when they were settled into his awaiting sports car and driving through the winding streets.

"I might as well be. I'm a bastard. Dukes and bastards are a time-honored tradition, in every culture, I should think. I am not royalty. Not by any real standard. But there are any number of people clearly willing to use this connection, and I would have told you he would be the last person to do it, out of a sense of self-preservation. But I suppose this is the problem with aging enemies. They figure perhaps they only have a certain number of years to even concern themselves with answering for the consequences of their actions. Why not see what happens?"

"All fine for him. But he's playing with your life."

"Though, in this case there is nothing for me to be ashamed of. Though I would suppose that vicious commentary about my mother will follow. Thankfully, she's dead. And none of this will be her problem."

"I'm sorry," she said. "I had no idea… When I chose you I miscalculated in more ways than I realized."

"I imagine you didn't wish to choose the bastard son of a twisted old man who also moonlighted as a gigolo to be the father of your baby."

"That's not what I meant," she said quickly. "I only meant that I didn't know how much the media would be able to discover. And how much they would use against you. They can be brutal and vicious, my mother instructed me on that early on."

"It doesn't affect me much," he said. "I have been brutal and vicious to myself in the public sphere for years. I found self-deprecation to be the best defense. But, it's not exactly a good look for the queen of a nation I don't suppose."

"Possibly not," she said.

"Did you always know who your father was?"

"I can't remember exactly when I truly became aware of who he was and what that meant. Yes. It was never a secret. Not for me. I think my mother wanted me to be aware. I think she wanted me to know that there was a certain amount of injustice at play. She wanted me to understand. Something that I appreciate greatly. Because it helped to shape me into what I was. It helped me understand where power came from. There are titles. And then there is money. And both bring their own kind of power. It's certainly better to have them together. One can be earned, and one cannot be. I decided never to waste my time caring about something that I could never go out and earn for myself. And so, I simply decided to work at getting money. Because I would be damned if the last word on who I was came from a man who didn't care whether or not I lived or died."

"I understand," she said. "I mean, I really understand now why you won't abandon your child. Why it means something to you. I'm sorry. It was so… I was only thinking of myself and my goals. Sometimes I get so focused on this idea of the greater good, and I remove the humanity from it. In this case, I decided that the greater good was something that I wanted. And I truly didn't think of you."

"It doesn't matter. What matters is that I won't be like my father. Ever."

"I believe it." She looked out the window, at the buildings that closed in around them, tall and brick, rebelling against the age that was beginning to crack at the foundation.

The farther on they went, the more faded the glory of the buildings around them. It did not appear that they were headed in a direction where Mauro would live, or have a club.

"Where are we going?"

He was questioning that himself. Questioning it because he had decided that he would take her to see, so that she had the whole story, but it was one thing to think it, and quite another to do it. He imagined that Astrid had never been near a slum in her life.

"It's the whole story. So that there are no more surprises. I think that is important to see."

Astrid was quiet after that, and he maneuvered the sleek car around the corner, until they reached a sparse, wasteland of an area that contained a crumbling apartment building, and tarp set up as tents around the property.

"If you're lucky, you live in there," he said.

"Oh," she said, her eyes wide as she took in the sprawl of humanity around them. "This is where you're from?"

"Yes." He cleared his throat. "I imagine you have not had an exposure to such things."

"No, I have. I've been involved in quite a few out-reaches worldwide where I went and distributed medical supplies and food. But… It's not the same as living in it. It's not the same as… Growing up this way."

"This is what I am. I have no shame in it, and I never have. The press is going to attempt to make it a shame-ful thing, and I'm sure that there are only more lurid de-tails of my sexual exploits to come. There will likely be women who spent wild nights with me in my club eager to tell their story. For all I know, more of my… Clients from my early years. These things will continue to hap-pen. As long as there is money or fame to be extorted, it will occur. It was one thing when I was selling sin. It's quite another in this position."

"It's all right," she said. "I… I did this to escape from the hold that the men on my father's council had over me. I did this to gain independence. What good is inde-pendence if I'm still held hostage by a desperate need to make myself look better than I actually am? My des-perate need to be something I'm not. Whatever the true nature of our relationship is… We are having a baby."

There was one last place. His house, if it still stood.

"Just a little bit farther," he said.

Their home was at the wall of a dead end, beneath an office building that he had never imagined housed businesses that were terribly legitimate. The place looked abandoned now, the windows boarded up, a notice posted on the side.

"This is where we lived," he said.

"This is your house?"

"Yes."

"Where does your father live?"

He turned toward the vast mountain that rose up above the buildings around them.

"There. He lives there. And he has a view of the whole city, down to the slums. While we had a view of those mansions up on the hill. And I knew that the man who fathered me was there. Somewhere. That he was there looking down on that very house, this very spot, and feeling nothing. It was motivating. And I…"

He parked the car suddenly and got out, looking around to make sure there was no one loitering nearby.

He had no doubt that he was well able to handle any attacker who might come out from behind the shadows. He had learned to defend himself against grown men when he was just a boy. Maturity, and years of hard labor in the gym, had only honed his physique further.

Plus, he was ruthless. He had learned to fight, not in arenas, but in situations that could very well have turned into life or death. That meant when he was under threat, he gave no quarter.

And should anyone step forward to threaten Astrid—to threaten his child—he would not hesitate to do what needed to be done. He took a breath of the air, stale down here, and warmer, boxed in by these tall, narrow buildings. And it reminded him of what it meant to be a boy. To be trapped here.

To be helpless.

He loosened his tie, feeling as if he was choking on the air around them.

He felt a hand on his shoulder and turned to see Astrid standing there. "Are you all right?"

"I'm fine. I haven't been back here, not since I left my mother's home. After that I went off to find my way, and once I had acquired enough, I sent for her. I bought her a house. One up there on the hill. So that she could look down on everything here, the same as he had done all those years. So much hard living. She did not last long after. I blame him. I always will."

"I don't blame you."

"I met him once. My mother told me which house was his, and I climbed the hill. I walked right up to that house, and I stood there on the front porch, full of the bravado of a young boy, just barely more than thirteen. Convinced I was a man. I knocked on the door, and I asked to see him. I thought they were going to send me away, but he heard me. He heard me and he came to the door. I thought that if I explained to him what our situation was... What my mother was forced to do..." That moment, that sick humiliation and shame, that deep, unmet need all seemed close to the surface now, rolling through his stomach like an angry ball of fire.

"He knew. And what's more, he made it very clear to me that my mother had not turned to prostitution as a desperate single mother. But rather, that was how she had found him."

"How vile," Astrid said. "How could he speak to you like that?"

"Oh, he took great joy in it. In making sure that I

knew that I was never going to be seen the way that he saw my half brothers and sisters. That my mother's blood made me unsuitable. But you know… It's his. It's his blood that I regret the most, not the blood of the woman who did what she had to, to allow us both to survive. Who cared for me, even when it was hard. No, I don't feel shame over carrying her blood. But when I think too deeply of his, I can feel my skin crawl. After that, I decided I would never covet what I could not have, not again. I took great pains to make sure that I could have whatever it was I pleased. I started making plans. I thought about all the places people went when they had money, and I figured that what I would want was a way to take the money of those people. Which is what I've done. Hotels. Clubs. Resorts and destination vacation spots. I appeal to those who have money to invest in fantasy. And with that I've built something real. With that, I will make a life for my child far and away what my mother was able to do for me, in spite of how hard she tried."

"Your father is a disgusting, opportunistic animal. We will give him no satisfaction with what he's trying to do."

"Oh, the press will give him plenty, I have no concerns about that."

"How unfair," she said. "How unfair that they all want to give you attention now."

"Let them," he said. "It makes no difference to me. It only proves that suddenly I have something that they want. Now my father can use me. How novel. All those years I could have used him. Well, fortunes of change."

He stepped away from the old house. From the tightness in his chest.

"I shall take you to my offices."

"Oh, really?"

"Yes," he said decisively. "I have spent a great deal of time in your domain, my Queen. It's time you came to mine."

CHAPTER TEN

MAURO'S OFFICES WERE impressive indeed. The contrast of the brilliant, steel-and-glass-framed building when juxtaposed against the slums they had just visited struck Astrid particularly hard as he ushered her into his office, paneless glass windows making up the entirety of the walls, overlooking Rome. Overlooking even the houses on the hills.

And she understood it. What it meant. Why it mattered. She understood what had shaped him.

And she felt…

It was a strange thing, to have this man let her in that way. She couldn't say that she knew very many people in such a deep way that she did him.

She knew no one in such an intimate fashion.

But his showing her the slums… The house. Talking about his father.

It was all new. This feeling for another person. This feeling like she knew him. Like she could feel the things he felt.

He pressed his hand to her lower back as he led her deeper into his office, and somehow as he did that, she felt as if he had wrapped his hand around her heart and squeezed it tight.

"These are the corporate offices. As you can see, I have a few."

"Yes. You do." It wasn't just a stark contrast to the slums, but to the palace and Bjornland, which was gilded and old-fashioned in every way. "The clutter of the palace must drive you crazy," she observed.

"I was thinking the same about you," he said. "You enjoy that restaurant we went to the night we got engaged. And it's quite spare. You also seem particularly fond of the ring I bought you."

She squeezed her hand into a fist, feeling embarrassed that he had seen through her so easily. "It is very pretty. Yes, I suppose the rooms in the palace are not necessarily to my taste."

"You should have them redone."

"That's simple?"

"Why not?"

"Because of tradition, and things. It's hardly… It's hardly appropriate to go changing everything right when you're crowned."

"Is it not?" he asked.

"I wouldn't think."

"You've been queen for two years."

"Yes," she agreed. "I have been."

"If you're not afraid to take control of your own destiny, you should be able to take control of your bedroom decor."

"Fair enough," she replied. "Perhaps I will do a bit of a redesign when we get back." She frowned. "If we… Are you coming back with me?"

It was such a vulnerable statement. So very silly. She didn't know why she was exposing herself to potential rejection like that. Especially considering he wasn't supposed to matter. But then, he wasn't supposed to have revealed such intimate and crushing things about himself either. He wasn't supposed to be human. That was the crux of the problem. The longer she was around this beautiful, god of a man, the more she saw his humanity. And that was dangerous in a particular way nothing else had ever been.

"I will be back intermittently," he said.

"I see."

"Though, I should make one thing very clear," he said.

"What is that?"

"That the idea that you might spend time in other men's beds is now off the table."

"Is it?" She tried to sound surprised, or maybe even mildly annoyed about his heavy-handed proclamation, but instead, she was certain that some of her hopefulness had broken through.

"After what happened on our wedding night... I should think that was quite obvious."

"What happened?"

"The explosion between us."

"It is as it ever was," she said, trying to sound casual. "Is it different than the first time? Is it different than it normally is?"

Of course, that last question revealed just how much she didn't know.

"It is never like that. Not with anyone else. And if you cannot feel how it was different than our first time..."

"I do," she said.

"Then surely you must know that this is a fact. There will be no one else."

"What about for you?"

"I don't want anyone else."

"And if you did?"

"I suspect we would have a discussion about it before anything occurred. I am nothing if not honest."

"So, should I wish to sleep with another man, we will have a discussion?"

"There will be no discussion. I would separate the man's head from his body."

"Well, that doesn't seem equitable."

"I didn't say that it was."

"I'm a queen," she said. "The rightful queen of Bjornland. You marrying me does not make you a king."

"But we are in my kingdom now," he said, a smile spreading slowly across his chiseled face. "And that is one reason I took you to see the slums that I grew up in. So you would understand. You think that you know because you have read articles. You think that you know because you have spent time in my bed. But unless you have seen where I was. You will not understand what it means that I am here."

So, he hadn't been showing her out of any desire to connect with her emotionally. She didn't know why, but that made her feel… She didn't like it. She wanted something more from him, and she hated that she did. She wanted something more from him, and the very idea of it made her feel uncomfortable. And also needy and vulnerable in ways that she didn't want to confront.

"I'm very impressed," she returned.

"I don't require that you be impressed. But you should understand. I am a man who sees no obstacle that he cannot overcome. If you think that you might win with me, *cara*, you are sadly mistaken."

The feelings that rolled through her body were tumultuous. She had no idea how to parse them all. On the one hand, his stubbornness, the fact that he was not intimidated at all by who she was, made her feel like she was adrift. She was accustomed to subtle challenges, not open ones. It also made her feel alive. Alive and particularly invigorated. That she could step into this place that was his, only his, as she had done that first night, and to be consumed by his world. By him. Even if only for a moment.

She wished that she could spend more time with him here. And maybe she would. There was no reason she couldn't split her time between Bjornland and Italy. Her ability to govern was not impacted by whether or not she was directly in residence in the palace.

But he hadn't said that he wanted her to. Instead, he had simply said that he would be staying here.

"There is a gala tonight," he said suddenly.

"Oh?"

"Not the sort of thing I usually bother myself with. In fact, I usually take great joy in turning down the invitations."

"All right."

"But we are in a different position now, are we not?"

"You are," she said. "I attend galas the world over, as a representative of my country."

"And I tend to sink deeper into debauchery at my clubs."

"We make choices."

"Well, now I'm going to make a different one. As we are making a show of solidarity, I figure there will be no better way of doing that than appearing so grandly upon the world stage."

"I suppose so," she returned.

"You are mine," he said. "And the world has only understood thus far, I think, that I might be yours. But they will understand after tonight."

She was his? But how did he mean that? And why did she want it to mean…? Why did she want it to have meaning?

The way he made her feel when they were alone in the dark was a heady, sensual rush that affected not just her body but also her soul.

It had nothing to do with performance and everything to do with… She didn't know.

She didn't know, and she hated not knowing. "That sounds ominous," she said, instead of any of the things she'd been thinking.

His dark eyes caught and held hers, and didn't let go. "You will understand too. After tonight. You will understand."

Mauro was not one to question his own decision-making. He never had been. There had never been time for any such things. He was a man of action, by necessity. He had never been one to Monday morning quarterback the decisions he'd made to propel his life in the direction that he wanted it. He was questioning himself now. If only a bit.

He was a headline the world over at the moment, and while in many ways he didn't mind at all, in others…

But he was set to beard the lion tonight.

His father would be at this event. That was one of the many reasons he had avoided things like this in the past, as much as he tried to pretend otherwise. He had allowed his father's presence to deter him from joining society in Italy for a number of years.

He had always told himself it was because there was no point.

He was not a man who dealt in galas, after all.

He liked to appeal to the darker, more sensual side of the moneyed set in the world. Liked to gather in the blackness, carrying out sultry, libidinous acts in the shadows.

He was going to have to work at changing the headlines. Not for himself, not even for Astrid, but for his child.

He did not deserve to see his father only as a horror, who was also the son of one.

He might not feel shame over what he was, but his child invariably would. And that would have to change.

He straightened the cuffs on his jacket and looked toward the room in his penthouse that Astrid had secreted herself in earlier. He had forced the issue of being the one to choose her gown, and she had been put out with him, as she had a stylist who was in charge of selecting all of the dresses she wore for public appearance.

Mauro had made the point—the excellent point, if he said so himself—that Astrid appearing in something a bit different would only support the narrative about their relationship being a defining one.

The gown he had chosen, with the help of his assistant, was exactly what he wished to see his beautiful, curvy wife in, but now she seemed to be hiding out.

"Astrid," he said. "We are about to pass the point of being fashionably late."

The door cracked slightly. "Do you care?"

"No. I like being fashionably late, because it makes people talk. But I thought you might care."

"I don't think I can possibly go out in this."

"It is nothing compared to that white dress you wore the night you first seduced me."

"That was different," she said archly. "I was not being photographed, and I was trying to seduce you."

"And tonight you are my wife. And we are in my part of the world, and I expect for you to present yourself in such a manner. I will wear any ceremonial dress that you require in your country. But you must indulge me here."

"Okay. So that is how it will work when we are in Italy, or when we are in Bjornland. But what about when we're in… Holland?"

"We will both wear wooden shoes. Now, show me the dress."

She opened the door all the way, and the tiger that he was barely keeping leashed inside him leaped forward.

He no longer wanted to go out. Rather, he wanted to spend the entire evening exploring the ways in which that gown clung to her body.

It was a burnished gold that set off a fire in her glossy red hair, the color picking up gold tones in that pale skin of hers, as well. It glimmered as it clung to each and every curve, the neckline a deep V that accentuated her lush body.

"It is a bit much," she said, breezing past him and moving to where her makeup bag was. She produced a tube of red lipstick, and applied it to her mouth, making her look even more of a siren than she had a moment before.

He brought her up against his side, and guided her toward the door, her figure fitting more perfectly against his than he ever could've imagined.

"When we come home," he murmured, as they got into the elevator, "I greatly look forward to stripping this dress off you."

"What exactly are we doing?" she asked.

"What do you mean? Right now, we are going to a gala."

"I mean... What are we doing? In private. Behind closed doors. Where we have no reason to be putting on a show. What are we doing? Because it was one thing when we had an arrangement, for the benefit of our son or daughter. It was one thing when we were putting on a show for the media. But this idea that we will spend our nights together... As if it's just an assumed thing... I don't understand the purpose of that."

He said nothing as they walked through the lobby of the spectacular apartment building he called his own. They were ushered into a limousine, and he took his seat right beside her, pressing his hand over the top of her small, soft one.

"I don't understand why we wouldn't burn out any chemistry that exists between us. People are so prudish about sex and attraction, but it's something that's never made much sense to me."

"I don't suppose it would. You used it as a commodity when you were young, but I did not. For me, it is about connection in some way, at the very least. It is inescapable as far as I'm concerned. I do not know of another way to see it. And I don't wish to put us in the position where things would become acrimonious between us should you decide... Should you decide that you feel an attraction for another woman. And what will happen when we decide to separate? What then? As I see it, it can only go two ways. We must decide that it is temporary, and that we are business partners. Or we must decide it's forever."

Forever.

He had never thought of anything in those terms before. Mostly because he didn't think very many steps ahead. He saw his goal, and he achieved it. And then he went on to the next. He enjoyed the excesses that he had at his disposal at any given time, with great relish. And he did nothing to concern himself with heavy things, things that pertained to the future. And she was asking him to choose. Nothing or forever.

He was a man who had no issue being decisive. And yet, he found this was one question he could not answer with an instantaneous snap of his finger.

Just another way in which this little queen confounded him.

The car rolled up to the front of the beautiful, historic hotel that the gala was being held in. The white marble shone pale in the moonlight, a beacon of all that he had ever aspired to as a boy.

And beside him there was Astrid.

A woman of pale marble, who wasn't cold to the touch, but warm and so very alive. So very enticing.

"We will speak more after the gala."

"We will speak," she said insistently. "I won't have you drowning out my common sense with your temptation."

Temptation. He would happily show her some temptation, and give her a very solid display on why they did not need to make such a definitive bargain between them.

He took hold of her hand, and pulled her forward, wrapping his arms around her and bringing her up onto his lap, so that she could feel the hardness and intensity that only she seemed to be able to create in him. And he kissed her. Not a slow tasting, but a fierce claiming. A promise. Of everything he was going to use to convince her that this heat between them needed to be thoroughly explored, and there would be no rationalizing that away on her part.

After all, she was the one who had ignited this need inside him. All of this was her fault. And her daring to try and put up a barrier between them now was something he could not let stand.

He cupped her face, taking the kiss deep, sliding his tongue against hers until he drew a fractured moan from her body. And then he pulled away.

"Yes," he said. "We will resume this discussion after the gala."

He opened the door to the limo, brushing past the driver, who was attempting to hold the door for them, and instead, held it open for Astrid before taking her arm and closing it behind them.

"You shouldn't try to do the poor man's job for him," Astrid said, clearly attempting to sound as healthy as possible and to seem unaffected by the kiss they had shared.

"You are my wife," he said. "I will be the one to hold the door for you. No other man need serve you."

"Very possessive for a man who isn't sure what he wants."

They said nothing more, because then they reached the top of the steps, and were ushered inside, where they were announced grandly, and in a fashion that Mauro would have taken a great kind of satisfaction in under any other circumstances.

He was here. Standing at the top, all these people he had looked up to all of his life, people who had kept him shut out of society, gazing up at him, as if he were the most important and powerful man in the room. Unlikely though he was, even without the inclusion of his new, royal bride.

But she brought that blue-blooded element he could not manufacture on his own.

She was carrying his child, a child who was the future ruler of a nation.

Nothing could elevate him more.

And yet, that wasn't the primary focus of his thoughts.

Mostly, he was thinking about her. Mostly, he was remembering the way her skin had felt beneath his hands.

The way she had sighed and moaned when he had kissed her. A pang of resentment hit him in the chest. That she should have such power over him. Over this moment.

He tightened his hold on her, her ultimatum ringing in his head.

They made their way down the stairs, into the center of the tangled knot of crows masquerading as aristocracy. Black dresses on the reed-thin bodies of the women, black tuxes and ties on the men.

Except for Astrid. Who was like liquid gold, shimmering before them all.

A prize. That was what he had fashioned her into. And yet, no matter how much he repeated that to himself as they circulated the room, as they made readings to those around them, Astrid with her royal ease, and him entirely absent of such a thing, all he could think was that he had revealed himself in many ways by his choices tonight.

Revealed the fact that he was not of the aristocracy, no matter that he shared half of his blood with it.

Because no one else would have dressed their wife as such an obvious prize, only to flaunt her importance.

And yet, she was beautiful. And she deserved to look as she did. As the most expensive, glorious woman in the room, and why should he have dressed her as anything else? Subtlety, he decided, might be best left to those born with money. He was not going to concern himself with it.

That was when he saw *him*.

Impossible to miss him. Broad shouldered, and taller than most of the men in the room, except for Mauro himself.

Age had not stooped the man's shoulders, and Mauro supposed that if he weren't quite so enraged at the mere existence of him, he might appreciate what that said about his genetics.

Instead, he only felt his stomach turned sour with the injustice of it all. Because his mother was dead and gone, and this man was able to stand tall, proud, well dressed and with his wife, as if he had not caused immeasurable pain over the course of years.

As if nothing troubled his conscience at all.

His eyes caught Mauro's and held them, and he whispered something to the woman at his side, who nodded in dutiful obedience, and separated from her husband, moving off to a cluster of women standing next to a tray of champagne.

Mauro gritted his teeth. "Well, it has been some time."

"Has it? I wasn't sure if we had ever met," his father returned.

"We did. I was a child. You had me thrown straight back to the slum I came out of."

"Oh, was that you? It's difficult for me to keep my slum bastards straight."

"And yet, you seem to know me well enough now."

"You've done well for yourself," he said, casting an eye over Astrid.

Mauro bitterly regretted involving her in this, the moment the old man's eyes began to roam over her luxurious curves.

Astrid, on the other hand, didn't seem regretful in the least. Astrid faced his father head-on.

"I'm Queen Astrid von Bjornland," she said, her tone frosty, her shoulders straight. Her hold on him tight. "I do not believe we've met."

"Dominic Farenzi, Duke of San Isabella."

"I see. And you are connected to my husband through accident of birth?"

She sounded perfectly civil, but he could sense she was feeling anything but.

"Yes. I had the impression you were connected to my bastard son much the same way."

Her lips curved upward. "Oh, no. I chose him. I chose him quite deliberately to be the father of my child. My heir. Because he is perfect, and everything I could possibly want, from a genetic standpoint and otherwise."

"I didn't realize the standards of perfection were lowered so."

"If this is the way that you expected you might leverage me and my status for your own personal benefit when you sought to announce your connection to my husband, you have badly miscalculated."

"You assumed it was about you? How very fascinating."

"I am queen of an entire nation. I assume many things are about me, and I've yet to be proven wrong."

"Is this what you have become?" his father asked. "Because at least when you were a boy you spoke for yourself. Now, you have this woman speaking for you." He shook his head. "But then, I am not surprised. It is the only thing that gave you any relevance in the eyes of the

media, and truly in the eyes of the world. One sin ped-
dler is essentially the same as any other. You are not only
uninteresting on your own, but unoriginal."

Mauro chuckled, and before he could grab hold of his
composure, reached out and grabbed hold of his father's
throat. "I see. I'm very sorry that I failed to produce a
surprise for you." He chuckled. "But you should understand this. If you assume that you understand me, you
will be bitterly disappointed. And if you think you can
stand here and speak to my wife, speak about my wife,
and face no repercussion, then you truly know nothing
about me at all. I have done a great many things in my
life that were rooted in calculation and self-service. But
Astrid is mine. Mine. And unlike you, I keep what is
mine. My child. My woman. You will not speak to her.
You will not speak about her. You will not sell any more
of your torrid stories to the press about my mother. If
you do anything to cause Astrid harm, I will end you.
Financially. Physically if I must. You could only lord
things over me when I was a little boy who had need.
You could only cow me, control me as long as you had
more power than I did. The tide has shifted, Father. And
now that I've made my position clear, all that's left to do
is for you to decide whether or not you want to push me.
I would suggest that you don't."

He released his hold on the old man, rage coursing
through his body. And he felt Astrid's calming touch on
his shoulder. He looked at her, the red, foggy haze of his
vision beginning to clear, and he saw that her expression
was filled with concern. "Mauro..."

"You reveal yourself," his father said. "That you would
stoop to physical threats. You might be able to put on a

suit, earn money, spend money, but you will always be what you were born. The son of a whore."

"Push me any harder and I may be the son of a dead man."

"Oh, I have no doubt. I have no interest in pushing you. I'm just making it clear, whatever narrative you think is happening, it is blood that wins. Time and time again."

"You're right about that," Mauro said. "It is blood that wins out in the end. And when mine triumphs, you had best hope it's not due to the fact that I spilled any of yours." He looked over at Astrid, who had gone pale. "Come, *cara*. I think that our time at this event has lapsed."

He had no more time for this. Had no more desire to engage in such a farce. He was going to end the evening now, and he was going to end it exactly the way he had intended on ending it before this miserable farce had began. She would see who he was.

He pulled her through the crowd, not caring that they had drawn curious stares. That they were now being subjected to scrutiny by all around them. He didn't care. He was not a good man. He was not a civilized man. He was not one of them. If it had not been apparent before, then it was apparent now.

He was Mauro Bianchi, and he was from the slums. If blood won out, then he was quite all right letting it show freely.

He signaled his driver using his phone, and by the time they reached the front of the hotel, the limo was there waiting for them. He ushered her inside, and she said nothing. That was unusual, as Astrid typically had a comment, or a snarky aside. Right now she seemed to have nothing.

Perhaps he truly had made her realize who he was. Made her realize what he was.

Now, perhaps she would find it undeniable. "I've made my decision," he said, once the limo began to move away from the hotel. "You're mine. There will be no discussion about any alternatives."

CHAPTER ELEVEN

ASTRID WAS STILL shell-shocked by the time they tumbled out of the limo and into the lobby of the apartment building that housed Mauro's penthouse. The way that his father had treated him, the way that he had treated his father…

She didn't know why she had expected anything else, actually. Mauro had all the trappings of a civilized man, but she had always known that underneath that exterior beat the heart of a barbarian.

She had not been disappointed in tonight's showing. Not on that score.

And then the way that he had… Declared his possession of her when they had gotten back into the car. But then, he hadn't spoken again. And he had not touched her.

She fidgeted, feeling restless as they stood in the lobby for a moment. Mauro seemed to take stock of his surroundings, looking for paparazzi, she wondered, and then he dragged her to the lift, the doors opening wide, as he moved them both inside. And that was when she discovered what he truly meant by being his.

He pushed her against the wall, the metal biting into her shoulder blades as he did. Then he gripped her chin between his thumb and forefinger and held her steady.

His eyes blazing down into hers. He was like a wild animal. A feral beast that she could neither soothe nor tame. One that looked completely and utterly bent on having her at his mercy.

She resisted. Everything in her resisted, because hadn't she been resisting such a thing for her entire life?

Until him. He was the beginning of that. The awakening of that desire. Feel a man's strength. To allow it to carry her own, if only for a little while. And now, even more, the temptation to allow it to overwhelm her utterly and completely.

It was intoxicating. To think that perhaps she truly could be his. She had belonged to causes. To an entire country worth of people. She belonged to Bjornland, she belonged to her duty. But to find another person who could carry all of that was a distantly hazy fantasy that she hadn't even been aware she'd ever possessed. She wanted it.

But she wasn't sure she was brave enough.

But she could see in him the anger, force, the will to bend her. To create the space that would require that submission. A space that would hold her. A space that would sustain her.

So when he kissed her mouth, she kissed him back, with all the ferocity penned up inside of her. There was no small amount of it. It was real and raw and wild. Something she had imagined might be beyond her.

But she didn't feel like another entity, not like another creature, no. Instead, she felt like she might be the truest, rawest form of Astrid. With no parents watching her every move, no press. No brother. No assistant. No council of angry men opposing her very existence.

As if she lived in a world created just for her, just for Mauro.

Not in the way she had felt when she had been pretending to be someone else, no. She felt like her. Like she was truly at home in her skin for the first time. Like she had become real, and now nothing on earth would ever be able to make her unreal. The elevator stopped, and the doors slid open, revealing his sleek and lovely penthouse, as light and view conscious as his office, with windows that she had been assured were made with one-way glass.

Affording him the view that he wanted, giving him the privacy he needed. As if reading her mind, he led her over to the window, and positioned her in front of him.

"Look at all that," he said. "All those glittering lights below. I can buy every single place and person those lights represent. Everyone. Here I am on top. And I have you."

She shivered, and he moved her hair to the side, exposing the nape of her neck. Leaning forward and pressing a firm kiss to her skin. "Yes. I have you. I want you to take that dress off."

Heat crept into her face. "Here? In front of the windows?"

"I already told you... No one can see," he said, his hand traveling down the line of her spine, stroking gently. He grasped the zipper tab that rested low on her back. "I want to see."

He drew it down slowly, the fabric parting, going loose and dropping from her shoulders, down to her hips, before it slid the rest of the way down to the floor.

The underwear she had on was whisper thin, barely there, and exposed the entirety of her backside for his enjoyment. Something he made no secret of as he reached out and grabbed her, squeezed her, growling in his appreciation.

"You're very beautiful," he said. "A beautiful trophy. All for me."

His words, rough and angry, should have upset her. Should have made her feel small and used. Instead, they sent a thrill through her body.

She was a great many things, but she had never been someone's trophy. She supposed it should make her unhappy.

But she was a woman with a great deal of power.

And within the broad scope of that power, knowing that she could call bodyguards in here at any moment and have Mauro dispatched handily. That she had an entire military at her command... That she had faced down leaders, heads of state and a great many men who had not wanted her in the position she held.

Yes, given all that, she could think of very little that made her feel threatened. It allowed her to sink into this. Allowed her to embrace it.

To give herself a moment where she was nothing more than an object for his enjoyment. A gift for him.

"I like this," he said softly, stroking her in the center of her back again. "My city laid out before me. My woman, laid out before me."

He advanced on her, pushing her closer to the glass, until her hip bones connected with the cool, smooth surface, her stomach, her breasts. Her thighs. Her palms were rested flat against it, and she looked out, having the strangest sensation that she was flying.

"You even carry my baby inside you," he said, his voice getting impossibly rough now. "You are mine.

Mine. In every beautiful, twisted-up way you possibly could be." He kissed her neck, her shoulder, gripping her hip, then the other as he continued to kiss her, tracing a line down to the waistband of her panties. He hooked his fingers in the waistband, tugging them down, before rising back to his feet and unhooking her bra, leaving her now completely naked, pressed against the glass. "The world is at your feet, my Queen," he whispered. "And I want you at mine."

He whirled her around so that she was facing him, the glass cold on her back. There was something about it that felt dangerous. This razor-thin pane between herself and the air outside. Between falling endlessly and safety. She began to work his clothes next. Wordlessly. In absolute obedience to his command. She undid his tie. Pushed his jacket from his shoulders and let it fall to the floor. She undid his shirt, her knees bending slightly with each button she pushed through the hole.

And then she did end up on her knees before him.

Ready to give him what she had last night. And more. Everything he wanted. All of her. She undid his belt, his pants slowly, taking his length in her hand and testing him, curling her fingers around all that heavy weight. He wrapped his own hand around himself, and pressed against her lips. She complied, opening to him. Taking him inside.

He bucked his hips forward slightly, gently, and she relaxed, allowing him to set the pace. Trusting him. Giving herself over to him.

He was big and strong, and he could hurt her if he chose to. But she didn't put up any defenses. She didn't do anything to protect herself.

She had seen what he was earlier, and still, she knelt

before him, offering him her throat, though she had seen him grab a man by his earlier.

His movements became less measured, more intense, and she let her head fall back against the glass as he found his pleasure, accepted his release as a strange, warm sense of satisfaction rolled through her.

She had been of service to him.

The idea made her giggle. And she didn't giggle. Particularly not after things like that.

She was buzzing, fuzzy. She looked at his body and saw that for now he was satisfied, but she found herself being pulled to her feet, lifted up into his arms. He clamped one arm around her waist, and urged her legs up around his hips, as he walked her back toward the bedroom. It wasn't any less private than the other room, large windows dominating the walls in there, as well. But there was the bed. Large and spare, with a low black headboard and a stark black bedspread.

"You will look beautiful against my sheets," he said, his voice low and harsh. "I wish to look at you." She moved over to the edge of the bed, uncertain as to how to proceed. "On your knees, facing the headboard."

She hurried to obey, getting into the center of the mattress and arching her back slightly, allowing him the full view of her body. He reached forward, pressing his fingers between her legs and teasing her where she knew she was slick with need for him.

"Turn around," he ordered.

She obeyed, still on all fours, but facing him now. She could see that he was hard again, ready for her already.

"Lie down on your back," he said. "And part your thighs for me."

Again, she did as he bid, lying back against the velvet bed cover and opening herself to him. Keeping nothing back.

She was trembling, her entire body shaking with the force of the strangeness of all of this. Of what it meant to give this kind of control.

"There," he said. "I like that. Just as I suspected. This was meant to be. You were meant to be mine."

"I am yours," she said. It felt like the right thing to say. And judging by the glint in his eye, it had been.

"You know," he said. "I told myself after that first time I met my father that I would never, ever allow myself to want without having. Ever again." He reached out, pressing his hand against her stomach, smoothing it gently over the slightly rounded bump there. "And so, I will spend my life having you, then. Because the alternative is to want endlessly, and I refuse it. I will not."

"Let me satisfy you," she said.

He growled, joining her on the bed, positioning himself between her legs and sliding inside her easily.

She gasped, arching upward, joining him in an intense, shaky rhythm that she thought might just break her apart. Might destroy them both. But she couldn't see another alternative. She needed him. Needed this.

She wrapped her legs around him and let him give all his weight to her.

And that was when she realized. The way that it worked. The push and the pull. The way he held her, kept her safe, and the way that she became the resting place for him.

Domination. Submission. Give. Take.

"Mine," he growled, as he stiffened above her, his body pulsing inside her. "Mine."

That last, possessive declaration drove her over the

edge, her release going off like a shower of sparks inside her.

And when it was through, she was shaking. Spent.

Weaker.

Stronger.

When it was through, she was his.

There would be no force on earth that could ever undo it.

"I hope you don't mind," Astrid said the next morning, sitting in the center of his bed with the regal bearing of an empress. The blankets were bunched up around her, her breasts exposed, her red hair tumbled down over her shoulders. She was clutching a coffee mug and managed to make it all look effortless and elegant.

She was such a compelling acquisition.

There was nothing, and no one, that had ever been part of his life who was quite so lovely or rare.

"You hope I don't mind what?" He was standing across the room from her, still completely naked, and he took satisfaction from the clear fact that she was enjoying the sight of him.

"I had a doctor's appointment settled in Bjornland. And, as we are here, I figured it would be easier to just have the doctor bring her equipment to us."

"Did you?"

"I didn't know when you would be through with your business here. I could have flown back, but Dr. Yang is going to meet us here instead. She's the best obstetrician in Europe, and we were going to have to fly her to be on loan anyway. Instead, she'll be bringing her equipment to us."

"My penthouse is going to be transformed into a clinic?"

"Yes," she said. "There is nothing untoward about it. People give birth at home. I might as well have my examinations done in a similarly comfortable environment. And, we won't have to contend with paparazzi."

"When do you expect her arrival? As I'm not the one meant to be in the hospital gown, perhaps I should get dressed." He bent down and retrieved his pair of dark slacks from the floor, where they had left them last night.

"Yes, perhaps you might want to do that."

"Though, we may have some time..."

It was only an hour later when the doctor showed up, and thankfully, Mauro had been able to put his legendary focus to the task and leave Astrid doubly satisfied by the time the doctor arrived. She had a warm bedside manner, and an efficiency to her movements that would have come across as brusque with most people, but with Dr. Yang it came across as a kindness. As if the time of the patient was being considered and respected.

He could see why Astrid had gone to the trouble of bringing her all this way.

"How have you been feeling?" the doctor asked.

"Well," Astrid said. "Surprisingly well. Only a bit of fatigue, and occasional nausea in the mornings, but nothing extreme."

If Astrid had been feeling nauseous this morning, she had hidden it well, and said nothing. The same with her fatigue. She was such a strong, self-contained woman, and he suddenly found himself overcome by the desire to bear some of that burden. To make it so she did not hide such things from him.

It was an ache that hit him square in the chest. A walnut-sized pain that rested there like a knot.

He didn't like it. Not one bit.

"Date of your last period?" the doctor asked.

Astrid rattled off the date effortlessly.

"Date of last intercourse?"

Astrid's face turned dark red. "That would be today's date."

The doctor didn't react to this, but Astrid was the color of a royal tomato, and Mauro took some amusement in that. It was a sweet thing, the way something like that could make her blush. It spoke of her inexperience, and of the fact that what was between them was somewhat singular.

Maybe even a bit miraculous.

That word, *miraculous*, was reinforced when the doctor had Astrid lie back on the bed and expose her stomach, squeezing some warmed gel onto it, where it was slightly distended. Then she placed the wand onto her skin and moved around, watery noise filling the room. The watery sound turned into a wish and whisper, steady and fast.

"And that's the heartbeat," she said. "Very strong. Sounds good." She moved the wand around. "It is a little bit early, but since you are sixteen weeks, we might be able to see the baby's gender. If you're interested."

"I am," Astrid said, her expression taking on a dreamy quality.

"I don't mind either way," he said. "As long as the child is healthy. It doesn't matter to me what gender." Dr. Yang and Astrid exchanged a glance, but he could not decode what it meant.

"Let me see," she said.

Suddenly, everything came into focus. The baby's head. An arm. A foot, which kicked as the doctor brought the wand down around the baby's body.

"It doesn't wish to be disturbed," Mauro said, that pit in his chest expanding, growing. As if a tree was growing from that walnut now. Becoming something large and hard and completely unmanageable.

"The baby doesn't mind," Dr. Yang said. "It's good that the baby is responsive. That's what we like to see."

He didn't know if he wanted to see it at all. It was suddenly so very real. This human inside Astrid. A child.

His child.

"We are in luck," she said. "There we go. We have a perfect view. You're having a son."

The mix of emotion on Astrid's face was strange. "I'm glad in some ways," she said. "His road will be easier. It's easier to be king."

"I would have liked to rub their faces in the fact that I was having a girl though."

She laughed. "That's a terrible reason to wish for one or the other."

He could understand what she was saying, and even the significance in her world. Producing a male heir was traditionally a valued thing. And Astrid herself was a defiance of that. But he couldn't think of that. Not now. All he could think of was that he was having a son.

A son.

A little boy, like the one his own father had taunted and sent away. A boy who would possibly look like him. Possibly look like his old man.

Redemption.

In a thousand strange and wonderful ways, this was

redemption. He craved it. And with that craving came something deep and unpleasant. Something he told himself he would not feel. Not again. This deep unending need for something he couldn't even define. This child made him hurt. And the woman in front of him, with her eyes shining so bright, she made him ache.

He felt as if his whole life had been turned inside out.

And he had been driven, driven to claim her, driven to claim the baby. He had been motivated by something he couldn't even put words to, but here in this small space, with that little life flickering on the screen in front of him, with that deep truth attached to him.

A boy.

A son.

That drive met with something different. Something dangerous. Something that had the power to wound and destroy. Something that he had told himself he wanted no part of for all that time.

It made no sense. He had her. Right here. He had the baby right here. So why did it hurt like this? Why? He could not fathom it.

"Congratulations," Dr. Yang said. She put her hand on Mauro's shoulder, and somehow in her expression he saw a wealth of things. Perhaps even sympathy, and he couldn't understand why she would feel sorry for him. Except that perhaps his own confusion was visible on his face. He despised that too. He was not a man given to confusion. He was not a man given to indecisiveness. Astrid had done something to him. She had… Damaged him in some way. And he hated it. He hated it.

"All right. I'll give you a moment with each other, and

to get dressed, and then I will have everything cleared from here, and leave you alone. The child is healthy. Congratulations."

And with that, she left them. Astrid sat up, wiping the jelly from her stomach with a warm cloth that had been placed by the bedside. "I expected that we would get to find out it was a boy. Not so soon. I'm glad... I'm glad we were together when we found out."

"You are happy?" he asked. The idea of her being unhappy with his son upset him even more than the idea of his own conflicted feelings.

"Yes," she said. "Really, his life will be easier. Easier because he's a boy. Easier because he won't have opposition to him. And I suppose what I hoped for was a chance to test out just how much we could modernize the country. But I cannot stand in his way for his gender any more than my father should have doubted me for mine. He will be a good king. We'll raise him to be."

They would raise him. Yes. They would. Of course they would. He gritted his teeth, squaring his jaw. "Yes."

"Are you all right?"

"I'm fine."

"I'm glad we're doing this together," she said. "I think I really wouldn't have wanted to do it alone."

"You won't be alone," he said, trying to harden his heart against the words.

"I guess not. Technically. I would've had nannies, and whatever else. But I am glad. I'm glad to have you. I'm glad our child will have you. Because a nanny is no substitute for a father. And what I did I did without thinking about the people involved. Not just you. But our child. It wasn't only you I would have deprived. And I'm glad things are like this. I'm glad that we'll be… I'm glad we'll be a family."

That word made him feel like he'd been cracked open. And after she spoke them, Mauro couldn't think of a single thing to say.

CHAPTER TWELVE

MAURO HAD GONE off to work quickly after the doctor visit, and Astrid knew that something wasn't quite right, but she also could not for the life of her figure out what to do about it.

Perhaps, Mauro had legitimately needed to go into the office. That was entirely possible. Or perhaps he was running from something, which she also suspected might be true, but didn't have a clue as to what she was supposed to do if that was the case.

The idea of him running was a strange one, but in many ways she understood. She had never been more terrified in her entire life than she was when she had seen that baby. So real and vivid on the ultrasound screen. A boy. Their son. There was something undeniable about that. Something real and heavy. And if he needed a moment alone after, she would have certainly understood.

Of course, he would likely rather die than admit that.

Which is why, she suspected, he had simply excused himself.

Because the man was too alpha to function, and God forbid he have a feeling in her presence.

That very thought made a smile that curved her lips upward. She supposed the same could be said about her.

But he made her want to be not quite so soft. Not quite so stubborn and closed off.

She wondered if he needed something from her now, and simply didn't have the ability to express it.

Then she wondered why on earth she was thinking about him when she had just gotten such momentous news about her life, her future. She was having a boy. That should consume her thoughts. Utterly and totally. And yet, she found that she was consumed with him.

She was lately. Quite a bit.

She had... Feelings for him.

If she was honest with herself she had for an impossible amount of time.

She had felt a strange sort of connection with him just looking at his pictures, and while she had initially told herself it was a response to his genetics, and then had told herself it was chemistry, now she wondered if it was something more. Something that made no sense at all.

And if it hadn't been since looking at the photos, it was definitely since the first time they had made love.

The way that he touched her. The way that he made her feel... It was all a strange kind of magic. He made her feel happy to be a woman, made her glory in the way that she had been made. Made her feel as if she understood and embraced her femininity for the first time, really and truly. When Mauro finally did arrive home, he was distant. He shut himself in his home office for a time, coming out only to ask if she was hungry for dinner.

When she said that she was, he set about cooking in the small, high-gloss kitchen. She watched his movements, sure and confident as he set about preparing their food.

"I didn't know you cooked," she said.

"I'm quite accomplished at it," he said. "I can make a fairly gourmet meal out of deeply underwhelming ingredients. A skill I picked up as a boy. Of course, now I prefer to make truly wonderful food out of excellent ingredients. It's always nice when you have the option."

"Well," she said. "Yes."

"I hope you like filet mignon."

"I think I can make do," she said, smiling. "I don't know how to cook. I've never had to do it. Everyone always does it for me. And I've never seen the point in picking up a skill when it can just as easily be done."

"Sometimes it's simply good to have the skill for the sake of it," he pointed out.

"I suppose. But there's always been… An idea around me that I could concern myself with more important things. And anything that's trivial… Well, anything that's a triviality I can leave to other people."

"I can see how feeding yourself might be considered trivial," he said drily.

"Well, you don't have to be ridiculous about it."

"I'm not being ridiculous. I'm being practical."

"What are you making? In all your practicality?"

"Filet mignon with a red wine reduction. And mixed steamed vegetables. Truly. Nothing overly elaborate."

"It all seems elaborate to me," she said.

She sat back and watched him work, not at all goaded into getting up and helping simply because he had taunted her about not knowing how to cook. She enjoyed watching him work. Anyway, she was a bit fatigued. Not terribly, but just a bit more than she was used to. But this time away with him had been… Well, it had been nice. Like a snippet of another life. A life she could have had if she had been just a regular woman. One who had met a man and fallen in love by chance.

In love? Was that what this was?

Her mind went blank for a moment, nothing there except for that one word, heavy, terrifying, looming above her.

Love.

Did she *love* him?

Her first instinct was to push it down. To hide. To never, ever admit to herself that she felt these things, let alone admit it to him.

But she saw clearly, suddenly, the fabric of her life. Her parents. Her mother's ferocity, and her unfailing need for Astrid to succeed, and her father's cool indifference.

And both of those things had a wall. A firm wall between her and Astrid. She was ideological for her mother. A point of contention for her father. And they had loved her. They had.

She supposed.

But the layers that kept them back from her... Pride. All of it was protective. And it had taught her to do the same. It was what she'd always done, and so much of it was because of her position, easy to sink into naturally. But so much of it had been to protect herself. From scrutiny, from criticism. From disappointing her mother, from failing in the eyes of her father, when he so clearly imagined that she would.

It all became so clear right then.

That no wall had ever healed. That no wall had ever truly protected. She had been concerned, from the beginning, that Mauro was the barbarian at the gate. But she had not imagined how apt that description was. Not really. And something had to change. Something inside her. It had begun, all those months ago, with that trip to the club.

Continued as they had grown intimate, as they had given and taken from each other, as she had found power in her surrender.

And perhaps now this was the next stage of that lesson. Strength in vulnerability.

In becoming the one thing she had always feared she might be.

Weak. Vulnerable. Open.

But perhaps it was the only way. Perhaps, it was the only path to what was real.

Something she had not considered, not truly, as she had started out this journey, was the fact that it was about more than simply gaining independence from a council. It was about more than living in defiance of her father's last-ditch effort to control her. It was about becoming more of a person than a figurehead. It was about defying some of what her mother had instilled in her, as well. The need to be perfect. The need to be a symbol.

She didn't want to be a symbol to her son. She wanted to be his mother. She didn't want to live her life as someone worthy of being carved onto a coin. She wanted to live her life. To do the best she could. To be the best she could, but to be her. To be Astrid von Bjornland, as she was. As she was meant to be.

Not in a constant state of trying to prove herself, not in an eternal struggle to appear worthy. No. She wanted to be herself.

She was flawed. She was strong. She was weak. She was angry. She was in love. She was filled with hope for the future, and terror about it, as well.

She was everything, not simply one thing.

And it would start here. It had to start here.

"Mauro," she said slowly. "I love you."

He barely paused in his movements. "That's only because I'm cooking steak for you."

She shook her head. "No. I am in love with you. I have been. For quite some time. And today... The ultrasound, the baby... All of it crystallized something for me. I cannot be the mother that I want to be, the ruler I want to be, the woman I want to be. If I'm going to be the best mother, the best ruler, the best wife, then I have to... I have to be different. I have to break the cycle."

"What cycle?"

"This cycle where I care only for my own feelings. Honestly, that I gave even a moment's thought to wishing he was a girl, to further my own cause, this cause that I've been fighting all of my life. It shows me that my parents impacted me in ways I wish they hadn't. I know my mother did. She meant well. She believed in me. But I was a battleground. I don't want to do that to our child. I don't want to live that way with you. I don't want to live the way my parents did. I want something more. I'm willing to give whatever I need to, to make that happen. I love you, and I think that... We can be happy. I think we can be wonderful, not just an arrangement. I think we could be everything."

He turned away from her, and went back to cooking, saying nothing. Doing nothing.

"The food is finished," he said, putting the steak on a plate and dishing vegetables beside it. "Let's eat."

There with him in the dining room in stunned silence, trying to focus, while emotions were spinning through her like cracks of light. Finally, she stood.

"I'm afraid," she said. "I have been. That my father

was secretly right. I wasn't strong. That's why I never doubted myself. I couldn't afford to. Why I went forward with my crazy plan to trick you into getting me pregnant. Because I had gotten myself to a place where I was so convinced that anything that I might want was a betrayal of what I needed to be. Well, I'm not doing it. Not anymore. I'm afraid. I'm afraid I won't do a good job. But I'm doing it anyway. I'm afraid I won't be a good mother. I'm afraid you will leave me. But I… I want it enough for me. For us."

He said nothing, only assessed her with cool, dark eyes. She moved down the table to where he sat. And, heart hammering in her chest, desperation pouring into her like a fountain, she dropped to her knees in front of him. "I'm your servant," she said. "Let me give you what you need."

CHAPTER THIRTEEN

MAURO COULDN'T BREATHE. He couldn't think. He had spent the entire day away at the office for a reason.

Because everything with Astrid, with the baby, had simply been too much for him to take on board. It had been too much for him to handle. And now this. Now she was throwing herself at his feet, confessing love, prostrate before him. And worst of all, worse than watching her kneel before him, was the fact that it intensified the growing ache inside.

He couldn't even blame the child, which ultimately he had rationalized as being a natural response. Very few men faced impending fatherhood without some sort of panic. But that wasn't it.

It was her. She did this to him.

And then, she began to strip off the dress she was wearing, began to reveal her body, and he could not turn away.

"Whatever you need from me... Let me give it. Let *me* be everything you need."

It was so perilously close to what he had wished he could get from her earlier today. That he could see that vulnerability, that he could understand what scared her, what drove her, what made her. And now, it was as if she was showing him, but not only that, was asking him to do the same.

He wanted her to stop. Wanted to tell her enough was enough.

Yet he found it impossible to turn away, especially as she revealed those pale, perfect breasts for inspection, especially when all of her soft, silky beauty was laid out before him. She took everything off except for her shoes, just as she had done that first night they were together.

She stretched out on her back, on the floor in front of him, her arms lifted over her head, her wrists crossed, her knees locked criminally together, as if it might spare some of her modesty. And he no longer hungered for the food on his plate. No. All the hunger he possessed was for her. Utterly. His desire like a living thing roaring through his body, right now.

No.

Part of him wanted to run away from, from that feeling she created inside, but that same part of himself would not allow it. Would not allow for him to admit she did strange and dark, magical things that no one else had ever done.

She terrified him. Him. A man who had sold his body to survive, who had spent nights sleeping on the street, wondering if the wrong kind of people would find him, and if he would wake up at all.

He feared nothing. And yet this one, fragile queen seemed to have the power to tear him apart from the inside out.

This woman who seemed to be able to give and take in equal measure. Who seemed to be able to take charge and then give her power over at will.

He didn't understand.

He did not understand how she had spoken to him as she had, so raw and real and broken. So revealing. As if she were bulletproof. When he could see full well she was not. All that tender skin so very capable of being destroyed.

And yet… Yet. He dropped to his knees, forced her thighs apart, exposed all of that luscious body of hers.

He should turn away. Should not take her in his current state of mind. It took all of his strength to even admit that. That she'd pushed him to this place.

And he had none left to resist.

He touched her breasts, her stomach, that tender place between her legs. Let himself drink in every inch of her beauty.

He held himself back, keeping a distance between them as he undid the closure on his slacks.

He gripped himself, stroking his hardened length twice while looking down at her.

Then he reached down, gripping her thigh and draping her leg up over his shoulder, repeating the motion with the other.

Then he rocked forward, one arm like a bar over her thighs as he gripped himself with his free hand and slid himself over the slick entrance of her body, before pressing his arousal against her opening.

She gasped, letting her head fall back, and he lost himself. Poured every emotion, every pain, every deep sharp jagged thing that was making him feel, into her. He wrapped them up, let it cut them both, and he let them both get lost in the animal need that was driving him forward, making him into a thing he didn't recognize.

A thing he feared was closer to real than anything he'd allowed himself to feel for decades.

And when he came, it was on a ferocious roar, with a bastard's body pulsing around his.

And he thought that maybe, just maybe, that had fixed things. That it had drowned everything else out. But then, she lifted her hand and touched his face.

"I love you."

And he could not endure it.

Astrid could tell the moment that she had lost him. The moment when she had pushed too far.

But what could they do? What could she do? She loved him. They were married. She was having his baby. They were bonded, whether he wanted that to be true or not. And she could see something more than a lack of love in his eyes. That wasn't what she saw there at all. It was anguish. It was fear. It was abject terror. And desire. A deep, unending desire.

To take what she had offered, she was certain of it. And yet, something was holding him back. She couldn't figure out what it was, couldn't quite say where the fear was coming from, only that it was there.

"Don't do this," she said softly.

"Don't," he said. "Don't act like you can read my mind because you shared my bed. Any number of women have done this with me."

She stayed right where she was on the floor. "Any number of women have submitted themselves to you completely?"

"It is only sex," he said.

"Is it? Because it seems to be something that terrifies you. I love you," she said it again.

"That isn't what I want," he said.

"I don't care what you want."

"No. You never have, have you? You find it so easy to make proclamations, to say that you're going to change because you now realize the error of your selfish, entitled ways, but you don't actually intend to do it, do you? Because the moment that it becomes inconvenient for you, you begin to tell other people they are wrong."

"That isn't what I've done," she said, pushing back, indignation and anger filling her. "I love you, Mauro, and if that offends you so very much you might want to ask yourself why."

"That is not what I signed on for when I signed on for this marriage."

"Yes. You only signed on for forever and said that I was yours. Why would I think a little thing like love would be a simple thing for you to accept?"

"You say that you want nothing, but in the end, you will," he said. "Nothing that I do will be enough for you, now that you've entered love into the equation."

"That sounds like baggage that we haven't discussed," she said flatly. "Because I never asked for a damn thing."

"This is not the way that I operate. It is not what I do."

"No," she said. "I know. You've done anything and everything to build yourself this tower. This place where you can look down on the world. And you seem to be fine as long as we can play games, and you can look down on me when I'm naked, and I give you everything that you desire. But now that I'm telling you there's more, now that I'm telling you I want more, you find that to be a problem?"

"You're asking for the impossible. You're asking for

something I can't give," he said, his voice hard. "I don't love."

"You're not going to love our child?"

"Dammit. I already do," he said, his voice hoarse. "But I…"

"But you can't love too many people, is that it? You can't open your heart any farther? Because you might be hurt?"

"You don't understand. I had to make myself hard. I had to build myself a tower, because no one would take care of me. My mother loved me, and she did the best she could, but when she was whoring herself out, she didn't exactly enact a screening process to make sure that none of the men she brought into her home tried something with her son. And no, none of them ever succeeded, but it wasn't for lack of trying. Yes, I had to become hard. So you cannot ask for me to open up my heart on command. I'm not even certain it's possible. More than that, I'm not certain I want to. I want to have this arrangement."

"More fortification. That's what you want. You marry me, you get that."

"That is not why I married you."

"You married me for our child," she said. "And certainly not anything to do with the fact that you keep hoping if you put enough Band-Aids on this wound you'll be all right."

"I am an infamous playboy," he said, his tone hard. "I am legendary for my ability to sleep with women and move on. What makes you think you're any different?"

"I know I'm different," she said. "I am a queen, and not just that, but I am *your* queen. You are the only man that I have ever knelt before, and the only man that I ever will kneel before. But until you can set down your own pride, and you can make yourself honest, afraid, vulnerable, we can't ever be. You're right about that."

"Are you issuing ultimatums?"

"Yes. As I said before, we had to either be forever or not at all. But to me, now forever is about love. Because I lived in a family where pride and stubbornness won. I lived in a home where there wasn't…love. Not really. I won't treat our child to the same. I will not. I won't treat you to the same. I deserved more. I deserve more, and I didn't get it. Because those around me were content to let it be. While I am not. Not anymore."

"And what will you do if I say no?"

"I will get on my private jet and I will fly back to Bjornland. You may come and see me again when the baby is born. But you and I are not a couple."

"I will not allow you to keep the marriage. I will not allow you to keep your front for the benefit of the world."

"I don't care. Or have you not been listening? I don't care anymore. It isn't about image. None of this is about image. I want you. I love you. I don't care how it looks. I don't give a damn if you were a prostitute. I don't care who your mother was. I don't care who your father is. I care about us. I care about our baby. I care about what we could be. And how much happiness we could have. How much more we could have."

She touched his face. "You were fearless once. You climbed up to your father's house and faced him when you were a boy, not having any idea what you might get in return. I'm standing here guaranteeing that you will have me. All you have to do is say yes."

"No," he said. "The divorce papers will be in the mail."

"Mauro…"

Astrid had to make good on her promise. And in her

last act of paying heed to appearances, she squared her shoulders, and held her head high. She collected her clothing, and dressed in front of him, hiding nothing. Then she walked out of his apartment, out of his life.

And only when she was in her plane, up in the air and alone, did she let herself weep.

But she knew she had made the right choice. Because she was the queen of so many. The hope of a nation.

But to Mauro, she had been a woman. To Mauro, she had been Astrid.

And Astrid wanted his *love*.

She would settle for nothing less.

Mauro was a study in misery, and he stubbornly refused to believe that he had any recourse in the matter. Astrid was being unreasonable. He called his lawyer in the middle of the night, in a fit of rage, and had divorce papers drafted.

And then had spent the next three days doing nothing with them. Nothing at all. The view from his office window was tainted, and he hated it all now because of her. Because of what she'd said. That he was using it to look down and hold himself above.

"Mr. Bianchi…"

He turned around to see Carlo rushing nervously into the room, with Gunnar von Bjornland striding in front of him.

"What are you doing here?" he asked his soon-to-be former brother-in-law.

"I should think that was quite obvious. Oh, but then I forget you don't know that I have a gun hidden in my jacket."

"Are you threatening me?"

"Yes. I knew that you would hurt my sister."

"To the contrary, your sister walked away from me."

"Astrid is a sensible woman. If she walked away from you, she had a reason."

"Yes, your sister is just so damn sensible. So sensible that she sneaked away from her minders, went to one of my clubs and tricked me into getting her pregnant. Then married me. Then left me when I refused to produce the correct words of love on command. Truly, it is a miracle that I was able to walk away from such a creature."

"I will concede that her tricking you into getting her pregnant is a problem. The rest… Why don't you love her? Everyone should."

The words hit him square in the chest, because actually he could only agree with them. Everyone should love her. She was strong, and her belief in him was the strange, unfailing thing. The way that she bonded herself to him, even as he told her about his past, the way that she stood resolute, as he showed her the slums that he'd been born in.

Truly, there seemed to be nothing he could do to lower himself in Astrid's esteem. After a lifetime of finding he could not raise himself in the esteem of others no matter what he did, it was a strange and refreshing thing.

"Is it that simple to undo a lifetime of not loving?" he asked.

"I don't know," Gunnar said. "I personally have yet to overcome much of my life. And I suppose it could be argued that no matter the situation with our parents, that we have had it easier. Astrid certainly had a different situation than I did. An heir and spare cannot, and will not have the same experience. But our parents were hard on her. And if they loved, they did not show it in easy, warm ways. If Astrid loves you, then it is truly an act of bravery. Not just because there has been nothing in our lives to suggest that love is something to aspire to, but because in Astrid's world nothing has been more important than maintaining that facade that she spent her entire life cultivating. That sense of total invulnerability. That sense of perfection. And then she married you. And we all saw those headlines about you. She went with you to Italy, she made a show of being yours no matter what, and I'm not sure that you can possibly understand what that means."

"Because I'm nothing but the son of a whore."

"Because you weren't raised to care quite so much. Your entire world never stopped and turned on your reputation. But for Astrid it did. You don't know what she has given up for you. How could you understand? And yet, she gave you the gift of her love and you threw it back in her face. If you divorce her and humiliate her on top of it…"

"Is that why you're really here? To prevent embarrassment?"

Gunner shrugged a shoulder. "My function in the royal family has never been to prevent embarrassment. Whatever Astrid is, I'm her opposite. My father always felt that I should be the one ruling the country, but I can tell you with great certainty that is not true. She is strong. Not only the strongest woman I know, but the strongest person I have ever had the privilege to be acquainted with. My sister is phenomenal, and you would be privileged to have her. Not because she is blue-blooded. Not because she is a royal, and you're not. But because she has come through our lives with the ability to love, which is more than I can say for myself. The strength in her… If you truly understood it, you would be humbled. But I am not certain that you can. Not unless you find a way to do the same thing she has done."

"I'm tired of receiving lectures from poor little rich kids who imagine that their emotional struggles somehow equal the emotional and physical struggles that I endured. Unless you know what it is to sell your body for a place to stay, I'm not entirely sure we can sit here and compare war wounds."

"Perhaps not," he said. "But then…" He shrugged. "So what?"

"I'm sorry?"

"So what? Your life was hard. Maybe it was harder than mine. Perhaps harder than Astrid's. Perhaps it is a struggle now, for you to figure out how to accept love. But so what? That part of your life is over now. You have money, you could buy whatever it is you need to make your life whatever it is you want, but the one thing you cannot pay to make better, or make go away, is the situation with my sister. That requires feelings. And it requires work. And in the end, life doesn't care how hard you worked for it. But it might mean more to you. If you figure out the way through. But you won't be given instant happiness simply because it would've been harder for you to sort yourself out than it might be for me."

Gunnar straightened the cuffs on his shirtsleeves, then treated Mauro to the iciest look he'd ever received. "Remember what I said. Do not embarrass my sister. Don't give me a reason to come for you."

And then, as he appeared, Gunnar walked out of his office. Carlo looked around the corner, his expression one of comical concern.

"Leave," Mauro said.

And Carlo vanished instantly.

Mauro was hardly going to listen to the ranting of a rich prince who wouldn't know struggle if it transformed into a snake and bit him in the face. But one thing kept replaying over and over in his head.

So what?

So everything.

Everything.

Because his life had been about struggle. Had been about wanting. And Astrid created more of that feeling inside him than anything else ever had. That ache. That sense of being unsatisfied. Unfulfilled. Of needing more than he would ever be able to have. A desperate hunger that could not be satisfied by food, by money. On that score he was right, as well. Because he knew that this was something that money could not solve. Knew that it was something he would not be able to fix. And that left him feeling…

Helpless. Utterly and completely helpless.

He hated that. There was no depth he would not sink to, he had proved that. He was willing to prostitute himself. He was willing to claw his way up to the top if need be. But there was no clawing here. There were no building towers. There was only…

There was only lowering himself.

As Astrid had said. Making himself into some debased creature all for her, and he didn't have any concept of how he might do that. Of what could possibly entice him to behave in such a way.

To leave all he'd created, to lower all his shields.

To make himself less.

Love.

The need for it, the drive for it… It was the thing that

was pushing him forward now. It was the thing that was making him miserable, the thing in his chest that made him want. And he did not understand how he was supposed to do it.

How he was supposed to...

It wasn't fair. She made him ache. She made him feel things, want things, need things that he had sworn he never would again.

Is she the one making you feel this? Or is it you?

And that was when the whole room seemed to turn.

And he wondered.

Perhaps it was Astrid who made him want. Perhaps it was Astrid who existed to fulfill the want that already existed inside him, and having her there, so close, and not allowing himself to have it all.

Maybe, she was not the problem. Maybe she was the answer to a hole that had already existed. To a need that had been present.

If only he was willing to cross the divide.

If only he was willing to admit that for all his power. For all that he had...

He could not fix it on his own.

He needed her.

He needed her. And he would do whatever he needed to get her back.

"Carlo," he said, his assistant appearing as if by magic. "Ready my plane. We're going back to Bjornland."

"As you wish."

CHAPTER FOURTEEN

ASTRID WAS NOT looking forward to this year's Christmas celebration at all.

It was a massive party, and in her mind, it was a total farce. There was nothing to celebrate. Yes, the impending birth of her son was joyous, but *she* was broken and alone, and it would take some time before she felt anything beyond that.

Still, all had been planned and arranged, and she was expected to participate whether she wanted to or not.

Things at the palace had changed.

In spite of the fact that Mauro was not in residence, her situation with the council was resolved.

While they would still exist, as long as the men wished to hold the office, she would disband it formally once they all retired, or passed on to the next life. And for now they existed as figureheads, symbols, more than anything else.

Which, in her mind, was much better than her existing as such.

The room was full of revelers, crystals dripping from each and every surface of the glorious ballroom.

The Christmas tree loomed large in the corner, a glowing beacon. At least it usually was. Right now the great golden glow mocked her. A symbol of joy and hope when she could feel none of it at all right now.

All of the decorations were ornate, in a way that she didn't truly enjoy, though she'd had her bedroom redone.

The thought made her smile, if somewhat sadly. Because it was something Mauro had said she should do, and even though he had hurt her, she knew that he was right.

And every night she wished that he were there with her.

Even though she shouldn't. Even though she shouldn't wish to see him again. Not ever.

Love, it turned out, did not fade simply because someone wronged you. Love, it turned out, was a terrible inconvenience.

The ball gown she was wearing was a gossamer, floaty confection that hung loosely over her curves, which was a necessity given that they were expanding with each passing day. That was another thing that made her miss him.

He was missing all of the changes, and it made her indescribably sad that this was the case. Guests were being brought forward to where she sat, being presented to her one by one. And there were any number of ushers dressed in navy blue suits, with gold epaulets on their shoulders, traditional dress for noblemen imbuing land.

Astrid was quite bored with it, and trying her best to appear engaged. It wasn't any of her guests' fault that she was brokenhearted, after all.

Out of the corner of her eye, she saw another of the greeters moving toward her, his head bent low. His hands behind his back. He did not have a guest on his arm. She looked at him, and her heart hit the front of her chest.

"What are you…"

"My Queen," he said, bending to one knee in front of her.

Mauro. He was here. And he was dressed as… One of the ushers.

"I had to sneak into your party," he said, his voice low, "especially as my name is mud here at the palace."

"Yes," she said, feeling dizzy. "It is."

"I had to come and find you," he said. "And I took inspiration for how from you. But I have something that I think belongs to you."

He reached out from behind his back, and produced her shoe. That crystalline beauty that she had worn and left behind the night she had seduced him at the club. "I believe this is yours."

"Yes," she said, her throat dry. "It is."

"You would permit me to see, if it fits?"

A bubble of laughter rose up in her throat. "If you must."

"I must," he said gravely. "Because the woman whose foot fits this shoe has something of mine. My heart. But more than that, my everything. I thought… Astrid, I thought that you made me hurt. That you made me incomplete, but that is not true. Instead, you revealed to me the empty space in my soul, and you are the only thing that can fill it. I blamed you, but you are not the problem. You are the solution. And so… Let me see. Do me the honor of showing me if you are in fact the woman who fits the shoe. Who fits that hole inside me."

She slipped her foot out of the shoe she was wearing and held it out to him, not caring that they were drawing stares, that everyone in the room had realized just who he was.

She could see that Gunnar and Latika were barely restraining themselves, allowing her to handle the moment, out of respect for her strength, she knew. But she also knew it was testing them.

She extended her foot to him, and he slipped it on.

A perfect fit.

"My Queen," he said. "I am kneeling before you. I am not in my tower. I am at your feet. And I must humbly confess to you that I love you. But I am a broken man who is nothing more than where I came from. But I love you. I love you, and I will spend all of my days trying to prove to you that I am worthy of that love. For I am nothing without you. I am nothing without this life. And it would not matter if you were a queen, or if we lived back in those slums I worked so hard to escape. Love was the thing that was always missing. And love is the only thing I cannot buy."

"Then it's perfect," she said, sliding out of her throne and dropping to her knees with him. "Because love is the one thing that I cannot legislate. Is the one thing that I cannot bend to my will. I cannot manipulate it, I cannot find an old law that would enable me to capture it and hold it in my hands. Love is all that I need. You are all that I need."

"I love you," he said.

"I love you too."

"You have to stay at this party?"

"It's my party. It's my birthday."

"Happy birthday."

"Thank you," she said, feeling light-headed and surreal, dizzy.

"We have this? Will we have each other forever?" she asked, whispering softly.

"Yes, my Queen. We will have each other, and happily. Ever after."

EPILOGUE

WHEN THE BRAND-NEW Prince of Bjornland came into the world some months later, the media instantly hailed him as perfection. A specimen of humanity that possessed his mother's regal bearing and his father's determination, but no one was half so infatuated with him as his father. And his mother.

"He is perfect," Mauro said decisively, laying him down in the crib that first night, pressing a kiss to his soft, downy head.

"He is," Astrid agreed. "Perfection. As is our life."

"I had thought that happiness was in the top of a high-rise building. Where I had finally overcome. Where I would finally prove to my father that I had value. I climbed up that hill and begged for him to love me, and received nothing in return. Though, I realize now that I did. I realize now that I learned something I needed right now. Our son will never have to earn my love. And there is nothing he could do to lose it. What our parents did to us... It was never us. It was them. And as for me... Happiness was never alone at the top of a high-rise. It is here. With you. With him. Forever."

For the first time in his entire life, Mauro did not feel like a boy from the slums.

Astrid made him a king. Not because of her title, but because she had given him her heart.

And he had given her his.

And that was truly the most powerful thing on earth.

* * * * *

COMING SOON!

We really hope you enjoyed reading this book. If you're looking for more romance, be sure to head to the shops when new books are available on

Thursday 26th December

To see which titles are coming soon, please visit

millsandboon.co.uk/nextmonth

MILLS & BOON

Coming next month

SECRETS OF HIS FORBIDDEN CINDERELLA
Caitlin Crews

She hadn't seen him clearly that night in September. That had
been the point. She had been bold and daring, and he had responded
with that brooding, overwhelming passion that had literally swept
her off her feet. Into his arms, against a wall. And then, in a private
salon, still dressed in their finery, with fabric pushed aside in haste
and need.

Too much haste and need, it turned out.

Even though she had watched him roll on protection.

But now, he wore nothing to cover his face. And he wasn't
smiling slightly, the way he had then. Those dark eyes of his
weren't lit up with that particular knowing gleam that had turned
her molten and soft.

On the contrary, his look was frigid. Stern and disapproving.

It made her remember—too late, always too late—that he wasn't
simply a man. He was all the men who had come before him, too.
He was the Duke, and the weight of that made him…colossal.

A decade ago, on the very rare occasions that he had looked
at her at all, he had looked at her like this.

But it felt a lot worse now.

"This is a surprise," Teo said, with no preamble. "Not a pleasant
one."

One of his inky brows rose, a gesture that he must have inher-
ited from the royal branch of his family tree, because it made
Amelia want to genuflect. She did not.

"Hi, Teo," she replied.

Foolishly.

"You will have to remind me of your name," he said, and there
was a gleam in his eyes now. It made her feel quivery in a
completely different way. And she didn't believe for a second that
he didn't know who she was. "I'm afraid that I did not retain the
particulars of my father's regrettable romantic choices."

"I understand. I had to block out a whole lot of my mother's marriages, too."

A muscle worked in his lean, perfect jaw. "Allow me to offer a warning now, before this goes any further. If you have come here in some misguided attempt to extort money from me based upon an association I forgot before it ended, you will be disappointed. And as I cannot think of any other reason why you should intrude upon my privacy, I will have to ask you to leave."

Amelia considered him. "You could have had the butler say that, surely."

"I will admit to a morbid sense of curiosity." His gaze swept over her. "And it is satisfied." He didn't wave a languid hand like a sulky monarch and still, he dismissed her. "You may go."

Amelia ordered the part of her that wanted to obey him, automatically, to settle down. "You don't want to hear why I've come?"

"I am certain I do not."

"That will make it fast, then."

Amelia could admit she felt…too much. Perhaps a touch of shame for having to come to him like this—especially after the last time she'd shown up here, uninvited. Her pulse kicked at her, making her feel…*fluttery*. And she was, embarrassingly, as molten and soft as if he'd smiled at her the way he had in September.

When he hadn't ventured anywhere near a smile.

"Never draw out the ugly things," Marie had always told her. "The quicker you get them over with, the more you can think about the good parts instead."

Just do it, be done with it and go, she ordered herself.

And who cared if her throat was dry enough to start its own fire?

"I'm pregnant," she announced into the intimidatingly, exultantly blue-blooded room. To a man who was all of that and more. "You're the father.'

Continue reading
SECRETS OF HIS FORBIDDEN CINDERELLA
Caitlin Crews

Available next month
www.millsandboon.co.uk

MILLS & BOON
A ROMANCE FOR EVERY READER

- **FREE** delivery direct to your door
- **EXCLUSIVE** offers every month
- **SAVE** up to 25% on pre-paid subscriptions

SUBSCRIBE AND SAVE

millsandboon.co.uk/Subscribe

MILLS & BOON
Desire

Indulge in secrets and scandal, intense drama and plenty of sizzling hot action with powerful and passionate heroes who have it all: wealth, status, good looks... everything but the right woman.